TEMPTING
FATE

TEMPTING FATE

LAURIE ALBERTS

Houghton Mifflin Company
BOSTON
1987

Library of Congress Cataloging-in-Publication Data

Alberts, Laurie.
Tempting fate.
I. Title.
PS3551.L264T4   1987   813'.54   86-27531
ISBN 0-395-43041-0

Printed in the United States of America

S 10 9 8 7 6 5 4 3 2 1

The author is grateful for permission to quote from the following works:
"Lullaby of Cape Cod" from *A Part of Speech* by Joseph Brodsky. Copyright © 1977 by Joseph Brodsky. Reprinted by permission of Farrar, Straus and Giroux, Inc.
"Elegy for Jane" from *Collected Poems of Theodore Roethke*. Reprinted by permission of Doubleday and Company, Inc.
"The Sentence" from *Poems of Akhmatova*, selected, translated and introduced by Stanley Kunitz with Max Hayward. Copyright © 1973 by Stanley Kunitz and Max Hayward. First appeared in *The Atlantic Monthly*. Reprinted by permission of Little, Brown and Company, in association with the Atlantic Monthly Press.

To
Alice Martell and Bill Strachan

The author wishes to thank James Michener and the Copernicus Society of America for their generous support.

The author also wishes to express appreciation to the following: the Virginia Center for the Creative Arts; Marlene Clarke for her wisdom and friendship; Connie Brothers, Jack Leggett, and Lee Goerner for their assistance; and many writing friends for their criticism, encouragement, and advice.

I write from an Empire whose enormous flanks
extend beneath the sea. Having sampled two
oceans as well as continents, I feel that I know
what the globe itself must feel: there's nowhere to go.

     · · ·

Preserve these words against a time of cold,
a day of fear: man survives like a fish,
stranded, beached, but intent
on adapting itself to some deep, cellular wish,
wriggling toward bushes, forming hinged leg-struts, then
to depart (leaving a track like the scrawl of a pen)
for the interior, the heart of the continent.

       Joseph Brodsky
     from "Lullaby of Cape Cod"

SUMMER
1974

———◆———

SHE WAS EAGER to get off the ferry. It was enormous and lush with lounges and restaurants she couldn't afford, filled with tourists and job hunters. The tourists oohed and ahhed at every passing dolphin. The job hunters came in two varieties: boisterous kids with backpacks looking for cannery work and summer adventure, and squat or rangy men in bulldozer caps and plaid shirts — their sleeves rolled up too high over their biceps — who sat chain-smoking while their wives alternately slapped kids and fed them from paper sacks.

These families could be found on the hard benches of a lower lounge that had no windows and resembled a bus station. They looked as though they had staked all their money on a ride north and a chance at Alaska wages, yet they had none of the hopefulness of the rest of the passengers. They seemed doomed to repeated failure and were beyond interest in the view.

Allie felt sorry for them in a distant sort of way. She, too, had spent her last dollars on a ferry ticket, but what she saw when she looked out over the grey water through fog that lowered and lifted, melding with the clouds, was the marvelous promise of her own future. It didn't matter that things hadn't gone well in the other places she'd lived — in Seattle and Denver, where in the past ten months she'd lost or left a series of menial jobs; in Connecticut, where she'd fidgeted through a year of college classes; and at home, in a decaying factory town north of Boston, where her ill-tempered father had recently lost his textile business to imports and the end of the war. (Vietnam had been his personal gold rush, combat belts his boom and bust.) None of it mattered. Stepping off the ferry, she would leave her history behind. She would be someone new; at twenty, an Allie she'd invent.

Coming into Vladimir Island at ten in the evening, the first thing she saw was the glow of a pink neon cross from a church steeple against the dark bulk of a fir-covered mountain. As they pulled closer, the town of Vladimir — the only one on the island — turned into a line of shacks with mossy shingled roofs on stilts over the water. The corrugated aluminum siding of canneries caught a blaze of evening sun, and an enormous Japanese lumber ship, the *Vladimir Maru*, dwarfed the docks. Even at this hour cranes were busy loading the ship with timber for Japan.

Vladimir had the false-fronted shops of any western town, but instead of sidewalks, raised wooden boardwalks ran alongside the unpaved street. Totem poles hinting of arcane ritual, a history of losses, stood rotting in empty lots. Allie shouldered her bag past a drive-in, the Totem; plenty of teenagers were hanging out, but there were no cars. The kids, half of them Indian, turned to stare at her with interest. The few cars that passed, stirring up dust that had formed out of recent puddles under the intense northern sun, sported bumper stickers that proclaimed JESUS SAVES and SIERRA GO HOME.

On the splintered boards of an abandoned cannery dock, the Vladimir High School band had set up its music stands to welcome a Canadian tour ship festooned with pennants which was just now steaming into port. Signs announced: WELCOME TO VLADIMIR, FRIENDLIEST TOWN IN ALASKA! and PLEASE DONATE FOR OUR SENIOR TRIP TO DISNEYLAND. A crowd of longshoremen, old Indian ladies, and little children had come down to the dock just to watch the show.

4

Allie wondered for a moment at the level of boredom that would compel people to turn out to watch a tour ship make its scheduled stop, or sent teenagers to a drive-in when they had no cars. Yet she could feel the hum of Alaska excitement. It was in the land itself, a lush, overgrown rain forest where bald eagles, as plentiful as gulls, swooped over the docks, and in the overtime clanking and screeching of the lumber mill with its piles of aromatic cedar and spruce and its plume of black smoke. She could read it in the brash faces of the fishermen and loggers who lurched along the boardwalks and into the bars, something that said: the sun won't go down, there's money to be made, we can do what we want.

She wandered down Front Street under a high Alaskan sun, filled with the mixture of dread and excitement that came from not knowing where she'd spend the night. She wanted something to happen. She was sure that at any moment someone would appear to offer her a place to sleep, a passionate touch, some piece of essential information.

In the past year she'd learned to depend not on the kindness but on the attentions of strangers. She was still flattered and confused at being noticed at all. She understood it as little as she had the fuss over rock music in high school, the way the boys she'd known seemed to be ecstatically transported by Jethro Tull or Cream. She had played along with them, closing her eyes in imitative rapture, moving her head in the same way they moved theirs, trying to follow the beat of a rhythm that meant nothing to her. The urgency that men seemed to feel around her was equally mysterious. Sometimes it made her feel powerful; sometimes she knew herself to be nothing more than a bull's-eye, a temporary target for their random desires.

In the eyes of the world she was a pretty girl, she knew because she'd heard it so often, but when she looked in mirrors and store windows (as she did every chance she got, always faintly believing that her image would not be there to greet her), she saw only flaws: a gross ripeness that she read as vulnerability — a body inviting assault. Her face appeared mushy, her lips too full. She would have preferred to be all angles, a resistant surface of self-protection. She loathed her body and picked at it mercilessly, clawing at cuticles, chewing the insides of her cheeks, grinding her teeth while she slept, covering herself in bulky men's clothes.

The only things she liked about herself were her olive complexion and her eyes. She equated her mother's pale, freckled, vulnerable flesh with weakness, and she liked to think she'd inherited power and strength along with the dominant genes for darkness from her father. She liked her eyes because they were large and black and had secrets of their own — she could hide behind them. If she had drawn a picture of herself, she would have sketched a pair of eyes safely divorced from her body, calm witnesses to the chaotic drama of her life.

The true secret, though, was that no matter what anyone did to her, no matter what happened, Allie was fully convinced of her ability to survive unscathed.

Vladimir, however, required little defense that evening; it was as friendly as the sign promised. The woman bartender in the Anchor Lounge, claiming to be half Cajun and half Tlingit Indian (it sounded to Allie like "Klinket"), set her up with a free drink for being "a long way from home" and because she thought Allie looked Indian. A young man holding a pool cue came over to her and introduced himself as "Frankie, Frank, you know, like a weiner?" and betrayed his handsome, slant-eyed face with a bad-toothed, goofy grin. He said he was Tlingit despite his blond hair and insisted that Allie should stay in town until the Fourth of July. Vladimir, he said, had the best Fourth of July in all of Southeast Alaska. Besides, they needed new blood in town. In half an hour she was offered the basement couch of a California couple up for the summer working in the cannery, and in the morning she was hired on as a waitress in a coffee shop with an ease that seemed like fate.

In the coffee shop, the other waitresses ignored Allie, sitting together in a corner booth gossiping under a swirl of cigarette smoke. Allie knew that as soon as someone newer came along, she'd be invited into the club and the other girl would be left out. For the time being, Allie was befriended by the fourteen-year-old Indian dishwasher.

Mistaking Allie for an Indian, the homely little girl, bulging out of her overalls, confided that she was trapped in Vladimir and desperately wanted to go home. She came from a tiny reservation island so small the ferry didn't stop there, and she couldn't leave until her parents, who fished all summer, came back in the fall to pick her up. Vladimir, population 900, had seemed like the big time to her, and she'd been eager to come and earn money. It turned out that she had to chambermaid all morning and wash dishes all night while her wages were being held for her parents. She had no money and no time to make friends. To her, everyone in Vladimir was a snob. Whenever the cook wasn't looking, the dishwasher caught Allie's eye and stuffed another dirty plate into the trash with a look of sour vengeance.

"It's different for you," the girl complained. "You ain't stuck here like me."

Allied pitied the exploited girl, but she agreed: it was different for her. Vladimir seemed friendly enough and she'd fallen in love with the boats.

All day long through the picture windows of the Takine River Inn, the boats kept leaving town. They slid across the grey, smooth surface of the sea, around the edge of Siligovsky Island, and disappeared. Pouring coffee, swabbing counters, Allie stopped to watch. She wanted to go too.

The boats were beautiful; they came and went with a logic of their own. And the men, sitting at the docks in their caps and woolen shirts cut off at the elbows, cleaning halibut or salmon, all seemed to know something, a secret that underlay their words: how to translate restlessness into purpose. It was as though they spoke a foreign language, as inaccessible as the clicks and clatters of the ravens perched in the trees and telephone poles all over town.

Allie believed if she was allowed to step on a boat and slide away, she'd learn to speak that language.

Now she was in the middle of nowhere, sitting on an overturned deck bucket while the thirty-two-foot *Ginny D.*, double-rigged for gill-netting and trolling, drifted with its engine off. Half an hour ago Digger had reeled the net off the drum over the guiding rollers, where it made a line in the water a third of a mile long: lead line, webbing, corks. The gill-net floated free, marked on each end by pink buoys. Digger leaned against the net drum, smoking. Allie wanted to say something, to ask questions, but she didn't know him very well, and ever since they'd headed out for the fishing grounds, he'd been tense and irritable, cursing other skippers for setting their nets too close to his. He was a bulky, broad-faced blond man in his late twenties who'd seemed jovial enough when she met him three days ago in the Anchor Lounge. He'd been a good times guy, laughing, buying her drinks, eager to hire her aboard.

She looked around. Sumner Strait was soft with fog, a grey-green spread of water bounded by Kupreanof and Prince of Wales islands. The other gill-net boats, waiting on their sets, bobbed gently. Allie began to forget what they were waiting for. Buoyancy lulled her, rocked her into a reverie near sleep.

Then Digger kicked in the engine. Using a boat hook and working from the cockpit controls, he captured the net marker and drew the net up onto the drum. The net, pulled from the water by the turning drum, shimmered seawater green, strung with kelp, red seaweed, glistening drops. A salmon surfaced. Snagged by its gills, it struggled and thrashed. Digger stopped the drum with a foot pedal, yanked hard, and the fish fell onto the planks. The drum turned again — two more salmon, females. They came up gasping, fighting, their sides imprinted with webbing, pink roe sacks popping, guts streaming in gooey arcs. When the fish hit the cockpit, they beat their bodies convulsively against the planks.

"Give me a hand," Digger ordered. "Put these gloves on, jump down here, and throw them in the bin."

Horrified, Allie could only stare. She didn't want to touch them. To do so would implicate her somehow. She'd never imagined that fishing would be such slaughter.

"Hurry up, goddammit!"

Then she was down in the middle of it, rain and seawater running over the tops of her boots, salmon slapping frantically against her shins and splashing jellyfish-laden water into her face. She grabbed a salmon but it thrashed free. She grabbed again, this time sliding her fingers into the yielding gills. Even through the rubber gloves she could feel the chill of its cold-blooded flesh. She clutched it against her chest and carried it to the bin, went back for another. Digger counted aloud: fifteen, sixteen, seventeen. The words "America gotta eat, America gotta eat" ran over and over in Allie's head, an apology, an idiot refrain.

Thirty-two hours into the gill-net week, with sixteen more to go, the rhythm was established: set the net, work the tides, watch the drift, pull in fish. Allie felt as though she'd never been anywhere else but here, sitting in the pilothouse of the *Ginny D.*, craving sleep, listening to the hissing of the kettle on the stove. Fog shifted down the sides of the mountains to fill the strait, then lifted, revealing the glow of sun, the hint of mountainous coast. The sky had blackened for a few short hours of Alaskan night, then lightened; it would soon be dark again. She hadn't slept. She envied all the sleepers in the world, especially Digger, snoring away in the bunk below.

Digger had taken off his watch, placed it in front of her, and instructed her to wake him in exactly forty-five minutes. It was her job to stay awake. There was plenty of time to sleep in the winter, he said; he had payments to make. Forty-five minutes. Just enough time to haul in the net before they drifted over the legal fishing line, close to a dangerous rock or into the riptide swirl of logs and kelp that could tangle the net and suck the boat down. The best fishing was near the rip, and Digger, sleeping while he waited for the fish to ride in on the flood, was cutting it close.

Digger. Allie was sick of him already, tired of his endless droning explanations, so that things that were important and things that weren't blurred together under the relentless weight of his voice. She was sick of his constant lament about Jeanine, a girl who'd come up with him from Seattle and then, when they reached Alaska, decided she didn't want to fish after all but wanted to go to Petersburg and work in the cannery. "Screw around with hippie fish packers is what she means," Digger complained. But he was still a romantic, he insisted; Jeanine had broken his heart.

It was hard for Allie to believe that although she had chosen Digger as randomly as one picked one's parents, which was to say she hadn't chosen at all, she'd been willing to entertain romantic ideas about him a few days back. It hadn't mattered who would hire her on as long as she found a boat, and Digger had seemed attractive enough in the Anchor Lounge, with his jauntily cocked white fisherman's hat and husky voice. He'd taken her dancing at the Takine Inn, on the other side of the red plastic accordion door, through which she'd only peeked at loggers doing a Frankenstein stomp to the tune of "Jeremiah Was a Bullfrog" while she filled the sugar dispensers in the coffee shop. But there she was, Digger's deckhand, sitting at a table full of skippers who bought her drinks, and suddenly she belonged.

When he took her down to the dock to see his boat, Allie was entranced. The *Ginny D.* was a narrow, old-fashioned wooden lady with a high graceful bow and low sweeping stern, a cupola pilothouse, a flying bridge, and a deck crowded with complicated gear. Digger pointed out the enormous net drum on the stern, the tall poles for trolling. Inside the pilothouse, Allie ran her hands over the spokes of the wooden captain's wheel, sat in the captain's seat, and looked out the curved, many-paned windows while Digger proudly displayed the screens for radar and sonar, the rolled charts overhead. Trolling lures — shiny reflective metal, painted teardrops, miniature rubbery squid — hung in neat rows on a line of filament on the back of the pilothouse door.

Digger led her down the stairs ("the engine lives under there," he said) into the fo'c's'le, a dark, narrow wedge of space redolent of diesel fuel. Dusky midnight sun filtered through brass-sealed portholes. To one side stood the galley table, and above it were shelves with wooden strips that kept the goods from sliding off: cans of condensed milk, catsup, a tub of butter, hardtack, maple syrup, a couple of heavy white ceramic mugs. Opposite the table sat a small, soot-encrusted kerosene stove, and beside it a miniature sink with a hand pump. A half-opened door revealed the head, and forward in the bow were V-shaped bunks with exposed grey mattress ticking, a life preserver glowing orange on the floor in the space between them.

Allie put her hands on her hips, and delightedly breathed in. She wanted this. It was a clubhouse for boys, an inner sanctum full of its own special order: male.

When Digger poured out two mugs of wine, winked, and suggested they "find out if they were compatible" before they sealed the deal, Allie agreed. The only way to learn was through osmosis; by accepting Digger's touch she would absorb everything he knew. Her desire was for the boat, but she was willing to blur distinctions, to believe that the man and the boat were one. Besides, she was afraid he wouldn't hire her if she said no.

Before he fell asleep Digger said, "You may be young, but I can see you weren't born yesterday," as though bestowing a compliment.

The next morning when she woke, hung over and embarrassed by the sight of Digger's unfamiliar bulk and by the thought of stepping out onto the dock where everyone would *know*, the sight of light shaped by a porthole and edged in brass was enough to keep her there. At least she was on a boat. Only when they were gliding away from Vladimir did she consider her recklessness. For all she knew, Digger might be an idiot who could drown her. But it was a risk she was willing to take. Sliding past Siligovsky Island with the diesel pounding under her rubber boots, wearing her brand-new Helly-Hansen fisherman's rubber overalls and rain jacket, Allie thought with satisfaction: I'm going through a one-way door.

That was how many, two, three days ago? Time had lost all meaning. This was the only place now, and the *Ginny D.* was the only boat in the world.

Sitting in the pilothouse under faint generator light, Allie wondered where all the other boats had gone. Yesterday, when the government plane had flown over to signal the start of the forty-eight-hour gill-net "week," fifty or more boats had crowded together near the legal fishing line, jockeying for position, skippers screaming threats and even waving rifles. Now they'd all disappeared. Once she heard the *dub-dub-dub* of a diesel engine, muffled by distance and rain. The Alaska State Ferry, lit up like a city, had cut through the strait, missing their net but sending the soup pot flying from the galley stove from the force of its wake. Was it possible that she had been on such a ferry only eight days before?

Now the only lights visible were those floating on markers at the ends of the net. Water lapped against the hull; little ducks quacked mournfully, caught and dying in the net. She could hear low-grade radio static and Digger's snores. The other gill-netters spread through the strait were as phantom as the salmon swimming beneath the boat. It was hard to believe that anything lived under there. In daylight the surface of the sea looked as flat and impenetrable as pavement. At night it glittered like a rain-slick road. But at any moment, life could leap thrashing out of the water, gasping for breath and hinting at secrets the way fragments of dreams shattered her sleep and left her breathless in the face of all the possibilities, the worlds she didn't know. The surface lied; the water showed nothing. "There's more creatures under there than walking the earth," Digger had said. How could she have known?

The water came as revelation and could exact a price. It would be so easy to fall in; the deck rails were only inches high. Every time Allie took a step, she held on to the rigging, placing each foot carefully on the slippery, slime-strewn deck. In that near-freezing water, a man could survive no more than twenty minutes, but if she fell in while Digger slept she wouldn't have that long; she'd be sucked under in her heavy rain pants and rubber boots. There'd be no second chance.

And sleeplessness was playing tricks with her. Last night she'd seen a face. Pale and sodden, it floated under the surface, long hair undulating in waves. "Just kelp," Digger had said, refusing to look. "Floating junk. You got to get used to going without sleep if you want to work on a boat." But Allie had seen it, kept seeing it, an image as vivid and recurrent as her mother's drowned man.

Seven years old, Allie's mother had run down to the beach to watch the hurricane of '38, as though it were something like a carnival. What her mother remembered best and loved to describe was the drowned man being pulled, blue and stiff, fingers clenched around the shape of a steering wheel, out of his car that had washed off the road. Allie had listened to that story so many times she'd begun to imagine that she was her mother watching that storm. Her mother had stood there and no one had come to take her home. She said that's why she feared the sea. Allie's mother feared the sea, and now she feared everything: crowds, driving, department stores.

Against her will, Allie pictured her mother on the other side of the continent, hiding from a world grown as threatening and infirm as the black water surrounding the *Ginny D.* They were both afloat in the middle of the night. Thinking of her mother left alone in a house where Allie's brother hid in his room, clamped under headphones, and her father paced the halls, haranguing them with obscenities, made Allie short of breath. It felt like drowning.

She sighed and stared at the sevenfold reflection of her face in the pilothouse windows. She was on a boat somewhere in Alaska, and the face in the windows didn't look like her own anymore. The eyes were lopsided, the skin too pale, and her black hair snaked out in a tangled mess. She touched her cheeks and felt dried seaweed and crusted slime. She needed sleep.

She let her head slide down on her arms but jerked up fast. No. If she fell asleep she'd never wake Digger in time. She could barely remember what she was staying awake for. Nothing made sense; she didn't even know where they were. She couldn't read the charts, and the pilothouse was a monument to her ignorance: the blank, unreadable face of the sonar, the compass's taunting roll. The two radios, marine band and CB, mumbled static and garbled words. Most of the time the voices just sounded like nonsense, even when they were coming in clear, but Digger wouldn't let her turn the radios off. He insisted that the fishermen were passing secret information to each other in code. For a moment two voices broke through, and Allie strained to hear.

"Read me, Joe? Do you read me?"

"Roger, Fred."

"Picking anything up out there?"

"Nah, looks pretty dismal, by golly. If this keeps up, I'll be spending the winter driving a rig. It's them damn Japs, cutting them off outside."

"We ought to torpedo the bastards, that's what we ought to do."

The voices drifted away. Day and night the radio transmitted voices crossing ocean miles, tangling in static: do you read

•

me, do you read me, do you read me? No one was asking for Allie. No one even knew where she was.

She checked Digger's watch. Thirty-nine minutes to go before she could wake him, fifteen more hours before they could sell their fish to a cannery packer boat, run into the nearby village of Point Baker, tie up, and sleep. The boat was rocking her gently, a lullaby of rigging creaking in the windless roll.

She tried to concentrate: compass, radar, radio, charts. Radio, compass, radar, charts. They were fishing in Sumner Strait, and soon Digger would get up to pull in the net. They were after fish and it all made sense, only Allie was tired now, too tired to hold up her head. She rested her cheek on her folded arms for just a moment, knowing it was wrong, a mistake, but the knowledge was far away. She closed her eyes, then gave in.

WHEN SONNY walked into the Port-O-Call Café in Petersburg with Henry, Frankie, and Duane, a withered old Norwegian halibutter twirled on his stool, stared at him, then spat a stream of brown snoose at his feet. Sonny knew it had his name on it. Duane was a big-bellied, long-haired white boy up from Seattle, and although Henry and Frankie were as much Indian as Sonny was, they didn't look it. Frankie had gotten blond hair from his Norwegian grampa, and Henry, little and sweet-faced and balding at twenty-six (whoever heard of a bald Indian?), looked out at the world through a set of baby blues. Sonny looked like any reservation full-blood. Sometimes he wondered what had happened to that quarter part of himself that came from his Yugoslav grandad, who'd jumped off a merchant ship in Vancouver and headed north, just to see the world.

Sitting at the table in the Port-O-Call, Sonny could feel the old Norsky's eyes burning a hole in his back. It made his shoulders ache. He wanted to get up and stuff the old man's can of Copenhagen down his throat, but he warned himself to let it go. Petersburg was bad news all around.

A middle-aged woman wearing a "Little Norway Festival" button came over to take their orders. Sonny couldn't get his eyes to focus on the menu, so he just ordered a T-bone and spuds along with everyone else. Tired and wired — that's how he always felt at the end of the fishing week: worn out but he couldn't sit still. A couple of stiff shots would take the kinks out of his shoulders, but that would get him going, and it would cost. They were all living off advances against a season that had just begun and didn't look too good. He wanted to save some bucks, but in Petersburg the only choices were the boat or the bar. At home in Vladimir he could lie low up at the house and watch the tube; here he had to do something to get the fishing out of his head. When Sonny closed his eyes, it played like a movie under his lids.

Sitting in the open power skiff, leading the net away from the sixty-foot seine boat, forming the circle to trap the fish, all Sonny could hear was the dull diesel roar and the engine's vibrations. He wore headphones to take instructions from his skipper and to keep from going deaf. When the headphones weren't squawking, Sonny talked to the fish.

He could feel them caught in the big web circle, milling, pulsing, scared. He could feel what they felt. If the guys knew, they'd laugh, say he'd gone crazy. He felt like a fool, like an Indian old-timer, like his grandmother with her stinking fish-head soup and her talk about eagles and ravens. "Don't talk to the ravens when you fish alone," she'd warned his father, but his father had only laughed. Then they found him face down on the beach with his boat adrift three miles away. Now Sonny was talking to fish and didn't know where he'd end up.

When the sun came out, the water sparkled so strangely it hurt his eyes and everything looked distorted. From his position in the power skiff, the big seine boat, the *Nancy M.*, seemed miles and miles away. He sat alone on the sparkling water, holding the net taut, waiting for the fish to ride in on the flood. Then it was rain again, rain down the back of his neck.

He led the net back to the big boat. On the boom the power block turned, hauling the net aboard. He backed off and idled while the *Nancy M.* heeled over with the net's weight. Jellyfish load, that's what they'd caught. He could see the boys on deck, their yellow slickers brilliant in the foggy gloom, their mouths moving, but he couldn't hear them. The block turned; they reached up. Seaweed, jellyfish, salmon, and rain fell into their open arms.

Frankie slapped Sonny's shoulder and Sonny jumped, snapping his eyes open. They were laughing and he grinned to be agreeable, waiting to catch the joke.

"What's that old coot looking over here for?" Duane wanted to know. He wiggled his fingers in a little hello and the old Norwegian looked away.

Frankie twisted around to see. "Oh, he's probably wondering how Sonny and me and Henry got through the box."

"What box?" Duane tilted his head with interest.

"Hey man, you been up here six months and you still don't know about the box?" Frankie was gleeful. "See, in Petersburg they got a box down at the dock, and everybody that comes to town's got to stick their heads in. If you ain't square-head enough, these squarehead Norskies won't let you in their town." Frankie cackled at his own joke like he'd just heard it for the first time. Sonny was amazed that Frankie always found life so entertaining. He'd laughed his way through first grade on up and probably right through Nam, though Sonny hadn't been around to see that one, thanks to his knee. "It was a gas killing them gooks," Frankie said when he came home.

Duane considered the information, then patted his lips in a little *woo-woo-woo* Indian call for the benefit of the old Norwegian, who was still sending Sonny hate stares.

The café door swung wide and two cannery girls dressed in jeans and down vests entered. Frankie said, "I'll take the redhead."

"Fat chance," Henry said. "You're too ugly."

It wasn't true. Except for his snaggly teeth, Frankie was good looking enough, just dumb. As long as the girl was dumber, he did all right.

The waitress returned with their orders. The girls took a table at the back of the room, but the redhead got up to buy cigarettes, and as she passed their table, she smiled right into Sonny's face.

"Did you see that?" Frankie hooted. "She likes you. Go for it, man."

Sonny had seen the girl give him the eye, but most likely it didn't mean a thing. Petersburg girls were generally more trouble than they were worth. The local Norwegian girls wouldn't give him the time of day because he was Indian, and the others, up from California or Washington or Oregon for the summer, were too hard to figure out. They came in the summer and disappeared when it started to get cold. Once in a while one of them would come on to him in a bar, but either they wanted to sleep with him because he was Indian (one girl told him she'd already had a black, a Mexican, and an Arab) or they'd drink his drinks all night, and just when he was ready to make his move, their cannery boyfriend would show up to take them home. The boyfriend, still wearing his stinking cannery clothes as though it made him more Alaskan, would want to shake Sonny's hand and invite him down to their place to get high. When the redhead walked by again, he dismissed her; longshots weren't his game.

"You're just going to let it pass," Frankie said disgustedly. "Sonny's too good looking a dude, he's getting spoiled. Can't you see she's begging for a heap big chief?"

Everyone laughed. They'd finished eating, except for Henry, who ate like a child, cutting his food into small, neat squares and following each bite with a swallow of milk and a look of satisfaction. He finished his last bite of potato, gulped his milk, and looked up. A white milk mustache clung to his upper lip.

"Jesus, ain't you been weaned yet?" Frankie smirked.

Henry wiped his lips with the back of his sleeve, and they were ready to roll. As they walked past the old Norwegian, he spat again, but Sonny didn't turn to look.

Out on the street it was drizzling, and the streets were puddled. Sonny walked carefully to avoid wetting his motorcycle boots. He liked to dress nice in town. He'd spent enough time in rain gear to last a life.

Above the tops of the cannery buildings and the neat white clapboard houses with their decorative shutters and trim, fenced yards, soft white clouds smeared the mountains. Sonny thought Petersburg looked too clean. Shop windows displayed the usual Alaska souvenirs: gaudy jade and gold nugget rings, silver clan bracelets carved in Tlingit designs — ravens, eagles, killer whales — miniature totem poles, and a large collection of soapstone carvings made by Eskimos in northeast Canada, farther away from Petersburg than Seattle by thousands of miles. In Vladimir they sold the same crap, but it annoyed Sonny that Petersburg, an Indian-hating town, should use phony native trinkets to rake in dough.

The streets were full of seine crews, jostling, laughing, headed for the bars. Gangs of four and five boys, they walked with their elbows stuck out, looking for trouble. Some were up from Seattle for the first time and wanted to flex their muscles. The full-blooded Tlingit and Haida crews off the Indian boats were the worst. Boys from the reservation islands still thought they were fighting a war, didn't know the Russians and then the Hudson's Bay Company had solved all that a long time back. Sonny gave them credit for being tough — you couldn't beat a reservation Indian for meanness — but all he wanted to do was have a few drinks and cool out. He walked along, glancing over his shoulder from time to time, uneasy and on guard.

"Fucking Seattle boats," Frankie said, looking around at the crews. "Ought to keep them down in Puget Sound where they belong instead of letting them come up here and take all our fish."

"Fish ain't out there," Henry said.

Sonny said nothing. It gave him a knot in his stomach to

think about the money he wouldn't be making if things kept up this way.

Duane disappeared to hustle pool as soon as they walked into the Harbor Bar. He was a good shot and was making a living at it in Vladimir before he got hired on the *Nancy M.* Duane's pool table grace, surprising in such a sloppily large kid, didn't carry over to the boat; he was always dropping lines or tripping on rigging and forever in the way.

Henry, Frankie, and Sonny pushed to the bar. The juke box was good and loud, which made Sonny feel better. He decided to stick to beer. The place was jammed. Seine and gill-net skippers sat in clusters, complaining about the most recent cuts in net-fishing hours; trollers argued bait and lures; packers from the cannery tenders sent drinks to skippers to keep their business; and here and there a cannery girl got more attention than she could handle. A few of the trollers and gill netters had their wives with them, or even a girl deckhand.

Sonny thought that would be the way to go, own your own boat and find some girl to help you pull in fish. How was it that guys from Outside like that phony Digger could come up here and make bucks and hire on girl deckhands, when he was still crewing and sharing a smelly fo'c's'le with a bunch of guys?

It burned him up to think about the nice-looking girl he'd seen Digger hire on that night in the Anchor Lounge. He'd been standing there when Lucille, the bartender, ran out on the street and dragged the girl in. She stood behind the bar in a red plastic raincoat, blinking in the sudden gloom, while Lucille introduced her as "Allie, that girl I told you about who wants to work on a boat."

The whole bar went quiet, the line of drinkers grinning slyly like they were listening to a dirty joke: here was a girl baiting herself on the hook. One of the mill workers stage-whispered, "Wish I had a boat." Somebody snickered. Digger just sat there, making the moment stretch. The girl didn't know which of the drinkers she was supposed to be meeting, and she searched the line of faces, puzzled and eager, like a dog lost in a crowd. For a second she looked right into Sonny's eyes as if to ask, "Are you the one?"

He wondered where she was from. She had to be Indian, with that black hair, those dark eyes, but there was something un-Indian about her too. By the time all the Tlingit girls he knew got to be her age, which he figured at eighteen, their faces had already hardened, shut down, and they always looked hurt or mean. Her face was too crazily hopeful, too innocent.

Then Digger leaned over the bar to check her out and started going on in that loudmouth voice of his, and it was all over. The girl was his property; the drinkers turned back to their drinks. Sonny felt impotent and angry in the face of Digger's luck, ashamed for the girl, ashamed for himself.

Henry had bought a round and it was Sonny's turn. He ordered another beer for himself, but Henry was gulping whiskey and starting up on his favorite theme.

"I don't care if we don't make a season," Henry insisted. "It don't make no difference to me. I just want to go out to Siligovsky Island, set my traps, and read my cowboy westerns. I don't need no fish to get by."

"Sure," Sonny said. Henry was telling his own truth, and Sonny envied him a bit for being so easy to please. The juke box stopped playing, and he went over to drop a few quarters and punch some tunes. The fishing movie in his head was fading, just a glimmer here and there of black web pulled up by the block, or a sparkle of water. It would start again when he tried to sleep, but for now he felt good, leaning over the bright flashing lights of the juke box, making choices, tapping his feet.

An old frowzy blonde wearing a white ruffled blouse with a beer stain down its front reached out from the last stool to grab his arm. "Hey," she said. "Hey you. You're such a handsome boy, you know that? You look just like my little John Junior. My little son John."

Sonny smiled.

"My name's Margaret," the woman said. "Will you do me a favor, honey?"

"What's that?" Sonny looked over his shoulder to see if Frankie was watching. Margaret dug around in her purse.

"I want you to play my favorite song, only I can't find my money. I know I got money here somewhere or they wouldn't be giving me beer."

Sonny pulled out some quarters. "What do you want to hear?"

"Oh, aren't you sweet. I want to hear 'Take the Ribbon from Your Hair.' I just think that's the prettiest song I ever heard. I always cry when I hear that song 'cause it's so pretty."

Sonny punched the right buttons. He hoped Margaret wouldn't get weepy. Why was it that some women got weepy, while his mom just got mad? He pictured his mother back in Vladimir, sitting in one of the bars and asking the same kind of favor, talking about her little boy Sonny. He wondered how she was holding up. If her boyfriend, Nick, was back in town from trolling she'd be okay, but when Nick was fishing and Sonny wasn't there to keep an eye on her, she got herself into trouble. She was just too lonely to stay home, she said. When he suggested she try bingo, she laughed in his face. They both knew it was more than time she needed to kill. These days she seemed to be as determined about going under as she always had been about keeping the family afloat. Thinking about it made Sonny feel helpless, like he'd been asked to fix something that couldn't be fixed.

"You're a nice boy," Margaret said. "I wish my Johnny'd been as nice as you. You know where that boy of mine is now? He's out at the Seventh Day Adventist logging camp, acting too holy to talk to his own mother. He says I got to go for the cure. Religion or no, that boy was always meaner than a weasel. You ain't mean, are you sweetheart?" Margaret slurped at her beer.

"Not me," Sonny said. He left her a couple of quarters and started back to his seat. A hand on his shoulder stopped him. It didn't feel friendly, and he dipped his shoulder to shake free before turning. Behind him, weaving, stood a Tlingit kid with ragged uncut hair tied back with a folded bandana headband and eyes so red they looked like something inside them had burst. Sonny recognized him as a kid who crewed on the *Kerri K.*, a boat from the Indian town of Kake.

"That your girlfriend?" The kid gestured toward Margaret.

Sonny's guts tightened. This one was too young, too drunk, and probably had a whole seine crew lurking in the shadows to back him up. Sonny didn't want this. He started to push past but the kid stuck out his arm.

"I ask you something, man. I want to know. That your girlfriend, huh?"

"My beer's getting warm."

"Hey, I think this old white bitch your girlfriend, man. I think you fuck old white cooze. Must be, Indian dude like you working on a white man's boat." The kid stumbled, far gone.

One punch. Sonny could take him with one punch, but he didn't feel angry enough to do it. He felt tired, although his stomach and fists were tense. All he wanted was to sit back down and finish his beer and listen to his songs on the juke box. His quarters were going to waste. He wanted to shrug it off, but now people were watching. It was no win. He knew that it was stupid to fight, but every time he walked away he felt shamed. It was some kind of code he couldn't buy into and couldn't buy out of.

"Hey," he said softly. "You got that right. Margaret's my girl. Come on over and I'll introduce you." He laughed, a tinny echo in his head.

Puzzled, the kid stepped back. Sonny ducked away and walked toward his seat, the back of his neck icy with chance, waiting for the blow. Laugh it off, just keep laughing it off.

"Somebody there got a problem?" Henry asked.

Sonny crushed his beer can. He was wired worse than ever now. What he needed was whiskey, not beer. Or better yet, a joint. "Shit," he said. "I could've taken him easy."

"Sure you could've," Henry said calmly.

"I could've. Easy. Where's Frankie?"

Henry nodded toward a table with a couple of cannery girls. "Gone fishing. Let's have another one here, what do you say?"

"Shit," Sonny said. He caught a glimpse of himself in the mirror behind the bar and sneered at his own reflection. A tough dude, a real tough dude. He ought to just go back to the boat and light up a number, but if he got up to go now, it would look like he'd been driven out. "I got to get away from this shit," he muttered.

Henry said, "We'll be back in Vladimir tomorrow."

"I don't mean that." It didn't matter anymore if it was Vladimir or Petersburg, and it wasn't a question of getting his own boat so he could be his own man. He wanted to go somewhere far away where he could try some different kind of life that he couldn't name. "Henry, you ever thought of getting out of here, going Outside for a while? You know, checking out someplace else?"

Henry shrugged. "I just want to go back to Siligovksy Island, set my traps, and read my cowboy westerns."

When the bartender came by, Sonny switched from beer to whiskey.

WHEN THE ROAR of diesel knocked her awake, Allie knew she'd blown it. Digger was standing in the cockpit, reeling in the net. "Get up on the flying bridge and shine the spotlight!" he screamed. "See how close we are to that rock!"

Allie clambered up the ladder and beamed the spotlight over the black water. She couldn't see anything, and her heart was pounding.

"Get down here! Hurry up!"

She scrambled back down the ladder, slipped on the last three rungs, and landed on an upended gaffhook. She yelped and sat down to pull it out of her boot. The gaff had gone through the sole, made a small cut in her foot. She couldn't remember when she'd last had a tetanus shot. She almost wished the cut was deeper so that Digger wouldn't be as mad at her as she knew he was going to be as soon as he stopped pulling in the net.

As a little girl she had stepped on a nail while playing barefoot in the basement. She was terrified, expecting a blow, since she'd been told not to take off her shoes. When her father swooped down the stairs, grabbed her up in his arms, and carried her in a rush back up, she was overwhelmed with amazement and gratitude. He'd come to rescue her. He loved her after all! But then he deposited her with a thump on the toilet seat in the hall bathroom and shouted for her mother.

He hadn't come to rescue her; he'd simply been afraid that she'd bleed on the wall-to-wall carpet.

Allie pulled her boot back on. It would probably leak now. She looked over at Digger, whose face loomed pale and frightened under the picking light. He was reeling in the net without stopping to pull out the fish. The whole mess of salmon and seaweed was loading up on the groaning drum. Digger leaped out of the cockpit, knocked Allie aside, and ran into the pilothouse. The boat rose from the water, cut a sharp turn that almost threw Allie from her feet, and roared full speed up the strait. Digger cut the engine. The stern lifted in the backwash, then settled in the trough. In the sudden silence Allie heard shorebirds and another engine far away.

"Do you know what the fuck you did?" Digger stood over her, his face so close it didn't look real. She noted details — blood vessels in his eyes, cigarette stains on his teeth — with the numbed fascination of an accident victim.

"I'm sorry," she whispered.

"Sorry? Do you know I could lose my fucking license if anyone saw us fishing over the legal line? You know we almost lost the net? You got two thousand bucks to pay for that net? You know how close we were? You almost killed us both!"

Allie shook her head. "I'm sorry."

"Sorry?" Digger grabbed her and shook her hard. "I could've fucking lost my boat!"

Allie turned her face away, bracing to be hit. She was an expert at this, shutting down, hardening inside herself so that she wouldn't feel the blow. She squeezed her eyes tight. He couldn't hurt her. None of them could.

"Fuck," Digger said. He turned away, kicked a pail and sent it clattering across the deck. When he turned back he looked drained. "Come on, we got to take care of that net. You better put some peroxide on that foot when we're done."

He climbed down into the cockpit and Allie followed, drawing on a pair of gloves. She no longer feared that he would hurt her, and in the absence of punishment, a new fear arose: he might fire her. It didn't matter that she couldn't stand Digger. She hadn't learned anything yet; she wanted to stay on the boat.

Digger reeled the net out slowly, reversing the usual process, picking out fish as he sent the net back into the water. The net was jammed with fish. Digger counted aloud: fifty-five, fifty-six. The fish were already dead, which made picking easier, but they were terribly tangled and squashed. Several times he had to stop and cut the net. Allie worked feverishly beside him, running back and forth to the bins, trying to prove her usefulness, a tiny plea in the face of her crime.

It took forever to empty the net. She grew sweaty under her rubber rain gear. Her foot throbbed.

Digger reeled the empty net back onto the drum, pulled off his gloves, and wiped his forehead with the back of his wrist. "Ninety-two fish. That was one hell of an illegal set. About five hundred dollars' worth."

Allie looked up in surprise. An hour ago they'd been yards from drowning and now he was talking bucks. "Digger? You aren't going to fire me, are you?"

He squinted at her. "Nah, not this time. But you better be more careful from now on." He tossed his gloves into a deck bucket and whistled. "Ninety-two fish. Jesus fucking Christ. You know, we might just be high boat this week?"

At noon, when the government plane flew over again, all the nets were drawn up out of the water. The large tender boats from the canneries bobbed on anchor while the gill netters circled, waiting to unload. When it was their turn, Digger climbed down into the hold and tossed the fish up on deck to Allie, who had to toss them one by one across the rail to the deck of the packer. The sun was out; Allie was hot and sweaty and her back ached. Digger kept yelling at her to be careful. He was afraid she'd drop a fish — a five dollar bill, he called them — between the two boats.

On the deck of the tender the packer's wife, a skinny woman in white plastic go-go boots, jabbed each fish in the head with a pointed fish pough, lifted it, and flipped it into the bins. The salmon were separated by species, weighed, then dropped into the boat's enormous slush-filled hold. The packer, Louie, wrote out Digger's check and they cast off.

"Did you have fun, honey?" the packer's wife asked as she tossed Allie their line. Exhausted beyond thinking, Allie wasn't able to make sense of the words.

"Well, we did it," Digger announced. "I don't know about the boats going back to Vladimir or Petersburg to sell to the canneries, but Louie said we brought in the biggest load. You're working on a highline boat!"

They ran up the coast, through a narrow channel, and into the village of Point Baker. "Now I'm going to show you the real Alaska," Digger said. "This is a place those turkeys off the ferry never get to see." Being high boat had made him expansive, but Allie knew this was the town Digger, the one she'd met in Vladimir. On the boat, pacing, smoking, consuming endless candy bars, cursing other skippers, Digger was a madman.

Baker had no roads, just a handful of cabins along the water's edge, a short wooden dock lined with gill netters and trollers, a floating post office in the middle of the channel, and a clapboard store and bar floating on cedar logs alongside the dock. Baker's thirty or so year-round residents commuted to the store by skiff. The ferry didn't stop there, and the only way in was by boat, or float plane if the radio was working that day. The whole village was supplied by a mail-food-oil barge that arrived once a week. Gill-netting season had swelled Baker's population, but even in winter the bar did well.

As soon as they had tied up and scrubbed the hold, Digger disappeared down the dock. Allie shed her rain gear and, without bothering to wash, climbed up onto the bow and fell asleep, cheek resting against the anchor cradle, sun beating down on her face.

She dreamed that she was little again, maybe ten or twelve. It was the time when they had money, when her father still owned a Cape Cod beach house and a cabin cruiser, and she was a captive on his boat. In the dream, her father was coming into a dock too fast, crunching wood, and blaming them for not fending off. Allie and her brother leaped around on deck, trying to tie lines, while her father shouted and the dockboys smirked.

"Hey, Jackie," Allie's father yelled at her mother, whose name was Emily. "Tell Jackie Kennedy there in the sunglasses to get off her ass and hand me that line."

Allie's mother went down into the galley to fix lunch. Allie followed her and caught her raising a large glass of Scotch to her lips. Her mother smiled weakly, put the glass down, and began to slice up leftover roast. Then blood was spurting over the bread slices, over her mother's white pants. Allie's mother stared at her cut finger in surprise. "Don't worry," her mother said, "it's just a little accident. I know I can't be drunk because my tongue hasn't gone numb yet. My tongue always goes numb when I get drunk. I'm in control." Allie began to cry.

Up on deck her father was shouting, "Some crew. About as much use as the tits on a bull!"

Allie woke confused and panicky, unsure of where she was. Her father's boat . . . but that boat was gone a long time ago, and she was working for Digger now. It felt like little consolation. How had she fallen in love with Vladimir boats when she'd hated boats all her life? Boats meant being trapped. But the fishing boats were nothing like her father's boat. They weren't fiberglass stinkpots for people with money who didn't know what to do on the weekend and so moved their fights from the house to the sea. They were boats with dignity, boats that made sense.

Allie climbed down from the bow. The sun had already slid

31

behind the high peak on the westernmost side of the channel, although the eastern side was still bright. Her face felt tight and sunburned, and her whole body ached. How long had she slept? In the galley she pumped cold water and washed her face, then stuffed her dirty hair into a watch cap, grabbed Digger's wool jacket, and walked across the sterns of two gill netters to reach the dock.

Country-western music blared from pilothouse windows, and she smelled spaghetti sauce. It was getting on dinnertime; soon she'd have to make something for Digger. On the dock a husky and a flop-eared hound growled over a bone. Behind the store the mountainous spine of Prince of Wales Island rose in a dark wall of hemlock and spruce choked with devil's club and stringy moss. Chimney smoke hung in the air. A couple of teenage boys wearing rolled down hip boots and wool caps squatted against the hull of a peeling wreck, passing a joint. One of them nodded toward the store and said, "He's in there."

Inside, three quarters of the store was stocked with open shelves of dry goods. At the other end, a plank thrown across two oil barrels served as the bar. Digger sat drinking with a group of fishermen dressed in black Oshkosh jeans, down vests, and plaid shirts. Allie realized with the thrill of the obvious that these men had always dressed like that; it was a uniform that college kids simply copied. She hung in the doorway, in awe of the fact that she was in a floating bar, in the midst of real Alaskan fishermen. She wanted to be welcomed in. She didn't know if she should turn around and leave or pretend she'd come to shop.

"Goddammit, Digger," one of the drinkers, a scrawny little gill netter with rheumy eyes, a hawk nose, and purple mottled checks, hooted. "You cheap bastard. Ain't you even going to buy your deckie a drink? Come on in, girlie. I'll buy you one."

Apparently, everyone in Baker already knew who she was. Digger looked smug, a real king, a highliner with a girl deckhand. He pulled up a seat for Allie next to a passed-out drunk who lay across the bar snoring, and made quick introductions: Alf, who had invited her in; Darryl, the bartender and general owner of Point Baker, a beefy man with Paul Bunyan forearms and mild eyes under a Marine crew cut; and a middle-aged troller from Vladimir named Nick.

Allie asked for a bourbon. She would have preferred a sweet mixed drink, but the bourbon made her feel tougher, more like one of them.

Alf winked. "It ain't like we get to drink with good-looking girls that often. Hell, we don't even get ugly girls out here. Hey Digger, what happened to the skinny gal who fished with you last year? You trade her in for a new model?"

"Jeanine," Digger said, turning morose. "She split."

"So you went and found yourself a little klootch that likes whiskey?"

"Allie ain't Indian," Digger said. "She's from Boston."

"Bah-stuhn? That right?" Alf grinned, revealing black stumpy teeth. Grubby long underwear hung out from the cutoff sleeves of his jacket, and his face was seamed with grime. "You must be one of them wops, then. I was sure you was Indian."

Allie shrugged. All her life people had been asking "What are you?" as though they had a right to know. Something about her darkness always intrigued or irritated them. It had annoyed her mother's family most of all, proof of what was in those days considered a "mixed marriage." Her mother's family, poor Boston Irish, had little to be proud of, but they felt themselves superior to her father's family of noisy, ignorant, and ambitious Russian Jews. Her father's family, for their part, rejected goyish grandchildren. Allie felt little affinity for either group and was in the habit of pretending to be what people wanted her to be, which meant what *they* were. Usually it meant Italian, French, or Greek; in Vladimir, it meant Indian.

Alf grinned slyly. "If you ain't wop, what are you? Maybe you're a little bit Jew?"

She'd never tell him.

"Come on," Alf wheedled. "What are you?"

"What are *you*?" Allie asked. "A Nazi?"

Alf raised a stiff arm and shouted "Sieg Heil!" then nearly laughed himself into apoplexy. "Hey, Digger," he said when he regained himself. "She's ornery, but she's kinda cute."

Allie snorted into her glass.

Alf grinned at her. "See how you are?"

Darryl folded his arms across his chest and looked thoughtful. "Boston, eh? You're a long way from home. I was in Boston in the Navy before they sent me on up to the Aleutians. I used to hang out in Scollay Square."

"Yeah?" Allie said. "Scollay Square isn't there anymore." She decided it wasn't worth explaining that she wasn't exactly from Boston.

"Let me tell you something, Allie." Darryl poured another bourbon for her and one for himself. Digger's voice boomed behind her in argument with Alf, something about the ferry cutting someone's net. Darryl leaned on his arms so that his face was uncomfortably close, thick and sincere. "Allie, this is the best fucking country — excuse my French — the best damn country you'll ever see. You're lucky you're getting a chance to see it now before it's all gone."

"What do you mean?"

"It used to be a free country up here, but it ain't gonna last. Fish and Game and the rest of them government jackasses are ruining it so a man can't be himself no more." He shook his head sadly. "They're taking it away from us. We're a thing of the past."

"How?" Allie asked. She felt anxious, as though something was going to disappear before she had a chance to be a part of it, but Darryl turned away to break up a block of ice.

"Anyone heard about the announcement?" Digger asked.

"Maybe tomorrow, maybe day after," Alf answered. "Hell,

there might not even be a gill-net opening. They might just shut her down."

"They *got* to give us an opening," Digger said in a threatening tone, as though he could bully them into it.

Allie looked from face to face, eager to understand.

"They ain't got to do nothing," Alf said. "Fucking Fish and Game don't care if we go broke. The whole thing's a fake if you ask me. There ain't no fish shortage, they just won't let us fish the right places. Fish and Game is in cahoots with the canneries, with the fucking Japs that own the canneries now." Alf nodded knowingly. "They're lying, saying there ain't no spawners in the creeks, but it's just a way to drive up prices. So what if the fisherman starves?"

"That ain't all of it," Digger said. "There's too many boats."

Alf ignored him, drained his glass, and thrust it forward for a refill. "Now the trollers, they got it easy. They're the goddamn last free men. Fish where they want to seven days a week with no one to tell them what to do. I should've got my trolling license when I had a chance, get out of this net-fishing racket. The goddamn last free men. Ain't that right, Nick?"

Everyone turned to look at the troller who'd been quietly sipping his drink. He was a lean, wiry man in his late fifties, with prominent cheekbones, curly grey hair, pale eyes, and a scar on his chin. He smiled into his glass and ignored them.

"Ain't that right?" Alf insisted. "Ain't you trollers the last free men?"

Late sunlight, refracting off the mountains and the channel, cut through the bar window, across the plank in a halo of splinters, and caught Nick as he looked up. In the oblique light his pale eyes were dazzling.

"That depends what to you means freedom," Nick said in a soft Slavic accent. "You think freedom means number of spawning salmon Fish and Game is counting in creeks? Okay." He looked down into his glass and smiled again. "To you, I am free man."

The men sat in confused silence. The sun dropped behind the mountain, leaving the bar cast in shadow. They were afraid, Allie realized with a surge of disappointment, all of them except perhaps for Nick, although she didn't really understand what he meant. They were afraid of losing their independence, their one-man, one-boat way of life. They blamed the canneries, Fish and Game, out-of-state boats, the Japanese, everyone but themselves. Yet the paradox of fishing was that it ensured its own end.

She felt alert with a sudden understanding that she couldn't express to the men around her because it would set her too much apart. Every fisherman was on a search and destroy mission; in performing his duties, he destroyed what he loved. Fishermen were like explorers who in mapping a wilderness betrayed it, made it into something else. Either they believed the supply of fish was limitless, as people must have once believed the land was limitless, or they knew it was running out and were intent on getting their share before it was gone. Knowing this made her no less eager to participate. There was a certain seductive element: the fascination of going down with a sinking ship.

"Ah, you're no better than the rest of us," Alf said to Nick, switching on the lights. "We're all just living off Jap welfare checks. Hey, Digger. She any good?" Alf nodded at Allie.

Digger grinned. "You talking fishing?"

Alf had hit the right note and the tension eased. They were back on safe ground again, comfortable at her expense. Allie felt uneasy, flushed to be the center of attention and yet insulted. She could feel a sickly, complicitous grin distorting her face.

"She does okay," Digger said. "Only she likes to sleep." Digger poked Allie in the ribs. She leaned away from him, bumping the passed-out drunk, who stirred, opened one puffy bruised eye, and gave her an evil glance.

"Hell, I'd never get out of the bunk if I had me a girl deckhand," Alf declared. "That net wouldn't even get wet."

"Alf," Digger protested, "you wouldn't even know what to do if you had the chance. Last woman you got close to was the nurse in the dry-out ward down in Ketchikan when she changed your bedpan." Digger laughed hard at his own joke.

Alf shrugged. "She wasn't so bad looking. Course, I did have the D.T.s at the time."

Everyone laughed. Allie noticed that the troller with the accent, Nick, was staring at her, not lewdly, like Alf, but steadily. She looked away in embarrassment.

"Hey!" The drunk that Allie had bumped into had roused himself and began banging his beer can against the plank. He stood up and waved the can in Allie's face. "Hey. D'you hear the one about the Canadian boat took out the female deckhand?"

"Hell with the Canucks," Alf grumbled. "Let them fish their own waters."

The big drunk banged his beer can on the bar again. It crumpled under the impact. "I *said,* did you hear the one about the Canadian boat took out the female deckhand?"

"Tell the goddamn joke," Alf said.

"Well, you see. It was like this." The fisherman looked around, then settled his gaze on Allie. "See, they came into port and the crew had thirty thousand pounds of halibut. But all that female deckhand had," he leaned his bulldog face close, "all *she* had was one pore little red snapper!"

"Red snapper!" The bar broke up.

"It's a bottom fish, see?" Digger explained. "Get it?"

"I get it," Allie hissed. The men roared again, showing their bad teeth with their wild laughter. The only one who didn't laugh was Nick.

She got it. It was suddenly very clear. She wasn't a deckhand, she was a *girl* deckhand. The joke was on her.

"Hey Digger," Alf snorted. "You shoulda kept the other one. This one ain't got no sense of humor."

Digger pulled money out of his pocket to show he was in

command. "Here, you need to buy anything, go ahead. You got everything you need to make dinner?"

Allie took the money and stood, willing to be dismissed. Her legs felt wobbly from the whiskey and the two days of bracing herself against the roll of the boat. Laughter followed her out the door. The boys were still squatting against the derelict boat, smoking. They nodded and offered Allie the joint, but she shook her head no. Baker was weird enough.

In the galley she cooked hamburger with onions and added it to a can of chili, which she left simmering on the stove. She set out two plates, two bowls, two spoons, bread. She heated water in the kettle for washing dishes, and then with nothing else to do, she stole a cigarette from Digger's pack and climbed up on deck to watch the light fade.

Thirty miles to the west the open Pacific would still be brightly lit. They would be heading out there to troll after the gill-net announcement came in and they knew where and when they'd be allowed to gill-net. Trolling. She didn't even know what it meant, just that it was something done with the tall wooden poles that stuck up from the back of the pilot-house, catching fish on hooks and lines instead of in nets. The real art, Digger had said. But the thought of trolling in the open ocean made her shiver. In comparison, gill-netting the protected waters of the Alexander Archipelago, bounded by islands, seemed cozy and safe. It was too soon to worry about that now. Hadn't it only been twenty-four hours since she'd been afraid that Digger would hit her, and then even more afraid that he'd fire her? All the decisions were out of her hands now that she was a deckhand; that was a choice *she'd* made. The only time it was in her hands was when she fell asleep. She hadn't even considered what could have happened if Digger hadn't woken up.

She could have drowned them both. Instead of remorse, she felt a strange excitement at the magnitude of risk. It really could have happened. What would it have been like? She remembered the face she'd seen under water — pale and sodden, long hair waving — and tried to imagine icy water closing over her own head. She kept turning the image over and over until she grew ashamed of the perversity of the attraction: fear that felt lascivious, fear that felt like sex. She thrived on it.

A salmon leaped in the channel, slapping the water and creating a ring of ripples; then the ripples receded and the darkness was complete. Down the dock an Indian family was having a party on a brightly lit houseboat. Someone came out on deck and dumped a pail of garbage overboard. Two boats away a baby began to cry. A figure appeared, just an outline in the darkness, holding the child, pacing up and down. Voices drifted out of the bar: Digger's booming bass, shrill laughter.

How had it happened that all of her days had added up to this, sitting on the stern of a boat at the Point Baker dock? Vladimir already seemed far behind, and the places before Vladimir more distant still. None of them seemed connected. Whatever had happened before didn't feel like her life. There was no narrative, nothing but a series of disjointed beginnings, nothing to make her feel whole. In the deepening darkness, Allie was overwhelmed by homesickness for a place she couldn't name. She drew in breath and gave up on the evening. Down in the galley of the *Ginny D.,* light broke the spell. Once again the world took on the hard, reassuring edges of the galley table, the V-shaped bunks, the bubbling of chili on the stove.

NICK WORKED the rock piles and kelp patches along the shores of Kuiu Island, trolling down to Point Decision where the automatic lighthouse boomed out its empty-hearted warning and the sea rose up in a swell. A straight shot to the outside waters. He had to put the stabilizers down, and quickly their blades tangled with kelp whips and junk riding in on the tide. The gulls wheeled large circles without diving or settling, a sign that there wasn't feed to bring in cohos. A couple of trollers ran past, their poles up, headed for the outside coast of Baranof Island and Sitka Sound. One was a Vladimir boat and Nick waved. He wondered if they knew anything he should, but decided to hang in.

The end of Sumner Strait, the pass between Coronation and Prince of Wales islands, formed a shipping route. All day long tugs appeared with loads headed for Sitka, moving so slowly it seemed they weren't moving at all, then suddenly they were gone with their raft of logs or their barges loaded with prefab housing or mobile homes. Nick got tired of turning his head left, right, left to watch for pulls on the tips of the poles while keeping one eye on the fathometer. When the poles dipped and the bells rang, it was nothing but trash fish, immature halibut, flounder, or brown bombers that he had to shake from the lines. There was too much chatter on the radio for anyone to be catching fish. He decided to cut across Sumner Strait and work through Sea Otter Sound before heading down to Noyes Island and the Pedro Grounds.

It was a brilliant day, good for traveling, with the sea at his stern rolling in from outside. He was spending too much time running between places, too much time not pulling them in. A man didn't get tired pulling in fish, but this endless searching made him weary as never before. Looking for fish gave him too much time to think. All day long he'd been haunted by uneasiness, as though he'd forgotten something important. He wondered if it was Vivian. The last time he was in Vladimir he found her sitting in the Takine River Inn. He stood in the doorway watching, trying to decide if he should turn around and go back to his boat. She had her back to him and was talking to the bartender, shaking her head while she rummaged in her big white plastic pocketbook. He was able to gauge the progress of her evening by the bartender's air of distraction, the way he looked away from Vivian in between bored nods. Although her brown shoulders rising above her low-backed jersey looked muscular and strong, familiar, Nick knew he was seeing something he had no right to: Vivian surrounded by bar stools, in all her raw loneliness and need.

He looked away to the bar's picture windows, where night refused to fall. The sun still glowed over the mountains, a northbound ferry was rounding the tip of Siligovsky Island, and a tiny red speedboat shot out to jump the ferry's wake. Reassured by the sight of distances much greater than the space between himself in the doorway and Vivian at the bar, he crossed the room to touch her shoulders. Vivian twirled on her stool, and he watched as her puffy, mascara-smeared, yet still beautiful face registered surprise, anger, relief, love.

"Damn you," Vivian said. "Damn you straight to hell."

It wasn't going to work. Not because Vivian expected him around more often — he was a troller, after all, and had to follow the fish — but she seemed to want something more definite, something she could hold on to, and that was something he didn't have inside himself to give. But this was an old story, nothing that should make him feel so ill at ease. When he closed his eyes and saw the face of the girl, he knew it wasn't Vivian at all.

Why should he care about a silly, dark-eyed kid? Just one of the pilgrims come to see the great American holy land, like the ones off the ferries with their guitars and backpacks. Only this one wanted to fish. He'd known she wasn't Indian when he saw her in the Anchor Lounge the night Digger hired her on. She couldn't be Indian with eyes like that. He'd felt shame for her up there on the auction block. Eyes full of hope, Byzantine eyes that lacked the Tlingit guardedness, the straight-lashed Oriental tilt. He'd known eyes like hers.

When the memory started to rise, Nick pushed it away, a catch in his throat. That wasn't a place he wanted to travel to now. He looked around for distraction, something to do, and saw that the pilothouse windows were smeared with salt spray picked up from when he'd been rolling in the waves near Point Decision. Nick grabbed a roll of paper towels and a bottle of Windex, set the automatic pilot, the iron mike, on a compass course, and, gripping the metal rail, worked his way around, hand over hand, to the outside of the pilothouse. He crouched, balancing, boots sticking out on the narrow ledge. The rise and fall of the sea was so familiar he no longer noticed it, an automatic compensation that made him wobbly every time he first hit land.

He sprayed and wiped, hanging on to the rail with one hand, the roll of towels under his arm, the Windex jammed between his knees. Inside the pilothouse, the steering wheel, governed by the iron mike, turned eerily by itself. A curl of smoke rose from the cigarette he'd left in the ashtray. Everything was in place: charts, compass, radio, sonar. A picture of his boat, the *Argus*, running without him, as though he'd been erased. The emptiness of the image struck him like a premonition. Nick stood quickly, knocking the paper towels out of the crook of his elbow. The Windex clattered on the bow, and one of his booted feet slid off the ledge. He clutched the rail with both hands, trying to find the ledge. Breathing heavily, almost in panic, he pulled himself up.

The roll of towels skittered in the waves and was dashed in the white curl of wake. In a few seconds it was far behind, a bobbing white speck. That was how far the boat would have left him behind if he'd slipped. His boat would have run on and on across the strait with its small load of salmon until it smashed up on shore. He could see it: the mountains bright with snow, the ocean glittering, and his boat moving on without him. He shook his head, trying to free it of the image, and carefully worked his way back into the pilothouse.

In the fading light at Shakan, Nick caught two king salmon and tied to the rotting pilings of an abandoned cannery. He shut down the engine and his ears rang from the diesel pound. The cannery was falling into shadows. He loved these old cannery ghost towns, hopes laid out in rotting wood. At one time, thousands of workers had lived in bunkhouses, danced in halls, worked the stacks and steamers now choked by weeds and devil's club. How quickly the land reclaimed its own. The workers' barracks had crumbled into ferns and thick green moss on a forgotten coast. There'd been fish in those days, the twenties; so much so that the men had come in with deckloads, their holds overfilled. But the bottom had fallen out of the market during the Depression when salmon sold at three cents a pound.

He'd been a uniformed schoolboy then, carrying a satchel of books across a Leningrad canal. He'd been Kolya, the diminutive of Nikolai. It wasn't odd to him to have had his name changed. After all, he was born in a city that changed its name twice in ten years: St. Petersburg, Petrograd, Leningrad. Nikolai, Kolya, Nick.

He put away his gear, laying the snubbers in a bucket full of soapy water to wash the smell of diesel from his hands. He hung the hooks on their string at the end of the cleaning table, covered the bait herring with another layer of rock salt to

44

keep them stiff. His two kings lay in a galvanized tub covered with a wet burlap sack.

He cleaned the first, placing it on the table, slicing out the gills, a fan of cartilage rich in oxygenated blood. Then a quick slice up the belly, releasing a slither of needlefish and herring over his gloved hand. The last supper. There was nothing more intimate than this, his knife in the creature's belly, taking intestines, liver, flipping them back over the salmon's head, making the swift, sure cut around the throat that released the whole mess in a solid handful. He slit the membrane holding the kidney and scraped the clotted blood with the spoon-shaped end of the knife. A clean, empty cavity. He turned for the bucket of water he'd dipped to rinse the fish, holding the creature on the slippery cleaning table with one hand. Emptied of innards, the dead fish suddenly jerked convulsively under his glove. Startled, Nick dropped the bucket of water, splashing half of it down his boots.

He laughed at himself. It wasn't the first time he'd seen such a thing, and still it surprised him. A lifetime reflex, only a reflex. A man could jerk like that too, emptied of life but still kicking; no heart, no liver or guts. Again he saw the empty pilothouse and the wheel turning of its own accord. Emptiness, yet motion. He understood.

Nick lifted another bucketful of seawater and rinsed the fish, rubbing in the direction of the scales until the fish was clean and all that showed was the empty belly and the simple hole in the head where the gaff had gone when he lifted it out of the water. He cleaned the second fish, then rinsed the last shreds of guts off the deck, little bruise-colored pieces of liver that caught in the scuppers and coiled lines. He lifted the hatch cover and climbed down into the hold to ice his fish, measuring the degree of melt from the day's sun. He refilled the salmons' bellies with ice, chopping the melt-hardened chunks with a shovel, and covered the fish. He pulled himself out of the hold with a groan.

With the engine off, Nick's hearing returned and with it the

sound of the wind bending spruce on the mountains and rattling the boards of the cannery shacks. A stream ran down
the slopes into the sea. Across the narrow inlet of Shakan Bay,
a whale surfaced. It's spouting roar was that of a lion. Nick
sat down with a cigarette to watch. The whale ducked and
reappeared. This time, when the whale went down, its tail
stood straight up for a moment, split flukes hanging in the
air, a signal that it would dive deep. Nick imagined its course
as it sounded: down, down, down in the darkness. What
loneliness. Whales traveled the lengths of continents, calling
out to each other in their strange, keening language. Their
voices reached halfway around the world. Did they mate only
once and remain true to their partners? He remembered
there'd been a time when he'd thought of a woman, Sophia,
across the globe: it is day here, and there, for her, it is night.
Here it is night and now she is rising from her bed. Nick
threw his cigarette angrily over the rail. The sun fell behind
the mountain and the evening was gone.

That night he dreamed of Leningrad: sun flashing off the
golden spire of the Peter and Paul Fortress, ice on the Neva
River. He was walking with Sophia past the railing of a
bridge. She wore a fur-trimmed coat and a soft fox hat. When
she laughed, her breath shot out in silvery plumes.

At the end of the bridge the road was filled with a moving
caravan of trucks. Dark green with the red star, they rumbled
past in endless succession, packed with uniformed soldiers.
Then Nick was holding a rifle and Sophia was gone.

He was standing in a bedroom filled with glaring light. An
iron-railed bed stood empty, a puffy white quilt thrown back.
A woman's bare shoulders, dark tumbling hair, an old-fashioned white linen nightgown. Sophia turned to face him, dark
eyes full of fear. When she spoke, he could see her lips move
but he couldn't understand a word, as though he'd forgotten
his Russian, lost his native tongue. "Sophia," he said but no
words came out of his mouth. "Sophia," he mouthed.
"Sophia!"

He woke, sticky with sweat. He fumbled for his watch, his cigarettes. The sky had already lightened and Shakan Bay looked glassily calm. It was three-twenty in the morning. Knowing that he would find no more sleep, Nick rose. He dressed, made coffee, pumped the bilge, started the diesel, cast off, and went out to look for fish.

"I'M SO HAPPY," Vivian crooned, leaning back on the couch. "I'm always so happy when my Sonny comes home."

Sonny winced. Across the room Brenda's tight, catlike smile curled tighter, although she didn't turn her head.

"That boy's a stick-in-the-mud," Vivian informed Jimmy Caldwell, who was seated between her and Sonny on the couch. "He didn't even want to come to your party. I had to beg him to come."

"Just got back in from fishing," Sonny mumbled.

"Hell with that," Jimmy exclaimed. "Hell with that. All wore out from fishing? Jeez, you boys are getting soft. Back in the old days we pulled those nets by hand."

"Yeah," Sonny said softly, "but you had a reason to pull them." Roaring up and down the straits, searching for fish, hauling water that spilled through the net, all they'd caught on the *Nancy M.* was jellyfish and seaweed. He didn't want to think about that. He'd rather be figuring his chances, watching Brenda pretend she didn't know he was watching, wondering how hard it would be to give his mom the slip.

"You're right," Jimmy conceded. "It ain't easy now either. A lot of good hydraulics do if there ain't no fish. I bet you're just all wore out from breaking those Petersburg girls' hearts." The old man cackled and put an arm around Sonny's shoulder, squeezing so hard his glasses poked Sonny in the side of the head. "You're a good-looking Indian. No shit. Us Tlingits got to stick together. No shit." Jimmy surveyed the crowded living room of his new housing project apartment with pleasure. There wasn't a single white person in the room.

Out of the corner of his eye, Sonny saw Brenda disappear into the kitchen, and, using beer for an excuse, he followed. He could feel Vivian's eyes on his back.

Brenda was leaning against the sink, hands on her hips and head tilted back so he could admire the perfect combination of angles and planes that shaped her face. She wasn't Tlingit but Oglala Sioux, raised on a Dakota reservation. As far as he could tell, she didn't give a shit about anything, and she'd spent a few days in jail her first month in town after breaking open her boyfriend's skull. She was as leggily beautiful and dingy in the head as the Athabascan girls he'd met up in Fairbanks the year he'd gone to college. She'd just shown up in town one day, all alone, which gave her a mystery and a bravado that Sonny found irresistible.

"Look who got back to town," Brenda said.

"You miss me?" Sonny reached into the fridge to retrieve a six-pack of Ranier.

"Boy, are you stuck up. You think I sit around waiting for you to come home?"

"I don't think nothing." Sonny popped the top on his beer and handed one to Brenda. He loved the way her collarbone came to two little points at the base of her smooth brown throat, points as sharp as her elbows. Her hair was styled in an old-fashioned way, fluffy on top and long in back, like they wore on the reservations. She reminded him of Indian girls in movies; he could almost see her riding a pinto horse across a flat land of tall grass and wide open sky.

"You're looking real good," he said softly, moving around to lean on the sink beside her. "The whole time I was sitting out there talking to the old folks I was thinking about you. You've been driving me crazy."

"Yeah? How come you didn't bring me nothing from Petersburg?"

A little warning light flashed in his head, but he chose to ignore it. "How come you didn't bring nothing for me?" he countered, grinning.

"You?" Brenda snorted. "You're the one who's always leaving town."

"I always come back, though. Don't I always come back?"

Brenda stuck out her lip. "You better bring me something next time so I won't think you're so stuck up."

Sonny slid his fingers up the inside of her forearm. "I'll buy you a drink right now if you'll come down to the Takine."

"What about your mom?" Brenda smiled cruelly. "She's probably wondering what's taking you so long in the kitchen. Any minute now she's going to send in the Coast Guard."

Sonny gripped Brenda's wrist, pulling her around to face him. A single strand of beads rolled under his fingers. She was the only Indian girl who didn't wear the silver Tlingit clan bracelets. He pressed the tiny beads into her wrist. "Hey, yes or no?"

"You gonna take me dancing?"

"Sure."

"What about your old lady?"

Sonny sighed inwardly. "She can take care of herself."

Brenda pulled away, rubbing her wrist. She looked bored all of a sudden, but shrugged assent. Sonny led her out of the kitchen.

"First I can't get him out of the house and now he don't want to stay," Vivian complained. She eyed Brenda, who stared back.

"Let 'em go," Jimmy Caldwell chided. "They don't want to hang around with the old folks." He winked and squeezed Vivian's knee. Vivian started to say something, but Sonny pushed Brenda past them and out the door.

"She's pissed," Brenda said. "She thought you were her date."

Sonny looked at Brenda sideways. She was right about his mother, but there was a meanness in her that made her have to say it. "She'll get over it," he said.

They walked quickly, without speaking. Brenda's heels clacked on the wet pavement. The projects were a good mile from town, and Brenda's long silence made him uneasy. He never knew what she was thinking, and there were no guarantees that things would go right. He'd have to steer her through hours of drinks, ease her along, work at keeping her from getting mad. He didn't even know what he wanted from her. He could get a roll in the sack, some friendliness, a place to rest his head, from any number of Vladimir girls, but usually what he got from Brenda was trouble. He was overcome with a vision of himself steering a course, not around rain-fat puddles on Nine Mile Road but through a treacherous maze of kelp islands and bow-cracking logs. It was like being on watch in a heavy fog when they'd been out for days and all he wanted was to find a safe way home. Now everything was turning into an obstacle course and it made him tired.

At the turn-off to Front Street, Brenda suddenly stopped. "I don't feel like dancing anymore. You want to just come up?"

He was going to be lucky after all.

Sonny followed Brenda up the rickety wooden outdoor stairs that led to her one-room apartment above the laundromat. Brenda's hair flipped left, right, left, and her small ass looked too good to be true rising up the stairs, but at the top when the door swung open, her room changed his mood. There was nothing but a narrow bed, a table with one straight-back chair, a Black Hills of South Dakota poster on the wall, and one shelf of junk. The overhead light was a glaring bulb. Sonny flipped off the switch and turned on the bathroom light, half-shutting the door.

"What's the matter, don't you like my place?"

"I like it," Sonny lied.

He sat on the edge of the bed and drew Brenda down beside

him. When he kissed her, she kissed back hard, then twisted away and flopped against the pillows. She watched him pull off his boots and hang his shirt and denim jacket neatly over the chair.

"I hate this fucking town," Brenda said. "I don't know why I ever came here. Fucking rain. You don't know what it's like back home this time of year. Everything's all gold-colored and there's horses. All you got here is stinking fish."

"Hey," Sonny said, lowering himself down on top of her, closing off her words with his lips. He didn't want to hear her dump on Vladimir; it was like listening to someone put down family. He could do it as much as he wanted, but when someone else did, it hurt because it reflected on him.

They took off their own clothes. Sonny's heart stopped at the fragility of her little boy rib cage and childish breasts. Brenda, thin and tense, looked as though her bones might snap right through her skin. She was strong, though. She caught him, held him tight, digging her nails into his back, thighs squeezed around his legs. Her bony hips met his in a frantic rising: bones beating bones, bones beating bones. Then Sonny stopped thinking, stopped watching her narrowed eyes and silent moving lips, shut out everything but the shivering in her thighs. Brenda was far away and he was self-enclosed, then simply empty as he let it all go.

He pulled out slowly and rolled beside her. He could hear the ticking of her alarm clock and wondered what time it was and why he hadn't noticed the sound before. Brenda lay still, head turned away, absorbed in her own breathing. On the wall the Black Hills poster glistened, caught in the light angling around the bathroom door. What kind of place was that? Gold-colored and horses, she'd said, but when he tried to shape a picture, all he came up with was a street of wooden shacks and dust: the reservation.

He reached over and pushed Brenda's hair from her face. She turned and kissed his palm, which encouraged him. "Why'd you leave that place?" he asked.

53

Brenda pushed herself up on one elbow and eyed him suspiciously. "I got in a little trouble."

He supposed the next question should be What kind of trouble? but Brenda was getting so edgy he wasn't sure he should ask. Anyway, it wasn't really *why* she'd left home he wanted to know about, but *how*. How did a person just up and leave the place he'd grown up in, where everyone knew him and where he knew who he was? He thought about telling Brenda how he wanted to go Outside, to the lower forty-eight, and try it himself, but she might make some comment that would make him feel ridiculous or take it personally and get pissed the way she got about him going out on the boat. There was no percentage in telling feelings. He got up and searched for his smokes.

"You got an ashtray?" Sonny asked.

"Over there on the shelf. There's beer in the fridge."

Sonny detoured into the bathroom, shutting Brenda in darkness while he pissed. It looked like a hotel bathroom, like the one in the flophouse in Juneau where he stayed once when he got too tanked up to make it back to the boat. Her toothbrush looked sad, standing alone in a paste-stained glass.

He found the beers but couldn't find the ashtray in all the junk on the shelf: underwear, magazines, a porcelain Eskimo hauling a line out of an ice-fishing hole, a Bible, a cereal box, and a doll with long black braids, leather dress, and cheerful brown plastic face. Sonny picked it up and smiled. He'd never seen an Indian doll before. His sisters, grown now with their own kids, had played with the usual dolls, blondes with curls. He wondered if his nieces played with Indian dolls. Probably not, since both sisters had married white men.

"Put that down."

Sonny looked over at her, puzzled.

"I said, put it down!"

He tucked the doll back onto the junk-filled shelf and raised his hands in a palms-out gesture of innocence. "No problem."

54

"That wasn't where it was." Brenda leaped from the bed, breasts bobbling. She grabbed the doll, rearranged its braids, smoothed its dress, and bent its legs into a sitting position. Carefully she set it on top of a folded sweater, then turned and glared at him.

He had no idea what she was so mad about, a grown woman messing with a doll. He glanced longingly at the rumpled bed. He wanted to climb back under the covers, pull her close. He wanted a smoke. He reached out to cup a breast. "Aren't you a little old to play with dolls?" he said.

Brenda twisted away. "Fuck you."

"Come on, it was just a joke. Be nice."

"You think you can make fun of me just because you're a hotshot in this little dump town." She glared. "That doll belongs to my kid!"

Sonny sighed. "I didn't even know you had a kid."

"You don't know jackshit."

"Where's your kid?"

"On the reservation. Where the fuck do you think?" Brenda stomped over to the bed and climbed in, pulling up the covers.

"I don't think nothing," Sonny said. So she had a kid. It didn't really surprise him. She'd been in Vladimir almost a year, and she had a kid she'd left behind and didn't see. It was information he didn't really want to absorb now, a secret he didn't want to share. How could he help her? She'd gotten away from home and now she was paying the price. He had that familiar feeling again, that he was faced with something he couldn't fix. He picked up his cigarettes, lit one, and sat down on the straight-back chair. He still didn't have an ashtray so he just sat there smoking, letting the ashes fall in his cupped hand. The plastic Indian doll smiled down at him from the shelf.

Of course Brenda had a kid. What kind of fool was he to think that people just up and left their homes without leaving all kinds of messes behind? There was always someone at home who needed you, who'd be screwed up by your leaving, whose loss was inevitably linked with your gain. It would be the same for him, except instead of leaving a kid he'd be leaving his mom, a woman who'd already lost too many men. It made him feel twisted and tangled inside, like he couldn't make a move without causing pain.

Sonny got up and tossed his cigarette in the toilet, rinsed his ash-filled hand. He brought a beer to Brenda. "You still mad at me?" he asked, squatting by the bed.

"Get lost," Brenda said, shoving the beer away, scowling. "You might think you're something special but I don't."

Sonny shrugged and stood up. He didn't need this.

Brenda wasn't about to let it go. She searched for the right phrase, then smiled in cruel triumph. "At least my mom don't have the hots for *me*."

Ten points. Sonny turned away and picked up his jeans from the floor. He'd hurt her by accident and she couldn't be happy until she was sure she'd hurt him more. He drew on his jeans, buttoned his shirt, slid into his jacket. Brenda turned over in bed and lay face down. Sonny pulled on his socks and boots, checked for his smokes in his pocket, patted his wallet, and walked out.

The rickety wooden staircase clattered underfoot. On Front Street the bars were loud and well lit, the people inside working at having fun. He walked past them, tired now and only wanting sleep. He should've stayed home as he'd planned. He took the turn-off and walked the slatted boards over the swampy yard to the house his father had built. It tilted like a ship run up on the rocks and left by the tide. It needed a new roof. He didn't want to start thinking about that.

The lights were off but Vivian was seated inside on the living room couch, facing the blank television screen. At first Sonny saw nothing but the red point of her cigarette, but as his eyes adjusted, he made out the dim outline of her face.

"You're home early," Vivian said.

"Who you waiting up for, me or Mike?"

Vivian shrugged. "It don't make sense to wait up for either of you. Mikey, I guess."

Sonny took two beers out of the refrigerator, wincing at the sharp light, brought a can to his mother, and sat down beside her on the couch.

"How was Jimmy's party?"

"Not bad. Better than sitting home. You could've stayed."

"Yeah, well." Sonny lit a cigarette and watched the red point of his alternate with his mother's as they inhaled, making the points glow.

"I don't like that Brenda," Vivian said.

"She's all right. She's just messed up like everyone else."

"You watch out for her."

Sonny laughed. "I thought you wanted me to go out with Indian girls."

"Not her."

"Don't worry about it."

Vivian picked up her beer can. "I wish you'd talk to Mikey. He's been tearing this place up and making a mess with all his friends. I told him I'd throw him out if he don't shape up."

"You won't, though."

Vivian sighed. "How can I?"

"I'll talk to him." Maybe he would, maybe he wouldn't. It wouldn't do any good. She worried about Mikey the way she'd worried about all of them, passionately, carelessly. She was doing the best she could right now, and he loved her for it. Or maybe he just loved her because he was used to loving her, because she was what he had. Sitting in the dark, he could feel her weight pushing down the springs of the couch, hear her rhythmic breath. He felt moored by her powerful presence, the two of them adrift in the darkness with their cigarette points flashing on and off like some mysterious code.

Vivian put her legs up on the coffee table and leaned back. "I'm real glad you're home, Sonny. I never sleep good when you're gone."

His chest tightened with a tiny crimp of panic, as though

there were suddenly less air in the room. He took a long swallow of beer, concentrating on the coolness spreading through his chest. "When did Nick head back out fishing?"

"Wednesday. Maybe it was Tuesday. It already seems like a long time ago. After he's gone it feels like he's never been here at all."

Sonny stubbed out his cigarette and lit another, remembering Brenda lying face down on her bed. How was he ever going to get out from under the weight of all the sad Vladimir women, the weight of the rain that had started again, a soft mossy pattering that seeped through the roof shingles and would soon drip right through the ceiling onto their heads?

"Hear that?" Vivian asked. "It's raining again."

Sonny inhaled deeply, blew out smoke. "Yeah," he said. "For a change."

THE BITE WAS ON and the trolling was good. Outside, past the last islands, the light play of shifting fogs and fiords was lost to sunshine and the open ocean swell. To Allie, it felt as though the sea was breathing and the whole world rode up and down on one breast. Sixteen hours a day she steered from the pilothouse while Digger worked the lines. He wouldn't trust her to pull in fish. Every troll-caught salmon was worth twenty dollars or more, and he feared she'd lose one off the leader or knock it off the hook. All day long she lived with the never-ending drone of diesel, the radio babble, and the ocean's roll.

She devised a game called wave catching to pass the time. She picked a wave and tried to follow its progress as it moved away, but the game always failed her; each wave was part of the whole. Somewhere she'd read that waves didn't actually move in any direction but simply up and down. Out on the open Pacific, with no coast to mark her passage, it seemed that the *Ginny D.* didn't move either, but merely rode the swells.

She never knew where they were. In the beginning Digger had tried to explain the radar and charts but she had merely pretended to understand. It seemed too complicated, or perhaps she didn't really want to know. But her refusal to take responsibility left her scared all the time. Every time she took a nap while Digger steered from the cockpit, she woke terrified that he'd fallen overboard. Without him she'd be lost.

It was a world without landmarks, a horizon that stretched farther west than west itself, to Russia and Japan. The continent to the east but no longer in sight called her back. She ached with the loss of land, a yearning as vague as nostalgia, as ponderous as gravitational force.

Yet trolling fascinated her. She was still amazed by the magic that summoned fish from the depths. The poles jutted out at a forty-five-degree angle, and two lines ran back from them; each line held six weighted leaders, each of them carrying a hook and bait or a lure at a particular depth. When a fish struck, the pole dipped and a bell rang, but it wasn't until Digger had reeled in the lines with the hydraulic winch called a gurdy, unsnapping and stowing each leader, that he knew which particularly lucky or artful combination of color and shape and depth had attracted the hungry fish. The gurdy turned, the line cut through the water, the leaders piled up, and suddenly a salmon appeared, a quicksilver flash of green and pink and blue.

Digger unsnapped the leader and played the fish as it zig-zagged back and forth until he got it close enough to gaff it in the head with a terrible crunch. It had to be the head, or the fish was ruined for sale. On deck the fish flopped, spraying blood, until Digger clubbed it still. Digger turned back to his gear, but Allie was drawn to the fish dying on deck. She kneeled over them, watching as they lost their colors, their iridescent brilliance ebbing with their lives. Sometimes she stroked them, spoke to them, begging them to come back. It was her job to slit them open and pull out their guts.

It seemed to her that the shimmering salmon, yanked from the water, battered, reduced to empty flesh, had something to tell her. There was a secret in the repetitious process of destruction, and if she could just figure it out, her life, which had always seemed so fragmented, would take on a clear and brilliant shape, the way the glittering pattern inside a kaleidoscope was formed from shards of broken glass.

Coming into Petersburg on a supply run, Allie stood on the deck of the *Ginny D.*, thrilled by a vision of white clapboard houses with rose-painted shutters, a long stretch of canneries, the ferry dock. For two weeks all she had seen were the cabins of Point Baker, abandoned canneries, and fish buyers' scows. The scows offered cold water showers and coolers stocked with browned lettuce, curling bologna, and beer. Everywhere they went there was only one topic of conversation — fishing — and she was Digger's deckhand.

Petersburg was the big time, and Digger had promised a night on the town. They'd eat in a real restaurant and shoot pool in a bar. She'd buy books in the drugstore, or at least magazines, stock up on fresh vegetables in the grocery store. She'd walk on land.

As they drew closer to the docks, Allie was overjoyed to see Frankie from Vladimir on the deck of a big steel seine boat, the *Nancy M.*, waving at her. Silly as he was, he was proof that she'd had another life before Digger; he was someone who knew *her*. She waved madly back.

The tides were running fiercely, and Digger threw the engine into reverse too late in an attempt to draw alongside the *Nancy M.* Instead of sliding around neatly, he had to go back into the channel and make a second pass. Humiliated, Digger turned on Allie in a voice that echoed over the docks.

"Why didn't you throw the line?"

"We weren't close enough!"

"The hell we weren't!"

On the second try, Frankie caught the line Allie tossed. "Some skipper you got there," he said, shaking his head disgustedly as he pulled them in.

Shamefaced and angry, Allie climbed down into the fo'c's'le, gathered up soap, shampoo, and a towel and headed toward the cannery for a shower. She was sick of Digger's bullying.

At the cannery, she stayed a long time under the hot water spray, washing away what seemed like weeks of dirt and the smell of fish, letting the warmth ease her anger. She dressed, wrapped a towel around her clean hair, and stood watching the cannery women in bloody aprons working on the lines.

The cannery was a damp, cold, corrugated aluminum structure with cement floors awash in water and blood. Fork lifts beeped and spun, carrying pallets of canned fish. Slabs of salmon moved along conveyor belts between the lines of women; another belt above the fish belt carried clanking, crashing cans; and steamers hissed deafeningly, filling the room with clouds of vapor. Over it all was the terrible stink of dead fish. How could the women stand it? Women's work — a nightmare of gore, degrading and dull.

There were few choices for women up here: be a waitress or work in the cannery, get married, and wait for your man to come home from the sea or logging camp. The Alaska that Allie wanted was closed to them. Compared to work like that, she felt lucky to be on a boat, any boat.

Fishing was often boring and bloody, and she was stuck with Digger with no say in where they went, but at least they were going somewhere, they were after something. If half the time was spent waiting, there was plenty of excitement when the fish were coming in. And then there was the danger — of accident, of storms. As long as there was danger, she knew something was happening, that her life wasn't standing still. Danger inspired her; it felt real.

When she was little, she had a recurring fear that would come over her at odd moments. Suddenly she'd feel uncertain of her own presence, as though she were just a thought process, a disembodied witness looking down on life from a great height. The feeling would escalate until she felt so alone she could be tumbling through space, millions of miles, light years away. Her heart would begin to pound, her face go white. Once she ran to her mother and asked in panic, "How do I know I'm real?"

"Of course you're real, sweetie," her mother said indulgently. "Just look at me. Don't I look real?" But when Allie looked, her mother's eyes had turned strange. They weren't mild and blue anymore but gel in lifeless sockets, and she had to turn away. Eventually she learned to divert her panic by silently counting one-two-three-four and on up to a thousand. Later she discovered that when she was walking on the edge of a precipice or standing on the deck of a boat without rails, in danger, she felt real.

Danger. It was a family joke. They had called the seat in the front of the car beside her father the "danger seat," because no matter who misbehaved, or even if no one had, the one in the danger seat got hit. Her father drove with the left tire over the middle line, swerving at the last minute as the oncoming driver honked and waved his fist. "It's *my* road," her father would say, grinning at their fear. Allie had liked to sit behind him, because when he started to hit, she was out of reach, and she couldn't see the road. Now it was Digger who was in the driver's seat; she was only along for the ride.

In the Petersburg Moose club, Digger sat toying with his steak, looking morose.

"Come on," Allie said, "you can't miss *my* cooking."

He shrugged and chewed at a hangnail. "Maybe I ought to just take the net off and store it at the cannery. It's hardly worth a one-day gill-net opening. We might as well just troll."

"Sounds good." Allie was impatient with Digger's mood, the quiet of this dull family restaurant with moose heads hanging above the red Formica tables, and maps of Alaska on the paper place mats. She wanted action. Every time the door opened she swiveled in her chair, hoping for an exciting new face, a reprieve, but it was just another glum Norwegian fisherman taking his wife out to dinner. In a land where men usually spoke at twice normal volume, the only noticeable voice was that of a fat woman in a lumberman's shirt threatening an undersized, hollow-eyed five-year-old at the next table.

"Kelly, if you don't finish every bite of that sirloin, I swear we're just going to leave you here." The mother made as if to get up and the child began to wail. Allie turned in her seat and glared.

"Come on," Digger said. "Let's get out of here."

Without much enthusiasm, Digger led Allie up the street to the Harbor Bar. The room was dimly lit, smoky, and full of seine crews, cannery workers, loud laughter, and juke box rock. The men standing by the bar, lounging about the pool tables, bumping into each other, gave off a certain energy, high spirits with a hint of leashed violence. Allie read it as fun. They were having it and she wasn't because she was stuck with Digger.

Digger steered her to a table full of dour seine and gill-net skippers arguing over whether or not they should just give up on the Alaska season and head back down south to try their luck in Puget Sound. Allie sat sipping her drink quietly, only half-listening, since she'd already heard this conversation many times. She turned to look longingly at the people shooting pool, the crowd laughing raucously up the bar.

A narrow-faced Seattle skipper in an orange Caterpillar Equipment cap, a man who drove truck in winter, began to expound angrily on the Indian fishing claims battle in the state of Washington. He jabbed the table with a mangled forefinger.

"They ain't going to win no way. Even if the judge gives it to 'em, we won't let 'em have it. We're fighting for our lives down there. The Indians are losers, and they're going to lose again."

Then Allie saw Frankie gesturing to her from a table across the room, and with the swiftness of a prison break, she got up and went to join him. Frankie was sitting with a couple of his crewmates from the *Nancy M.* — Sonny, who merely nod-

64

ded hello, and Henry, who smiled shyly — as well as Louie, the Whitney-Fidalgo Company packer Digger sold his fish to out by Point Baker. Louie had an Amish-style beard and, on the fishing grounds at least, a stern Nordic demeanor. He'd never said two words to Allie when she was pitching fish to him, but now he pulled out a chair for her with a flourish and paid for her drink.

"Allie!" Louie roared. "It's great to see you without those rubber overalls. Did anyone ever tell you you're a pretty girl?" He focused his gaze at breast level. Allie had taken off her jacket and was wearing jeans and a pale blue turtleneck.

"Never," Allie said, smiling. "You're the first one, Louie. Hey, where's your wife?" She looked around for the skinny woman in go-go boots. It wouldn't pay to be on her bad side. Rumor had it that she'd once stabbed Louie during an argument.

"Who cares? Where's your boyfriend?"

"Digger isn't my boyfriend," Allie protested. "It's just a job."

"Sure it is," Frankie said, grinning slyly, glancing at Henry and Sonny, although the two of them remained expressionless and silent. "Ain't you never heard the saying? You got to screw to crew."

"Is that how you got your job?" Allie asked brightly, and they all laughed. Tonight she didn't care if she had to listen to the same old stupid girl-deckhand jokes, had to suffer Louie's chest-level gaze. At least they were willing to forget fishing for a little while; at least they were having fun. She sipped her bourbon gratefully and bummed a cigarette.

Then Digger was standing behind her. "How's it going, Louie? Guys? Hope you're doing better than us out there." His voice sounded falsely hearty. "So, ah, Allie, we're going to head on back to the boat now."

"You go ahead," Allie said. "I think I'll stay up here for a while."

"Will you guys excuse us a minute?" Digger clamped her

arm above the elbow and almost lifted her from her chair. He drew her over to the bar and whispered furiously. "What are you trying to pull? It don't look good, you hanging out with those guys."

"Hey, I'm just having a little fun. Do you mind?"

"Yeah, I do. What do you want to hang out with them for? They're a bunch of losers. None of them can get it together enough to own his own boat." He crossed his arms emphatically over his chest, sure that Allie would be convinced. Only men who owned their own boats were worthy companions.

Allie looked over at the table where Frankie and Louie were laughing. "I like them okay. What difference does it make?"

"It makes plenty of difference," Digger said. "You want everyone laughing at me, saying my deckhand's running around in town?"

"Digger, you don't own me off the boat. I'm going to stay up here."

"Not if you want to work for me, you won't."

Allie gaped in surprise. He'd thrown his trump card, the bastard. She considered mutiny, wavered, and gave in. Quitting would mean walking away without a place to sleep or a job. It wasn't worth it. Goddamn him. She hadn't even had a chance to finish her drink.

Allie followed Digger down the Petersburg streets to the docks, refusing to walk beside him, feeling childish, petulant. The sun was still infuriatingly high overhead, the sidewalk crowded with people on their way to a good time. They clomped onto the boat in silence.

"Look," Digger said, hunching at the galley table, his head in his hands. "I'm sorry about tonight."

Allie climbed into her bunk and refused to answer. Wasn't this the way her mother always did it, powerlessness and then the sulk, the cold shoulder? Subterfuge and subversion, never the direct attack. She hated herself for not standing up to him. It was all the more inexplicable because she had always been

66

the one who had fought with her father, the one who had stood there saying no over and over again as his hand shot out repeatedly to slap her face.

"I know you wanted to have some fun," Digger said. "I can understand that, after all these weeks. I promise when we get to Vladimir I'll show you a good time. But in Petersburg I just can't get in the mood. It's this Jeanine thing." Digger looked up from the table, his face awash in misery. "I saw her in the cannery today."

Allie rolled over and hid her head under her pillow. In the bar, he wanted her to play the role of girlfriend, to save face, and now he wanted sympathy because he was heartbroken. Who did he think she was, his goddamn friend? She was his deckhand, period. Ever since they'd starting trolling, they'd been so exhausted that sex wasn't even an issue; they just fell into the bunks for a couple of hours until the alarm went off again. They didn't have to pretend to be lovers.

The last time Digger had shown any interest in sex was when they'd been tied to the Baker dock, waiting for a gill-net opening. Allie had gone off that day with a shy sixteen-year-old boy on his rickety old troller with its tin-can smoke stack to pick up crabs from the community crab pot while Digger mended the net. It was a beautiful, peaceful ride through the channel, and Allie knew for the first time what fishing could be like with a reasonable man. That night there was a crab feast on Digger's boat. Allie and five men sat around cracking crabs with their teeth while the juice ran down their chins. Soon the conversation turned to prostitutes and pussy, the men eyeing her enviously. When the last of them had lurched off the boat, Digger was inflamed with the knowledge that he had what they wanted, hot with their horniness. Allie went along with him because the presence of desire itself overwhelmed her; she confused power with passion.

Now their relationship was not unlike that of some long-married couples who coexist in a balance of familiarity and dislike, a marriage in which the husband always gives the orders. She was Digger's deckhand; she would do what he said, but she didn't have to feel sorry for him.

"Allie?" When Digger received no answer, he undressed, lay down heavily, and soon broke into loud, mournful snores.

There was no way she could sleep. Light filled the portholes, and the sound of Digger's breathing infuriated her. She ought to quit. But if she did, she might end up in the cannery. And if she found another boat, there was no guarantee that another skipper wouldn't be worse. Allie felt trapped and restless, and she thrashed for what seemed like hours, until finally she got up, dressed, and went out onto the deck to smoke. It was just getting dark, and the masts and trolling poles of the tethered boats formed a gently waving forest against the streaky, purple sky.

Light, music, and voices spilled out the open galley door of the *Nancy M.* Allie put out her cigarette and lit another. Over the music she heard the unmistakable sound of someone peeing, and looked up to see Frankie balanced on the seine stacked on the stern of his boat.

"Hey," Allie said.

Unembarrassed, Frankie turned and zipped up. "Hey yourself. Why don't you come on over? We're having a party. Or do you have to ask your skipper first?"

"The hell with him."

"Whoa!"

Allie clambered over the rails and followed Frankie into the brightly lit galley, where the boys she'd met in the bar, Sonny and Henry, and a drunk girl were sitting at a table littered with beer cans, ashtrays, and a dope pipe fashioned out of a toilet paper tube and tin foil. The girl was slender but had a fat face, a kewpie doll Angela Lansbury with a missing tooth, and she was singing loudly along to a tape of the Stones' "Satisfaction." Frankie introduced her as Shelley.

Allie looked around at the gleaming galley and whistled softly. They had all the comforts of home: a full-size refrigerator, a six-burner gas stove, lots of Formica, and a stainless steel double sink with hot and cold taps. On the *Ginny D.* the kerosene stove was smoky, a nightmare to light, and she had to pump cold water by hand. "Wow," she said. "I must be working on the wrong boat."

"Hey," Frankie said proudly, pulling a beer out of the fridge for Allie and sliding into the seat next to Shelley, "we travel in style. We even got our own shower."

Allie sat beside Frankie, across from Henry and Sonny. "I *know* I'm working on the wrong boat."

"Digger's got a nice boat," Sonny said. "Where's your high-liner skipper?"

"Asleep. Dreaming about his long lost love."

"Hey," Frankie said. "I thought that was you. What'd you do, have a lover's quarrel?"

"Give me a break. It's just a job. Do you think I could get a job on a seiner like this, cooking or something?"

"No way," Frankie said. "What skipper would hire a girl on with a bunch of guys? They'd be fighting over her. And where would you sleep, huh? Down in the fo'c's'le with the boys, or in the stateroom with the captain?" He leered. "What you ought to do is just hang it up and collect your Indian money. You don't need to fish."

"I *want* to fish," Allie said, hoping she still meant it. She'd want to fish if it weren't for Digger. "Anyway, what's Indian money?"

"Ain't you Indian?" Frankie was surprised. "It don't matter, though. You look Indian enough to pass. Don't she?" He turned to Sonny and Henry for confirmation. They nodded. "You only got to show a quarter blood, or you could get yourself a little papoose and collect on him. I'd help you there, hyuk, hyuk."

Allie rolled her eyes.

"Henry and Sonny and me all get it," Frankie continued. "Two thousand easy bucks from the Native Claims Act. I already put a down payment on a pickup."

"It's getting popular to be Indian all of a sudden," Sonny said into his beer.

Something in his tone surprised her. Bitterness? Not exactly. Irony.

"Hey," Frankie said. "How does a Tlingit tell time?'

"How?"

"With a Klawock! Get it? A Klawock!" Frankie slapped the table with pleasure.

"Klawock is an Indian town on Prince of Wales Island," Sonny explained. "See what happens when you hang out with the same guys all your life? You have to keep listening to their jokes."

He smiled, and Allie realized for the first time that he was handsome. In the bar she had hardly noticed him, dismissed him perhaps out of some shameful sliver of racism, because of his darkness, because he looked Indian. He had classic Tlingit features: high cheekbones, short arched nose, glossy black hair, and a closed-up face. When he smiled, his face was full of contradictions. It was an all-American smile, dimpled and flashing, yet intriguingly, his flat black eyes remained the same.

"You gals are lucky tonight," Frankie said. "Our skipper flew back to Vladimir to see the wife. He don't allow women on board. He thinks if anyone gets laid it'll change our luck."

"We could use a change of luck," Sonny said, standing up to get more beers.

"I could use getting laid." Frankie raised his eyebrows hopefully in Shelley's direction.

"I could use more smoke." Henry reached across the table for the dope pipe. He lit up and passed it around.

Shelley studied Allie thoughtfully over the rim of her beer can. "Allie don't look Indian. She looks Eye-talian. They got lots of Eye-talians where I come from."

"Where's that?" Allie asked, half out of interest, half in an attempt to deflect the usual question about her origins.

"Oregon. A little dump called Marway that nobody ever

heard of. I come up every summer to work the canneries. It's better than punching a register at Safeway."

"She's one of them Okie ridge runners," Frankie said. "Oregon hillbilly. They like to run around in the hills with shotguns."

"Am not." Shelley pouted.

"Where are you from, Allie?" Sonny asked.

"Originally? Back east, but I lived for a while in Colorado and Seattle." Coming from "back east" seemed like a shameful admission, as though it were so far away in miles and spirit it meant she could never be a part of this world — Petersburg, Alaska; a fishing boat tied to a dock. Even though she'd lived there, the words *Colorado* and *Seattle* sounded false to her own ears.

"Colorado," Sonny said, shaking his head. "I don't know why you'd want to trade in a sunny place like that for this rain forest. Everybody's growing moss up here."

Things hadn't gone so well for her in Colorado. She'd taken up with a carpenter who was playing cowboy with a couple of friends on an old ranch thirty miles from Vail. The three men paid her a pittance to cook and clean for them while they worked at a construction site. She had to wash dishes in the cold water of a creek encrusted with gypsum, and all day long she was alone with the sagebrush, the flat-topped mountains across the valley, and the eerie, relentless light.

The men — her carpenter, a car-crazy guy from L.A., and a Vietnam vet from Detroit — designed a system to pump water to the house. After work and on weekends, they dug trenches to reroute the creek and built wooden carrying troughs for the water. The Saturday they finished they all got drunk. The vet cornered her in the kitchen and screamed in her face, "You know nothing, nothing, *nothing.*" Then he ran around in the sagebrush shooting wildly at rabbits. The next morning Allie was the first to wake. When she went down to the creek to look at the system, she discovered the carrying troughs floating on the water. The creek had rerouted itself, and the banks, cut in two feet toward the house already, were crumbling fast. She gathered her things and walked out to the highway before anyone woke.

"Hey, this is God's country, boy," Frankie informed Sonny. "Heaven on earth. You wouldn't live no place else."

Sonny didn't argue.

"You know, these Alaskans think they're something special," Shelley said. "But I wouldn't want to stay up here in winter. They're all crazy, especially the fishermen. I went out on a gill netter once. You listen to the way they talk on the radio?" Her voice went nasal in imitation. "By golly, might as well hang it up. Over. Roger. Negative. Japs got all the fish."

Allie laughed with recognition. "Yeah, and the wives passing meatloaf recipes?" Half the radio talk was probably just an attempt to make contact across the miles — loneliness turned to communication fetishes. She and Digger had made a visit to a Seventh Day Adventist logging camp to see a guy he knew. It was a little company town of pale green cabins, enormous bulldozers scattered about like oversize toys. A nervous wife offered cocoa, two shy kids flattened against the wall, gawking at them, and the husband, looking out dreamily at the vista of mountains and ocean beyond his window, only wanted to talk about the faraway places he'd raised on his ham radio set. Newfoundland. Hawaii. Brazil.

"You shoulda seen this guy I fished with," Shelley continued. "He drank a whole bottle of vodka before we even got the net out. I had to steer us back to town, and I never even been on a boat before. Hey, where's that pipe at?"

"Digger doesn't drink when he's fishing," Allie said, "but he gets real nervous."

"Digger's no fisherman," Sonny said.

"What do you mean?" Allie looked up at him quickly. What did he know that she ought to?

Sonny merely shrugged.

"He's too hungry," Henry said. "He wants it too much."

"He's got a nice boat," Frankie said.

"Who'd want a boat?" Henry had slipped so low in his seat his chin was almost resting on the table. He looked like a child who needed a parent to put him to bed. "A boat's just a hole in the water you throw money into. I got enough trouble taking care of myself. I don't need no boat to take care of. I just want to go out to Siligovsky Island, set my traps, and read my cowboy westerns."

Frankie said, "Morgan's got a boat and it ain't hurt him none. Allie, you ever meet Morgan back in Vladimir? Squirrelly little red-headed dude? He used to fish with us before Duane. This year he bought himself an old wreck of a troller and he's pulling them in like crazy. He even got himself a girl deckhand out by Sitka. Me and Henry and Morgan all grew up together, but Morgan's the only one got his own boat."

Sonny refilled the pipe. "Morgan," he said, musing. "He used to have a motorcycle with no brakes. One day he drove it into the cannery to visit his girlfriend, only he couldn't stop and he drove it right off the cannery dock into the bay and came up laughing. Crazy Morgan."

"Remember the time we pulled a shark up in the seine?" Frankie laughed. "Morgan stuck a broom in its mouth just to see if it'd bite. Toothpick city! You shoulda seen it."

Allie wished she had. It didn't matter if Frankie was silly, Henry a child; she wanted to be one of them, one of the boys who had known each other all their lives, always known where home was.

"Morgan's lucky," Sonny said. "Lucky with cards, lucky with women, and now he's lucky with fish. He's got his own boat, and the rest of us are sitting around staring each other in the face, and we'll probably be doing the same thing when we're sixty."

"Not me," Henry said, getting up and pushing past Sonny. "I'm hitting the sack. You guys can stare each other in the face if you want to, but I think the ladies are a lot better looking. Hey, tell Duane not to dump his stuff on me this time when he comes in."

Sonny rose to change the tape. Allie admired the white stretch of shirt across his shoulders, the taper down to narrow blue-jeaned hips. The tape crackled with static and then Mick Jagger's insinuating moan: "Factory Girl."

Frankie passed her the pipe and turned to whisper something to Shelley. Shelley giggled, pretended to smack him, but kissed him instead. Allie inhaled deeply, feeling the smoke circle around inside her chest and then rise to her head.

Sonny leaned forward on his elbows. "So you came up here all by yourself?" He looked at her steadily, waiting for an answer, and Allie met his gaze. His lips were rather thick, turned slightly upward in a sensual, private grin, his eyelids half lowered. There was something sleepy and sated about Sonny, something embracing beer and grass and the relief of obliteration, yet his black, unreadable eyes seemed to hold a promise. She turned away.

"I came here by myself," she said. "Sometimes I hooked up with people for a little while."

Sonny was still looking at her across the littered table. She could feel the current running between them, an insistent little buzz of attraction that made her shy. She looked away from him again, down at the ashtray on the table. It was attached to a little red and white anchor-patterned sandbag to keep it from sliding off the table in high seas.

She twirled the ashtray, imagining Sonny, Henry, Frankie, and the mythic Morgan out there in their rain slickers, working together as a team. She was jealous. She wanted to be like them, one of the boys instead of Digger's girl deckhand. She was a sidekick, like those girls who rode around on the backs of motorcycles with Hell's Angels, girls who probably wanted to be driving the motorcycles themselves. If they couldn't be what they wanted to be, they settled for being wanted.

Sonny had said something but she hadn't caught it. How

long had she been sitting there not answering? She felt light-headed, stoned. Frankie and Shelley were locked in an embarrassing clinch beside her. Allie looked back down at the twirling ashtray, and suddenly she was dizzy, in danger of getting sick. "I'll be back in a second," she said to Sonny, and stumbled up and out the galley door.

Out on the deck the air was cool and fresh, and her head no longer whirled. She sat down on the rail and waited for her heartbeat to slow down. That was the trouble with dope. It always made her inner processes so noisy, the rush of blood in her veins unbearably loud, the pound of her heart echo in her chest.

Night had finally fallen. Across Wrangell Narrows a few cabin lights glittered. The water in the middle of the channel was black, but nearer it danced with light, reflecting the lamps on the docks. Allie sat listening to the comforting lap of water against hulls, the creak of rigging, a light breeze gently rolling the boats. Sitting alone, she could almost believe it was hers, that she was a part of this place.

"Are you okay?" Sonny stood above her on deck, his white shirt glowing in the dark.

"Yeah. I just needed some air. It was getting a little steamy in there."

Sonny laughed. "Yeah, it was." He sat down on the rail about a foot away, pulled out a pack of Marlboros, and offered Allie one. "It's nice out here."

They sat for a while, looking across the darkened *Ginny D.,* across the Narrows, at the lights. Above a ridge of mountains, stars could be seen. Allie leaned forward to drop the cigarette overboard — it was making her woozy again — and noticed that the water between the hulls of the *Nancy M.* and the *Ginny D.* was alive with green sparkles, tiny underwater lights. "Look," she said. "It's like a city down there."

Sonny leaned forward. "Phosphorescence. It comes from algae or something. It's bad because it sticks on the net and shows the fish where not to go."

"It's pretty, though." Allie dipped her fingers in the cold water, stirring the sparkles, then stuck her numbed hand between her thighs. She looked up at the stars and then down at the phosphorescence, trying to reverse them in her mind's eye so that she could pretend she was upside down — like swinging on a playground swing and leaning back until you were lost and dizzy and couldn't tell the sky from the ground. She loved that feeling of falling, falling.

"So, you liked it out there?" Sonny asked.

"You mean fishing?" She was flattered by his interest, but how could she put it into words that Sonny would understand? "I like trolling better than gill-netting," she said, "but I wish we could just stay Inside." It wasn't a matter of liking it — she'd been amazed, bored, entranced.

"You got seasick?" Sonny raised his hands in a palms-down balancing gesture to indicate waves.

"Sometimes, but it wasn't that. Maybe I got *land*sick. You know, like homesick for the land? I think being out there made me a little crazy. I was starting to talk to fish. They're so beautiful when they're coming in on the line, fighting, such gorgeous colors, blue and green and pink and silver, and then, as soon as you get them aboard they start to fade . . . Did you ever notice that, Sonny? How they lose their colors as soon as you take them from the water?"

"I know what you mean. I trolled one summer after my dad drowned."

She turned to look at him. After his dad drowned? It was information that made him more estimable in her eyes. She believed that people who had suffered terrible losses — concentration camp survivors, veterans — were privy to information she needed, information that would rub off on her if given the chance.

"Talking to fish," Sonny said, shaking his head in amusement. "Are you sure you aren't just a little bit Indian?"

Not unless you think Indians are one of the ten lost tribes, Allie thought. She shook her head no.

76

"I was sure you were Indian when I saw Digger hire you on."

"You were there?" She was pleased that he remembered her, but a little embarrassed at the thought of what it must have looked like to him. She tried to remember the faces of the men lining the bar that night. It seemed like years ago.

"Talking to fish," Sonny said. "that's not so bad. It's the ravens you've got to watch out for."

"Why?"

"They play tricks on you. In the legends, the raven is the spokesman when Tlingits talk to God, but the raven is also a jokester. Tlingits can only talk to God through an animal that plays tricks." Sonny's smile was clearly visible, a disarming flash of white. "No wonder we never get what we want."

"Do you believe in all that?"

He threw his cigarette overboard and lit up another. "Old wives' tales."

"Where'd you learn about it? From your family?"

"Nah, nobody talks about that stuff anymore. I read about it up at the library, back in Vladimir."

Allie pictured Sonny sitting in a library, reading about legends. He knew things, wanted to know. It was a picture she liked. She could feel him sitting there in the dark beside her, a presence alert to her presence.

A lone duck flew a trajectory across the darkened sky, quacking mournfully. Sonny raised his arms as though sighting along an imaginary rifle barrel, following the sound. "*Kat*choo, *kat*choo," he said. Allie was shocked. It was the sound all little boys made, pretending to shoot guns. A silly, touching gesture, yet under it lay a sharp little crackle of violence that widened her eyes, quickened her breath.

"Missed," Sonny said, lowering his arms.

"I can't believe you did that." Allie wanted to shame him for the shameful way it made her feel: fear, desire. "What would Donald say?"

Sonny laughed sheepishly. "I was just trying to put it out

of its misery. It must have lost its flock. They don't usually fly around alone like that, especially at night."

The duck quacked on faintly in the distance. A lucky duck, Allie thought. Better to be lonely than blown away.

"Sonny, do you like to hunt?"

Sonny considered the question. "I used to. I used to love to hunt snow geese when they flew in over the flats by the mouth of the Takine River." His voice sounded muted, suddenly shy.

Allie imagined him carrying a rifle, walking the muddy flats at low tide, the mainland mountains snowy behind him and the sea stretched out ahead. It was cold and ice crunched under his boots; his breath shot out ahead.

"But then one day I just couldn't do it anymore," Sonny said softly. "First you take their freedom when you knock them out of the sky, and then you got to go up and wring their necks while they're flapping around on the ground. And all the time they're fighting to live up to the last minute."

Sonny turned to face her, but Allie saw that everything he said was turned inward, as though he were speaking to some secret part of himself. "And then you take that from them too. I just couldn't do it." He looked down, shrugged. "I guess my family isn't that hungry yet."

Allie held her breath. Who was he? A beautiful Indian boy who read about legends in the library, who shot imaginary rifles but was too tender to hunt. The contradictions made her alive with longing, edgy with hope. She didn't know if she wanted him, or if she wanted to *be* him.

Sonny shrugged again. "I know people think it's funny that I won't hunt."

"You shouldn't be ashamed to think like that," Allie said. She understood. He was at once completely a part of this place and yet a stranger to it. She could feel him there beside her, sharing an intimacy of soft lapping waves and twinkling lights. Any moment he was going to reach across the distance and then everything would start. And when he did, she would fall backward into his touch.

78

Sonny stood up abruptly. "I'm talking my damn fool head off. Give me a little beer and I get talking." He peered across the channel, where the blackness was fading into purplish streaks — crazy, middle of the night dawn. "It's already getting light. That skipper of yours just might wake up and wonder where you've gone to." He tap-danced a nervous little shuffle on the steel deck.

"Yeah," Allie said too quickly, to mask her regret. "We're heading out early in the morning. I better get some sleep." She stood up, awkward with disappointment, not sure what to do. Should she shake his hand?

Then with a touch so swift she almost didn't believe it had happened, Sonny reached out and pressed a finger to her chin. "Watch out for Indian boys and whiskey," he said with a grin.

THE PARADE was still going by. Sonny stood weaving in the sunshine, watching the last floats. WOOD PULP PRODUCTS — WE DEPEND ON THEM! JAPAN, OUR NEIGHBOR TO THE WEST. Neighbor, Sonny, thought. Shit, they own the town. OIL — ALASKA'S BRIGHT FUTURE! That float, representing support for the pipeline they were going to start building up north, displayed some kids dressed in caribou costumes struggling back and forth over a culvert pipe. One of the caribou had taken off his mask and was crying. FUTURE LOGGERS OF AMERICA! A flatbed truck was littered with stumps and little girls in hard hats and bikinis waving papier-mâché chain saws. Sonny waved at his second cousin Sally. The floats moved in fits and starts. Kids spun by on bicycles with red, white, and blue crepe paper strung through the spokes. Then the fire engine and a caravan of beeping, honking backhoes, road graders, and a snow plow signaled the parade's end. It was a short parade, though, and it headed back through town for a second run. Frankie caught Sonny's eye, pantomimed smoking a joint, and they ducked behind the supermarket to light up with Henry and Morgan.

Front Street was jammed with strangers: loggers in from camps, tug and fishing boat crews from all over, tourists off the ferry. Sonny dodged sticky wands of melting hot-pink cotton candy, blinking at the colors. Girls walked by in halter tops and shorts. The white girls from Vladimir had legs as pale as slugs yanked out from under rocks. Only the tourist girls had tans. Frankie and Morgan called out to them, but the girls, wearing big dumb-looking hiking boots, wouldn't even turn their heads.

They slipped into the Anchor Lounge to cool off, and Morgan ordered dive-bombers. Sonny dropped the shot glass into his beer and watched the foam spill over. He laughed and gulped it down. He'd been up all last night partying and probably would be up all night again.

"Awright!" Morgan said. Henry wiped beer foam off his lips with the back of his sleeve. Frankie belched.

"Hey, Smiley," Morgan called out to the bartender, who didn't look smiley at all. "Hey, Smiley, get the lead out. Can't you see we need another round?"

"Don't pick on Smiley," Henry said. "He don't look too good."

Smiley scowled but brought the shots and glasses. His upper lip was beaded with sweat, and his skin had turned an even deeper shade of yellow, a sign that he'd fallen off the wagon again.

"Nobody in here looks too good," Morgan said. "Hey Alf, hey Ole, why aren't you two old farts out there chasing hippie chicks? You ought to be finding yourself deckhands, har har!"

The old diehards squinting out at the sun with distrust turned to look at Morgan. It must have been eighty degrees outside, and they were still wearing their wool shirts and long johns. Sonny figured they preferred the rain.

"Why'nt you go home and ask your mama to change your diapers," Ole said.

"Awright!" Morgan crowed. "Ya wanna come and help?" He swiveled on his stool. "Hey, look at that big ugly lunk over there."

Sonny turned to see an out-of-town logger leaning over a can of Ranier in a booth behind the pool table.

"Hey you!" Morgan got off his stool and pulled himself up

to his full five foot five. "Hey, I like your hat. How come you're wearing a fisherman's hat?"

The logger, whose new white cap made a shining contrast to his mud-smeared face, turned his head slowly in their direction.

"He's an ugly cocksucker, ain't he?" Morgan stage-whispered.

"Take it easy, Morgan," Sonny warned.

"Hey, where'd you steal that hat?"

The logger rose slowly. "Whadju say?"

"He said he wants to buy you a beer," Henry piped up. "Jeez, Morgan, you want to get us all killed?"

Morgan giggled. "Yeah, I want to buy you a drink, you big ugly hunk of whale shit!"

Then they were out on the street, dragging Morgan away from the Anchor, laughing. Sonny caught sight of his mother and Nick up the street. Vivian was waving at him, and she had her other hand hooked into Nick's belt loop. It was a relief to see them together, a reprieve from responsibility, but the way her breasts swelled up out of her low-cut blouse made him ashamed. Why did she always have to look so big, so noisy, so *there*? He looked over his shoulder nervously, embarrassed in front of the boys. Behind her, the volunteer firemen were hosing down a stretch of unpaved street for the tug-of-war. Two teams were lining up.

"Sonny! Sonny! Over here," Vivian called.

"Uh-oh," Morgan said. They wandered over.

"Mikey's going to be in the tug-of-war," Vivian exclaimed. "Don't you want to come and watch your little brother?" She hugged Nick happily. "Oh, I just love holidays, having all my men at home." Nick's angular face expressed amused tolerance.

Sonny forgave her. The fragility of her happiness pained him. It hung on too thin a thread, on something as tenuous as the loop of Nick's belt. And still she wanted more. It wasn't enough for her just to have Nick around; she needed them all together, needed to put her arms around all of them and hold them tight so it would feel like a family. She was so afraid of losing them, the way she'd lost everyone else, that she squeezed and squeezed until they all got bent out of shape.

"What about you, Sonny?" Nick asked.

"What about what?"

Nick gestured toward the worthless piece of muddy ground over which the two teams were struggling. People cheered. Vivian yelled, "Attaboy, Mikey. Show 'em!" Mikey, laughing and grunting, slid into the wallow and came up covered with mud.

"Sonny don't like to get dirty," Henry said. "That's why he's our skiff man. He don't want to get fish slime all over his pretty face."

"Is that it?" Nick asked. Sonny couldn't help squirming under Nick's pale blue gaze, couldn't help taking it as some kind of veiled reference to the fact that he didn't have his own boat. Maybe he was just being paranoid. All he saw in Nick's face was curiosity, a wisp of a smile.

"Sure," Sonny said.

The onlookers began to cheer more raucously as Mikey's team was pulled over the line.

Vivian groaned. "You want to come over to the landfill and watch the logging contests with us? Choker setting's going to begin real soon."

"Maybe later." Sonny hardened himself against the plea in her voice. Mikey appeared, wiping mud off his face, and when Vivian turned to console him, Sonny slipped away.

Out at Kutl Park the Takine Inn Sluggers battled the Vladimir Lumber Bumpers on the softball field. Husbands and boyfriends hooted the women players from the sidelines, and then it was time for the men to play. Sonny wasn't on a team. He would have played if he wasn't out on the boat all summer, but he didn't like to do anything if he didn't have a chance to be good, and he'd never had a chance at summer sports. His father had started taking him out gill-netting when he was only nine. He'd worked him like a man, right from the start, keeping him up all night.

It had never occurred to Sonny that maybe that wasn't fair. It was just the way it had been, as consistent as the rain that fell all winter, as the tide that came in to cover the derelict boats rotting on the low tide mud. He'd feared his father; he'd been his father's slave. Once when he was eleven he fell asleep on watch while gill-netting, and his father knocked him overboard in a fury. He pulled him out of the freezing water right away, but after that Sonny knew his father was capable of anything. The key was to work silently, not ask questions, anticipate his father's mood, and be ready to duck.

He quit watching the baseball game after the second inning. It was too hot and dusty, and the sun glinting off the ocean right behind the outfield fence hurt his eyes. It was cool and shady up at the picnic shelter under the hemlock trees, and he could look down at the baseball diamond with the proper perspective, dismissing it all as a silly combination of tumbling colors and muffled shouts. He sat down at a picnic bench and opened a beer from the six-pack he'd carried along.

It didn't seem like any time at all had passed, but three of his beers were gone, the softball games were over, and everyone was crowding around the picnic shelter, eating salmon baked in foil and potluck salads, and cracking beers. Someone had backed a pickup right up to the shelter, and its stereo speakers blasted rock. Sonny liked the noise; it added to his buzz. He felt like he was inside some kind of buffering private cloud and could just sit back and watch everyone go through their party motions from a great, safe distance.

Henry appeared with a six-year-old in tow. "Billy here's my best pal," he said. He was breathing hard from a game of tag, and the longer strands of hair he'd combed across his bald spot were hanging down on one side. He looked happy. He'd make a great daddy if he wasn't too shy to find a girl.

Sonny worked on his beer.

"You coming up to the party at Eddie's later?" Brenda stood before him, cocking a hip and pushing her hair over her ear with a nervous, sexy gesture. Sonny studied her, weighing the angle of hip against the trouble he knew he was in for if he agreed. "Could be," he said without enthusiasm.

Brenda got huffy and stalked away. A few minutes later he caught sight of her down the road, hanging off some guy who worked the green chain at the lumber mill. Maybe it was a performance for his benefit, maybe not. He didn't care; he just wanted to keep inside his buzz.

A few feet away, Morgan was wrestling with Bobby Gill. They pushed and laughed and pushed and laughed and then their faces grew red and angry and Morgan called Bobby a cocksucker and Bobby took a swing at Morgan's nose and they were pulled apart. Then Morgan and Bobby were laughing again, arms around each other's shoulders, and Sonny shook his head. Crazy Morgan didn't worry about whether or not he should fight.

Nick sat down beside Sonny, making the bench creak. Sonny automatically looked around to see where his mom was, but she was leaning over the food table, laughing with Henry, who had his arm around her neck. Sonny relaxed a fraction, although Nick's presence put a serious dent in the ease he'd been cultivating with the last few beers. He turned and offered Nick an Oly from his dwindling six-pack. Nick accepted, raising his can aloft.

"To independence," Nick said. Sonny didn't know if he was joking. Independence Day. He'd never thought about it like that. It was just the Fourth of July, Vladimir's biggest day of the year. Get drunk, raise hell, deal with the hangover tomorrow. That was about it. He didn't know what to say, so he just sat staring out at the water where the chip barge sat tied to a mooring, three pyramids of pale wood chips waiting to be hauled to the mill where they'd be loaded on a Japanese ship and taken to Japan. Wood pulp products. Japan, our neighbor to the west.

"It's kind of a joke when you think about it," Sonny ventured. "A bunch of Vladimir Tlingits running around celebrating red, white, and blue."

Nick sipped his beer. "In Russia, when Stalin was putting millions in camps, we celebrated May Day and anniversary of Great October Socialist Revolution. When there is holiday, it is good to enjoy."

Sonny looked at Nick out of the corner of his eye. Maybe he was right: don't sweat the questions, just lay back and enjoy it. It seemed to him that Nick understood everything, that if there was one person in Vladimir he could talk to, who would understand all the jumbled craziness in his head, that person would be Nick. But things had gotten so complicated he couldn't talk to him anymore.

When Sonny trolled with Nick the summer he was sixteen, the summer his dad drowned, everything was simple. Nick gave him his own side of the boat, let him pick his lures, work his own lines, and keep whatever he caught. Everybody else only gave their deckhands a percentage, but Nick didn't care about making money, he just loved to troll. Nick thought Sonny had a real talent for trolling and was all hot on helping him get his own boat. He was a lot more like a father than his father had ever been, and he gave him the first praise he'd ever known.

When fall fishing started, Sonny had gone back on the seiners because there was more money to be made net fishing, and his family needed the bucks, but even so he'd really wanted to be a troller. He'd started saving for a boat, but somehow it never happened. Now he was twenty-five and still crewing with the guys, and he couldn't shake the feeling that he'd let Nick down, that he'd blown it somehow.

He wanted to turn and say, "Hey, Nick, I'm really going to get that troller after all." But Nick wouldn't believe him and he wouldn't believe himself. Here he was trying to save money so he could get out of town this winter, the roof on the house needed fixing, and the seine season was the worst anyone had ever seen. He'd have to take a loan to get his own boat, let alone gear and licenses. There might not even be any new licenses if the limited entry law went through, and how would he pay a loan back? He didn't know if he wanted to be a fisherman anymore. Maybe he wanted to be something else that he didn't know about yet but had to leave Vladimir to see. He wanted to tell Nick about that, but he'd just sound like another bullshitting Indian who'd had too many beers; he'd just feel dumb.

There was no percentage to telling feelings. With a twinge of shame he remembered the girl off Digger's boat and how he'd talked to her about ravens and snow geese a few nights back. Something about her got him talking, and now it felt like his words were drifting around out there and he couldn't call them back. Some people thought photographs stole your soul, but he thought the way to lose yourself was by talking. Why had he given so much away?

She was a strange girl, knocking around on the boats like that. Talking to fish. Landsick. He couldn't figure her out but he liked her. She was pretty in spite of herself, wearing those oversized men's clothes, no makeup, smoking so awkwardly, like a teenager trying to be tough. Yet she'd had the guts to come up here all by herself. It didn't add up. He'd wanted to lean across and kiss her, to feel her soft fleshy lips, to put a hand on the back of her black-haired head and pull her close, but what could he do with Digger tied alongside? He didn't need any trouble.

That night he lay in his bunk, imagining the feel of her under his hips, his hands on her breasts, everything soft where she'd tried to cover herself in hardness. He wanted to drive himself into her, open her up so that he could know what she meant, and the frustration of it — the guys snoring in the fo'c's'le, the sky already light outside, the thought of her with Digger — somehow tangled up with the frustration of wanting to go somewhere, to just pick up and take off and leave everything behind like she had until his desire for her got mixed up with his desire for leaving, and left him sweaty and sleepless and pissed off. Anyway, she was from Outside; she'd be gone like the rest of them when it got cold.

He glanced sideways at Nick, who was puffing on a Pall Mall and staring calmly out at the ocean beyond the softball field. He gave up on the idea of trying to say anything and cracked open another beer.

AT KELLY COVE, the wind bent the tops of the spruce, and the masts on the trollers tied to the buyer scow's floats rattled and dipped. On the other side of Noyes Island, a sou'wester gale whipped the ocean into swells. Allie had wanted to go back to Vladimir for the Fourth of July, the best Fourth of July in all of Southeast Alaska. She wanted to see a parade, to see Sonny, but Digger wanted to get the jump on everyone else. He loved the thought that he'd be the only one fishing. Then a storm blew up and there was no fishing and no Vladimir, just a party at the cove and two days tied to the scow.

Fourth of July at Kelly Cove: a dozen trollers had built a bonfire on the five-hundred-foot stretch of pebbled beach on the protected side of Noyes Island. They shared salmon baked in seaweed and booze bought tax free at the friendship stores on the Canadian border when they'd come up from the south in the spring. A couple of kids wearing life preservers raced around the cove in skiffs with outboard motors and set off dinky firecrackers.

Digger was standing around with a bunch of skippers, talking fish, and Allie sat by herself on a log, staring into the fire, until a man with a triangular flattened nose and widely spaced teeth — a face like a battered jack-o'-lantern — came up and introduced himself as Dirty Don, the mayor of Port Ellis.

"You know why I'm mayor?" Don inquired.

"Why?"

"Because I can beat up everybody else in town."

Allie didn't think it was such a feat, since Port Ellis had only twenty-five residents, some of whom had to be women and children, but the guy had hands like baseball mitts, so she didn't argue. "So how come they call you Dirty?"

"Hey," Don said, "you're kinda cute. You want to go up a creek and spawn?"

At that moment Don's wife, a short, fat Indian woman, came rushing down at him, threatening to kill him, and Allie laughed so hard she fell backward off her log.

On the deck of the *Ginny D.*, the last Kelly Cove drunk was searching for his boat. "I know she got to be here somewhere," he muttered. "I sure as hell didn't come by bus." A deck bucket clattered. Allie giggled. She hoped he wouldn't fall in.

Digger moaned. He pressed his lips to hers, his bulk on top of her. They were making something, not love. Steaming up the portholes, drowning out the howl of the wind with the huff of their breath. She clung to Digger's sweaty flesh. It wasn't that she desired him, but tied to a float in the middle of nowhere while a storm blew, she needed something to hold on to, the way people made love with strangers in bomb shelters during a blitz. Digger pounded *thump, thump, thump* and he was done. Allie lay still, feeling her heart slow down. The air cooled. Digger's snores rumbled against the planks that curved up to meet in a point behind their heads.

A sudden gust hit the boat, rattling the rigging. Above it all was the eerie, heartbreaking cry of the wind; the sound of all the sorrow in the world. What if the boat broke loose from its mooring while they slept and they drifted out to the stormy open sea? As kids, she and her brother had held trash can covers into the wind and sailed down to the beach to see the boats that had cracked up on shore in a storm.

Storm — that was a game she'd played with her brother. The rules were simple. They could be in the middle of anything — watching TV, playing Monopoly — when one of them would suddenly shout out "Storm!" Then everything would be thrown into the air, all order shattered, and they'd run into her bedroom closet shrieking. There they hid, clutching each other. They loved that game, and had had no idea that they'd been playing house, as house was played in their home. It was the perfect metaphor for her father's nightly return.

There'd once been a storm she'd loved. She was only eight or ten, and her father had run his cruiser across Nantucket Sound to Martha's Vineyard. When the storm blew up he refused to stay over and miss a day of work. Her mother, afraid of the waves, chose to ride the ferry back, but she sent Allie and her brother along with their father.

Years later Allie asked her mother why she had let them go with him, wasn't she afraid they'd drown? Her mother was surprised by the question. "You wanted to go," she said, "and I didn't want you to be afraid of things like I was. Besides, I believed your father could handle it."

That was the myth they lived by: her father as powerful as Poseidon. But what a wonderful storm it was! The waves and rain crashing against the windshield, the wipers sluicing, sluicing, coming back for more. The waves rose right over their heads to smash at the stern of the boat. They heaved and rolled and bucked, the inboard motor sucking air when the waves lifted the stern, the compass whirling crazily, like the nighttime sky of her dreams. At one point the ferry passed them, the huge boat rolling, floundering, her mother a little figure in a raincoat, waving, gripping the rail. But Allie stood beside her father, holding the wheel while he read his charts, thrilled.

It was the only time she'd ever seen him happy. He'd been angry every other day of her life, an anger that seemed to well up from some implacable dissatisfaction with everything around him — his work, his family, himself. But that day in the storm he stood there making his jaw jut and retract, jut and retract, his only sign of pleasure. Maybe the danger relieved him of the misery of living inside himself, or else he loved another chance to exert his will.

When they slid between the two long stone jetties into the safety of Falmouth Harbor, the waves had receded into a fierce white chop, and light rain tapped on the windshield. She was swept by loss; she didn't want it to end. She didn't want her mother waiting dockside with the car, ready to say the one thing that would start the day's fight. She wanted a storm that would go on forever, her father huge beside her, hands on the wheel, the ocean rising overhead, and the two of them held in its turbulence, riding on its crest.

IN THE TAKINE INN, a band from Oregon replaced the local boys in honor of the Fourth. They played bad rock interspersed with country-western, the same tunes punched on the juke box in between sets. Nobody cared. It was something to move to, and everyone in Vladimir wanted to move. The dance floor heaved and shook.

Nick sat out the rock numbers, content to sip his bourbon and watch Vivian kick up her heels. When the music played slow, he held her close, breathing in the scent of her perfume. It was much too sweet, but it didn't matter. He liked the way she looked tonight, the way she smelled. Her breasts billowed against his shirt front; her cheekbones, wide as a Tatar's, pressed against his shoulder; the heft of her broad back felt warm and solid beneath his hand. It was this, Vivian's solidity, large as life, larger than life, that brought him back.

That morning he found her wrapped in a chef's apron, dishing up fried chicken at the Volunteer Fire Hall to benefit the Native Health Clinic, looking calm and regal above the aluminum pans. Her joy at the fact that he'd made it back to town for the Fourth made him cautious. It contained too much its opposite: in leaving he might take too much away. But Vivian was strong. He believed in her strength as much as he believed in her need, her sorrow. He believed in her voice, softly humming with the band, the heat of her skin so real. Nick twirled her and pulled her close: their dance.

Back at the table he bought her sweet creamy ladies' drinks — brandy Alexanders, white Russians. He talked fishing with the trollers; Vivian leaned back in her chair, eyes half closed, wriggling her shoulders, basking in the warmth the way everyone sucked in the sunshine that first spring day.

Jimmy Caldwell stopped by on the way to the men's room and put an arm around them both. "Nick, you old dog," Jimmy said, "you goddamn troller. What you doing stealing my sweetheart here?" Jimmy cackled. "I'm just kidding. No shit. You ain't Indian but you're still good people. No shit."

"Quit messing my hair, Jimmy," Vivian protested. "C'mon, Jimmy, let's dance." Vivian and the old man disappeared in the crowd.

"He was better to me than my daddy ever was," Vivian said when she came back and settled into her seat. Nick agreed. It was a story he knew, how Jimmy and his wife had taken her in after her father drowned and her mother burned to death at home. Jimmy'd been one hell of a seiner, too. Now he carved Tlingit war paddles and totems, not for money, but because it was something he liked to do, and he was the only one who remembered how to do it.

"Look over there at Sonny," Vivian said.

Sonny sat at a table across the room with Frankie, Henry, Morgan, and Duane and a couple of local girls. Laughing, flashing dollar bills in liar's poker.

"Just look at him," Vivian said. "Trying to pretend he don't know I'm here. I'm just gonna go over there a minute and remind him."

"Vivian. Let him be."

Vivian narrowed her eyes. "What are you getting worried about?"

Why couldn't she leave him alone? He wasn't a boy anymore but a grown man. She let the youngest one, Mikey, run wild. He was too young to come into the bar, but he was probably out in the parking lot right now, drinking beer and smoking marijuana with his friends. But Sonny, the first-born, the one who looked like his father, Sonny she couldn't let alone.

Nick put his hand on Vivian's and pulled her up for another slow song, for diversion. When the band struck up a faster tempo, he was grateful that Henry appeared to whisk Vivian away. Nick wandered up to the bar. He talked cohos, herring on hooks versus spoons and hoochies. He turned with a fresh bourbon and another sweet concoction for Vivian, to see her draped over Sonny's shoulder at the other table. Sonny sat blank-faced, shaking his head no. Nick flashed with rage. He dismissed the possibility of his own jealousy, called it disgust.

Vivian flounced back, annoyed. "That boy," she said.

"Why must you always to follow him? You make him to be ashamed."

Vivian slammed the table with a fist, upsetting the thin-stemmed glass of brandy Alexander. Beige cream ran across the Formica table, diverging into two paths. "Goddamn you, Nick. Who gave you the right to tell me how to raise my kids? I might not be the best mother in the world, but I sure as hell didn't get any help from you — or nobody else, neither."

"Vivian, he is not kid now."

"Don't you tell me what he is!" she shouted. "You ain't a part of my family. You don't want to be."

There it was, the truth under her anger. He didn't want to marry her and she knew it. Heads were turning. The barmaid lurked with a rag, eyeing the spill. Across the room, Sonny sat rigid with humiliation at the sound of his mother's voice. Nick knew he should have kept his mouth shut. She was right; it wasn't his business, but he couldn't keep from saying, "Okay. Vivian, that is enough."

"The hell it is! What do you know about families, anyway? What kind of family do you have? You tell me. If you ever had one, it didn't keep you from running off and leaving them all behind in Russia. You're a goddamned one to talk."

97

Nick paled with anger, with the accuracy of her aim. It wasn't something he'd ever discussed with her, or with anyone. Forgetting that he'd already paid for the drinks at the bar, he drew out a ten and placed it on the table, pushed back his chair, and stood up.

Vivian's expression wavered, anger giving way to fear. "Nick?" she whispered, then her anger returned. "Go on," she said. "The hell with you. Walk out on me, too. Go get on your boat and leave everything behind. That's what you really want to do anyway, ain't it? Well you can just go to hell."

No, it wasn't what he wanted. He wanted peace, as elusive as fish. He wanted things simple. He wanted to sit back down beside her and drink the drinks and continue to celebrate Independence Day, but it was too late for any of that. He picked up his wool jacket and walked off.

"Fuck you," Vivian yelled at his back. The lights dimmed and the sky was split by great gunshot bursts. People ran to the windows where fire hung in the sky — a burning carnation — and then fizzled into the bay. Fireworks. Nick walked out, the taste of sulfur, acrid and bitter, in his mouth. Behind him in the Takine Inn, a chorus of voices went "Ahhhhhhhhhhhhhhhhh."

Sonny watched his fingers shaking on his coffee cup. He should have tapered off sooner, or cut back down to beer. Now it was a long run to Chatam Strait for a two-day opening with a queasy stomach and a pound in his head. He pulled out change along with a handful of worthless Fourth of July Queen Contest raffle tickets. The raffle was yesterday, maybe the day before. It scared him not to remember. First prize was a trip to Hawaii. Hawaii wasn't where he wanted to go. Nice enough weather, but who needed another island? Second prize was a rifle with a scope — Henry's jacklighting uncle Izzie got that — and third was a side of beef. He didn't know what to do with the stubs, so he stuck them back inside his pocket and left a tip.

In the drugstore he studied the newspaper rack, looking for something to read on the boat. The *Seattle Post-Intelligencer* carried a lead story on Nixon and Watergate, with a full-face picture of the president. It was in the news every day, but nobody ever talked about it. That's Outside, they said. We got our own problems. What do you expect from down there?

Sonny studied Nixon's face. The guy was a bastard, but he probably could have gotten away with it if he hadn't pushed too hard. To have everything like that and screw it up didn't make sense. Playing within the limits of chance was the name of the game. He tucked the paper under his arm and kept looking.

The *Vladimir Eagle*'s souvenir Fourth of July edition was already out. A lot of parade pictures, and who won the choker-setting and log-rolling contests. Then inside, the usual stuff about the lousy spawner count, the decline of Pacific salmon, the need for limited entry in licensing boats. If they did that, nobody who hadn't owned his own boat would be able to get one now unless he could get the money to buy out someone else's license. It looked grim. Sonny let his eyes wander past girlie magazines, *Sports Illustrated*, a two-week-old *Time*, something called *Rocky Mountain West*.

On the cover of *Rocky Mountain West* a young man and woman in shorts and hiking boots stood on a red rocky ledge. In the distance a city with tall buildings spread out below, massive yet inviting. The girl wore a halter top and the boy was shirtless. They had tans, sun-streaked blond hair, and faces silly with health. The Rocky Mountain sunshine looked harsh, brilliant; the sky behind their heads unbelievably blue. Hype, Sonny figured. Some garbage to sell hiking boots. Still . . . He picked up the magazine and flipped through the pages.

Inside was a spread on Denver, the city depicted on the cover. Denver nightlife, Denver mountains, the expansion of Denver industry, and the boom in Denver jobs. In every picture the sky was exquisitely bright, the clouds white cream puffs — none of that brooding Vladimir fog. The idea of constant sunshine made him wonder: at those altitudes he bet it would even feel stronger, you could take more in through your pores. He wanted to live in a place like that, dry and pretty, with the city right there for you when you wanted to climb down off your mountain and boogie around. The women were probably nice, too, not all edgy and angry like Vladimir women, like Brenda or his mother. It wasn't their fault but something the island did to them, making them wait for their men to come back from fishing. In Vladimir both men and women had to drink away the rain and the darkness when it got cold. But Denver . . . He had to make it down there this winter and see for himself. If only they could make a decent season. If only he saved his bucks.

"Hey, boy, you looking or buying?"

Sonny turned to see Frankie grinning across the aisle, holding aloft a copy of *Penthouse*. Sonny closed his magazine quickly and stuck it back on the shelf. He wasn't about to bring it down to the boat, where the guys would ask questions and turn Denver into a joke.

"You ready to roll?" Frankie called.

Sonny picked up his duffel, while the word *Denver* repeated itself inside his head like a prayer.

"DIGGER?" Allie stepped onto the deck of the *Ginny D.* and leaned in the fo'c's'le door. "They didn't have Wheat Chex so I got you Rice Chex instead." She started down the galley stairs but Digger appeared, blocking her path. Behind him stood a cannery girl in a bloody apron and headscarf, her mouth set in a grim line, arms crossed in front of her chest.

"Uh, Allie, this is Jeanine."

"Hi," Allie said. The girl met Allie's greeting with a belligerent stare. So this was Jeanine. After all Digger's heartbroken rhapsodies, she'd expected a princess, not this thin-lipped, Appalachian girl. She turned to Digger. "They said they'd deliver the food by twelve-thirty. Is that okay? I told them we're pulling out at one."

"Listen," Digger said. "We're kind of in the middle of an important discussion here."

"Yeah?"

"We need a little privacy, understand? Why don't you just go back uptown for a while?" He looked at his watch. "Jeanine's got to go back to the cannery in half an hour."

Too surprised to protest, Allie backed out the fo'c's'le door. It wasn't until she was halfway up the dock that she realized that Digger was in the wrong; he had no right to tell her to get lost in front of that girl. They should've gone somewhere else. Now she was supposed to go back uptown and amuse herself until they were ready to allow her back on board.

She saw Sonny's boat, the *Nancy M.*, tied beyond the ramp behind a shrimp trawler, and, eager for a chance to express her indignation as well as for a chance to see Sonny, she detoured away from the ramp. She hadn't seen any of the crew since before the Fourth of July, which was more than a month ago. Once, coming through Wrangell Narrows on the way to Petersburg for a new steering chain, the *Ginny D.* passed the *Nancy M.* heading out for a seine opening. Allie stood on deck waving, in the hope that Sonny might be watching from the pilothouse or the galley.

No one was on the deck of the *Nancy M.*, but she found Frankie in the galley slicing potatoes into a pot roast. "Hey," he said cheerily, "how's life?"

"Lousy." Allie flopped down at the galley table and lit up a cigarette. A cribbage board, cards, and a score pad were spread across the table. S.M. was winning against F.T. Allie fingered the pegs. It was all fun and games for them.

"Where is everybody?" She refrained from mentioning Sonny's name, but she glanced around surreptitiously, hoping he'd appear out of the fo'c's'le or the pilothouse.

"Uptown, doing errands." Frankie dumped an overloaded ashtray and set it in front of her. "So you're lousy, huh? Poor baby. What's the matter?"

"Digger," she said disgustedly. "You know what he just did? He kicked me off the boat for half an hour so he could have a little chat with his old girlfriend. Do you believe that shit?"

Frankie laughed. "He got tired of you, huh. What's the matter, weren't you any good in the sack?"

Allie groaned. "Don't you get it? It's a job. As long as I work for him, the boat's where I live. He doesn't have the right to tell me to get lost."

Frankie continued slicing potatoes into the pan. "Don't worry, you'll find yourself another boyfriend."

"It's got nothing to do with boyfriends! Digger *isn't* my boyfriend."

Frankie shrugged. He was growing bored with the conversation.

The galley door opened. A heavyset man with small blue eyes and muttonchop whiskers leaned in, gave Allie an unfriendly glance, turned to Frankie. "We could use you out here on deck for a minute." He let the door bang shut.

Frankie put his knife down and winked. "Our skipper don't like women aboard, remember?" He grinned, as though this were a joke Allie would appreciate, and ushered her out the door.

On deck, Sonny stood atop the piled black seine, guiding the power skiff as his skipper winched it aboard. He looked up, startled when he saw her. Allie lifted her hand in a quick little wave. There was no way to read the emotion behind his eyes. Shyness? Embarrassment in front of his skipper? Simple surprise? If only he'd given her some indication. She ducked her head and hurried away.

Why had she been so dumb as to tell her woes to Frankie? Now he'd turn it all into a joke for his crew, for Sonny, telling her tale with his particularly insightful slant. Hyuk, hyuk. Why hadn't she just kept her mouth shut? She was an idiot, and she still had time to kill.

Allie hung around the drugstore, blindly gazing at gruesome corpses in *Police Digest* and cute little seals in *Alaska Magazine* until enough time had passed for Jeanine to go back to her cannery line. Back in the galley of the *Ginny D.*, she found Digger staring morosely at two untouched tunafish sandwiches set across from each other on the table. Apparently, Jeanine had made lunch for him in an act of reconciliation. Allie felt irked. The groceries had arrived, but Digger had done nothing about them.

"That wasn't right, throwing me off like that," Allie complained, dropping a box of groceries with a thump on the galley floorboards.

Digger lifted the top slice of bread from his sandwich and looked at the exposed tuna salad, as though an answer might lie under there. He sighed unhappily. "Yeah, I know, but it was the way things worked out."

"Well, you don't look very happy, considering."

"I got a lot of things to think over."

"Next time you might think about me, you know. I live here too."

Digger made no reply.

At one in the afternoon they untied from the dock, gassed up, and headed out for a six-hour run to Point Baker. Digger steered moodily in the pilothouse, accompanied by staticky chatter on the marine band. The water was calm, and since there was no roll to make her seasick, Allie stayed below, alternately listening to Digger's collection of pop and country-western tapes and napping, storing up sleep for the twenty-four-hour gill-net opening.

Before they turned away from Sumner Strait and cut into the channel that led to Point Baker, Allie went out on deck to watch the evening end. To the west, the sun was falling into the sea in a blaze that spread out over the water and backlit the trees on the mountaintops. There was a harsh autumnal tinge to the sunset. The calm water rippling away from the bow looked colder than ever, a hint of winter in an August evening. It was frightening how much shorter the days were now. She shivered at the thought of the outside waters, the waves forming and reforming there. Yet the more inhospitable it became, the lovelier this land looked. It filled her with a longing she couldn't identify.

Inside the channel the spruce leaned toward the boat, blocking the light, and the water was still and black. They passed a tumbledown cabin on a spit of land separated from the rest of Baker by a small lagoon. A derelict boat lay on its side on the seaweed-covered rocks that served as the cabin's front yard. The boat's name was painted on the stern in red: *Hope*. Two little mulatto kids in spiky pigtails and life jackets stood on the rocks watching them chug by, open-mouthed in stunned amazement, as though they'd never seen a boat pass by in their lives. Rumor had it that a black woman abandoned by her fisherman husband lived in the cabin with her kids. Allie couldn't imagine why she remained there. Perhaps she was still waiting for her man to return; perhaps she'd given up all hope, and the cabin was the perfect expression of her desolation. Allie waved to the children but they didn't respond.

The Baker docks were much emptier than usual, the gillnetters and trollers tied only two deep. A lot of the boats hadn't shown up for the opening. Either they'd headed south to try their luck in fishier pastures or they'd decided not to gill-net at all but rather, if they were double-rigged, to troll until it was time to fall-fish for dog salmon up by Juneau. Although it meant more fish for the boats that were willing to go after them, there was something grim and disheartening about Baker without the crowds.

Digger didn't make his usual jaunt to the bar to check out the fishing gossip but hung around listening to sad songs on the tape deck while Allie made dinner. When they were sitting across from each other at the galley table, separated by a pot of spaghetti and a salad, Digger cleared his throat.

"Look," he said, "there's something I got to tell you."

Allie held a canister of fake Parmesan, the best that Petersburg had to offer, poised above her plate.

Digger chewed at his upper lip. "I'm going to take Jeanine back on board. She's been thinking it over and she realizes she made a mistake."

Allie put the Parmesan down in a sudden, panicky rage. "Are you kidding? Digger, she doesn't want to fish with you. She probably saw me in the cannery and just wants to get me off the boat. She'll fish with you three days and quit again."

"Don't talk about Jeanine that way, Allie," Digger said in a pained voice. "You don't know her. She's a very special person."

"I bet!"

"Now don't be like that. I told you all along. I'm a romantic and I got to follow my heart."

"Great! So what does that mean? I'm supposed to switch jobs with her and go stuff fish in cans?"

"Listen, I'll be fair with you. I'll let you fish this opening with me, and when it's over, I'll take you back to Petersburg and give you ferry money to Vladimir, if that's where you want to go."

"Thanks a fucking lot! Why didn't you tell me in Petersburg when I had a chance to get off and find another boat if I wanted to? What's the matter, you didn't want to fish alone and Jeanine couldn't pack her bags in time?"

"It wasn't like that. I didn't tell Jeanine I'd take her back. I told her I had to think it over, and I been thinking it over."

"Well, that's just great!"

"Come on," Digger said, "be reasonable. You can make some bucks with me tomorrow. You're just jealous now, but you'll get over it. We had some good times."

"Jealous? Of you?" Allie pushed her plate of spaghetti across the table so hard it almost landed in Digger's lap, got up, and headed for the door. "Digger, you're such a jerk."

"Where are you going?" he called after her unhappily.

"None of your business, since I don't work for you anymore."

She stomped up the stairs and slammed the door. She didn't know where she was going, only that it felt better to storm away, to leave in a fury, than to sit across from him and accept her fate. She was riding high on the reckless thrill of anger. For the moment, it didn't matter where she went.

She headed down the dock, accompanied by the echo of her own footsteps, which began to sound less angry and more forlorn with each step. The boats looked unapproachable: doors shut against the evening chill, smoke from kerosene stoves rising from their stacks. She could hear bilge pumps doing their duty, spilling bilge back into the sea, and even that steady suck and slurp seemed suddenly poignant now that she was about to lose it. She wouldn't get to go fall fishing in Juneau. It wasn't fair, after she'd put up with him so long.

At the end of the dock she stopped, hugging her arms to herself, caught in indecision. What choices did she have but return to Digger or go to the bar? She turned back, and then, on the stern of a boxy fiberglass gill netter, she saw a young man working over the rollers with a wrench. In the near-dark she'd almost missed him, but he flicked on the picking light, illuminating the top of his head with its thin pale hair and the glittering net on the drum.

"Hi," Allie said.

The man swiveled to look up at her. He was about Digger's age, with a round, freckled, Howdy Doody face; his eyebrows and lashes were so pale it looked as if he didn't have any. Homely but harmless, she decided.

"Hi," he said.

Allie took a breath, jumped in. "You need a deckhand?"

His mouth fell open in surprise, and he uttered an embarrassed little snort. "Well, that's an idea. Are you a deckhand?" His voice was soft, modulated — unusual in this land of loud guffaws.

"Yeah. But I need a new boat."

"You fish with Digger, don't you?"

"Not anymore."

"Well . . . What do you think, Sherlock?" He turned and addressed a large brown hound lying on its side on deck. "You think we need a deckhand?" The dog raised its head, then flopped back with a thump. It beat its tail against the planks a few times in response to the attention. Allie felt a wave of impatience. There was something cloying about a grown man conferring with his dog.

"Sherlock says he doesn't mind." The man smiled, revealing tiny, pointed teeth. "Why not? I could use some help. By the way, my name is Steve Tucker." He leaned across the rollers to give Allie his hand. A fisherman's hand, calloused, strong.

"Allie Heller."

"Welcome aboard. I'm having dinner over on some friends' boat. Why don't you get your things, bring them onto the *Miranda* here, and come along?"

Hallelujah! Allie wanted to jump up and down on the dock planks. Here was proof again: no matter what happened, she always landed on her feet, always found someone new to take her in. She was invincible, and Digger could go to hell. "I'll be right back," she said.

Digger was lying under the sleeping bag in his bunk, holding a copy of *National Fisherman* in front of his nose. He put it down quickly when she came in. He looked relieved to see her, but his expression turned anxious as she set about gathering her things. He sat up in his bunk. His T-shirt looked too small to contain his bulky chest, and his head sat on his shoulders with little assistance from his neck. She'd never before noticed just how brutish Digger looked.

"What are you doing?"

"Moving. I'm working on the *Miranda* now." She smiled. Digger looked stricken.

It served him right, she thought. Let *him* be humiliated now in front of the fishermen of Baker; they'd think he lost her to another man. It was the perfect revenge, and she felt only triumph. Whistling, Allie stuffed her clothes, rain gear, books, and toothbrush into her duffel bag and left without looking back.

Steve's boat wasn't as pretty as the old-fashioned, graceful *Ginny D.* The *Miranda* was all squared-off angles, fiberglass and plywood instead of teak and brass, a box built over a hull. A serviceable boat, efficient and easy to maintain but lacking in style. On the shelf above the bunks, however, mixed in with back issues of *National Fisherman,* Allie noted a dog-eared copy of *Don Quixote* and Bronowski's *Ascent of Man.* Better to have a skipper with class than a boat with class, she supposed.

Steve's friends, a couple from Port Townsend, Washington, named Joanna and Jim, lived on a freshly painted wooden gill netter–troller. A baby slept in a cradle suspended behind a lacy curtain, spider plants hung in front of the portholes, and the galley smelled deliciously of garlic bread and tomato sauce.

"This is Allie," Steve announced. "She's going to be helping me fish."

"It's about time," Joanna said. She looked too old to be a new mother. She had a plain, angular, pleasant face, a greying ponytail, and deep smile lines around her eyes. "We were beginning to think Stevie had given up on society altogether in favor of that dog."

"Sherlock *is* society," Steve said.

"Excuse me." Joanna winked at Allie and kissed Steve's cheek.

Jim looked remarkably like his wife, more of an academic than a fisherman, with steel-rimmed spectacles and a briar pipe. He was doing a crossword puzzle at the galley table, but he got up to shake her hand when she came in. Allie sat down across from him at the table and put her hands demurely in her lap. She felt awkward in the midst of this cozy little domestic scene. It had been a long time since she'd been around "nice" people, and she feared that in Joanna's and Jim's eyes she might appear to be a boat hopper, a fisherman's groupie. She wanted them to like her, and having been Digger's deckhand didn't seem like much of a character reference.

"Where are you from, Allie?" Jim asked. Behind his glasses, his eyes were clever, probing.

"Back east. Not far from Boston."

"Is that so? You and Stevie were practically neighbors. Did he tell you he went to school back there?"

"No."

"Stevie's the Yale man of the fishing fleet. He's our college boy." Jim grinned at his friend.

Steve looked abashed. "Jim likes to pretend I'm the only one who ever went to school, but he and Joanna have a couple of degrees between them, and he's still working on another, so don't let him fool you with that Yale stuff."

Allie turned to study her new skipper. She was impressed — not that Steve had gone to Yale, but that he'd gone to Yale and ended up here, owning his own boat. It made her feel closer to him, as though they shared membership in a special little conspiracy of superiority: those who knew both worlds.

"I went to school in Connecticut too," Allie said. "Wesleyan." Immediately, the baldness of her assertion embarrassed her. She was such a chameleon, always trying to be like the people around her. In the Baker bar, in front of Frankie or Sonny, she'd been careful to avoid the subject of college, and here she was tossing off credentials. "But only for a year," she amended.

"Look at that," Jim said. "Stevie found himself a college girl who knows how to wear a halibut jacket."

Allie couldn't figure out if Jim was simply kidding or being sarcastic. Was he making fun of her? She looked into his grey eyes but couldn't tell. The halibut jacket was something she'd had for years, although she hadn't known what it was called. It was a simple brown wool jacket with a double flap over the shoulders that she'd bought in Boston. She'd been surprised to see that all the fishermen wore them, although they usually cut off the sleeves at the elbows so the cuffs wouldn't get caught in their gear.

"What are you studying, Jim?" she asked, eager to divert the conversation away from herself.

"Social work. Do-gooding. I was working as a juvenile probation officer, and I'll probably end up doing it again, the way fishing's going. I'm trying to get my M.S.W. to be a counselor. We're incorrigible Peace Corps types, out to change the world and all that shit."

Steve said, "Joanna works as a school librarian in the winter, or she did until a few months ago." He nodded toward the cradle.

Allie liked Steve for including Joanna, liked how these friends knew one another, their jokey tenderness. Jim's sardonic tone was directed at everything, not just at her. She began to relax.

Joanna spooned a generous serving of lasagna onto Allie's plate. Allie leaned over the steam. It was wonderful to have someone serve her for a change.

Joanna stopped to look at her with a furrowed brow, a bowl of salad cradled in her arms. "Allie, aren't your parents worried about you up here all alone?"

Allie said, "They don't know where I am." It seemed like an irrelevant question.

Joanna shivered with horror. "Now that I'm a mother I see things a little differently. I never used to mind the bad weather, but now I'm always worried about the baby. It's tough being a parent, being afraid for someone else all the time." She went over to the cradle and fussed with the baby's blanket. "Your parents must be worried sick."

They were sick already, Allie thought and smiled to herself. She actually envied the baby in the cradle, as she envied the closeness among Jim, Joanna, and Steve.

"So, have you guys made a decision?" Steve asked, looking up from his lasagna.

Joanna and Jim glanced at each other. Jim said, "We're still hashing it out."

Steve turned to Allie and explained. "They're trying to decide if Jim should go on up north for fall fishing next month and send Joanna and the baby home by plane, or if he should just bag it and run them down the coast. It's a real gamble."

"Why wouldn't you fish?" Allie asked.

"I've got a lot of debt on this boat, Allie," Jim said. "I might do better to just head home and look for a regular job, at this point. School will just have to wait a little longer. There's no guarantee that the fish are going to show up, or that Fish and Game will let us go after them, if they do. I'm not sure I can chance it, now that I've got other considerations."

"I can go back to work," Joanna said uncertainly. "There's day care, you know."

Jim shook his head. "Not for my baby. Not after we waited so long."

Joanna put her hands on her husband's shoulders. They looked veiny, almost gnarled in contrast to the smooth gold wedding band. She looked weary, old. "Well, none of us know what's going to happen," she said. "It could still all turn around."

Jim smiled wryly. "Right. There could be an earthquake. Nuclear disaster. Why decide now?"

"You've got to admit, there's got to be some controls," Steve said earnestly. "There's too many boats, plain and simple." He turned to Allie. "In the past five, ten years everyone wanted to get into the act because there was so much profit in gill-netting. Trolling takes patience and knowledge, but anyone can throw out a net and get lucky. Then there's the growth of the logging industry. The clear cutting is ruining the streams for the spawners. If the fish can't go back to their home streams, they can't spawn. I've hiked these mountains, and the streams are ruined, half of them. Choked with log falls. There's got to be more control, but the timber industry's got a lot of power in this state."

"Why don't the fishermen organize — you know, do some lobbying up in Juneau?" Allie asked. It was a question she'd been pondering for some time. All she ever heard was complaints and never any solutions. Why didn't they join together and buy up the canneries themselves, go cooperative so they could set their own prices, instead of blaming the Japanese?

"That's a good question," Steve said. "Unfortunately it goes against their natures. One man, one boat, the last independents. Fishermen are great at helping out their friends, but forget organization. That's why we got into this crazy business, so we wouldn't have to compromise with anyone. Only now it's getting away from us. It's a sad thing. All we've got now is what somebody called 'the sustaining illusion of independence.' You're lucky to get a chance to see it before it's all gone."

Everyone kept telling her that. She knew she was lucky — lucky to be in on the end of an era, luckier still to be sitting aboard this boat eating lasagna with Joanna and Jim and Steve instead of working for Digger. Lucky to have a new skipper who actually considered her opinions. She wanted badly to be a part of it all, to have something at stake, as they did.

"Well, we aren't going to solve it all tonight," Joanna said firmly. "How about dessert? There's blueberry pie, hand picked."

At the end of the evening, when Steve went up the stairs ahead of her, Joanna kissed Allie's cheek and whispered, "You know, Stevie's wife just left him this April, and we've been really worried about him fishing alone all the time. We're so glad he has you to keep him company now."

Allie flushed with pleasure; Joanna had offered her the gift of acceptance.

On the *Miranda*, Allie and Steve undressed chastely with the lights off, each turned away in his bunk.

"I really liked your friends," Allie said, lying on her back, looking up at the planks above her head.

"Yeah, they're fine people. And they're in a hard place right now. Well, we got a long day coming up." Steve rolled over. "Better get some sleep."

Allie tried to sleep, but Sherlock, who was stretched out in the vee between the bunks, kept uttering high-pitched little whines.

"Shhhh," Allie said.

"Just try to ignore it. It's been a while since he's had to share me with anyone else, and he's jealous." Steve reached down to pat his dog and addressed him in baby talk that made Allie wince. "What's the matter, wittle boy? What a good, good boy. Who's my good boy?"

Allie tried not to feel disgusted. Was she jealous of a dog as well as a baby? Steve was a nice guy and probably just lonely, as Joanna had said. People who lived alone with animals always got gooey like that. She pulled the covers over her head, but she couldn't sleep. It was distracting, listening to the whining dog and the breathing of a strange man only inches away. It made her edgy, not with desire but with possibilities. It was too bad Steve wasn't more attractive. She'd noticed at dinner that he had funny-looking hands, stubby fingers, and spatula nails. She wondered if he was attracted to her. It was hard to tell, because he was obviously a gentleman, and they really did have to get some rest before the gill-net opening. Although she wasn't attracted to him, it seemed important that he be attracted to her. If he wasn't, she wouldn't know who she was.

She tried to will herself to sleep, counting backward from a thousand, but she was wired with excitement. Almost by accident, she'd stumbled upon a new life, a much better life than the one she'd had with Digger. Tomorrow was a gill-net opening, twenty-four hours. After gill-netting, she supposed that she and Steve would troll, since his boat was double-rigged, and then they'd probably go up to Lynn Canal and Juneau for fall fishing. After that, who knew?

Steve's attitude toward fishing was completely different from Digger's. He remained calm, addressed Allie politely, and explained every move — why he was setting his net near a certain point of rocky shore, how he'd be changing his net soon to a lighter color to match the pale, glaciated waters up near Juneau. When they pulled in the first set and Allie waited to gather the fish and toss them in the bin, he asked, "Didn't Digger ever have you help him pick?"

"No. He just had me throw them in the bin."

"It's a lot faster and easier if we work together. See, you stand across from me, over there on the other side of the net, and we stretch it between us. It unsnags a lot faster that way, and whoever gets to the fish first grabs it. Teamwork. We always did it that way when Ellen was aboard. Didn't we, Sherlock?"

Allie stood in her rain gear across from Steve, pulling the net rapidly toward her as he pulled it toward him, and the salmon, snagged by their gills, practically jumped out of the stretched net and into her hands. It was fun working together like that. With Digger she'd been a virtual slave, stuck with the dirty work. Maybe when they trolled, Steve would let her work the lines. She grew excited at the prospect, and she worked feverishly, stretching the net, tossing away the tangles of seaweed and the stinging jellyfish.

The salmon — dogs and humpies this time of year — were discolored with graffitilike swirls of pink and green and purple, and they looked deformed, their spines arched, their mouths twisted. They barely resembled the beautiful, graceful fish that had fought the hook so valiantly when Allie and Digger trolled.

"When they're ready to spawn," Steve explained, "they stop eating and you can practically see their bodies begin to decay. Have you ever seen them heading upstream? The mouth of the stream is black with them, thousands of dorsal fins, and then there they are, fighting their way over boulders, struggling up through falls. It's enough to make you believe in destiny."

Allie looked at him across the net. He had a black gob of seaweed stuck to the side of his snubby nose, and she wanted to reach over and wipe it off for him. With his olive rain jacket hood framing his face, his blue eyes bright against a background of grey sea and mist on the mountains, he looked almost appealing.

At two in the morning, with the sky black and rain falling, they pulled in a set and unloaded under the picking light, then set the net again to wait for the changing tide. Steve suggested she take a nap; he'd wake her in half an hour to change places. Sherlock would keep him company on watch, he said. Exhausted but happy, Allie went below to the bunks, pulled off her boots, rubber overalls, and jeans, and immediately fell asleep.

She woke to the sound of a zipper unzipping.

"Take it easy," Steve said sharply. He was standing at the end of her bunk, pulling off his jeans. His bare chest, pale and sunken, glistened in the dim light cast from the pilothouse.

Allie struggled up, still half asleep, bumped her head against the low bunk ceiling, and slid back down under the open sleeping bag. "Is it time for me to go on watch?"

"Not yet."

Steve slid into her bunk on top of her. Allie froze under his weight. He hadn't kissed her or caressed her, had whispered no tender word nor said anything to make his intentions known. She wasn't afraid of him, but she was shocked. If he'd approached her, she probably would have accepted him, even tried to muster some response. She would have supposed it came with the territory. But this cold grappling for her underpants, this wordless lust, left her stunned. She put her hands against his shoulders in a stiff, uncertain gesture: not a protest, not an embrace.

Steve pulled her underpants down roughly and entered her, thrusting with harsh, repetitive jabs. With every lunge he uttered an ugly little grunt: *unh, unh, unh.* Allie felt nothing.

She lay there, still, unresponding, until he came with a final repulsive groan, and then he pulled out. He lay sprawled on top of her, and his weight seemed suddenly unbearable, crushing. She touched his thin hair, plastered now to his sweaty skull, in a tentative gesture, a question. He jerked and shuddered like a horse shivering off flies, then roused himself. In the half-light he pulled on his jeans with his back turned and left without a word.

Allie lay under the sleeping bag, curled into a small fetal ball. She could feel the wetness of his ejaculation running down her legs. He hadn't asked, hadn't done anything about birth control. She tried to remember where she was in her cycle, but she couldn't keep the numbers straight. A terrible emptiness came over her, a cold that mixed with the cold of his semen on her legs, and all she could hear was his grunting *unh, unh, unh,* and she kept seeing a vision of his stubby fingers. If only he'd said something to her, just one kind word, she wouldn't feel so bad. She just couldn't understand what he'd done, or the way he'd done it, almost as though he were angry at her. She pulled the sleeping bag over her head and tried to fall back into sleep, but she couldn't. Finally, she got up, wiped herself with a towel, dressed, and went into the galley to pour herself a cup of coffee from the pot on the corner of the stove.

Steve leaned down the fo'c's'le stairs from the pilothouse. "You can take over now," he said in a flat voice. "I'm going to take a nap for half an hour."

They fished out the morning quietly, politely moving around each other, stretching the net between them without their eyes meeting, loading the fish in the bins. Steve seemed to go out of his way to avoid any accidental contact, and he barely spoke. Allie kept looking for the word, the touch that would set things right, that would make sense of what had happened. It almost seemed as though she'd dreamed it, it was all so unlikely, so unexplained.

When they tied up at the Whitney-Fidalgo packer to sell

their fish, Louie raised his eyebrows. "See you got yourself a new boat," he said. Allie couldn't look at him, could only stare down at her boots, at the twisted salmon littering the deck like the dead after battle.

They headed back into the channel to Baker, past the tumble-down cabin where the abandoned black woman lived. It was high tide, and the derelict boat, the *Hope*, lay half submerged on the seaweed-covered rocks. The children in life jackets and pigtails were nowhere to be seen.

At the dock, Steve instructed Allie to scrub the hold and went off to take care of an errand. The hold was slimy and slippery with fish gurry, scales, and blood, and she was so exhausted her scrub brush kept slipping off the messy walls. It seemed to take forever to soap and scrub and rinse the boat with the dock hose, but finally she was done. She climbed out of the hold, scales stuck to her face and hands, smeared with guts, and pulled herself out of her rain gear. She sat down on a deck pail and lit up a smoke.

"You're done already," Steve said, climbing across the rails to stand before her. "That's great." His voice sounded overly cheerful, and his eyes were focused somewhere over her left shoulder. "Listen, here's your check, for your percentage, and you were a real help. I'm sorry that things didn't work out better."

"What do you mean?" Panic rose in her chest, a nauseating wave.

"I guess I don't really need a deckhand after all."

Allie folded the check in half, into quarters, then opened and smoothed it, reading it without seeing the numbers, her share. She said nothing. It felt hard to catch her breath.

"You must have noticed that we were rubbing each other the wrong way," Steve said evenly.

"I didn't notice that. I thought we got along all right." Someone else was talking, using her voice. She sat on the deck pail, beside the brush, the bottle of detergent. What had she done? Hot tears came to her eyes. Soon everyone would know that she'd been fired: Joanna, Jim, Digger, the whole world. The tears ran down her cheeks, and she wiped at them with the back of her dirty hand.

"Come on now," Steve said. "Don't cry. It's not such a big deal. I'm sure you'll find another boat."

She didn't want to find another boat. She liked fishing with him. It was the nicest day of fishing she'd ever had. What had she done wrong?

"Come on now, chin up." Steve turned around to see if anyone on the dock might notice her crying. "Listen, I've got to make a supply run. I'll give you your choice. Where would you rather have me drop you? Petersburg or Vladimir?"

Allie stood outside on deck through most of the trip to Vladimir, letting the light mist fall on her face, watching the hypnotic curl of wake behind the boat, the soft fog lying in strips at the base of the mountains. It was chilly, but she didn't want to go inside. The water had a strange greyish sheen, almost clay-colored, and it seemed as though she could just step out and walk away. That's what she wanted to do, to walk across the surface of the sea, away from Steve in the pilothouse, away from herself.

What had she done wrong? She couldn't figure it out. Had she chattered too much, told him too much about how bad it was fishing with Digger? Had she neglected his beloved dog? Maybe he was still broken up about his wife and wasn't ready for another woman?

She turned it over again and again, but all she could come up with, finally, was that he'd simply used her; he'd done something he was ashamed of and had to get rid of her so that he wouldn't have to face his shame. And then he'd made her clean the hold before he told her. Somehow, that struck her as the biggest outrage.

What had she done? She'd allowed it, allowed it all. She

felt a sudden rage, against him, against herself. She wanted to shout at him, "You're ugly, and you talk baby talk to a dog, and you grunt when you fuck, and you can't do anything to me," but he'd already done it. Period. Now she was returning to Vladimir, jobless, with no place to go, in disgrace.

Riding on the stern of the *Miranda,* looking out at the perfect curl of wake that turned over and over upon itself, as though it couldn't wait to get away from her too, Allie was overwhelmed by the knowledge of how many times this had happened before. It was such a familiar feeling. She'd never been allowed to be innocent.

"Where are you going, you little tramp?" her father had asked when she was dressing to meet a boy for a first date. "Out to tramp around again?"

Alone with her father in a restaurant, she'd sat helpless, filled with a sickly feeling of complicity while he stared at her breasts with his sly, awful grin.

"You're not as good looking as you think you are," her father said. "You know, you're not my type."

Loving her father had robbed her of any anger.

And when she began to sleep with boys, her mother said, "*I* could never be like you. *I* respect my body too much."

Allie was honestly puzzled by her mother's remark. How could she respect something that had nothing to do with her? What was there to respect?

In the dark, at ten, they came into Vladimir, sliding into the narrow channel between the line of tugs and the fishing boat dock. Allie performed her last duty, leaning out to tie the stern line while Steve swung the *Miranda* in close. The water glittered black under reflected light, and for a moment she imagined herself under there, down in the cool darkness. How easy it would be, how simple.

Steve turned off the engine.

She picked up her duffel and started to climb over the rail.

"Hey, wait," Steve said.

For one wild moment she imagined that he was going to apologize, perhaps even change his mind. She was filled with the wild hope of reprieve: he'd realized his mistake. She put her duffel down.

"I was wondering." Steve hesitated. "Do you have a place to sleep? You know, I'm staying at my friend's house, so if you need a place tonight you can use the boat. Of course, I'll be leaving early in the morning, so you'd have to get off then."

She hated him. She hated his pale, homely face illuminated by the dock lights, his fucking tone of concern. His ugly fingers caressing Sherlock's ear. She hated his dog, too.

He seemed embarrassed. "Well, uh, do you need any money? I mean, until you get that check cashed?"

Allie looked into his blue nice-guy eyes and silently wished him dead. He was worse than Digger. Digger was an oaf who didn't know any better, but this was a civilized man. Without a word she picked up her duffel and clambered over the rail. On the dock, generators hummed and bilge pumps sucked away, doing their monotonous jobs. She walked through pools of yellow light, past lit portholes and galley windows. On the deck of a boat, someone with a harmonica was playing a mournful tune.

Allie started up the steep slats of the ramp, and then she stopped. She couldn't face it. She just couldn't go into the bars to find someone to take her in. All she wanted was a private place to curl up for the night, a place to lick her wounds. Tomorrow she'd figure out what to do. Now she was just too tired, too numb.

At the end of the floats, near the outhouse that sat over the bay, she discovered an abandoned, unpainted two-decker riverboat riding low in the water. It listed, with a couple of broken windows on the day deck and a row of flapping stateroom doors.

"Anyone home?" she called out, but the riverboat was obviously empty, a derelict still afloat. She climbed aboard, and the boat rolled gently underfoot. She chose a stateroom — a narrow cell with a bunk and a door that closed — climbed into her sleeping bag on a mattress that smelled of mildew, and fell asleep to the sound of sloshing bilge.

WINTER

1974–1975

———◆———

N ICK TIED ALONGSIDE the cannery dock and waited for Emory to lower the hoist. His hands, numb from handling the stiff, wet lines, were raw and deeply cracked. He blew on them and watched his breath condense in the chill November rain.

Emory, dressed in an orange snowmobile suit and rubber overalls, guided the metal basket over the dock and eased it down on deck. Nick drew on rubber gloves, climbed down into the hold, and began to pitch fish.

"Hey, Nick, looks like you got yourself some competition."

Nick looked up to see Emory grinning in the direction of the bay. A little flat-bottomed skiff, a Boston Whaler, swung around the bulk of a Japanese lumber ship tied in front of the mill. A figure in rain gear sat hunched in the stern, one hand reached back to the tiller of a tiny outboard engine. Two sport poles jutted out of pole holders fastened midway on either side of the skiff, their lines trailing.

Nick turned back to the task of unloading salmon from his hold. It wasn't a remarkable sight; half of the trollers in town had started out that way, hand-trolling for winter king salmon. There was little overhead, and for a boat with less than six horsepower, commercial licenses came cheap. It was a cold and risky business, though; skiffs like that were easily swamped.

"She's been up here a few times selling good-looking kings." Emory shook his head in amusement, let loose a brown gob of snoose that fell neatly between the rails of Nick's boat and the pilings of the cannery dock. "One day she brought in a thirty-pounder cradled in her arms like a baby. Wonder how she got the thing aboard."

She? Nick turned to look again. As the skiff drew even with his boat, he saw that indeed it was a girl. She wore a blue wool cap pulled low over her forehead, and it took him a few seconds to recognize her: the girl he'd seen fishing with Digger back in the summer, the one with Sophia's face. For a moment he was filled with pained confusion. Like déjà vu, an unbidden fragment of his inner life, of memory, had appeared suddenly in his line of vision. Yet he couldn't pass her off as a neurological quirk, an accident of body chemistry. Across the water, the small *put-put-put* of her tiny outboard was clearly audible, insistently real.

When had he last seen her? In August probably, and then one day Digger showed up in Baker with another girl. A few days later Digger was fishing alone, and that was that. He'd just assumed, if he'd even thought of it, that this one had gone back to wherever it was she came from. But here she was, fishing for herself now, working her own commercial licenses.

The skiff skittered away across the grey water, leaving a ripple-sized wake. In a couple of minutes it was nearly lost against the vastness of the bay.

In the office Emory wrote out his check, tracing the numbers in his account book with a stumpy, nailless forefinger. The cannery echoed with emptiness, floorboards slick and clean, steamers silent. Now that net fishing was over, the cannery had cut back to its winter crew, just a couple of Filipinos and cold-storage women freezing the troll-caught salmon in icy blocks along with deer shoulders and moose rumps, the autumn harvest.

"There you go," Emory said, tearing off the check.

Nine hundred and forty pounds, reds and whites, and a

couple of little halibut he'd decided to keep although he couldn't sell them. At one time he would have brought them to Vivian. It seemed there should be someone to bring a fish to when a man got back to town.

He thought of that woman in Ketchikan last month. A woman with red-gold hair going down the street with him at three A.M. Pretty face, maybe forty-five, with too much makeup but not a whore. Her hand on his arm, leading him, but when they got to her house, she wanted to cook him breakfast, didn't want to get him into bed after all. He put his arms around her at the sink, under the baleful glare of a small, hairless dog — what was it, a chihuahua? — the desire almost sickening after so long.

She led him into the bedroom, sat down on a floral print spread, and turned to him. "Well, I might as well show you now, in case you want to turn tail and run," she said. Pulling up her frilly blouse, she reached behind her back, the bra slipping off to reveal one breast full, somewhat fallen, with its staring nipple, and the other side nothing but flatness like a small boy's chest, ribs lined through the skin, and a great, long diagonal scar.

"Bet you're surprised," the woman said. Rita — her name was Rita. "You probably want to run out of here now, huh?"

In answer he laid her back and kissed the line softly, his right hand on her remaining breast, moving it while his lips traced the scar, then her mouth; her relief one long moan under him. In that moment he loved her — for revealing herself, for what she'd lost. But afterward, she said, "Where you from anyway? You talk funny."

Revulsion, desire.

At the Potlatch Café, Nick hung his coat on a peg and took a seat at the counter. It was mid-morning; the breakfast crowd had thinned. In the back of the pale green room, a very young, very angry Indian girl was struggling to pull a parka on her unwilling child. Smiley Ferris sat alone at a table, hunched over a plate of eggs, forking them into his mouth in a furtive, mechanical motion, eating with the desperate hunger of a drinker coming off a binge.

Nick opened his *Seattle Post-Intelligencer* and began to read. Dottie, the Indian woman who owned the coffee shop, set his cup of coffee in front of him. "Hi, Nick. You just get back in?"

"Uh-huh. How you are Dottie?"

"Keeping on. You want the usual?"

"Sure."

Dottie lingered, wiping around his place until Nick looked up questioningly. She was a thin, nervous woman not given to wasting time. "I guess you heard by now," she said.

"Heard what?"

"About Vivian. They had to bring her on up to the hospital last night." Dottie turned away, started mixing mayonnaise into the lunchtime vat of tuna.

"What for?" Nick waited, trying to calm the clench of fear in his chest by concentrating on the swift jab of her spatula, the stack of silver Tlingit clan bracelets clattering on her wrist, the diminishing swirls of white as tuna and mayonnaise became one.

"She took some kind of fit up at the Takine. Seeing things, talking crazy. She was climbing the walls half the night. You know how she's been drinking the past few months."

Nick pressed his fingers to his eyes. The news didn't really surprise him; what did was that it had the power to make him feel so suddenly beaten, so guilty. Would it have been different if he had stayed with her?

"I hate being the one to tell you, Nick. I know you ain't seeing Vivian no more, but I thought you'd want to know."

"Yes."

"I mean, you'd hear it from the regular gossip . . ."

He waved her words away, pulled out change, and set it beside his coffee cup.

"Nick, don't you want your eggs?"

.   .   .

Sonny was just coming out of the lobby door of the hospital when Nick went in with a two-pound box of chocolates under his arm. Sonny looked startled to see him, but he stopped, let the door close, and they faced each other in the glass entry. Sonny's eyes looked puffy and tired, ringed with black circles. Nick fought an impulse to put his arm on Sonny's shoulder, to give him a hug.

"I just came back this morning," Nick said.

"Yeah, it must be all over town by now."

"How she is?"

"Pretty quiet. They got her all doped up." Sonny fumbled for cigarettes in the pocket of his down vest. Nick pulled out his own Pall Malls and they stood in the entry smoking, watching the slanting rain beat against the glass. Across Airport Road, fog struggled to free itself from the fir trees. Living in Vladimir in the winter was like living inside a cloud.

"She's going to have to lay off for a while," Sonny said. "I just hope this will scare her into listening. If it doesn't, she's going to end up dead."

They were silent, the words claiming space between them. Finally Nick said, "Perhaps it would be better if . . . You think she will want to see me?"

Sonny opened the door and dampness poured in. "I don't know, maybe she'll be glad." He hunched his shoulders against the prospect of going out into the cold rain. "You know I don't blame you, Nick." Then he was out, walking toward town, head down, cigarette cupped in his hand.

Nick threw his own butt out the door. It sizzled against the puddled asphalt. Blame him for what? For Vivian's misery or for leaving her? Either way, it raised the question of fault, set it between them. Blame was something Nick knew all about. He knew the parameters of his own guilt and would never allow himself to forget it. It was as familiar to him now, after almost thirty years, as the shape of his face in a mirror, the scar on his chin. For a second he saw Sophia, then the Sophia-faced girl out in the rain in that little skiff. But this was self-indulgence. What Sonny was saying was that he blamed himself.

Eleanor, the receptionist, a brittle woman with hair that looked like egg whites lacquered in stiff, permanent peaks, and a face as waxy as Lenin's in his tomb, pursed her lips disapprovingly when he asked for Vivian. She led him through the hall, her footsteps echoing, harsh, angry, followed by the meek squish of his own rubber boots. She'd once been married to a local doctor who'd been caught propositioning patients in the office while Eleanor sat outside at the desk. The doctor had moved on to another town, but Eleanor, permanently embittered, had remained, punishing everyone else for her shame.

Vivian was sitting up in bed, propped against pillows, playing with the remote control of a TV set suspended from the ceiling. "Well, what do you know?" she said in a flat voice. "You get sick, you find out who your friends are. Hello, stranger."

Nick kissed her cheek, held out the box of candies. Her usually vivid face had been drained of life, turned to fragile brown pottery. When she moved her lips to speak, she seemed in danger of fracture.

"You didn't have to." Vivian took the box and held it against the sheets. "So, sit down. Or are you in a rush?"

"No rush." After all these months, she was still afraid of his leaving. It made him ashamed. He lowered himself into the bedside chair. "I wanted to bring for you halibut, but I thought, maybe for nurses it would not be such great pleasure." He smiled, feeling the tight falseness of his own face.

"Yeah, you always brought me fish, didn't you? I got to give you that."

"Vivian, how you are feeling?"

"They got me all shot full of dope so I don't feel nothing right now. It's not a bad way to be. You ever have the D.T.s, Nick? Nature's little way of telling you to slow down." Vivian laughed. Nick had a horrible image of her face breaking into pieces, fragments on the sheets.

"I really got to get myself together, Nick. The kids are all worried. Sonny wants me to promise I won't go out no more when I get home. I told him I can't make no promises. You should be able to understand that."

Nick accepted the jab, let it pass. The TV gabbled on inanely — a sale on pork chops at City Market, football scores from the lower forty-eight.

"Sonny wants to send me up to my cousin Emily in Juneau for a while, keep me out of trouble. Did I ever tell you about Emily? She's the one who made good, married a white doctor. I'm supposed to take a little vacation, do some shopping, see the picture shows."

Even sedated, lying here in this cool white room with chrome and the smell of Lysol, her body spoke to him. Why hadn't he loved her? Maybe if he'd been able to love her, she wouldn't be here now. Fool, did he think himself so powerful he could save her from herself? In any case, he hadn't tried because he knew he couldn't. To love her would require not more of something, but less of what he'd already known, an absence of history. He wanted to love her, but all he could do was reach out and touch her hand. Vivian looked down at it lying there on top of her own, white over brown.

"You know, Nick, I been having the strangest dreams. Last night, maybe it was this morning . . . I dreamed I was a little girl again and I was out with my folks at fish camp. I used to love that, all of us being together and working like that, camping in the shelter, running the smokehouse and the drying racks. That's when we really lived like Indians, you know? But in the dream, Mama and me were keeping things nice at camp, waiting for Daddy and the boys to come back in the boat. Mama said, 'Vivvy, you run on down to the beach and watch and see when your daddy and the boys come in, so I can start supper. You just holler when you see them.'

"So I went down to the beach and I started playing with the rocks, making these little houses, pretending that I was making the house I was gonna live in when I grew up and fell in love and got married. Sounds pretty funny, doesn't it, but I used to believe all that stuff was going to come true, just like other little girls. Then I saw the boat coming and I hollered to Mama.

"Daddy and the boys were all on deck — I don't know who was steering — and the deck was just covered in fish. It looked like they'd caught so many they'd filled up the hold and had to bring in a deckload. Only it wasn't salmon. I don't know what they were, all these beautiful colors: bright blue and pink and purple. I started waving and waving. Daddy and the boys waved back, but then they just kept going. They didn't stop. The boat kept going by, with me waving, and them waving, and all those pretty fish on board. I started hollering, 'Come back, come back.'"

Vivian leaned back against the pillows, rested a moment, then leaned forward, suddenly urgent. "I know it's just a dream and it don't mean nothing, but it seemed so real, Nick. Them all alive again like they'd never drowned, waving at me. I was so happy when I saw them. And then when they kept going . . . I wanted to go with them." She lay back again and shut her eyes, spoke to the ceiling. "Now I feel like some part of me was on that boat, gone to wherever it was they went to. Like something's missing and I'll never get it back. I bet you think I'm talking crazy."

Nick shook his head. It seemed there was just too much sorrow, that even he could not face it anymore and that if he didn't turn away from it he'd be consumed. Softly he said, "I do not think you are crazy. I too have such dreams."

"You?" Vivian snorted in disbelief. "Sometimes I wonder about you, Nick. I think, 'That man's worse off than me.' You know why? 'Cause you don't need nobody. Don't you ever miss nobody, Nick? I wouldn't be talking like this if I weren't all doped up, but I missed you, Nick. I missed you bad and I still miss you. Damn, I hate that, missing you."

Nick let out breath. In his own chest something was turning to fragments, something broken and ragged, so that his breath caused him pain. "I miss you, too."

"Yeah?" Vivian studied him. Then she lay back and stared at the ceiling. "It don't matter though, does it? It don't make a damn bit of difference."

Nick sat quietly. There was nothing he could say to contradict her. He missed her, but he didn't love her. He felt for her pity and guilt, not love. Vivian was a prisoner, as much as he'd been a prisoner in Germany during the war, as much as the millions had been in the camps back in Russia. She was as helpless to walk away from whatever it was that was holding her down, destroying her, as he'd been helpless to walk beyond first a border, then barbed wire and machine guns.

Vivian shut her eyes, closing him out, closing out his inability to reply, which they both knew was his answer. "You know, I'm feeling real tired, Nick. It must be this dope they're giving me. I think I'm just gonna take a little nap. It was sweet, you stopping in."

Nick stood, kissed her cheek again, and set the box of chocolates on the bedside table. When he got to the door, Vivian said softly, "You know, I never thought things would turn out this way. It's all been a surprise to me."

Nick walked wearily back along Airport Road, a two-lane asphalt strip gouged out of the forest on the back side of the island. In the summer blueberries grew in the low-lying land alongside the road, where now fog settled and tangled in brush. One day he'd gathered berries for Vivian and she'd baked a pie. She'd worn a white peasant blouse with a drawstring neck, and they'd finished a bottle of wine. Laughing, he'd held her, heard the beat of her heart, seen the purplish stains of blueberries on her lips, her teeth, and known that his own must look the same. Was it possible they'd been happy? It seemed as long ago, as out of reach as Vivian's fish camp.

He'd gathered blueberries as a boy, but in Russia the forest was easy to walk through, as though time itself had spaced the fir trees and the thickets of birch, had left a soft springy moss to sit on. Strange that the forest itself should be gentler in a land no less violent, no less wild. One step into the forest here and it was all brambles and thorns, decaying logs, enormous leaves, hanging moss. In Russia there were pools in the forest, dappled with light filtering through the leaves, the gentle province of nineteenth-century landscape painters — Levitan, Repin. Russia, Russia. He knew better than to cry for what could not be regained, yet who could argue with the persisting image of blueberries in a white enamel milk can, and in the autumn, fluted yellow mushrooms in a basket, a bouquet of brilliant leaves?

Even now he could smell wild mushrooms frying, pungent and haunting, as vivid as life, more powerful than the scent of wet fir on either side of him, or of the fish that never washed off his hands. Mushrooms frying, sharp, earthy, somehow entwined with the odor of decaying leaves, of horses' sweat, of fear. Then he remembered.

He was in the forest with his babushka, his grandmother, gathering mushrooms. She was carrying the basket, bending over to dig at the earth, her behind so wide in a faded blue wool skirt it took up his whole field of vision. He wandered ahead, bored with her snailish pace, and then through the latticework of birch he saw them, or perhaps he smelled them first: the sweat of the horses, damp leather, hunched silent men.

"Kolya?" his babushka called out, and when she straightened up, hands on her lower back, she saw them and he heard her sharp, frightened gasp. "Idi syuda, come here!" she whispered.

How long had it taken them to pass? Forever, it seemed.

He stood there holding his breath while his babushka mumbled a terrified prayer and held her hand over his mouth. Twigs snapping under hooves, the creak of saddles, the rasp of a man hawking phlegm. What side were they on? Were they the tattered remains of the whites? Valiant red guards? He couldn't remember now. It was the civil war, and he was no more than four years old. Yet how clearly he remembered the prickle of his babushka's hand running over his shaved head, her urgent words in the silence when they'd passed: "You must thank the Lord our Savior, Kolenka, Kolushka. You must give thanks for being spared." And his own fierce tears, his anger. Didn't she know he wanted to go with them? Miserable as they were, they seemed the very embodiment of bravery and purpose: men on horses, traveling. Like Vivian in her dream, he felt bereft when they were gone.

For what now did he give thanks? Mud underfoot as he hit Front Street, rain on the back of his neck, the shape of the boat harbor coming into view. In all this vastness, he'd somehow made his world too small. For what had he been spared?

The thing to do was to gas up his boat and buy his groceries so that he could head out early in the morning. He never felt as though he were really back from fishing until he was ready to leave again.

At the bottom of the ramp beside the spigots and the dock hose, he saw the girl from the skiff cleaning a king salmon, a small shape in dark rain gear kneeling on the planks. He stopped and watched as she slit the salmon's belly.

"Nice fish," Nick said. "Fifteen, sixteen pounds. You will sell?"

"Yup." The girl didn't look up from her work.

"You are using bait or lures?"

"Choked herring on a treble hook."

Nick smiled. He went down the dock to his boat and dug through his gear until he came up with two wooden lures in the shape of herring that he'd carved himself. The girl was rinsing her salmon under the hose, brushing away the last shreds of vein and clotted blood with a bare red hand. He squatted beside her. "Try these. Perhaps they will bring to you luck."

She stopped rinsing and turned to look at him. "Hey, thanks." Her smile was a child's smile, grateful, full of delight. She was so young, as young as Sophia when they'd first met at the institute, with those same dark eyes, the full lower lip, the broad cheekbones. Yet she wasn't just the image of Sophia but somehow herself: a girl in rubber overalls and a blue wool cap, with a king salmon she'd just caught lying gutted between her rubber boots. Tiny opalescent fish scales clung to her forehead, and black strands of hair fell from her cap. He wanted to reach out and brush the scales off, to wipe a thin streak of blood from her cheek, to warm her cold red hands between his own.

She flipped the lures, weighing them in her palm. "I'll give them a try."

Nick tipped his cap, stood up, feeling the crick in his knees as he straightened. He headed back down the dock to his boat. Her name was Allie. He remembered all of a sudden from the Baker bar, from the night Digger hired her on at the Anchor. He shook his head at the pleasure he'd gotten from the encounter and called himself an old fool.

ALLIE WOKE to voices clacking in a language she couldn't understand. Ravens, she realized, opening her eyes, ravens on the roof again. She could hear their footsteps, light and rapid overhead. What time was it? What time had she come in? She couldn't remember, but from the look of her clothes strewn about the riverboat bunk, it must have been late. She pulled the covers over her head to block out the sight of last night's confusion. Even under the blankets she could hear the riverboat rattling with wind, with rain, then a siren and the rumble of the fire truck moving up the street. She sat up straight, listening intently until the siren passed the harbor, passed the houses and boats of everyone she knew.

Fires. Fires and drownings. There wasn't enough road to kill yourself, just nine miles, and then the dead end where you had to turn around and go back. Last night she'd dreamed again of driving on a superhighway, a thousand miles straight. It was her Vladimir dream that had started as soon as the summer was gone and the darkness set in.

In the summer, the sun had never gone down but had merely become fainter somewhere around midnight or one and then brightened, so that when she walked home in her rubber boots over slippery boardwalks, it was as though there'd never been a night, just a duskiness through the bar window, a moment of darker clouds when the steam from the lumber mill blew more ghostly against the dark bulk of Siligovsky Island across the bay.

"Why are you still here?" Sonny kept asking. "Every time I get back to town I expect you'll be gone but you're still here." Thinking of Sonny made pictures from last night fall into place. The bar closing, another party. Whose? Riding in the back of a pickup, and the Indian girl beside her saying, "No white people allowed," not knowing about her, letting her pass. A weird feeling, guilty and exciting, like being someone else. Sonny knew what she was, but he didn't tell. At the party, he came over to sit by her on the couch.

"See those paddles up there on the wall?" he asked, pointing. "They're war paddles. See the carvings? Every one tells the story of a battle. Those old Indians knew how to fight."

Allie nodded, eager to keep him talking, eager to keep him beside her. He'd never been so close, and she could barely look into his half-shut eyes, his beautiful face.

"Yeah, the old-timers could fight, all right. It took the Russians a long time to beat them down. They used to go everywhere in these big old canoes, up and down the coast as far as California, making raids. My great-grandmother had a Flathead slave girl brought back as spoils." Sonny took a swig of beer. "I could have had all that."

"What would you want a slave for?"

Sonny muttered, "I would have been a chief."

Every Indian would have been a chief, Allie thought. But maybe it was true. Sonny descended from nobility, a leader.

"See that old Norwegian over there?" Sonny shifted his attention to a big-bellied old man sitting half asleep in a corner. "That's Lester Bergsen. He's the toughest fisherman in this town. One time he was on a drunk with some fishing buddies, and they ran out of booze on the boat. The three of them drank compass fluid and gasoline. One guy died, one went blind, but it didn't bother Lester at all. He's as mean as they come, but he was one hell of a fisherman. He married an Indian girl."

Allie understood. Sonny wanted the war paddles, but he admired the white men who'd come up here and taken it all away, turned everything to power skiffs, hydraulics.

"War paddles," Sonny said, shaking his head. "Shit, now we got bombers that are so damn accurate you can send death anywhere you want. All you got to do is push a button. Megadeath. It's all done by computer. It's amazing the stockpiles we got." Sonny laughed, a dazzling flash of white. "What is it about you that makes me talk my damn fool head off?"

Allie looked down at her feet. Where had he learned about the bombers? Up at the library, where he'd read about ravens?

Sonny reached over and pinched her lip between his forefinger and thumb. "You got a beautiful lower lip."

Allie looked into his eyes, searching. They were flat, black, unreadable. "What's the matter with the top one? Don't you like the top one?"

Sonny laughed and leaned against the couch.

What did he want? He wanted war paddles, hydraulics, bombers. Did he want her now?

He wanted a beer. He left her sitting there on the couch, the feel of his fingers still burning on her lip. Through the open kitchen door she saw him lean down to kiss a local girl. Then she was stumbling back to the riverboat in the dark, on rain splattered pavement, alone.

"Get up," Allie told herself but didn't move. If it was this light out, it was too late to be in bed. She wished it would blow so hard she'd have an excuse to stay under the covers reading library novels until the bars opened at noon. But already the wind had died down, and all she could hear was the soft, mossy fall of the rain. Where was her tide book?

She turned on the little space heater, which glowed red but did little more than warm the air six inches in front of itself while the rest of the bunk stayed cold enough for her to see her breath. She pulled on her jeans, thermal top, sweater, woollen socks, and rubber boots. At least she had electricity;

the river boat had little else. But then it was hard to complain when she was given free rent in exchange for checking to see that the automatic bilge pump was working. If someone had the time and the money, the riverboat could be converted into a wonderful floating house. It was a shame it wasn't used anymore for its original purpose, but the Takine River had silted up over the years and was only navigable by boats that drew less draft than this one. It was a ride she would have loved to take, all the way up into Canada. They said the climate changes from rain forest to desert over a course of ninety miles. Still, there was something frighteningly dead-end about traveling up a river that became narrower and smaller until it was only a stream, a headwater, and there was nothing to do but get out and walk. It felt too much like being trapped.

The riverboat, the *Emily Jane,* had a wreck of a galley with an enormous gas stove she was forbidden to use. There were six staterooms — all similar to her own narrow cell, with a bunk and two-tone painted walls, green waist high, white above — a couple of nonfunctioning toilets, and on the upper deck, a common room empty of furniture. It had a lot of windows covered in opaque plastic, and a hideous orange shag rug, the one and only attempt of the riverboat's current owner to renovate. Allie's favorite place was the pilothouse, a cubicle forward of the common room, with its captain's chair, fine old captain's wheel, and great view of the fishing boats, the tug dock across the channel, and the shrimp cannery dock. Allie loved to sit up there late in the afternoon until she got too chilled or the windows steamed up from her breath.

She pulled on her rubber overalls, climbed down the stairs, stepped onto the dock, and headed for the outhouse, which sat suspended over the bay at the end of the floats. There were few boats this time of year, so many gaps between the ones tied to the dock. All the Seattle boats were long gone. Only the trollers went out now, along with a couple of the big seiners like Sonny's, which had converted their gear for herring fishing. Out of habit she looked to see if the *Nancy M.*, Sonny's boat, was still in town and felt relief when she saw that it was.

At the end of the dock the outhouse floated in the water, blown off its stanchions in last night's wind. Allie stared at the half-sunk plywood box, the exposed white seat cover, and laughed. What if she'd been in there, pants around her ankles? What a way to go, down with a sinking outhouse. She'd have to use the restaurant's toilet until somebody fished it out and set it back up.

High tide would be 12:02, and the best fishing at slack tide, an hour before and after, so she had time for a cup of coffee. Allie left her two sport poles, pole holders, bait bucket, and tackle box in the skiff.

When she walked into the Potlatch Café, everyone turned to stare. The women — Morgan's mother, in her pantsuit and neatly coifed blue hair; Helene, the librarian, purse-mouthed and wrinkly, with her mother, a tinier, wrinklier version; and an Indian woman with lank hair and harlequin glasses — lowered their voices. The men stared back at their egg-encrusted plates. Allie felt apologetic. Her Helly-Hansen rain gear was an affront to their morning coffee. It wouldn't have been if she were a man.

She hung her jacket on a peg, tucked her wool cap into the sleeve, and, rubber overalls swishing, took a place halfway down the counter between the cluster of women at one end and the skippers huddled at the other. She smiled tentatively at a seiner who'd bought her a drink last night, insisting to his buddies that she was going to clean up the winter catch. Now he didn't know her. Everyone was shy when the booze wore off.

Dottie came over to pour her coffee without saying hello.

"Where was the fire?" Allie's question rose as much out of a need to use her voice and hear another one reply as out of interest.

Dottie seemed annoyed. "Mary Lepteris's shack on Nine Mile Road. Burned down before they got there."

Allie wanted to ask if anyone was hurt, but Dottie had already moved away. She'd hear it later anyway, in the bars. She gave up on conversation and stared out the window hoping to see someone she knew walk past. Hoping for Sonny. A skinny crew cut kid with a rifle over one shoulder took long, awkward strides down the slippery boardwalk planks. Across the street, a man in a business suit stepped out of the office of the Raven Motel, a ranch-style building with mobile homes in back for rooms. The man looked at the rain and stepped back inside.

Vladimir men walked by, wearing green, brown, or blue wool halibut jackets, rain oozing off their hunting caps, down their necks. Nobody in Vladimir wore a raincoat. The men strode up the boardwalk with their knees turned outward, bowlegged and broad, their shoulders stooped. A couple of Indian kids played with the new automatic doors of the laundromat across the street, opening and closing them with solemn pleasure.

Allie turned back to the sickly green of the Potlatch, her head aching from the *ping ping ping* of the pinball machine being raped by a teenager. On top of the freezer, hamburger buns lay defrosting, crystals turning to water inside the plastic bag. In her bait bucket, the herring would be doing the same. She should've remembered to take them out last night. The thought of threading frozen herring onto hooks with her bare fingers made her grip her coffee cup tightly, twenty-six cents' worth of warmth. She had to remember to try those carved plugs.

"So Dottie, did you order your rug yet?" Helene asked.

"Yesterday. Kind of a rust color with brown flecks. It'll look real pretty with the drapes."

"Sears or Montgomery Ward?"

Down the counter a gill-netter was bitching about limited entry.

"Sears," Dottie said.

Allie listened intently, waiting for the word or phrase that would explain everything. They could have been talking in code like the fishermen on the CB. If only she listened hard enough, if only she'd been allowed to listen here her whole life, the words might make more sense; she might feel she belonged.

Even if she understood what they were saying, the women would never talk to her. She'd learned that working in the cannery in August, where the women wouldn't acknowledge her presence. She'd broken the rules by going out on the boats, and they wouldn't forgive her that. Every day at break she stood alone on the cannery dock watching the fishermen unload, looking longingly out at the water, while the other women crowded around the coffee table chatting. The table was heaped twice a day with boxes from the bakery, and many of the cannery women were hugely fat. They gobbled donuts, wrinkling their noses at the salmon stink on their fingers which never seemed to wash completely off. At lunchtime they walked uptown together to eat at the Potlatch or the Five and Dime, and she followed along alone as far as the Anchor Lounge.

She could go in there only during the day because Lucille, the bartender who had made her welcome her first day in town, had threatened to kill her. Back in the summer, Allie made the mistake of playing a game of pool with Lucille's man, a no-good gambling logger, and one of Lucille's regulars, out of loyalty or boredom, reported her crime. "You're just after him," Lucille insisted, "because things didn't work out with Digger." In Vladimir, intentions weren't important; what mattered was how things looked.

Dottie made the refill rounds, put down the pot, and picked up two large triangular knives. When she raised them high overhead, a stack of clanking silver clan bracelets fell down her arms to her elbows. Allie watched transfixed while Dottie sharpened the knives one against the other in a furious scraping blur. Dottie's face expressed the peculiar inward grace of a juggler or magician. The bracelets rose and fell, rose and fell in rhythm. When she stopped, it sounded as if someone had slammed a drawer full of silverware shut. On her own left wrist, under the men's thermal undershirt and wool sweater, Allie wore a silver Tlingit clan bracelet, but she kept it hidden. She was ashamed of her desire to buy a place in town from the jewelry case in the drugstore, ashamed that she'd chosen Eagle, Sonny's clan.

Dottie put down the knives and became again a woman wiping counters. Allie paid for her coffee, leaving too large a tip.

The skiff, as usual, lay deep with rain water. Allie bailed the boat, then baited hooks, bending the half-frozen herring into the proper shape, threading the hooks one through the eye, one through the tail. She pulled the leaders tight enough to make the arced herring flip and shimmy under water like live, swimming fish. Free meals for the flounder and tom cod, bottom fish that came up after her bait. In a week, she'd only caught a single king she could sell.

"You guys are ruining it for me," she told Sonny at the party last night. "The kings aren't coming in to shore now that you herring seiners are picking up all the feed with your harbor sets. I'll be glad when you're gone." That was a lie; the bars would be empty when Sonny left town, but she had to say it, just as she had to fish. She was afraid of becoming too much like those women who wouldn't talk to her, always waiting for a boat to come back in.

"What do you want to go out and sit in the rain for?" Sonny wanted to know. "That's crazy, and its dangerous. A good-looking girl like you could clean up on tips. Why don't you work in the bar?"

"I want to fish," she insisted, flushing from the compliment, angry that he didn't understand. And if he thought she was so good looking, why had he disappeared with that other girl?

A float plane taxied through the channel, its engine winding up like the loudest chain saw in the world. Allie dropped a herring to cover her ears. The plane, passing between a line of tugs and the fishing boats tied to the dock, with no visible change of intention, suddenly lifted itself, pontoons dripping, out of the water and into the air. Her skiff bumped against the dock from the force of the plane's wake. Circling once, dipping its short, fat wings, the plane rose, rose, then slid into the thick grey clouds. Leaving looked so simple.

Allie pulled the cord on her Evinrude six-horse motor ten times before the engine caught, sputtered, and died. She adjusted the choke and tried again, bracing herself so that if the cord broke, she wouldn't fall overboard. Finally, in a cloud of blue burned oil and gas fumes, the engine consented to run. Maybe she ought to talk to Henry about it. The skiff and the engine were his, on loan. What if it just conked out while she was fishing two miles from town?

Chugging along slowly, she passed the shrimp and salmon canneries and the lumber mill, where the *Vladimir Maru* dwarfed the dock. She'd been aboard last summer, guest of a longshore foreman who wanted to take her out. The Japanese captain gave her a tour of the pilothouse, explaining their electronic ballast system. What impressed her most was the Buddhist altar sitting beside the sonar. Computers to keep them balanced, and a belief in prayer . . . She lacked them both.

She passed the Takine Inn — who might be inside now, eating fried eggs, watching her through the picture windows? — the Alaska State Ferry terminal, a stretch of beach with a cabin, and then she was beyond the tip of Vladimir Island, and no one could see her at all.

She placed the poles in their holders, snapped on the leaders, and reeled out, letting the herring flip for a moment just under the water to see if she had baited the hooks correctly. The lines made a new, refractory angle. She sent them down, guessing at the proper depths, trolling slowly while the rain fell on her head. Above the bay a bald eagle made slow circles. They were as common as seagulls here, hanging around the docks, disgracing themselves with little undignified squawks. She liked the ravens better. Click, clack, clatter. But Sonny was an Eagle. The clans descended through the mother.

If only they could be together, Sonny would tell her something important, something she needed to know. He wanted to tell her, she knew it. Why else would he seek her out? He circled her, then shied away, as though something had scared him off. Something perhaps in the way she chain-smoked, fumbling and inexpert, a habit she'd picked up on Digger's boat. Or something in her face that marked her as clearly as Sonny's features marked him as Tlingit. She suspected that the mark was fear.

Fear blew down the mouth of the Takine River with the colder air and sat over the bay like a fog. Fear followed the eerie line of demarcation between river and sea — serpentine, frightening, dividing icy black ocean from silty green river in a roiling swirl. Fear lay in the distance between the channel marker where she fished and the wisp of lumber mill smoke that marked Vladimir. Northward, up the Takine River, the mainland mountains stood snowy and jagged, a thousand miles of nothing but wolves and moose and snow running straight to the Arctic. And under the skiff there were things she couldn't see, could barely imagine: canyons, caverns, undulating fronds, a drama of swallowing jaws. When her lines went down in this water, instead of refracting they simply disappeared. Yet life leaped up, gasping and insistent, all the time.

Allie shook her line, hoping to dislodge the fish, but the bastard flounder had swallowed the hook. The fish was ugly, with two eyes on the top of its head and flesh that felt like sand instead of scales. She didn't want to touch it. Its eyes, unused to light or air, stared into hers without emotion, but the frightened fish thrashed, opening its jaws so wide she could see the hook embedded in its guts. "You are a *dead* fish," she said. "There's nothing I can do." Wasting the hook and sinker, she cut the leader. The flounder fell back into the milky swirl.

Trash fish. Flounder and cod. As a child, she fished for them with her father. Off the coast of Cape Cod they anchored and rocked on the surface of the bobbing blue Atlantic. Her father would bait her hooks with sea worms, and hand her a drop line while the boat rolled in the swells. The line would go down and down forever, and when it hit bottom it felt so close. She got seasick every time, from the rolling waves, from the gasping fish they pulled aboard, from the sight of her father's merciless knife as he cleaned fish off the stern.

Did he still carry a fish knife under the seat of his car for protection? He lived in a world full of arguments with strangers, fights over parking spaces, a world ready to attack.

Now he sent letters in answer to her single post card. At first he wrote, "If you wanted to go fishing, I would have taken you, but you wouldn't go with me. When will this foolishness stop? When are you coming home?" Later his letters were nothing but lists: watch out for hooks, watch out for pulleys, watch out for lines. She felt a sad, mixed triumph: finally, she had the ability to make him scared.

But she wasn't afraid of hooks, of pulleys, of lines. She wasn't afraid of drowning. She was afraid of the mountains, of how big it was here. The fog and the sea looked the same, and northward the mountains stretched on forever. The vastness cast an eerie spell. No, she wasn't afraid of drowning, she was afraid she wouldn't care.

"Twenty-one dollars and sixty cents," said Smiley, inspecting Allie's cannery check. "Easy money." He cashed it and gave her change, minus the price of a bourbon and water.

"It's not so easy, sitting out there in the rain."

"Wish I had the time to go out and pick up winter kings. I'd show you how to do it. Trouble is, I'm always stuck in here."

Allie ignored him. Smiley always complained.

"You know, I never get any time, but I'm going to stop one day and take a vacation. Then I'll really get away." Smiley stood behind the bar, hands on hips, imagining it.

There was no one else to talk to in the Anchor but a couple of loggers shooting pool and an old Indian lady muttering to herself in a back booth. Allie relented. "Yeah? Where would you go?"

"I'm gonna go to Ireland."

"Ireland?"

"Yeah, Ireland. I'm gonna get me a fancy bike like the ones the kids ride, and just bike up and down those beautiful country roads. I've read all about it. I know everything about Ireland there is to know."

Allie tried to picture Smiley sitting in the library reading *National Geographic* or something. It made her like him more, but she couldn't really see Smiley, with his jaundiced complexion and his crew cut wheeling down an Irish lane. "Hey, that's great. When are you going to go?"

"Oh, soon's I get a vacation."

"You could get some time off." Allie was suddenly insistent, as though Smiley's dream were her own. "You probably haven't taken a vacation in years. Why don't you ask for it? I bet summer would be the best time to go."

"Yeah," Smiley said vaguely. "I dunno." He turned away to pour a beer.

"Come *on*. If you really want to go to Ireland, you should go."

He leaned over the bar, almost whispering, close enough that she could see the blood vessels in his eyes, the sweat on his upper lip. "Well, you see, Allie, I just got this feeling. Kind of a warning or something. I can just see it. There I'd be, getting off the plane in Ireland . . . and I just got this feeling about something bad. Like I told you, I read a lot about Ireland, and, well, they got a lot of IRA terrorists over there. It'd be just my luck, I finally get there, and I get shot stepping off the plane." Smiley shook his head sadly.

Allie looked at him in wonder. It was the most elaborate excuse she'd ever heard. It made her angry, like her mother's excuses for why she couldn't get dressed and go out of the house anymore, how she would've come to visit Allie in Denver if she weren't afraid to fly, how she was going to go shopping but first she had to clean the drawers.

"I am gonna go," Smiley said loudly. "One of these days there I'll be, just wheeling down those beautiful country roads."

"Sounds good." Allie picked up her drink from the bar and wandered away to the pool table, where her quarter was coming up next.

The door to the Anchor opened, and Nick came in carrying a bundle under his arm. He looked slight and a little stooped in his wet brown wool jacket.

"Hey, you brought it," Smiley exclaimed. "Awright!"

Allie watched as Nick opened the bundle on the bar. It was a patchwork leather chessboard with hand-carved chessmen, but in the place of kings, queens, knights, and pawns were fish of various species on little wooden bases. Tiny halibut, salmon, flounder, crab. She went over to get a better look.

"They're beautiful," she said, turning a carved salmon in her hand. "Where'd you get them?"

Nick continued to set the chessmen in their places. When he turned to answer, she was mesmerized by his pale blue eyes. "In winter is not so much trolling. When I have time, I carve. It is something to do."

"He could just give up fishing altogether and make a living carving," Smiley said. "That would be the way to go."

Allie wondered what fisherman would want to give up fishing.

When they started to play she lost interest. She didn't know the game and it appeared dull, too much thought between actions. The loggers over at the pool table looked drunk enough that she might not completely humiliate herself this time. She lost two games of eight ball and won one, sitting out the games between her losses. From time to time she returned to the bar for another bourbon. Smiley seemed to be steadily losing the chess game. Allie was losing track of how many drinks she'd had.

The drinking had started in August when she was working at the cannery, taking her lunch break at the Anchor Lounge. Booze, she soon learned, made the afternoon pass more quickly. Looped on three drinks and an empty stomach, she stood at the conveyor belt while the cans crashed, the steamers shrieked, and clouds filled the room. If she drank enough, the cannery became a grotesquely fascinating place.

At the heads of the lines a guillotine chopped off the salmon heads. An oil barrel under the blade caught the heads, which were saved as bait for the halibutters and crab men, or for the occasional old Indian lady who wanted to make fish-head soup. After the guillotine came the gut pullers, fin cutters, deboners, and chunk slicers, a sinuous line all the way down to the end, where the less deft — like Allie, who couldn't be trusted with knives — stood ten feet from the deafening hiss of the steamers, stuffing chunks in cans. All she had to do was open the gate to her bin, let chunks of salmon plop in, reach for a can from the belt, stuff it, weigh it, pop in a salt pill, and pass it along.

When things became too dull, she filled every other can with bones, sprinkling on a little flesh to hide the secret. Sometimes she stuck in a stray fin as a surprise for the phantom Iowa dietician who would open the can. Where would they all go? She thought of hiding messages: "Help! I'm being held prisoner in a salmon cannery in Vladimir, Alaska!" but that would have raised the question of just who, or what, was holding her there. It was a question she didn't have to consider as long as she stopped for lunch at the Anchor Lounge.

When she'd been drinking it was all funny, even the fact that the woman across from her on the fish line wouldn't meet her eyes, or that if they'd wanted to talk they wouldn't have been able to hear each other above the din. She sang at the top of her lungs and no one heard her. It was funny: she'd started out fishing and ended up stuffing fish in cans. It was funny until the booze wore off. It never lasted the whole afternoon. Then her feet were clammy inside her rubber boots, her fingers were frozen, the concrete floor rose up to smash her aching legs, and the smell of dead fish was as close to her skin as sweat. It was enough to send her back to the Anchor for another drink as soon as she got off shift.

Now she had no shifts to worry about, and except for when she was trolling out of the skiff, she was in the bars all the time. How many whiskies had she had? It seemed important to keep count, especially in the afternoon, but it wasn't afternoon any longer. At five o'clock, the mill whistle blew at Vladimir Lumber. Swing shift mill workers put on their hard hats, paid for their beers, and filed out. Day shift men, grimy and tired, wandered in. A row of fishermen now sat watching the changing of the guard. Smiley was washing glasses and the men were giving him a hard time.

"How'd the chess game go?" she asked.

"Maybe I'd have a chance if I didn't have to keep jumping up for these jokers. Probably not. I ought to know better than to play chess with a Russky."

So that's what he was. Allie wandered down the bar to where Nick was tying the carved chess pieces back inside the leather bundle. She climbed up on the stool beside him, lit a cigarette.

"Allie the hand troller," Nick said. "Do you play chess?"

"No. I don't know how."

"You would like to learn?"

"No, I couldn't. I'm lousy at anything that takes strategy."

"Tactics or strategy?"

"What's the difference?"

"Strategy is big picture, over time, and tactics means your next move. Trolling requires strategy, does it not?"

"Well, I never said I was good at it." She took too large a gulp from her whiskey but managed not to sputter. She caught a glimpse of herself in the mirror behind the bar and looked away in disgust.

Nick smiled. "So," he said, setting the bundle on his lap. "You mean you do not want to be good troller? Trolling is much like playing chess. You have opponent. You must study him, learn his ways. You become his intimate, think his thoughts. Then you play him, so" — he raised a hand as though holding a leader and gave it a little jerk — "right into your hand."

"Jesus, Nick," Smiley said, stopping to dump Allie's ashtray, "I won't want to play with you next time. You're giving me the creeps."

Allie turned away. Through the window, the street looked black, but only a little while ago, it seemed, the grey gloomy drizzle outside had appeared bright in comparison to the bar's darkness. Who did this guy think he was? But he was right. She was a lousy troller because she couldn't imagine how the fish thought, she could never figure out what was going on under the surface, and she didn't try hard enough to figure it out. It was like being a deckhand for Digger and refusing to learn to navigate, or shooting lousy pool. She had a good eye, and her partners tried to improve her game sometimes. Shoot high, they'd say, and the ball will follow; shoot low and it'll come back to you. Try a little left-hand English. But she went on shooting blindly, letting the cue ball go where it may.

"Allie. I will teach you to play chess," Nick said firmly.

Allie shrugged.

"You have courage to sit in such little skiff, to fish alone. I admire your courage. Why you want to sit all day in bar? There is nothing so interesting here, I assure you. Come to my cabin, on beach past ferry dock. You will find, no problem. I will teach you to play, okay?"

Why was he so insistent? Why had he bothered to give her his own carved plugs? No one paid her that much attention innocently. She was flattered, uneasy. "Maybe someday."

"Allie. Tell me. How you found your way to this little island?"

"I guess I kept going west, and when I couldn't go west anymore, I headed north. This seemed like a good place to stop for a while. There's nothing back there."

"Nothing?" Nick threw his head back and laughed.

His laugh revealed nice curves from cheekbones to mouth, exposed a missing tooth. She wondered how he got that scar, a raised white line from the corner of his mouth to his chin.

"Nothing?" Nick repeated. "You are young to have used up already whole continent."

Allie flushed. That was what she'd done, exactly. "And you? You didn't come from here either."

"No, no." Nick grew serious. "I came from Russia."

"Yeah? My grandparents came from Russia, on my father's side."

"So you are Russian girl. Perhaps I felt it. From what city they came?"

"I don't know. I don't think it was a city, probably just some little village." All she knew of Russia was her grand-mother's favorite story: how as a little girl she'd had to lie quietly under a pile of grown-ups in the basement of a Christian neighbor's house; how she'd kept silent, wanting to cry out that she was smothering, while the Cossacks walked in their heavy boots on the floorboards overhead.

"And I come from Leningrad, very beautiful city. Very beautiful. You should see it someday." He sighed and stood up to go.

"Nick, do you ever think about going back there? You know, think about going home?"

"I am home," Nick said.

Sonny sat in a borrowed pickup outside the ferry office while Vivian went in to buy her ticket to Juneau. In the back of the truck her suitcase lay under a tarp, protected from the winter drizzle. It was eleven A.M. and he still felt he should be sleeping; fishing for herring messed up his head. They fished at night, waiting for the herring to rise to the surface to feed. The odd hours threw them all off. No one was eager for a shift at the wheel and they bitched all the time, but the hold filled up with slithering fish and he had money in the bank. Money for escape.

Vivian trotted out, holding a hand over her freshly set hair to ward off the rain.

"Looks like you're the only one heading north," Sonny said. He figured anyone in their right mind would be heading south this time of year. Either to refute him or to prove his point, Avie Morris appeared, heading north to Petersburg for a weekend jail sentence. Vladimir didn't have its own jail anymore, so Avie had to serve his drunk-and-disorderly in Petersburg. He was drinking straight from a fifth of whiskey in preparation for the dry weekend ahead, and when he saw them, he waved from his Chevy, raising the bottle. His kid, Junior, who'd just gotten his license back after a six-month DWI, was at the wheel.

Sonny and Vivian sat watching the ocean in front of them

as though it were a TV screen displaying a boring but hypnotic program. The ferry had just come around the edge of Siligovsky Island.

"You going to keep after Mikey when you're in town?" Vivian asked. Her voice was even, but she was clenching the handles of her pocketbook.

"Sure."

"I don't want to get back from Juneau and find out he's wrecked the house."

"Hey, don't worry about it. You're supposed to be taking it easy, remember?"

"Sonny, *you* got to quit worrying. They got bars in Juneau, too, you know. You got to have some faith. I admit things got bad for a while, but we been through worse than this before. We'll come out of it like we come out of everything. Your old mom hasn't gone under yet." She patted his knee.

Sonny turned to look at her. She was trying to put up a good front, but he could see how shaky she was. She hadn't had a drink in the three days since she'd gotten out of the hospital, but who knew how long that would last. There were bars in Juneau, bars on the ferry. Now she was fussing with her lipstick in the rearview mirror like some half-sick warrior putting on war paint, getting ready to face another battle.

Back at the house he'd sat on her bed watching her pack, averting his eyes from the sight of her dingy, washed-out underwear, her nightie with a ripped hem. The cardboard and vinyl suitcase with squared edges and dented sides was the only one they owned; he'd taken it north that year he'd gone to the university up in Fairbanks on a Bureau of Indian Affairs scholarship. He'd used it only one other time, when he was seven and ran away.

There'd been a fight of some kind, and his father had hit his mother again while Sonny and his sisters — Mikey hadn't even been born yet — stood flattened, mute against the kitchen wall. When his father stomped out of the house and his mother retreated to the bedroom, locking the door, Sonny sneaked up to the attic and found the suitcase, filled it with a sweater, jackknife, a jar of peanut butter, the scouting compass his grampa Pandel had given him for Christmas, his father's hammer, and a box of nails. He left his mother a note with instructions to meet him that night at a derelict boat on the beach past the ferry dock. With the certainty of desperation, he planned to rescue her, take her away to some unknown place where they'd be safe.

The derelict boat lay on its side two hundred yards past Nick's cabin, a troller that had sunk, been washed ashore, and was covered occasionally by high tides. By the time he reached it, his arm was aching from the heavy suitcase, yet the glory, the gravity of his mission, urged him on. He couldn't fail.

He spent the afternoon trying to patch the holes in the boat's sunken hull, but the nails kept splintering through the rotten wood. He worked until his hand was numb and his jeans were soaked from kneeling on damp planks. He believed if he only tried hard enough, he could make it float when the tide came in. When his mother found him it was nearly dusk, the sun falling across the bay, the air beginning to chill. She climbed aboard, and the sight of the purple bruise on her cheek and her swollen eye sent him into furious, hopeless tears.

"It's okay, honey," she kept saying over and over. "Honey, it's okay." She took the hammer from his hand, put her arms around him, lay his head in her lap, and rested her soft cheek against his. She'd never spoken to him so gently; they'd never been so close. The two of them huddled there like that on the warped deck, warming each other, until the tide came in and began lapping against the planks.

They walked wordlessly home together, carrying the suitcase between them like a shared secret, weighted by grief, past barking, chained huskies, lit houses, the dark Vladimir streets. He felt weary, terribly old, a shell-shocked soldier returned from battle or a Rip Van Winkle who'd slept for twenty years. It was the same Vladimir, yet everything had subtly, irreversibly changed.

Sitting beside his mother in the borrowed pickup, Sonny was overcome with a sudden desire to lay his head in her lap again, to let her cradle him and stroke his hair as she had on the derelict boat. He wanted desperately to return to that moment, to have her, even bruised and battered, larger than him, to hear her say, "Honey, it's okay." But she was a sick and shaky woman in need of someone larger and stronger, someone who could offer her comfort. She needed him.

The ferry was suddenly there, towering white, blocking the view as it sidled up to the pilings. Vivian opened the truck door. "Well, here goes nothing," she said.

Sonny leaned over and kissed his mother's cheek, got out and pulled her bag from under the tarp. Avie came over and offered them both a swig from his bottle. Sonny looked anxiously at Vivian. She shook her head no, then turned to him with a warning glare. "Just don't go preaching at me. You know I can't stand that."

At the gangplank she stopped and gave him a big hug. "It seems funny, me being the one leaving this time."

"You take it easy up there. Promise?"

"I can't promise nothing, Sonny."

He watched Avie and his mother recede down the plank into the ferry's belly, Avie hauling her suitcase. He sat for a while in the pickup while the windshield misted over and the ferry pulled out, churning the sea in yellow waves. Avie's kid roared out of the lot, tires squealing. Vivian was gone.

Sonny drove the pickup slowly down Front Street past the Five and Dime, the Potlatch. He wasn't ready to give it back yet. It wasn't often he had the chance to view Vladimir through a windshield, from the height of a driver's seat. He wanted to drive somewhere, but he couldn't think of a single place to go, so he just drove out to Nine Mile and turned around.

.   .   .

The Takine Inn was mobbed. Balloons hung from the ceiling, and the band, Bob and Gina from up north, was already in full swing when he walked in. Gina weighed in at two-fifty, wore a lime green muumuu and little red and white light bulb earrings that flashed on and off as she sang, and banged away at her electric organ. Bob, the drummer, was as skinny as Jack Sprat and hardly visible behind the fifty-pound Matanuska Valley cabbage that sat like a trophy on Gina's organ. Gina was belting out her Vladimir song:

Oh, I like humpback salmon, I like humpback salmon,
Cohos, humpies, dogs and kings.
Whatever you call them, we just haul them in!
Oh, I like humpback salmon, I like humpback salmon,
Caught by the Vladimir fish-er-meeeennnnnnnn!!!!!

The drinkers screamed "Yeahhhhhhhh!" They were having a good time tonight, and Sonny was in the mood to join in. He decided to skip the beer and go with whiskey. He had one, then another before he saw Henry and Allie sitting together at the end of the bar. He wandered over.

"Hey, Allie," Henry said, wrapping his arm around Sonny's throat. "You know this big dumb Indian? He's good people. He's like my goddamn brother."

"You feeling good tonight, Henry?" Sonny looked over at Allie, who was hiding her face in her drink. She was wearing a dress for once, some kind of soft blue knit thing that gave her a shape he didn't even know she had. Why did she hide herself in those men's clothes all the time? "I almost didn't recognize you without the rain pants," Sonny said.

"Yeah," Henry agreed. "Allie's a real lady tonight. Tonight she's the prettiest girl in Vladimir." Henry put a hand on the back of Allie's head.

Allie ducked her head slightly, but she smiled over her glass. She was wearing lipstick, Sonny noted.

"Just tonight?" she asked.

"You usually keep it a secret," Sonny said.

Allie flushed and fumbled with her cigarettes. She smoked too much, even more than he did.

Henry said, "I been telling Allie how I got to get out of town, set my traps, and read my cowboy westerns."

"Henry's getting tired of pirate westerns," Allie said.

For a second Sonny didn't get it, then he laughed. What other kind of westerns were there besides cowboy westerns?

Henry said, "What?"

Allie said, "So how come if you want to be out there so bad you're sitting in here?"

Henry shrugged. "You know how it is. Can't live with town, can't live without it. Hey, Allie, you want to dance?"

"It's a polka, Henry. I don't know how to polka. How about in a little while?"

"See how you are? Okay, I'm gonna find me a partner, but I'll be back. Don't let this big dumb Indian steal my seat." Henry staggered away, far too drunk for so early in the evening. Sonny slid onto Henry's stool.

"He likes you," Sonny said. "You better watch out or you'll break his heart."

"He never talks to me when he's sober."

"He's shy. Afraid of girls."

"Not like you, huh?"

Sonny grinned. "Depends on the girl." He leaned over to light her cigarette. He felt buoyant as the balloons, light and ready for whatever might happen, the music rising inside him like bubbles, making his foot tap gently against the bar rail. It felt good to be sitting at the bar talking to a girl in a blue knit dress. "You know, every time I get back in from fishing I see you in town and think, 'That girl's still here.' I keep expecting you'll be gone."

"How do you know I just won't stay here forever?" Allie ran a hand through her black hair, pushing it off her forehead, a flaunting little gesture. "Maybe this is the place I've been looking for all my life."

"You won't stay here. There's nothing for you here."

"What do you mean?" She looked up anxiously.

It was just something he knew, like he knew that Henry was going to end up wandering around the streets alone at four in the morning. Whatever had made Allie restless enough to bring her here would take her away again.

Allie pushed her empty glass back on the bar so the bartender would give her a refill. "There's still things I want to learn here. I haven't used this place up."

And when she'd used this place up, she'd leave. He knew it better than she did. He paid for Allie's drink and bought himself another. He watched the way she drank, leaning her head back, throwing the whiskey down the back of her throat. She didn't drink because she liked it; she drank fast, to get drunk. Yet her hands were narrow and graceful on her whiskey glass, her black hair was shiny, reflecting the light when she leaned down to pick up a matchbook.

"What do you think you can learn here?"

"How people live. You know, where I come from, nobody knows anybody. I never went into our next-door neighbor's house, and I wasn't allowed to play with anyone who didn't live on our street. The Nice Street. We were supposed to be better — what a joke. Here, everybody knows everybody, and they care. Like Henry, lending me his skiff, or Nick, giving me lures."

Sonny looked around the crowded bar. He knew every face, knew all their secrets, more than he wanted to know. Henry on the dance floor flinging his arms in frenzied joy, Frankie trying to hustle Morgan's cousin up from Oregon, Eleanor from the hospital in a booth with her girlfriends, glaring at people having fun. "I can't figure it," Sonny said. "I bet you had everything back there, lots of money, lots of guys hanging around."

"What's money got to do with anything?"

"Plenty. You know, when I was a kid, all I wanted was a washing machine so I could be like everyone else, not just some ragtag Indian. I used to iron my own shirts before I went to school."

"Why didn't your mom do it?"

"She had enough troubles." His words were getting away from him; he knew he must be getting drunk, saying things he'd regret tomorrow, but he wanted to just go with it, let things slide into whatever shape they would.

"Poor Sonny." Allie reached over and touched his knee, a friendly gesture that sent rays of warmth up his thigh to his groin. She said, "You know, there's lots of ways of feeling poor."

He supposed there were, though he couldn't imagine what way she could feel deprived. A girl from the Nice Street.

"Hey you two, break it up!" It was Smiley, crowding in close, an arm on each of their shoulders. He was off duty and off the wagon, by the look of it. Sweat stood out on his forehead and beaded his lip.

"Smiley, when you going to Ireland?" Allie asked.

"Soon's I get a vacation, I'll be off."

"Ireland?" Sonny said. "You going to show them what Alaskans are made of?"

"Damn straight. I'll be cruising down those country roads, just me and those pretty Irish maidens, sitting in the sun." Smiley ordered them a round, laid a conspicuous hundred dollar bill on the bar, and left a huge tip.

Sonny said, "He's flying high. He'll end up in the dry-out ward again." He thought of his mom on the ferry and wondered if she'd started drinking. Maybe he should've gone with her. He pushed the thought out of his mind.

"I don't have the heart to tell him it rains a lot in Ireland, too," Allie said.

"Ireland." Sonny shook his head. "Who'd think Smiley Ferris would want to go to Ireland?"

"Oh, everybody's got a place they want to go. You know, your mom told me she always wanted to see New England, see my part of the world. She's got this dream about white churches and stone walls and seeing the leaves change color in the fall."

Stone walls? That was a new one. He never knew his mother had a place she wanted to go. What was it about Allie that got people to tell their secrets? Something about her eyes, intent, interested, urging him on, or the way she leaned forward and seemed to listen with her whole body. Nobody listened to him as she did. "There's a lot of places I'd like to see," Sonny said.

"Yeah? Like where?"

"I always wanted to go crabbing in the Aleutians. Morgan and Henry went up there for a while. There's great money, the trouble is, they lose forty boats a year up there. It's not that I'm scared, but my women have already lost too many men. It wouldn't be fair to them to take the chance."

Allie waited, stirring the ice in her glass.

"And . . . I'd really like to go Outside and see it for myself. See how the rest of the world lives."

"I didn't know you wanted to go Outside, Sonny. Where would you go?"

"Oh, I don't know. I was thinking maybe Denver." It was the first time he'd ever said the word aloud. It felt risky, like saying the name of a girl he liked, as though he might jinx it.

"Why Denver?"

"I don't know. It just sounds nice, all that sun, and I heard there were jobs down there."

"I lived in Denver once but I didn't like it that much. The people were too healthy or something."

Sonny laughed. "I wouldn't mind that. Is that why you left?"

"Not really. I didn't want to live in a city, and then I had trouble with a job. I blew up a Kwick Lunch truck."

"A what?"

"You know, one of those quilted metal camper trucks that carry food to construction sites? I guess you've never seen one, but they've got them down there. I was a Kwick Chick, a Goody Girl. I lied and said I knew how to drive a standard shift, which I didn't, and then I blew it up by mistake by putting it into the superlow grandma gear and revving it up to about five million rpm's trying to get up a muddy hill because the guys wouldn't walk twenty feet down to the truck. Shot a rod right through the block." Allie smiled at the memory. "You should have seen it, this geyser of oil all over the place, and the guys laughing at me."

"So you got fired, huh?"

Allie grinned. "I was going to be fired anyway, because my route was losing money. I used to get stoned while I was driving, and get brilliant ideas for short cuts across muddy fields. And if I didn't like the guys, I wouldn't stop. Plus, I wouldn't push the crappy food. My boss wanted me to say, 'Hey boys, there's some mighty fine hot sandwiches in the back!' He thought I lacked the right attitude. When I blew up the truck, I just locked the money belt in the truck and started walking. I figured, 'Oh, well. Time to move on.' I moved to the mountains after that."

Sonny laughed. She did whatever the hell she wanted. He leaned over and picked her glossy black hair off her shoulder and weighed it in his hand. "I was sure you were Indian the first time I saw you, until that time you came over the boat."

"How come you hardly talked to me last summer?" Allie asked.

"You were Digger's deckhand."

"So? He didn't own me."

Sonny shrugged. "Digger's a damn big guy. I didn't want any trouble."

"Oh, come on."

"I mean it. Everybody wants to fight me all the time, especially whenever I leave town. I'm big, and there's always some asshole trying to prove himself. I know it's dumb to fight, but if you don't, people think you're yellow. I can push my weight around if I have to."

"What do you care what people think?"

Maybe she really didn't understand. If she cared, she'd never be out in that skiff making a joke of herself, while all the other girls in town were sitting under dryers in curlers. Sonny shrugged.

"Well, Digger isn't here anymore," Allie said. She stared down into her glass, suddenly shy at her own words, her invitation.

Sonny looked at her sitting there in that blue dress, eyes lowered, worrying the straw in her glass, and he wanted her. He wanted to tell her about his plans for Denver, to fill her up with all his words, the words he'd never told. He leaned over, brushing her ear with his lips. "I'm talking my fool head off again," he whispered. He could smell the shampoo in her hair, a fresh cool scent, and underneath it, something spicy, warm, the odor of her flesh. "It's dangerous talking to you."

Allie shivered and released pent breath. She turned to look at him sideways, from under her lashes, her eyes clouded. She wanted him. He'd known all along she'd wanted him but now he was sure. Why had he waited so long?

"Hey, Allie!" Henry shouldered his way up to the bar, grinning and sweating. Dancing had helped him work off the farthest reaches of his drunk. "Allie, you ready? They're playing our song."

Allie got up from her stool in a trance, knocking her cigarettes onto the floor. She turned to look back over her shoulder at Sonny.

"I'll be waiting for you right here," Sonny said.

Sonny, Allie thought, while her skiff slapped on small winter waves. Across the bay, bumper boats shunted a raft of logs around the hull of a Japanese ship, and longshoremen in caulk boots, raising peavey poles, leaped from log to log. She watched the men, and their every muscular flex and stretch was that of Sonny above her; the rocking skiff was the rhythm of the bed where she woke beside him to the whispering hiss of a stereo receiver and its one dumb green glowing eye.

It wasn't Sonny's room; it belonged to his little brother, Mikey, who was out with his buddies getting stoned. It was a teenager's dream room filled with purple and green psychedelic hard rock posters. Last night she hadn't bothered to ask why Sonny chose Mikey's room. She would have preferred his own room, to learn more of Sonny, but it was too dark, too drunken, too wordless, and when they entered the house she'd been stunned. The lit up kitchen had shocked her, awed her. It was so fabulous in its neglect: whining husky, dirty dishes, dismal army barracks wall paint, and the odor of leaking gas. And in the middle of it all the big white shiny washing machine like a statement: "Sonny grew up here."

Sonny slept on his back, arm thrown up over his head as though warding off a blow, throat taut and stretched backward, eyes shadowed by tired circles, unaware of being watched. So beautiful, she thought, feeling safe for the moment because he was still asleep and it was only waking that was dangerous; in comparison, sex was easy.

His skin was the color of her deepest summer tan, his armpit hair straight as an Oriental's, his chest smooth and well muscled. She watched him sleeping and watched the clock that would wake him in twenty minutes and send him down to the harbor, to the boat that would take him away.

Out in the skiff at noon she saw his boat pass, the steel seiner stacked with net and corks, the power skiff — Sonny's skiff — riding on top of the net. Now a shrimp trawler cut a line in front of her, its trawl hanging off the side, piled high with pyramids of shrimp, on top of which sat three black ravens, feasting, enjoying the free ride. Allie made slow, looping turns; the lines trailed out behind the skiff, herring flipping silvery under the sea on one side, and on the other swam one of the painted plugs she'd got from Nick, and she thought: Sonny. Remembering the underwater darkness of the sleeping bag Sonny had spread over them and the taste of his skin and its smell, she suddenly remembered sitting next to a dripping boy in the back seat of a station wagon while her mother drove them home from the beach years ago.

Fifteen, angular, a skinny virgin, Allie had sat beside a boy who saved her from her father's wrath by scubaing to the ocean bottom to find a piece of topmast lost when a sailboat tipped. She found the boy amazing not only in his skill and courage but in his very dimensions, a foreign geography of broad-boned borders, of dripping, muscular flesh. And sitting beside him, growing damp from the damp of his cut-offs, she smelled an odor rising off his skin. More than the ocean, it was a smell like ozone, like the sky after thunder and lightning, charged and wet and full of promise. She didn't think sex, didn't know enough to think it. She didn't have a word for that odor and could only sit next to a dripping boy, flaring her nostrils, galvanized with the scent of all the mysteries, everything she didn't know yet but was hell bent on finding out.

And Sonny smelled like that, like all the promises, like everything she still didn't know. Pressing nose, lips, forehead to his chest, she'd been convinced that when Sonny entered her she would enter the knowledge of what it meant to grow up in this house, for Vivian to be your mother, to have found your father face down on the beach, to live like Sonny, here.

Sonny, she thought, feeling an ache in her chest, in her arms, in her thighs a ripple, while the skiff shimmied on strangely sparkling water and weak winter sun shone on the snow-shaded logging cuts on Siligovsky Island. Sonny, she thought, and then her outboard whined, gurgled, choked, and went dead.

She knew immediately what she'd done, in fact she'd known it a second before it happened, but she'd been too slow, too sleepy and stupid with Sonny to not do the stupidest thing a troller could do. In turning, she'd run over her own line. With the engine dead, the sound of the bay grew suddenly loud and distinct: the clank of the cranes lifting the logs; the saws in the mill screeching; the cries of gulls and eagles; the slap of waves. She turned and tilted the outboard engine into a horizontal position. She could see the propeller tightly wound and tangled with nylon line, but she couldn't reach it. When she leaned over the stern, water poured in over the transom of the low, flat-bottomed skiff. She sat down quickly and bailed, then tried again. Same result. Shit, shit, shit, shit. What a jerk she was. She'd even managed to troll past slack tide, and the outgoing tide had already carried her fifty feet farther from shore, toward the straits and the open ocean. Shit.

She took her poles out of their holders, laid them in the skiff, and picked up a ridiculously undersized yellow plastic oar. After five minutes of frantic paddling, she hadn't managed even to stay where she'd been but had drifted farther out. If she screamed, would anyone hear her? That would be the last thing she'd do. She'd drift out to sea before she'd yell for help after doing something so dumb. She reached for the propeller, bailed, reached, bailed, paddled. A seal popped up fifteen feet away and swam backward with infuriating ease, watching Allie closely. "Fuck you," she said, slapping the water with her oar. Maybe she could just paddle until the tide turned and she'd be carried back in? But her arms already ached from the effort.

She was still paddling, stubbornly but with no effect, when the longshoreman came out to rescue her in a steel bumper boat. He was laughing. She'd probably made his day. "Throw me your line!" he mouthed over the diesel roar of his little metal bathtub, and Allie did as he ordered. She stared at her rubber booted feet in epic shame as he hauled her back to the dock. There she lay on her belly for an hour and a half, slashing and unwrapping twisted line from the outboard prop, while a steady parade of fishermen stopped to crack jokes about what she'd caught.

UNDER THE LITTER of frozen pizza boxes, beer cans, and bills on the kitchen table, Sonny found a post card from his mother, asking him to call. The card, with a picture of the state capitol building, wasn't dated, and he had no idea how long it had been sitting there, since he'd been out two weeks on the boat. "Hey, Mikey," he called, "when did we get a card from Mom?"

Mikey didn't answer. He was sitting in the living room smoking a joint, watching a soap opera with the sound turned off and the stereo blasting, feet up on the coffee table. Sonny went into the living room and waved the card in Mikey's face. Mikey grinned amiably. "Oh, yeah. Mom wrote," he said.

"When?"

"I dunno." He held up the joint. "You want to get stoned?"

Sonny went back in the kitchen and dumped his dirty clothes out of the duffel into the washing machine. The post card read, "I'm kind of involved up here and don't know when I'll make it home." Maybe she'd met some guy and would stay on good behavior the way she had when she first met Nick. Something like that probably wouldn't last too long, but it would buy him time. Maybe time for Denver . . .

He poured in the detergent, set the knobs, and went back into the living room to take a hit off Mikey's joint.

. . .

Sonny worked his way through the Anchor Lounge, Jimmy's Bar, and the Lone Wolf. Jimmy's was a white man's bar, according to his mother, and Sonny rarely went there. The Lone Wolf was for old-timers. But he stopped in each of them, looking around, going through the motions of buying cigarettes from the machine, saying the hi-how-are-you's, moving on. He was looking for Allie, but he wouldn't let himself know it until he found her.

She was sitting up by the bar in the Takine Inn, and she spun on her stool when he entered. She smiled, then covered it with nonchalance, turning back to her cigarettes and her drink. He went straight over and sat down beside her.

"I was thinking about you out there," he said.

"Yeah? What were you thinking?"

In the wheel house reading the radar, in the power skiff hunched against the wind and cold, in his bunk, he'd imagined the curve of her breasts, her roundness, no hard edges like Brenda, everything smooth and resilient. He saw her eyes fastened on his, the way she kept smiling, smiling when he moved above her, like everything he did made her happy.

"I was thinking, I never been on that riverboat of yours. When do I get an invitation?"

Allie turned to him, her eyes wide, deep, startled by desire, and he almost couldn't believe them. How could anyone want him that way? He looked away to the half-empty room. It was Tuesday night and there was no live music, just the juke box playing an awful song about how God didn't make little green apples. The Takine was decorated for Christmas three weeks early, tinsel and cutout Santas gracing the mirror and the bathroom doors.

"Let's go," he said.

Sonny bought a bottle in the little store at the back of the bar, and they went out. While they were in the Takine it had begun to snow, and now all of the ice patches on Front Street were dusted with half an inch of powder. Sonny put an arm around Allie's waist to steady her, although she was wearing her rubber boots and he was the one likely to slip in his hard motorcycle heels. Every fifty feet the streetlights caught the large flakes in their beams, making white, dancing cones of snowy light. A man appeared under a streetlight, and as he came closer they saw it was Nick. He looked into their faces, touched the brim of his hat, and continued on. He was either heading for the bar or his cabin. For the first time it occurred to Sonny that it might be lonely being Nick.

"He's an interesting guy," Allie said. "He wants to teach me to play chess."

"Just be sure that's all he wants to teach you." Sonny slapped her butt.

"Oh, come on. He's old. Why do you act like you hardly know each other?"

"I like Nick all right."

"But you always clam up when he's around. I've noticed it."

"You notice too much," Sonny said.

They stopped at the platform above the docks, lingering to look down at the boats with their snow dusted rigging — a post card picture, a Christmas card.

Allie walked over to the streetlight and stood under the beam, sticking out her tongue to catch the illuminated flakes. "Once," she said, "my mother told me a story about snow. She was little, and her mother was giving her a bath. Usually her sisters did it, washing two kids in the tub at a time since there were eight of them, but this one time it was her mother. My grandmother was humming, my mother looked out the window and there was snow coming down. It looked real pretty in front of the streetlights. My mother told me that every time it starts to snow she feels happy." Allie moved out of the light into the darkness, so that Sonny couldn't see her face.

Sonny leaned against the rail. He didn't know what to say, what the story meant.

Allie punched at the snowflakes. "Now she's fucking afraid

of her shadow. She won't even go out of the house."

The word *fucking* hung in the air, harsh and ugly against the muffled softness, the gentle hiss of falling snow. It jarred his ears when she swore, as though she were trying to talk like somebody else, like one of the boys. He was afraid of her sudden anger.

"Come on," Allie said. "I want to slide down the ramp."

The tide was out, and the ramp was steep and treacherously slick with snow. It was divided vertically: half of it slatted for easier walking, half without slats for dolly loads. Even the slatted side would be rough going tonight.

"You're crazy," Sonny said. "You won't be able to stop when you hit bottom. You'll fall in the bay." Every winter they lost a couple of drunks who fell in the freezing water, too tanked up to make it back to their boats.

"Sure I will," Allie said. She took a running stride and went flying down the slick boards, arms flapping. She hit the floats with a thump and then slid across the boards, leaving a track, and stopped herself, laughing, against a gill netter. Two feet to the left there was no boat to stop her; she would have gone in. He shook his head.

"Hey Sonny!" She called up. "Try it. It's great."

He worked his way carefully down the slatted side, holding on to the rail. He didn't want to make a fool of himself, falling on his ass.

"Chicken! I want to do it again!"

He waited while she hauled herself up the slats, and when she came flying down this time, he grabbed for her, but her momentum was too great and she knocked him over, falling on top of him, laughing. She kept laughing, laughing, until he heard hysteria in her voice. He rolled over and pinned her to the planks. Her nose was cold and wet against his cheek, and there was snow in her hair and eyelashes. "Shhhhhhh," he said. "Shhhhhh."

Allie struggled, still giggling. "Get off me, Sonny. I'm freezing. My ass is all wet."

"You'd be a lot wetter if you knocked us both in."

"I said, *get off!*"

She thrashed under him, suddenly wild to get free. For some reason he thought of the snow geese, after he'd shot one, out on the flats. She was a wild girl looking to drown herself, and she didn't care if she took him along. He didn't know if he should be mad at her or if he should just make love to her right there, under the glare of the dock light, until she was quiet and peaceful and empty of fight. He pulled her up and brushed her off and followed her down to her boat.

ALLIE LAY beside Sonny in the bed at his mother's house. His arm was around her shoulder, and she held his hand in front of her face, turning his ring. It was gold with a circle of rough nuggets surrounding a leaping fish, and underneath, the word in gold: ALASKA.

"I bet you don't know what kind of fish that is," Sonny said.

"Of course I do. I'm not that dumb. It's a salmon."

"Yeah, but what kind?"

"I don't know what kind." She pushed his hand away in exasperation.

"A coho! And you thought you were so smart."

"I never said I was smart," she said.

"No, but you think it, don't you?"

In answer, she leaned over and bit his shoulder. Sonny pinned her with little effort, so that her arms were stretched out on the mattress and there was nothing she could do but move from side to side, laughing, while he shoved his knee between her legs. "I give up," she said, "you win." Sonny released her.

He flopped back on the pillows beside her. "I used to fight like crazy when I was crewing on Jimmy Caldwell's boat. I went out with him seining that time my dad drowned, and then after I trolled with Nick in the summer, I went back with Jimmy fall fishing."

"You trolled with Nick?" Allie was fascinated. She knew that Nick had been his mother's lover, but not that Sonny had trolled with him. She wanted to push him further, to learn more, but she was afraid he'd shut up, the way he did when Nick was around. And if he stopped talking, he'd get out of bed and pull on his jeans, and then everything would change and be awkward between them again. All the time she lay in bed beside him, listening to him talk, she feared the moment when he would get up and leave.

"Yeah. I was going to be a troller, get my own boat." He shook his head as though to clear the idea away. "Anyway, I was fishing with Jimmy Caldwell, and he had this nephew Billy. I don't know why, I just never got along with him. We were just a couple of kids, but we were always duking it out all over the net and the rigging. Jimmy'd laugh and laugh. I was a hell of a fighter then. I was fast, real fast."

"Now you're fast with women." It bothered her when he talked like that, as though he wanted to be more of a fighter and needed to convince her, or himself, that he was tough. He was ashamed of his gentleness.

Sonny threw a few punches into the air over her head. "Left, right, left. I could really hold my own." He put his arm around her shoulder again. "Fishing with Jimmy Caldwell. That was a long time back. You know, I always felt bad that I didn't go out gill netting with my dad that time. If I'd been there with him, he wouldn't have drowned."

Allie kissed the beautiful rise of his bicep lying against her cheek. "It wasn't your fault, Sonny. He wanted you to seine, to make your own money."

"Did I tell you that? You remember everything, don't you? Are all the girls back east like you? Maybe I don't want to go down to Denver and check it out after all."

Allie didn't want to hear about Denver, about other girls. If Denver was just a lot of empty talk, she'd think less of him, but it would be awful in Vladimir if he really went. She turned back to study him anxiously, propping herself up on one elbow. Something was happening to her that she didn't like. Every time Sonny left town to go fishing, it was as though her life stopped and couldn't start up again until he came home. "Denver isn't exactly back east," she said.

"You know all about it, huh? I forgot you were a Denver Kwik Chick." Sonny pulled her arm out from under her, grinning, so that she fell back on the bed. It was a relief when he climbed on top of her and ended the discussion.

ALLIE NEVER KNEW a plane could be so little and fragile; how could this toy hold them up? She sat in the back of the four-seater Cessna, behind Sonny, who sat in the copilot's seat. Coopie, the town chiropractor and a reputed hero flyer in Nam, had agreed to fly them to Juneau. Pudgy and amiable, with a pomaded, overgrown crew cut and a face like a softened pumpkin, Coopie was going to Juneau to see a lawyer. He was being sued by a Seattle woman who claimed he'd given her a spinal workout while drunk. Allie and Sonny planned to take the ferry back to Vladimir, since Coopie couldn't drink the night before he flew, and he wasn't certain when he'd have a dry day.

"Ready for take-off, over," Coopie said into the radio, and received a squawking clearance as well as a warning not to blow his money on those Juneau whores. "A bit of the personal touch at Vladimir International," he said, turning around to wink at Allie in the back seat.

The airport was international in name more than function, a nod in the direction of the Canadian border, which lay across the channel behind Vladimir Island, thirty miles into the mainland.

They swung around slowly, wings dipping, bouncing on the gravel runway, picked up speed, the engines whining and the entire plane shaking as though it would rattle apart, and then with a last bounce they lifted into the air. Allie sucked in breath. She loved the feeling when a plane left the earth, that instant of recognition, a tangible change of state. Most of the events in her life merely blurred together, and she'd always thought if she could just put her finger on the moment of change, her life would make more sense.

When had she slipped over the line? Up until her senior year in high school she'd been such a good, good girl: doing the family laundry, her homework finished days in advance, and her clothes, carefully coordinated outfits, laid out the night before. And then all of a sudden she was hitchhiking after school — Route 3, Route 128 — just to see what would happen.

"Scared?" Coopie kept his eyes on the dials. "You got nothing to worry about as long as we don't hit the mountain coming into Juneau. This part's a piece of cake. Soon's we get up to altitude, I'm going to let Sonny take over."

"Coopie's a funny guy," Sonny said.

Allie studied the back of Sonny's neck. Did he regret inviting her along on this outing, or was he simply nervous about seeing Vivian? If only she knew what he was thinking; if only she could be sure he wanted her as much as she wanted him to. She sighed and looked down at the tip of Vladimir Island becoming small beneath them, the curl of mill smoke miniaturized, as though rising from a cigarette.

They crossed the mouth of the Takine River, the shallow delta beige against the darker sea, the line where she fished a brilliant contrast from above. Then they were into clouds and fog, flying so close to the mountaintops she could see sinkholes and bogs puddling the peaks. Even the mountains are full of water, she was thinking when they broke through to startling sunshine. A few thousand feet below, the distance from the Takine Inn to the boat harbor, Vladimir lay locked into its damp sorrows under a weight of low-riding clouds. It seemed like a trick, a hoax, to have sunshine so close, yet out of reach. If you lived in Vladimir, she thought, maybe it was something better not to know.

"Okay, Sonny," Coopie said. "She's all yours."

Sonny turned to Coopie with an expression of alarm.

"No sweat," Coopie counseled. "Here's your altimeter, tachometer, and air speed indicator. Pull the wheel back to bring up her nose, push it forward to put her down. You just keep her right where she's at now. Don't worry, I ain't stepping out for a coffee break."

Allie was afraid that Sonny wouldn't chance it. She'd do it herself, but she'd seen him hesitate and knew that part of him that wouldn't take risks. She'd seen him sit in the Anchor Lounge watching the guys banging away at the new fooseball table, curious, aching to try it, but unwilling to do so until he'd watched long enough to figure it out, terrified of making a mistake. Take the plane, Sonny, she whispered silently. *Do it!*

Sonny put his hands on the wheel and Allie relaxed, breathing, thank you, thank you. He sat rigid in his seat, eyes on the dials, waiting for the plane's nose to dip or the wings to shimmy but nothing happened; they kept on cruising with the clouds below in a flat grey layer and the sun bright, sparkling on the windows where moisture had frozen into delicate crystal patterns.

"Now my life's in your hands," Allie joked.

Sonny gave her a quick glance over his shoulder. "Then you're in a shitload of trouble," he said. But she could feel his excitement, read his triumph in the set of his shoulders, the angle of his neck when he turned back to the controls. His triumph was hers; it was as though she'd given him her will. A moment later, she felt oddly disappointed. It wasn't such a big deal. Wasn't he something like a little kid who sits on his father's lap in the driver's seat, holding the steering wheel? Coopie was there all the time. It would have been a big deal only if Sonny had refused.

·   ·   ·

They shared a cab into town with Coopie. After months of Vladimir, Juneau, with its boxy government buildings slammed up against the mountains, came as a surprise. Looking out the taxi window, Allie felt disdain for the business-suited, briefcase-toting bureaucrats — they weren't Real Alaskans — mingled with excitement at the sight of stop lights, flashing neon, a Salvation Army Santa, a department store window full of spangled party dresses, the faces of strangers. In Vladimir the ferry only arrived three times a week in winter, usually just to unload food and machine parts, and no one new came to town.

Coopie dropped them at the Baranof Hotel with a promise to steal a dance with "Sonny's lady" that night at the Red Dog Saloon. Allie glanced at Sonny to see how he'd taken it. Was she "his lady"? He looked dazed, still riding high on the thrill of playing pilot.

The Baranof was plush with red carpets, flocked red and gold wallpaper, chandeliers of clustered glass tubes, and hung with outrageously priced acrylic landscapes by local artists. A regular big city hotel, expensive and tacky. Sonny paid in cash at the desk and took their key up to the room.

Allie inspected the "Sanisealed" bathroom, pulled the accordion drapes on a view of early dusk over Juneau high rises, bounced on the aqua spread of one of the big double beds. "Hey, this is really nice," she said.

"What did you think, I was going to bring you to a flophouse?"

"Of course not." Actually, she wouldn't have been surprised if he had, and she wouldn't have refused, either. She would have gone wherever Sonny asked her to go. "When are you going to call your mom?"

Sonny waved the question away. "Later."

They went down to the hotel bar. It was a businessman's bar, decorated with fake Tlingit and Haida masks on one wall, and on the other a collection of fishing nets and glass floats that looked like escapees from a Cape Cod cocktail lounge. Allie was reminded of her mother's lobsterman phase of interior decoration, the buoys and lobster pots she'd crowded into their summer house.

Sonny ordered a double shot of Jim Beam for himself and a single for her. He looked ill at ease and kept glancing over his shoulder, a habit that made her anxious. She wanted to distract and entertain him, to captivate him with herself and pull him away from his thoughts. She wanted him to focus on her; when he looked away, she felt as if she disappeared. She wanted to say, Look at me!

At the table behind them, two men in suits were loudly discussing the question of clear-cutting timber. "The thing is," one of them said, "it isn't just the erosion problem. It's been documented that logging is ruining the salmon streams and injuring the harvest." Allie turned to look. He was an eager, scraped clean young fellow, a junior conservationist, a Fish and Game type. She was unpleasantly reminded of Steve Tucker and her brief stay on the *Miranda.*

His companion had the bloated face and baggy eyes of the disillusioned. "Freddy," he said, "when you've been up here a little longer, you'll see that logging and fishing are not even in the game anymore. This land's shot. She can't regenerate fast enough. We got bigger stakes coming up. It's a sad fact, but the fisherman is like the Indian up here; he's picturesque, but he's an anachronism, a thing of the past. I'm talking priorities, Freddy. I'm talking oil."

Allie looked up at Sonny. He sipped his drink without changing expression, as though he hadn't heard. She pushed back her chair and turned to give the oil enthusiast a furious glare. "You ought to look around and see who you're talking about if you're going to talk in such a loud, asshole voice," she said. She slammed her chair against their table and stalked out.

Sonny caught up with her in the lobby, where she was pretending to be entranced by a lurid painting of sunset over Mendenhall Glacier. She was about to apologize for making a stupid scene, but when she saw he was laughing her anger resumed.

"I bet they thought they insulted *you*," Sonny said. "You little Boston klootch."

"They did. Aren't you pissed off? He could've bothered to look around a little before shooting his mouth off."

Sonny met her eyes, then looked at the painting. "Maybe he was telling the truth."

Sonny didn't really believe that, did he? That as a fisherman, as an Indian, he was an anachronism, a picturesque thing of the past? She felt angry at him for his lack of anger, because if he saw himself so diminished, what could he be for her? She needed him to see himself larger. She needed to believe in him.

"What do you want to do now?" Sonny asked.

"I don't know, let's go to another bar, some regular place." It seemed there ought to be something else to do in Juneau besides go to a bar, which was all anyone did in Vladimir, but right then she couldn't think of what it might be.

They got their coats from the room and went down to the corner, slipping on city slush, to a dark little dive called the Timberland, where no one was wearing a suit. Sonny joined a fooseball game, and Allie won a game of eight ball. At seven they walked up the street to a Chinese restaurant with satiny red wallpaper and tasseled pagoda lamps. Allie drank mai tais out of a yellow mug with a paper parasol, and she was tipsy before the food arrived. Sonny stuck to Jim Beam.

"This isn't real Chinese food," Allie said, pushing suspiciously brilliant green peppers and too-pink shrimp in a gloppy sweet sauce around her plate with chopsticks she'd asked for and then felt silly using. Sonny used a fork. She preferred the spicy Szechuan food she'd learned to like in college; this stuff reminded her of Sunday family trips to a gas station–turned–Chinese restaurant on Route 3, everyone fighting over who'd get the last pork strip.

"I thought you wanted to come here," Sonny said.

"No, no, I didn't mean that. I'm glad we're here." She turned her attention away from the food to the Chinese waiter dodging between the tables with his laden trays, his expressionless face. What were his private thoughts? Was he figuring the tips he'd make that night, plotting a rendezvous with a lover, or simply despising them? She leaned forward over the table and spoke low. "I wonder what makes them come up here? It must be weird to be one of the few Chinese in Juneau, Alaska."

"Jobs," Sonny said, dipping a spare rib into hot mustard and gnawing at the bone.

"There must be plenty of waiter jobs in San Francisco or Seattle. Why would anyone go to a place where no one speaks their language, where everyone looks different?" She shot Sonny an embarrassed look. In Juneau, as an Indian, *he* looked different. "You know, my father grew up like that," she said hurriedly. "The only Jewish family in this little town on Cape Cod. They were always out of it, the misfits."

Sonny put his fork down. "Is that what you are? Jewish?"

"Just half. My mother's regular white bread American."

"I got a lot of respect for your people. They didn't let anyone kick them off *their* land."

Who knew if it was their land? With Sonny it was always a question of power, of who won and who lost. Allie reached for a spare rib. "I don't think of them as *my* people. Technically, I'm not even Jewish, since the religion goes through the mother. They wouldn't claim me."

"You're a half-breed," Sonny said with satisfaction. "Like me."

Like him. She felt a leap of hope, the same she'd felt when Sonny's mother reached across a table in the bar to take her hands and said, "You look like my Sonny. You could be his little sister, you know?" If she were like Sonny, he might want her more; she'd fit in.

"You know what I'm afraid of?" Sonny downed the last of his Jim Beam. "I'm afraid that if I did go Outside, to Denver,

I might feel like a Chinaman in Juneau. It's not that I can't push my weight around if I have to, but I might not know who I was. At least in Vladimir, I know everybody. I know who I am."

Allie winced. He wasn't who he thought he was in Vladimir; only she knew who he was, the real Sonny, the one who didn't have to worry about pushing his weight around. If only she could release that part of him, show him who he was.

"I never knew who I was at home, so it doesn't matter where I live," she said. Her voice sounded too tough, too flippant. If it didn't matter where she lived, why had she traveled so far from home? Why was she still in Vladimir?

The waiter removed their dishes, brought fortune cookies and the bill.

"For better luck, wait until autumn," Allie's read.

Sonny's said, "Use caution choosing friend."

Wait until autumn? She couldn't wait that long. She wanted something to happen now. She wanted Sonny to fall in love with her. Then she'd know who she was. But Sonny's fortune was even worse, warning him against her.

"I bet he gave us lousy fortunes because I said something nasty about the food." Allie crumpled the paper strips into the ashtray while Sonny carefully counted the twenties in his wallet and paid the bill.

Out on the street in a cold light mist Allie asked, "What should we do now?"

"We could go to a bar," Sonny said.

"How about a movie first?"

"If you want to."

They walked along, peering into shop windows, searching for a place to buy a paper so they could read the movie schedules. The stores were open late for Christmas shopping, and some had mechanical displays like the ones in the stores in Boston when she was a child — Santa's workshop elves pounding nails relentlessly a fraction beyond the edge of a piece of wood, and Swan Lake dancers twirling across a mirror dusted with plastic snow. She remembered crowds, cold air and Boston slush, shuffling between large overcoated bodies to get close enough to press her nose to the glass. Her mother there beside her, holding her hand. Was it possible? It was only later that her mother stopped going out of the house.

Her father hadn't allowed them a Christmas tree because of his family, but every year as consolation he drove them all into the city to see the trees lit up on Boston Common. How elegant they had looked, each lit with a single color, white or blue — not like the garish, multicolored blinking lights in the windows of the houses of their neighborhood. Was is possible that they'd had a family tradition, a ride in a car to see something as simple and lovely as illuminated trees in a park? A ride without a fight? And in summer, she remembered, her mother had taken her for a ride on the swan boats in the Public Garden. Sunshine, throwing popcorn to the swans on the murky, feathered water, the sound of the creaking paddles, her mother's big, pointy sunglasses glinting in the sun — it hurt to remember that; it hurt so much it made her chest constrict. It was easier to believe it had all been bad. If it had all been bad, she wouldn't have to miss them; she wouldn't have to feel that something was lost.

"Wait." Allie stopped to read a flyer posted on a door. It announced a free performance of the University of Alaska Traveling Renaissance Dance Troupe, sponsored by the Alaska State Council on the Arts. "Want to check it out?"

Sonny glanced at his watch. "It started half an hour ago."

"So what? Let's just watch for a little while. It might be funny, and it's free. If we don't like it, we'll walk out."

Sonny followed Allie into the hallway, up a flight of stairs to a lobby where a woman wearing an Emily Dickinson hairdo — severe center part, bun at the nape of her neck — a wool suit, and a large, hand-cast silver pendant dangling between her tweedy breasts stood behind a table heaped with programs. The woman looked inordinately grateful to see them. When they entered the hall, Allie knew why: the room was half empty. The metal folding chairs were dotted with women akin to the one with the programs, along with a couple of shanghaied husbands, the kind of men who wore galoshes and combed their hair over their bald patches.

"Juneau culture vultures," Allie said.

"Shhhhh," Sonny said and pushed her toward a seat.

The room was hushed save for the sweet, slow, processional beat and trill of the Renaissance music played by four costumed musicians at the edge of the stage, and the soft shuffle and thud of the dancers' feet. Women in long purple, crimson, or forest green velvet gowns with flat washboard bodices that mashed their bulging breasts dipped and curtsied with men in equally brilliant tights, pantaloons, and codpieces. The women favored the men with attention, then turned away in exaggerated, choreographed flirtation. The couples marched around and around the small square of stage, their passions orderly, contained. Allie turned nervously to Sonny, who was staring glassily at the stage.

"Too bad we aren't stoned," she said, trying to make light of her error. Why had she dragged him in?

A woman beside her, who'd been leaning forward in aesthetic ecstasy, turned and glared.

The truth was that the music was lovely. The steady courtly beat overlaid with sweet piping melodies made her want to tap her toes, to hum; it filled her chest with lightness, a visceral joy. But with Sonny beside her she couldn't relax. What if he was bored? She was as bad as her mother, who'd hauled her to the theater, the ballet, to concerts, because no one else in the family would go, and her mother was incapable of going alone.

The last time they ever went anywhere together, Allie was in the ninth grade and her mother had bought tickets for the Royal Danish Ballet in Boston. They parked in a pay lot and were hurrying down Washington Street, Christmas shoppers bumping into each other on the sidewalk, the brick walls of

Jordan's and Filene's rising above them. They were late, as her mother was always late, a battle between fear and desire, then, indignity of all indignities, as they walked down the sidewalk, a pigeon crapped on her mother's head.

Filene's was open late for Christmas, and they rushed into the ladies' room, where her mother, nearly in tears, stuck her expensively set hair under the tap. Her mother had taken it as some kind of judgment, a cosmic commentary: *This was not meant for the likes of you.* It was the beginning of the end. Thinking of it now as the dancers dipped and bowed and the men showed off their well-turned calves, Allie wanted to laugh to protect herself against the pity she always felt for her mother, the pity that would drag her down and keep her inside the house where her mother lived, afraid of the world. She could feel the laughter rising in her like hysteria, like the laughter that always preceded the family explosions when the hitting began.

"Come on," she said, grabbing Sonny's sleeve, "let's go."

"We can't until there's a break," Sonny whispered back.

"Yes we can." Allie stood and squeezed past the knees of the lady beside her, who uttered an annoyed "Tsss."

"Sorry," Sonny said.

Allie rushed past the startled program lady. "Lovely," she said. "Too bad we have to run." Outside, she leaned against a wall and breathed in the cold, wet Juneau air. Sonny clomped down the stairs behind her and pushed the door open.

"What a joke," Allie said.

Sonny shrugged and lit a cigarette. "It wasn't that bad. I never saw instruments like those. What were they?"

Allie turned to face him in surprise. "Well, the string one, like a guitar with a bent neck? That's a lute. And the funny sounding horn that went *nheeeeee* real high? That's a krummhorn."

"A crumb horn?" Sonny laughed. "How do you know these things?"

Allie fished a cigarette out of the pack in his breast pocket and struggled to light it with a damp match. She gave up and lit it off the point of Sonny's. "Well, my mother was a culture vulture too. She was always trying to raise herself above her origins, which weren't very glamorous." She disliked the tone of her own voice, putting her mother down when it was the one part of her mother she respected, the part that was drawn toward beauty. Culture vulture. She was using her father's disparaging term.

One time her mother enraged her father by buying a bronze sculpture — a piece called *The Firebird,* by a Russian exile — three hands of differing character reaching toward an abstract shape in flight. Her mother came downstairs in the morning to find her sculpture defaced: Allie's father had put gloves on the hands, tying the fingers back to make obscene gestures, three hands giving the finger to the sky.

"Crumb horns and lutes," Sonny said thoughtfully. "You grew up with that stuff, didn't you? You can make fun of it, but that's because you take it for granted."

"It doesn't mean *any*thing to me," Allie said fiercely, as though Sonny might argue the point and in doing so would prove something shameful about her, something that would set her apart, keep her from being one of the boys, show her as weak.

"I can't figure you out," Sonny said. "You want to play fisherman and wear those rubber boots and go out in that skiff, but it doesn't make sense. You were raised like a real lady."

Allie spun around, suddenly furious. "Right, I was raised like a real lady. My mother took me to the ballet and the opera, and my father called me a smartass cunt and fucking bitch. And I was a real lady sitting in the emergency room, with a belt buckle in my eye, lying to the intern who wanted to know who did it!"

She threw her cigarette in the gutter and stomped away, angry at Sonny, angry at herself because she'd dumped it on him and she didn't believe in talking about it, because talking about it made it seem as if she was after sympathy or that she was talking about someone else's life. When she talked about it, she didn't *feel* anything. How could it have been her life?

She was lying. She was always lying. She lied to the intern, saying her wound was an accident. She lied in school, wearing the eye patch. She lied to herself, because that time it hadn't been her father, her father had been the one who'd taken her to the hospital. She could never admit her mother also beat her, because if her mother had hit her too, there was no one, there'd never been anyone to save her, and anyway, her mother was weak, she couldn't help it.

"Hey," Sonny called out, trotting to catch up. "Hey, hey."

Allie turned around. "Hey, what?" Then without warning, she broke into angry tears.

Sonny put his arms around her. "Hey," he said. "Hey, it's okay."

Allie allowed herself to lean against him, just for a moment. He was being so nice. If only she could stay like that, leaning against him, if only she could just give up for a little while and let him take care of her. She was tired, tired. She'd been holding herself up all her life.

Sonny wiped her face. "You aren't so tough as you try to be, are you? You aren't so tough after all."

Allie wasn't tough, she was tired.

"Come on. We're going to walk over to the Red Dog and find Coopie and show them all how to boogie. We don't need those lutes or flutes or whatever they are. What do you say?"

This time, she let him lead the way.

At the Red Dog, a surging, smoky, crowded bar with sawdust on the floor, they found Coopie sitting with a bottle blonde in hot pants named Monique. Coopie was drunk already and kept saying, "Allie, you're good people. If Sonny don't take good care of you, you just let me know. You just call old Coopie."

Monique drummed her long, purplish, lacquered nails on the table, got up to make a call, and didn't come back.

"Let her go, the bimbo," Coopie said. "Who needs these Juneau bimbos, anyway? We got better ones back in Vladimir. Vladimir's the best fucking town in the world!"

Allie drank and danced with Coopie, ignoring his hands on her buttocks, turning her head away from his floral aftershave. She danced with Sonny until the room began to whirl and the colors blurred into bourbon, blurred into mai tais. Then she was lurching down the darkened streets, singing Sonny the theme song to the TV show "Mr. Ed" — "People yackety yak and waste the time of day, but Mr. Ed will never speak unless he has something to say" — and laughing because Sonny knew nothing of talking horses, since television had arrived in Vladimir only a few years ago.

When they made love on the aqua bedspread, she was sure that if she could only keep him there in bed with her, at his tenderest, she'd never lose him. She linked her legs behind his back, held him, watching his closed eyes, thinking, Sonny, Sonny, stay with me please.

Sonny whispered so softly she almost didn't hear his amazing words: "I could fall in love with you if I don't watch out."

Sonny, she thought, don't watch out. Live dangerously.

IN THE MIDDLE of the night, Sonny woke with his arm over Allie, his nose between her shoulder blades. Light from a building across the street cut through a crack in the drapes, illuminating the rise of her shoulder, the curve of her waist and hip. He listened to her breath against the pillow, felt the heat of her back against his belly, his knees tucked behind hers. When he cupped her breast, Allie stirred but didn't wake. He wanted to roll her over and force himself inside her, to pin her to the bed, but he was afraid he'd slide in and out without her even knowing, without leaving a mark. She was like some kind of train rolling along on her own little track, and whatever was happening around her didn't really matter, because when the whistle blew, she'd be gone.

Who was she? He could hardly believe the things she'd told him out on the sidewalk about eye patches and interns. How could those things have happened to her when she seemed so untouched by it all? With her innocent, unlined face and her willfulness, it seemed as though she'd never lived through anything, that for her everything lay ahead.

Holding Allie in a Juneau hotel room, Sonny felt lonely, as lonely as he'd ever felt, and scared. She turned his head around by making him want things he knew he'd never have, by making him want her. There was no percentage in it. He was going to get swallowed in the process, and he had to do something to keep himself safe. He had to watch out.

Sonny slid out of bed without waking her and poured himself a drink from the bottle of bourbon they'd bought on the way back to the hotel. Then another. When he climbed back into bed, sleep simply came.

He woke with a hangover, knocking his watch off the bedside table as he looked for it, not knowing for a moment where he was. Allie sat propped on an elbow, watching his face. How long had she been sitting like that? It gave him the creeps. A few years ago he was on an outing upriver, walking through a clearing, and came face to face with a wolf. His chest filled with adrenaline: he tasted metal on the back of his tongue. He didn't move and the wolf didn't either; it looked him straight in the eye, appraising him. When he reached for the pistol on his hip, the wolf trotted away slowly, all the time looking back at him over its shoulder as if to say, I know who you are. He'd been bettered. Although Allie's eyes were as dark as his own, nothing like that yellow-eyed wolf, it felt the same.

Sonny said, "Don't you ever sleep?"

Allie smiled. "No. Never."

He pulled the pillow over his head and groaned. When he woke again, it was after one and Allie was sitting in a chair by the window with an open book in her lap, still watching him.

"I didn't want to wake you so I did a little shopping. There's a great bookstore up the street." She held up her book. How could she look so clear-eyed and healthy when she'd been up all night drinking and had had less sleep than he? He needed a tomato beer for his aching head. He needed to call his mother.

Allie went down to get him a cup of coffee, and Sonny dialed Vivian. Her voice sounded faint, almost faded, and she didn't even bother to ask when he'd gotten in, or give him a hard time for not calling sooner. She just asked him to drop by at seven. It was so easy, it set his nerves on edge.

On top of the dresser he saw a stack of books that Allie had bought. *Notes from a Hunter's Album* by someone called Turgenev, *Play It As It Lays* by Joan Didion, Charles Dickens's *Hard Times*. He'd only heard of Dickens, and that was from a sixth-grade adaptation of *Oliver Twist*. Schoolteacher books. Sonny sighed and got dressed.

Out on the street the temperature had dropped, and everything that had been wet with mist last night had turned to sharp, crackling ice. Each step sounded like glass splintering underfoot. They stopped in at the Timberland, where Sonny drank two tomato beers and felt his nerves unjangle, the pound in his head decrease. Allie chattered on about what they should buy for Vivian, about sending a Christmas card home. Sonny nodded without really listening, concentrating on the wash of beer down the back of his throat, the easing of his mood. After a third, he was ready for the escalators, the glittering Christmas ornaments, the fluorescent confusion of Macher's department store.

Allie helped him select a soft grey angora sweater with pearl buttons at the throat for Vivian, and they waited while the gift was wrapped. Somewhere above them in department store heaven, Burl Ives was singing "Have a Holly Jolly Christmas."

"Let's play dress-up," Allie said. "You pick out something for me to try on, and I'll choose something for you."

He felt silly looking through the racks of ladies' dresses with Allie grinning at one elbow and a plump, fiftyish saleslady at the other, babbling on about how she loved to see men "shopping for their gals." The saleslady was wearing a candy-pink version of the sweater he'd just bought for his mother, adorned with about fifteen gold chains.

Sonny settled on the one thing he figured Allie would never choose herself, a strapless black semisheer cocktail dress that would have belonged in Vegas if you added a few sequins.

"Every man's fantasy," Allie said, holding the dress in front of her skeptically, but she took it into the dressing room. The saleslady lingered beside him, humming in happy anticipation of a sale.

"Pretty girl," the woman said. "You two make a real cute couple."

Sonny said, "Mmmm."

"Ready?" Allie called out from the dressing room. She hummed a drum roll, then emerged barefoot and struck a pose.

"Stunning!" the saleslady pronounced, hurrying over to fuss with the fit. "Just some heels, accessories, and I bet you'd be lovely with your hair up."

Allie winked at Sonny and held her hair off her shoulders, piled on top of her head. "What do you think, Sonny? You think I'd be a big hit at the Takine Inn?"

He couldn't speak. She looked beautiful, like a picture in a magazine, her shoulders smooth and pale above the dress, her neck surprisingly long and elegant with her hair piled up. The Takine Inn, what a joke. Where in Vladimir would she ever wear a dress like that? He knew at that moment as clearly as if he'd read it in print: he'd never be able to keep her. She was playing games with him, playing dress-up like she played dress-up in Vladimir, wearing rain gear and trolling out of a skiff. She could slide in and out of whatever costume she wanted, but he was going to be the one left in the audience.

Allie flopped her hands at her side, letting her hair fall. "He doesn't like it," she said to the saleslady.

"Of course he likes it," the saleslady hissed, giving him a nasty look. "He's a very lucky guy."

"Nope, he doesn't." Allie turned back to the dressing room. She re-emerged in jeans and sweater, carrying her parka over her shoulder. The saleslady had already disappeared to greener pastures. Allie took Sonny's arm. "How come you didn't like it?"

"I did."

"No, I could tell you didn't. Anyway, it's your turn now."

He didn't want to play this game anymore.

"Come on, it's only fair, you got to see me looking silly."

Sonny feared that the salesman knew he had no intention of buying the things that Allie had picked out, a suit with shirt and tie. He felt like a kid about to be caught reading smutty magazines at the drugstore. He hadn't worn a suit since his youngest sister's wedding, and that was rented in Ketchikan. The dressing room was a cubicle with no mirror and a saloon door. His head started pounding when he leaned over to pull off his boots, and he felt like a fool by the time he had the pants zipped, the shirt buttoned, the tie knotted.

"I chose *herring*bone tweed for you," Allie called to him. "I thought you could relate to it."

Sonny pulled the tweedy wool jacket on with a shrug and stepped out.

"Hey, you look great! Come over and look in the three-way mirror." Allie pulled him to a mirrored alcove. "You look like an exotic foreign businessman, a millionaire from South America!"

Sonny stared into the mirrors, transfixed by his own handsomeness. For a moment, he believed her. There in the reflection was someone else's broad shoulders in tweed, the sharp, clean angles of an expensive shirt collar, neat pleated pants. And then, above it all, as if to mock him, his own dark Tlingit face with its too long hair and his own startled eyes. Who was he kidding? He looked ridiculous, like a monkey wearing a tuxedo, a pug-nosed Indian playing dress-up. Sonny pulled the tie from his throat in disgust.

"Come on, Sonny," Allie urged. "Don't you see how great you look?"

He turned away from her as though he'd been walking along the edge of a land fault, as though he'd just averted disaster. "Game's over," Sonny said.

. . .

At twenty to seven he left Allie sitting on the bed watching the evening news and headed down the elevator. She'd offered to come along and he'd almost let her, but decided against it. Who knew what he'd find? He started after a cab, then changed his mind and ducked into the Timberland for a couple of quick shots to put him in the mood for the visit ahead. He felt the way he did after fishing, both weary and nervous. What was he afraid of? That he'd be confronted with some mess he'd have to take care of, or simply the awkwardness of seeing his mother after all this time, the mixture of love and pity and shame that always twisted his stomach when he was in her presence?

At the bar he sat beside a pimply kid who insisted on buying him a drink and telling his life's dream of rowing a boat from Juneau to Seattle.

"Why would you want to do that?" Sonny asked, trying to keep himself from turning around to look behind him, trying to force his eyes to stay on the kid's pustular face.

"What do you mean?" the kid huffed. "Jeez. Just so I'd know I'd done it."

"Sounds good," Sonny said diplomatically and pushed his glass back on the bar. He had to get out of there. It was already seven-twenty.

"Damn right it sounds good," the kid insisted. "Damn right!"

It wasn't until he was halfway to Emily's house in a cab that he realized he'd left Vivian's Christmas present under his bar stool, and he had to ask the driver to turn around and take him back. He grabbed the wrapped box from under the caulk-booted feet of the kid, who was droning on to the bartender about how the main thing was "to have a goddamn good radio, so's I never lose communication."

By the time he made it to Emily's house it was almost eight. Emily lived in a split-level ranch house with a winding flagstone path and a Christmas wreath on the door. Sonny stood on the top step, staring at the red plastic bow on the wreath. Just ring the bell, he told himself, but he felt unable to do it. His mother peeked through a window at him, smiled, and opened the door.

"Sonny!" She hugged him, pulled him into the hall.

"Sorry I'm late," he mumbled. He held out the wrapped box. "Merry Christmas, anyway."

"Oh, you're sweet." She kissed him and set the box down on a hall table. "We don't have much time now, since I've got to get somewhere by eight-thirty. Look at you!"

Sonny followed her into the living room, catching a glimpse of himself in the hall mirror: a stranger's face in a stranger's house. It felt weird to have his mother playing hostess in a house he'd never seen. "Where's Emily at?"

"Night shift at the hospital. She's real disappointed to miss you, and Bob's on call tonight. Let me get you coffee."

Vivian hurried into the kitchen, and Sonny sat on the couch with his jacket still on, looking down at his boots on the plush beige wall-to-wall rug. A Christmas tree stood in one corner with stacks of wrapped boxes beneath it. The living room furniture all matched: a long, low couch and squared off chairs in a beige two tones darker than the rug; a blond coffee table with matching end tables supporting white pottery lamps with little plastic dust covers over their fluted shades. A painting of Juneau harbor hung over a fireplace that held three precisely cut logs. Framed photographs on the mantle: Emily's dark Tlingit face, Bob pale and grinning. It all looked so clean and normal. How could his mother be comfortable here?

Vivian came back in with a tray bearing two delicate cups of instant coffee and a can of evaporated milk. "Sorry, this is the only milk we've got in the house right now. I meant to get to the store."

Since when had she started apologizing? It wasn't her style.

Vivian lit a cigarette, put it down. She moved in nervous,

jerky little motions that he wasn't used to. Her eyes looked tired and there was a soft, putty cast to her skin. She'd gained weight.

"You look good," Sonny lied.

"I'm getting fat." She patted her rounded belly. "Ever since I quit drinking I been eating candy like crazy. I heard that drinking gives you a sugar imbalance, so you crave carbohydrates, you know?" She picked up her cigarette again and fumbled with it.

The coffee tasted foul. What he needed was another straight shot. "So where you got to be in half an hour?" He glanced at his watch. It was already eight-fifteen.

"Kind of a meeting. Well, not kind of. Listen, I thought you might come with me and see it, and then we could talk after?"

"Sure." He couldn't imagine what kind of meeting, but since he was an hour late, he had no right to squawk.

"Great. You know, we better run." Vivian jumped up, her lit cigarette forgotten.

"Don't you want to open your present?" Sonny felt a little miffed that she'd forgotten that, too.

"Oh, Sonny, of course I do. I got a present for you, too, and one to take back to Mikey. I'm mailing packages to the girls. But let's open them when we get back, okay? We're going to be late."

They walked quickly along the icy sidewalk, Sonny taking his mother's arm. Vivian prattled on about the part-time job she'd landed as an aide at the hospital, something Emily had arranged. It bothered him that she'd taken a job; it sounded so permanent.

"There it is!" Vivian pointed to a Catholic church across the street. A church? Maybe it was bingo, but she'd never gotten excited about bingo at home. At the basement entry, Vivian said, "Just try not to judge. Try to listen. Okay? I just want you to know what I'm into."

They entered a dreary basement room with metal folding

chairs facing a table behind which hung a scroll: THE TWELVE STEPS OF ALCOHOLICS ANONYMOUS. Sonny stared at his mother in amazement. This was what she'd gotten herself into? There was AA at home in Vladimir, a group of sad sacks who met in the church and tried to convert everyone into holy rollers. He couldn't believe his mom had turned into one of them.

The room was crowded with people chatting, hugging each other, looking far smilier than he'd have expected at a club for losers. He felt self-conscious, afraid that people would mistake him for one of their own, and at the same time like an intruder, in danger of being caught and thrown out.

"Let's sit up close," Vivian said, leading him to the third row. "I want to be able to hear good."

When Sonny sat down, a young man his own age in a business suit turned and stuck out his hand for a shake. "I'm Joe," the guy said, pumping away, giving Sonny a big, gap-toothed smile. "Is this your first time? I haven't seen you here before."

Sonny shrugged ambiguously to get the guy off his back. He'd never shaken hands with a guy in a business suit in his life. In front of him sat an Indian woman wearing maroon stretch pants, knitting with huge needles, the size of those giant pencils kids in second grade love. The item she was knitting from orange wool closely resembled an airport windsock. On her left sat a grizzled fisherman with a rum blossom nose and a dirty halibut hat. His eyes were closed, and he looked in danger of nodding off. To the right of the knitter, a young woman with shag cut auburn hair sat rigid in her seat. She wore a stylish wool blazer, narrow grey wool skirt, nylons, high heels. She kept sliding her foot nervously in and out of one of her shoes. Probably a secretary in one of the government offices. What was she doing here?

The meeting hadn't begun, and already a dense cloud of cigarette smoke lay trapped under the low watt bulbs suspended from the ceiling. A fifty-cup electric percolator was making loud gargling noises at the back of the room. The walls of the church basement were drab yellow, spotted with water stains. Inane slogans hung at intervals over the peeling plaster: First Things First, Keep It Simple, Live and Let Live. Sonny sighed and stared ahead, keeping his eyes off his mother.

A middle-aged man with the flattened nose and scarred face of a logger sat down at the table. "My name's Stan and I'm an alcoholic," he said.

"Hi Stan!" everyone in the room, including Vivian, shouted cheerfully. Sonny cringed.

"I want to welcome you to the Thursday night meeting of the Saint Ignatius branch of Alcoholics Anonymous. AA is a fellowship of men and women whose only requirement is a desire to stop drinking and a commitment to help others to stop drinking. Anyone is welcome, but we do ask that if you've had a drink in the past twenty-four hours, you refrain from sharing in the open discussion which will follow the qualification."

Sonny leaned away from Joe, wondering if the whiskey he'd had at the Timberland could be smelled by the people around him. Vivian must have smelled it, but she hadn't said anything. She sat staring ahead, her eyes fixed on Stan.

"And now, to share with us her experience, strength, and hope, please welcome Lillian S." Stan started clapping and was joined by the entire room. Sonny clapped mechanically, trying not to look at his watch. How long was this going to last?

A round-faced, grey-haired, bespectacled elementary schoolbook version of a grandmother took a seat beside Stan. "My name's Lillian and I'm an alcoholic," she said.

"Hi Lillian!"

Sonny's skin crawled. These people were such morons. Look Dick. Look Jane. See Gramma Drink.

"Hi. Well, my story goes a long way back, just like me, ha-ha. I was a drunk for thirty-seven years, until AA and my higher power helped me to put the plug in the jug and find serenity and a new life. I been sober now twelve years, one day at a time, and I call myself a grateful alcoholic." Lillian beamed.

Grateful? What was this shit?

"When I first started drinking, it was the twenties and I was living down in Frisco and it was the thing to do, flappers and jazz age and all that stuff. And I did it all, believe me. Then I met a man who was a big drinker too, which I thought was just dandy . . ."

Sonny began to drift off. Who needed this? Everyone in Vladimir and probably half of Juneau had a tale about how they started drinking. So what's new? He looked around the room. They were all, including his mom, leaning forward in their seats as though this old broad Lillian was going to tell them their fortunes or something. He studied the scroll behind Lillian's head.

1. We admitted we were powerless over alcohol — that our lives had become unmanageable.

Okay, he could see how his mom could relate to that.

2. Came to believe that a power greater than ourselves could restore us to sanity.
3. Made a decision to turn our will and our lives over to the care of God as we understood him.

He just couldn't believe his mother had gotten religion. She who always said she couldn't stand preaching, who hated the hypocritical Vladimir holy rollers worse than anything. She was ready to believe in fairy tales now?

Lillian was still droning on. ". . . It was about that time that I got out of my third rehab down in San Diego, and when I started drinking again a week later, that's when I finally bottomed out and became ready to turn my will and my life over to a power greater than myself. I said, 'God, it's your turn, 'cause I can't do it myself.' I won't say it's been smooth sailing, but as I say, I'm a grateful alcoholic, 'cause I've been given a chance to learn how to live."

Everyone began to clap wildly. Sonny didn't get it. She was a drunk, and then she wasn't a drunk, but she hadn't explained how she'd gone from one state to the other. It was connected to something called "bottoming out" and "higher power," but that kind of faith was impossible, something for people who'd knocked a few teeth off the gears in their brains. They hadn't just stopped drinking, they'd stopped thinking.

Stan held up a small basket and said, "We have no dues or fees but we do have expenses, so please give as generously as you can." The basket moved down the first row, and everyone started digging in their pockets. Sonny put a dollar in as it came by. Joe in the suit gave him another gap-toothed, too friendly smile. Vivian touched his knee. Now people were raising their hands like kids in school. Lillian called on the Indian woman sitting in front of him. She put her knitting down.

"I'm Maureen and I'm an alcoholic," she said.

"Hi Maureen!"

"Hi. I just got to share that I'm feeling so low today I think I ain't gonna make it. I been getting drink signals, you know? I can't even turn on the TV, 'cause I'm afraid someone's gonna be lifting a glass. I'm scared I'm gonna slip."

"You got yourself here, Maureen. You're taking care of yourself," Lillian counseled. "Remember, it's one day at a time. You only got to not pick up a drink today."

"I'm John and I'm an alcoholic." A voice from the back of the room.

"Hi John!"

"I'm Chris and I'm an alcoholic."

"Hi Chris!"

"I'm Vivian, and I'm an alcoholic."

"Hi Vivian!"

Sonny stared ahead, his heart pounding.

"Hi. I want to share tonight that my boy Sonny's sitting beside me and . . ."

Sonny flushed with shame, the eyes of the room on him.

". . . I'm real happy about that, real happy. But it's hard. There's so much fear coming up now, fear I guess I always had but I never let myself admit it, I was always covering it up with the booze. I don't know. I feel real bad about the things I put my kids through, and I feel bad that I can't go home for Christmas, but I know I'm not ready yet. Anyway, thanks for letting me say what's on my mind."

Vivian reached over and took Sonny's hand. He stared ahead, unable to look at her. Her hand felt soft and damp and repugnant. He knew he should squeeze it, pat it, do something, but he couldn't.

It was time for the anniversaries, everyone clapping like maniacs for years, months, days of sobriety as though for dollars on "Let's Make a Deal." Sonny suffered through a hand-holding rendition of the Serenity Prayer with Joe clamped onto his hand like death. "Keep coming back," Joe said.

Sure. In a million years.

All he could think of was how he wanted to be out of there and someplace comfortable, like the nearest bar. Vivian wanted to introduce him to her "sponsor," a skinny little white woman with the bright bulging eyes of a terrier. Then he had to wait for her to go through a hugs and kisses routine with people who wanted to take *his* hand and welcome him to this club he had no intention of joining.

They walked back toward Emily's, ice cracking under their boots on the sidewalk, past houses cheerily lit with blinking Christmas lights. Sonny was silent. He just didn't know what to say.

"So what did you think?" Vivian asked.

"I guess if you think it helps . . ."

"You don't have to approve, Sonny. It's something I *got* to do. You know, for the first time I really feel like there's people that understand me, you know, people are on my side?"

Hadn't he always been on her side? He felt vaguely insulted. "So now you got God on your side, too," he said.

"I don't know about God, Sonny. I really don't know what I believe, I just know it works. Before AA I was killing myself, and I'm not killing myself anymore, at least for today. You know, two days after I got up here I started drinking again. Emily promised she wouldn't call you if I went into the hospital rehab. Without meetings, I don't know where I'd be right now. I don't know about God, I just know I can't do it on my own. I think of the group as my higher power, or as my sponsor says, I just call it G-O-D — good orderly direction. It doesn't matter what you call it as long as you surrender your will."

Surrender? That meant giving up, not giving a damn, letting everything fall apart so that everyone could make fun of you and make you feel like a fool. Surrender was *not* the name of the game. He never thought he'd see the day when his mother gave up like that. He turned to look at her. "So you aren't coming home for Christmas?"

"I really wish I could. I know they got meetings at home, but I got to get ninety days and ninety meetings in sobriety first before I make any changes. I know it sounds selfish, but there's only one thing I care about now, and that's not picking up a drink, one day at a time."

Did they all talk the same bullshit? He felt resentful and ashamed of himself for feeling that way. Why did he feel like he'd somehow been tricked, aced out? He should be glad she wasn't drinking. It was no skin off his nose.

Vivian offered to make him a sandwich at Emily's, but he refused. Eating was the last thing he wanted to do. Vivian opened her present, oohed and ahhed, and kissed him. He dutifully opened his: a shearling vest and matching shearling gloves. Where did she think she was getting the money for all this? It shamed him to think that Emily might have paid. Then he remembered. Her job.

Vivian clutched her sweater to her chest. "Sonny? You haven't seen Nick around, have you? I keep wondering how he's doing."

In fact, he had run into Nick a few days ago in the Potlatch, and Nick had asked him to give Vivian his regards, but for some low reason he didn't feel like passing it on. "I don't know," he said. "Okay, I guess."

Vivian sighed and stood up, started fussing with the coffee cups, the ashtray. Sonny gathered up his gift and the one for Mikey. At the door he allowed his mother to kiss him, but he didn't feel anything. Vivian kept on apologizing for not having made him dinner, for not coming back to Vladimir with him. "I just wish I could make it all up to you," she said.

He steeled himself against her words. If AA was supposed to be helping her, why was she suddenly so weak and pitiful? Why was she turning into someone he didn't know?

The cab she'd called for honked on the street. "Take it easy," Sonny said, turning into the cold Juneau air with relief. He watched her waving at him from the doorway as the cab drew away.

Allie was sitting up in bed reading one of her new books when he walked in. She looked happier to see him than a person ought to look. "How'd it go?" she asked. "How is she?"

"Okay." He sat down on the end of the bed with his back to her and struggled to pull off his boots. Leaning over made his head whirl.

"Just okay? Is that all? Has she been drinking up here? When's she coming home?"

"I said, she's *okay*. What are you, the FBI?"

"Sorry," Allie said softly. He could hear the hurt in her voice. Why was she apologizing when he was the one who should? Everyone was apologizing tonight. He'd been late for

Vivian, late getting back, thanks to another stop at the Timberland, and now he was biting Allie's head off for asking perfectly normal questions.

He relented. "She's going to stay up here a while."

Allie crawled out of the covers and reached a hand out to stroke his back. "You know, I missed you, Sonny. It wasn't fun without you. I watched the dumbest sci-fi movie on TV and got a burger in the coffee shop. You wouldn't believe how much it cost. You know, I was thinking. Maybe next time we could go visit your sister in Sitka. I've never been to Sitka." She kissed the side of his jaw, then pulled back. "Sonny, did you go drinking? Why didn't you come here first and get me? I would've gone with you."

He wanted to say, Because I didn't feel like it. Why didn't she just back off? There was no point in doing anything else mean, so he got up and dropped his shirt on the bed. "I'm going to take a shower," he said.

In the bathroom he ran the water hot and stood under the nozzle, letting the room fill up with steam. He didn't feel like turning it off and having to face her questions and her hopeful eyes, which were sure to be hurt now. There was something about her that almost begged to be hit sometimes. What did she want from him, anyway? She was trying to turn him into some kind of answer, the way his mother had tried for years, but it wouldn't work. One of these days Allie would wake up and see that he wasn't the man in the suit, he wasn't an exotic businessman from South America, he wasn't whatever it was that she was trying to turn him into. And one thing he knew for sure: he didn't want to be around to see what it would be like when she figured it out. He was going to be the one left with nothing, and he didn't need to see that at all.

He finally got out of the shower, and wrapped a towel around his waist. The mirror was obscured by steamy condensation. He wiped a circle and stared at his reflection. His face wouldn't take shape. He realized he was drunk.

"I'm Sonny and I'm an alcoholic," he whispered at his

blurred reflection. "Fuck you, Sonny," he answered himself.

He sat down on the closed lid of the toilet and put his head in his hands. He was trapped, trapped in Vladimir, trapped into a twelve-hour ferry ride back to Vladimir with Allie tomorrow, trapped inside himself. If he could, he'd just sit in this steamy room and never come out. He waited and waited until the light switched out in the bedroom and he waited some more. When he finally went in, Allie was either asleep or pretending to be, which was good enough for him.

"**I** DON'T CARE. Even if you are the orneriest barmaid at the Takine Inn, I'll hire you on my boat," Morgan said. He grinned, displaying greenish, fuzzy teeth. He had a pale, freckled, boyish face that was puffy from drinking; a Huckleberry Finn gone to rot.

"No, thanks," Allie replied. She stood, leaning her elbows on the counter of the waitress station at the end of the bar, beneath a sagging Christmas garland and shiny cardboard lettering that announced "Happy New Year!" It would be New Year's in a couple of days, and Sonny hadn't yet come back from fishing. He didn't even know that she'd taken the barmaid job.

She was still hand-trolling out of the skiff occasionally, but now that she was working nights it was harder and harder to get up in time for the first tide, and it was difficult to get motivated when she hadn't caught a king in weeks. It seemed the fish had just disappeared, gone off to deeper waters, perhaps, or moved down the coast. The truth was that since running over her lines, she'd lost enthusiasm for fishing more than half a mile from town. She hated to think she'd lost her desire to fish, but instead of salmon, now Sonny was always on her mind.

Sonny was the place she lived inside her head, the country to which she traveled. Every boat whose running lights were visible through the condensation on the Takine's picture windows might be his. Every head of shiny black hair, every Indian face down the sidewalk, was a herald of hope. Every time the bar door opened . . .

She'd gone over the details of the trip back on the ferry a hundred times. Maybe it was just the aftereffects of seeing his mother, but he'd been silent and distant the entire trip. Panicky with anxiety, she'd watched his face for clues and had been too solicitous, too eager to get him coffee, unable to shut up and leave him alone. The more he withdrew, the more she needed him there.

"Come on, sweetheart," Morgan persisted. "I'll pay you twenty percent. I know that cheapskate Digger only paid you ten, and my bunks are guaranteed better, har har."

The bartender, Linda, rolled her eyes. She was a thin, pleasant Indian girl with a round face who always dressed in smart, coordinated slacks and blouses she ordered by catalogue. She'd grown up with Sonny, Henry, Frankie, and Morgan and didn't think much of them. Allie tried to elicit stories of Sonny's childhood from her, but Linda just shook her head and said they'd always run around like a pack of rats.

Allie glanced at her only customers, a logger and his family in a side booth. They had come in for dinner hours ago, and now the children lay crumpled against each other, sleeping while their parents leaned across the table, talking low and fast above the wreckage of T-bone steaks and catsup-splattered plates. She considered going over to pick up the dishes; it wasn't her job but the waitresses in the restaurant had already gone off shift. There wasn't much to do on this Tuesday evening, and so far she'd only made six bucks in tips. On a good night, or on weekends, she might make fifty or seventy, but she could see the way this night would go.

"So how come you're so ornery?" Morgan asked.

Allie sighed. "Just my nature, I guess."

"See how you are? Hey, did I ever tell you about when

Henry and me were fishing for crab up in the Aleutians? That's one gloomy place."

"How come Frankie and Sonny didn't go?" Allie asked, blushing at the need to speak Sonny's name, to hear Morgan corroborate his existence.

"Sonny was up in Fairbanks, in college, and Frankie was in Nam shooting gooks. Anyway, one time we were in this bar, and I got arguing with this guy who had a wooden leg. The bastard kept saying Southeast wasn't even a part of Alaska, just the leftovers of British Columbia that the Russians threw away. He was getting on my nerves. I just kept buying him drinks, and when he passed out, I went down to the boat and came back with a hammer and nailed that sucker's wooden foot right to the goddamn floor! No shit!"

Two seats down the bar a big, bad-natured halibutter in a red flannel shirt and suspenders frowned at Morgan. As far as Allie could tell, all halibut fishermen were nasty; it required a certain kind of man to fish for something that weighed three hundred pounds and had to be shot when pulled aboard.

"You know," the halibutter said, "I think I heard as much shit out of you as I can stand tonight."

A little ripple of interest went through the audience, which consisted of a toothless old-timer, two mill workers, and Nick.

"Hey, you big tub of lard," Morgan said. "Why don't you drink your beer and keep your trap shut? I got to teach you a lesson?" Morgan squared his blocky little shoulders and cocked a fist.

In two steps the halibutter was on top of him, holding him aloft by the collar. "Wise up, you little punk, or I'll squash you like a bug."

"He's a big sucker, ain't he?" Morgan stage-whispered. He giggled. "Uh, negative on that lesson."

"You guys just cut it out," Linda said, "or I'll throw you

both out of here. You're all just bored and acting like a bunch of babies."

Morgan began to sing "Baby Love," and the halibutter lurched back to his stool.

The door opened and Allie spun around, hoping, but it was only six Japanese businessmen in black suits with skinny ties who had come to town to survey their holdings, either the cannery or the lumber mill.

"Good tippers," Linda whispered, nodding in the direction of the Japanese, who took a round table in the center of the room.

Allie went over and got their orders. "Six Chivas. Four on the rocks, two straight up," she told Linda.

"Cheezus," Morgan said. "They're getting rich off us."

The halibutter turned to give the businessmen an evil look. "Bastards are ruining the bottom fish with their goddamn factory boats and their forty-mile nets. Picking everything up off the bottom, dragging it all to shit."

In the face of the yellow peril, Morgan joined forces with his enemy of a moment before. "What we ought to do is blow them off the face of the earth," he said to the halibutter. "Them and the fucking Russkies. No offense, Nick."

Nick smiled sardonically.

"Torpedo them!" the old-timer said, his first words of the evening beyond "whiskey and water."

"Maybe I ought to go over there and see if they want to engage in a little hari-kari," Morgan offered.

"You will *not*," Linda warned.

Allie carried the drinks over to the Japanese. One of them reached up and tried to touch her breast as she leaned over with her tray. She considered slapping his hand but decided not to start an international incident. Good tippers. She turned away to pick up empties and another order from the logger and his wife. The logger's haggard wife was insisting, "It couldn't be helped. Honest to God, Arlie, it just couldn't be helped." She didn't even seem to notice Allie's presence.

Wiping a table that didn't need it, Allie looked up at the sound of the door opening and saw Sonny walk in with his arm around Brenda.

It felt like being kicked in the chest. She was swept by nausea, a heart-pounding wave that took away her breath. Head down, she grabbed the plates off the logger's table, dropping a bone on the floor, and rushed into the kitchen, where Herbie, the feeble-brained dishwasher, was mopping the floor. The little Indian girl had gone back to her island.

"You got more for me?" Herbie bitched. "Those damn waitresses never clean up before going off shift. It's about time I made a real stink." Herbie shook his mop in annoyance, spraying grey water over his shoes.

Allie lowered the dishes onto the gleaming aluminum counter, bent over, and lay her head on her folded arms beside the dirty plates and the spray nozzle. Her back shook.

Why did he have to be such a bastard? She knew he cared about her. And now she had to go back out there and serve them drinks?

"Hey, honey, I didn't mean nothing, it ain't your fault," Herbie said nervously. "Hey, honey, forget it, don't cry." She stood and wiped her eyes with the back of her wrist.

"That's better, sweetheart," Herbie said cheerfully. "Look on the bright side. I'm the one's got to wash up this mess."

"What?" She gave Herbie an uncomprehending glance and headed back out.

Sonny and Brenda were still standing at the bar talking to Morgan. Brenda smiled evenly at Allie. She was wearing a Black Hills of Dakota T-shirt and no bra. She was pretty — a long-boned, slender Indian girl — but there was something tough about her, something crazy in her eyes. The kind of girl who'd want to fight.

"Hey, Sonny," Morgan said, "you met my little sweetheart Allie here? She's gonna be my deckhand come spring. I'm gonna hire her on."

Was it possible that Morgan didn't know? She thought

everyone in Vladimir knew everyone else's business. Had she and Sonny been that discreet?

"You'll get rich fishing with Morgan," Sonny said, shuffling nervously. "He's a highliner." He didn't even have the nerve to meet her eyes. "So what happened to hand trolling? You finally get smart?"

"Something like that," Allie said. Her voice was flat, dead in her own ears. What had she done to be punished like this? She watched Sonny and Brenda take a table at the back of the room.

"Hey, what are you, anyway?" Morgan inquired. "Some kind of gypsy with those big brown eyes?"

"I'm Swedish," Allie hissed. "Can't you tell?"

Nick gave her a glance.

"Damn, you're hard to get along with," Morgan said. "See how you are?"

Linda opened the register and handed Allie a pile of quarters. "Here," she said. "Why don't you play us some music?"

Allie punched every he-done-me-wrong song on the juke box.

Overnight, it had snowed, just the tiniest dusting in town, but the logging cuts across the bay were shaded white. Allie wanted it to snow and snow, to be enveloped by a white blanket so she wouldn't have to feel anymore. On Front Street the puddles were frozen. She took a skid and remembered something from her childhood: lining up behind a row of girls with bony knees on a cold New England playground to take her turn sliding across a frozen puddle. How mysterious the thin black ice had seemed, with its shatter lines and the silhouette of a trapped leaf. She'd imagined whole worlds under there, hidden from view, like the worlds under the sea.

When she was little, there was so much snow. They dug tunnels and honeycombs into fifteen-foot snow banks heaped by the plow, and when the snow was soft and deep they fell backward into it and made angels, waving their arms and legs. Jane O'Malley, from across the street, said you could see angels if you looked into the sky before it rained, but all Allie could see were tiny pinpoints, floating circles like dust on the surface of her eyes.

Her father had played a game with her on the ice behind his factory, making the car spin and twirl on a frozen puddle, howling, to make her scared. She loved it, sitting silent beside him, the heater blowing hot air on her frozen toes, the windshield jagged with ice. She sat entranced while the headlights inscribed a magic circle and they spun and spun and spun.

Now these pieces of her own history seemed so distant. She almost believed she'd never lived anywhere else but in Vladimir, never thought of anything else but Sonny — Sonny and Brenda in the Takine Inn last night . . . It made her scared. Without Sonny she'd have nothing to fill up the spaces.

Front Street ended in a pile of gravel just past the ferry terminal, giving way to a path that cut through alder thickets, hemlock, and frozen tufted muskeg, running along a stream rimmed with ice. Her breath shot ahead in frozen vapor. The branches hung low and dark, then opened suddenly to brightness, the expanse of pebbly beach and glittering bay. Steam rose off the ocean like a great cauldron of soup. She stopped and felt the weight lift. It seemed she hadn't been out of the artificial light of a bar in years.

A few hundred yards down the beach Nick's cabin sat under a curl of chimney smoke. It was a box of weathered clapboards surrounded by piles of driftwood and stacked cut logs. Up close she saw that log slices had been set into sand to make a path. Her mother, who had always wanted a railroad tie patio, would have approved. Around the cabin lay fuel cans, splitting mauls, saws, a rain barrel, carvings. One of the carvings looked like a Jimmy Caldwell totem; the rest were larger versions of Nick's chess set, a hierarchy of perfectly shaped fish.

Allie hesitated, decided that anything was better than the bar today, and knocked. No answer. She heard a halloo and turned to see Nick appear from behind a half-rotted boat, dragging a large piece of driftwood and carrying a chain saw. She walked toward him, preceded by plumes of breath. "You've got the best view in town," she said.

"I pay for it. No water, no electricity, but it is worth it, I think. So, you decided to become chess player?" He smiled, his blue eyes bright against the red of his cold cheeks. Even in his down parka he looked angular, a small, stooped man barely taller than she.

"I guess."

"Good. First I will give to you tour." He waved toward his cabin. "My house." He gestured toward the ocean, the beach. "My yard, my museum. I will show to you petroglyphs."

"What?"

"Pet-ro-glyphs. Rock carvings. They are everywhere here at low tide. Look." He pointed to a rock with a flat surface about ten feet away, jutting up from the sand. Allie went over and saw the faint outline of an etched face with round eyes and a gaping mouth. She walked farther and found a killer whale, then other rocks with curlicues and figures of abstract design. Some were in sharp relief, others were worn smooth by the tide.

Nick sat down on a log and lit a Pall Mall. A seal bobbed past, swimming on its back. When Nick raised his hand to toss the match away, the seal ducked under the surface. Allie sat down beside him. "They're amazing," she said. "Where are they from?"

"No one knows. There are theories. Some say they are eight thousand years old, made by people from Siberia who walked across land bridge when Russia and Alaska were one land."

"What do they mean?"

"No one is sure. Some anthropologists say they were sites of blood sacrifice."

Allie shivered. "Ugh. What a thought."

Nick laughed. "I would not mind to die in such lovely place. You know, Allie, I have my own theory. I think they say, 'Remember.' To where those people went? We do not know why they left. Perhaps war, bad fishing, who knows? They lived here, they left, and rocks speak for them. I like it. My little Stonehenge."

Remember. Allie looked out at the bay. It was the same view those carvers must have seen, save for the channel marker where she used to fish and the logging cuts on the islands. Clouds had come up and the falling sun cut through them, turning the light oblique. She committed this picture to memory: late afternoon in winter, a day in her life that would never return. It seemed like memory already. Why did this land break her heart? Even in this moment of perception, it felt as though it were something she'd already lost.

"Alinka, you are freezing?"

She nodded. Her toes, even in double socks inside her rubber boots, were numb. They walked back to the cabin in the falling light. The tide was just past slack and starting its creep up the beach. The swirls and designs and faces would soon be under water. She remembered the face she'd seen that first time, fishing with Digger, the face so much like her own. "Nick, did you see me from your cabin when I was fishing in the skiff? I used to pass right by here."

"I saw you."

They reached the cabin door, and when he opened it, the heat from his oil drum stove was welcoming. Allie took off her jacket and boots and stood holding her palms over the ticking metal while Nick bustled about with a kettle. It was a one-room cabin, with a spectacular picture window view of the bay. In one corner stood a neatly made narrow bed with a fluffy comforter. Against the wall was a dining table with hand-carved chairs. There were two overstuffed chairs by the stove, a low table with a chess set in mid-game, dark landscape paintings on the walls, and a shelf full of hardbound books, volumes of poetry in English beside Cyrillic titles: Eliot, Roethke, Neruda. Allie ran a finger across the books' spines, trying to imagine this fisherman, Nick, reading poetry.

Nick set the kettle on the stove and carried a tray of cups, cookies, a tiny china teapot, and a bottle of Hudson Bay 151 proof rum to the table. "You will have rum in your tea?"

"Sure." Allie's fingers felt better now, but her toes pinched as they thawed. She sat in one of the two armchairs and propped her feet up in front of the stove.

Nick poured the tea, a strong solution, from the china pot, and then added water from the kettle and a dash of rum. He said, "This is very good rum. It does not freeze when I am gone." They sat in the armchairs staring at the stove, and Nick lit a cigarette. Allie felt groggy and relaxed from the heat and the rum. She wouldn't mind living in a cabin like this. She could call it home.

"Allie. You look very much like woman I knew long ago."

"Everyone tells me I look like someone they know. I guess I have a common face."

Nick smiled. "You are fishing for compliment? You know you do not have common face. It is not common but familiar. Perhaps your eyes are to blame."

Allie put her cup down. What did he, a grey-haired man holding a teacup with gnarled, veined hands, want from her? Everyone always talked about her eyes. All the old drunks wanted to tell her their tales because she had "sympathetic" eyes. But she wasn't really sympathetic, only curious. She hated it when people misread her appearance. When she was a teenager, men had begun to say she was sexy, strangers on the street would follow her, ask her out. She began to act the part without believing the role. It was their idea and she was an impostor. Finally, it was easier to wear bulky men's clothes. Now she was afraid Nick was going to reach out and touch her and ruin the afternoon, and afraid he wouldn't, because that was the only way she knew how to be with a man.

"Yes," Nick said thoughtfully, "you resemble her very much. But perhaps it is something else I feel. You are to me familiar, because you remind me of myself, long ago. Allie, we are both fish out of water."

"What do you mean?"

"Alyusha, tell me. Why you are in Vladimir?" He tilted his head like a dog hearing a whistle in a frequency too high for human ears. He was tuned to some secret vibration of hers, some fluttering heartstring she'd tried to damp. She was afraid he might tell her something about herself she didn't want to know.

"You sound like Sonny," she said, hating herself for bringing his name up. "He's always asking why I'm here." Sonny, Sonny. What had she read once, about how we always stick our tongues into a toothache, needing to domesticate the pain?

"What do you answer?"

"I don't know. I keep thinking there's something I haven't learned yet, something I need to know."

"And you think Sonny will teach you?" Nick stood and opened the stove door. Embers flashed bright. He wedged in a few more chunks of driftwood and slammed the cast iron door shut.

"Maybe. I don't know." She slipped low in her chair, to protect herself against the question.

"Perhaps you expect too much?"

"I don't expect anything from anybody," she said, but the words rang false in her ears. She expected everything all the time, no matter how many times she didn't get it. "Listen," she said. "Sonny's got a lot more going for him than people know, but he thinks he has to fit in. He could be someone, if it weren't for Vladimir."

"You have such contempt for this town you have chosen?"

"I don't have contempt. I love it here." Love-hate. The old merry-go-round, the only one she knew. She was getting confused. Why was she defending Sonny when Nick had witnessed the scene last night? She was humiliating herself. "I don't care about him now," she said. "It's obvious he doesn't give a shit about me."

"I do not think that is true," Nick said gently. "Sonny cares, in his way. Allie, you think I speak badly of Sonny? I like Sonny very much, but I am thinking now of you. I knew you were in trouble the first time I saw you."

In trouble . . . If he saw it, then Sonny had seen it, and maybe that's why he'd done what he had. There was something wrong with her that people could see when they got close enough. It was something she'd always suspected. She was like a vase that had been knocked off a shelf and broken, then glued back together. From a distance she looked fine, but up close all the little cracks and the glue showed. Sonny had known . . .

Allie looked into Nick's eyes. The black points of the irises seemed to shift eerily inside the pale blue — a kaleidoscope, eyes of fractured glass. She was suddenly angry. "Why did you invite me here if you think I'm in trouble? What are you, some kind of social worker who likes being around messed-up people? Or are you just trying to get laid?"

Nick put his head back and laughed. "A fair enough question. Alinka, I am not so bad as you think, though I am very bad. I am selfish. I invite you because I like you. I want that we should be friends. Let us begin again." He rose a bit stiffly from his chair and bowed. "I wish to make your acquaintance. I am called Nikolai Alexandrovich Kerelinsky."

Allie stood and took the hand that Nick proffered. "Allison Elizabeth Heller."

"Very pleased," Nick said. They shook hands solemnly. Allie warily smiled.

He went to the table and lit a kerosene lamp suspended on the wall. From a shelf he took the bundled chessboard he'd brought to the Anchor and began to smooth out the patchwork leather. Allie examined a painting of a dark canal, statues of horses rearing wildly on a bridge, grey sky, a Cyrillic signature. "What's this?"

226

"Leningrad. Anichkov Most — Bridge — and Fontanka Canal."

"You bought it here?"

"I painted it here. From the heart, or as they say in Russia, from soul."

Allie tried to imagine Nick walking along that bridge, past statues of rearing horses. How different his life must have been in that world: no petroglyphs at low tide but wrought iron railings, cast bronze.

"Nick, why'd you leave there?"

"You are not so eager to learn chess?"

"I am, but I'd like to know."

"It is long story and not pretty."

"Please tell me. You said we're alike."

Nick sat down at the table and slowly set the chessmen into place. "Well. When I was young man, there was great patriotic war for fatherland. You say World War Two. I was finishing then training at institute. I was scientific illustrator, little bit artist, but only little. Then I was soldier. I was taken prisoner, to Germany. Perhaps now I am alive because I was prisoner, who knows? You know how many died in Russia during the war? Twenty million. Why they died is another story. I am not speaking of Stalin's camps." Nick looked up.

"And?"

"I was two years prisoner. When we were liberated, there was great confusion. It was Americans who freed us, by the way. I heard many things in camp, many rumors. I heard that Russian soldiers were being sent home, and there they were also imprisoned, shot as traitors. It was considered collaboration to be prisoner."

"How could that be possible? It isn't fair."

"Fair?" Nick snorted. "It was Stalin. He disowned his own son for such crime. So, I heard rumor, maybe true, maybe not true. I decided I would not go home. Allie, do not think I did not love my country. I love her still. But I also wanted to live.

And there was something else which is difficult to explain you. I saw for me chance. All my life I never was beyond Baltic until war, and here was chance to see world. You cannot understand what it means to grow up and think you will never in your life see another country, never go beyond frontier." Nick pressed a finger to the windowpane and drew a squiggly line in the rime. The hollows under his high cheekbones filled with shadow in the flickering light of the lamp, and his eyes looked black now. "So, home to be shot, maybe, or chance to see world. What would you choose?"

Although she couldn't imagine facing such a decision, it was a question with only one answer.

"So, I arranged. It was not so difficult. Europe was chaos. I got false papers, I slipped through. Switzerland, France. But everywhere I went, I wanted another place. It was like disease, you know? Mania, to keep moving. I traveled west, farther west, to America, and finally to here. Alaska was not even state then, only territory. I came to this island and I thought, now there is no place farther to go. Across that sea, Russia again. I was at end of Western world. And so I am here."

"And you've never been . . ." she started to say "home" but stopped herself, remembering his words at the Anchor Lounge: I am home. "You've never been back?"

"Never. To them I am criminal. I betrayed." He smiled bitterly.

"Do you miss it?"

"Very much."

So the two of them were fish out of water. Then why did he call this place home? "Nick, what about your family. You must have had family. Were you married back there?"

"I was." He tapped the chessman on the table. "But that is enough history for today. Soon it will be late, and your lesson has not begun. You see, I arrange pieces so. King, queen, knight, rook, pawn. Now I will explain you rules. Alyusha, you are ready?"

So they began.

"Hey doll, over here!" Morgan called. He turned to Sonny, Frankie, and Henry as Allie passed with her tray. "You get the feeling she don't like us?"

"Maybe she don't like you," Henry said. "I don't blame her. I don't like you."

"Hey doll, we're thirsty," Morgan insisted.

Allie came over to the table. "Yeah? What do you want?"

"What are you giving away?" Morgan asked.

"Look, I'm busy. What do you want to drink?"

"Hey, don't get hostile. I like my women hog-style, dog-style, any style but hostile."

Frankie cackled in appreciation.

"Give me a break," Allie said.

"Boy is she a sweetheart," Morgan complained. "What's the matter? I thought she liked you, Sonny."

"Not tonight," Sonny said.

Allie didn't look at him.

"Don't let these turkeys bother you, Allie," Henry said. We'll have a Jim Beam straight up, two Olys, and a Ranier."

Over at the barmaid station, Allie leaned on her elbows. Sonny came up to the bar and sat a few stools away. "You aren't still mad at me, are you?" he asked, leaning toward her with a supplicating grin.

"I'm not mad, I'm just dumb," Allie said, slapping the counter with her bar rag. She'd worked the whole of New Year's Eve, running with trays, watching him out of the corner of her eye as he sat with Frankie, Henry, and Morgan, pushing past him without a word. He hadn't been with Brenda, he hadn't been with anyone as far as she knew, unless he'd gone off to a party when the bar finally closed. She'd just gone back to the boat to collapse.

"Oh, come on. I've known that girl a lot longer than I've known you."

"You don't know me," Allie said.

"Come on," Sonny urged. "Don't be like that."

Allie ignored him.

"So," he said in the direction of Linda, who was tending bar, but loud enough for Allie to hear, "we've hung it up for the season. No more herring. Now I'm a free man."

"Yeah?" Linda asked, searching for beer in the cooler. "What are you going to do with your free time?"

"Oh, I don't know." Sonny looked back at Allie and smiled. "Catch up with friends."

Allie didn't respond.

Sonny shrugged. "Maybe I'll see about going on down to check out Denver. You know, take a little vacation."

Allie looked up, suddenly furious that he thought he could humiliate her with Brenda and then come back in the bar a week later and pick her up like that.

"Denver? That's a laugh," she said. "You'll never go to Denver. You'll just spend your whole life talking about it."

Sonny's mouth opened in surprise, gaping like a caught fish, a wordless sucking for air that made her hate him, made her want to yank the hook and rip at his guts.

"You're as bad as Smiley with his Ireland," she said. "Always talking but he'll never go because he's too goddamn scared to leave this town."

She picked up her drink tray and stomped away from the bar. When she returned, Sonny was gone. Linda removed Allie's empties from the tray.

"Allie, what did you have to go and say that to Sonny for? Maybe it's true, but that doesn't mean you have to say it. You're getting so hard, you know? Were you always like that, or is it something this town is doing to you?"

Allie put her head in her hands. "I don't know why I said it. I don't even *want* him to go to Denver."

S<small>TAPLETON</small> A<small>IRPORT</small> was full of Mexicans who looked like Indians, but they were short and noisy and chattered in high-pitched, accented English or Spanish Sonny couldn't understand. There were blacks — more than he'd ever seen — and blondes, too; not the pale washed-out Norwegians of Petersburg but glowing sunburned blondes carrying skis through the airport crowds. And there were big Marlboro men in ten-gallon hats like walking ads.

Sonny asked his cabbie to suggest a hotel. "How much you want to spend?" the guy wanted to know, and when Sonny told him, thinking in terms of Alaska prices, the driver looked back at him in the rearview mirror and raised his brows.

The Downtowner Hotel was a new high-rise with an enormous, glittering lobby, a round bar full of business suits and a three-piece band. It reminded him of the Baranof in Juneau and for a moment he wished Allie was there with him so that he wouldn't have to go up to his room alone. How had things turned so ugly so fast? He hadn't really meant to hurt her. He hadn't even known she was working as a barmaid, although it didn't surprise him to come back to town and find out. She wasn't making any money trolling. Of course, all he had to do was show up in any bar in Vladimir with Brenda and everyone in town would know in ten minutes. Why had he done it? He didn't really understand, except that Brenda had approached him and it suddenly seemed easy. All Brenda needed was attention. Allie wanted him to be someone he couldn't be, someone who would travel to Denver, and the irony was that he'd let her anger force his hand. Now here he was, in Denver, alone.

He opened the curtains in his room, but it was dark outside and he couldn't see the mountains. He didn't feel like sleeping, so he took a shower and spruced up to go down and check out the bar. He didn't know what to do about his money, so finally he put all his cash in his wallet and his airplane ticket home in his suitcase. He had fifteen hundred dollars to spend.

In the bar he drank a Coors and ate peanuts from a dish. The Coors tasted watery; he didn't know why everyone made such a fuss over it. The bartender was a busty redhead with small, hard eyes, a lot of rings, and a QT tan. Sonny wondered why she needed to fake a tan in Denver. Bartending nights, he supposed, she slept in the daytime and missed the sun. For the first half hour she smiled at him without engaging his eyes, but she warmed up as the night wore on.

"Where you from, honey?" she asked.

"Alaska."

"Alaska! No kidding. I thought you were Mexican. You look big for an Eskimo. Hey, is it true that people up there live in igloos?"

He waited until the bar closed, but the bartender only gave him a free one "for the road" and turned on the lights. Sonny went back to his room and looked through the advertising leaflets on the bedside table — car rentals, businessmen's services, travel brochures. It was his first night in town, and it seemed that something should happen, but he didn't know what.

He awoke in Denver, but he couldn't see it. His hotel room faced east, away from the mountains. Out on the street the sun was bright, and the air was cold and dry. He walked west until he got a view of the mountains. Smog lay in a pink swatch against the foothills. He took a city bus across town to the eastern outskirts. It reminded him of Fairbanks with its low buildings, rows of prefab condos, apartment complexes, housing developments, and winter-killed grass. He walked back into town and up and down the streets until his feet hurt.

In the Denver Art Museum he saw an exhibit of southwestern Indian art — blankets, turquoise and silver jewelry, rugs, weavings. None of the people walking around and looking at the objects was Indian. Culture vultures. What was he doing there? He went out and bought himself a burger and tried to figure out what to do.

In the afternoon he took a bus tour up into the mountains to see Central City, an old mining town. The bus had tinted windows and was filled with old ladies and a few mothers with whining kids. As they began to climb, snow appeared along the road until the banks were piled high. Central City didn't look like much: a tourist trap like Skagway, north of Juneau, near the Chilkoot Pass. Central City had an Old Opry House, cutesy saloons, and a place to buy genuine gold nugget jewelry. Heading back to Denver through narrow, winding Clear Creek Canyon, Sonny felt excited when the mountains gave way in a great opening. He expected the ocean, but it was only treeless plains.

That night he went out to buy some dinner but instead ended up in a honky-tonk bar, where he watched hard-hatted construction workers joking over the pool table and envied their smoky camaraderie and girlfriends in the booths. He drank too much, went back to his hotel room, and fell asleep with all his clothes on. He dreamed of ravens chattering on a tree outside his window. The ravens began to speak, but it was a language he didn't understand. In his dream, Allie was walking down the street in her rubber boots and rain pants. "Where are you going?" he kept asking her, but she wouldn't say. When he woke he had a hangover, and cars were honking on the street below.

CUTTING DRIFTWOOD with his chain saw, Nick hit a knot and the whining saw kicked back and up, missing his face by inches. He put the saw down on the hard-packed snow, squinting against a vision of metal grinding flesh. He sat on a stump and searched under the layers of down and wool for a Pall Mall. He was sweating, but his fingers striking the match began to freeze. It was too cold to be standing outside cutting wood, especially when he had enough wood cut for the next two years. Even the bay had frozen, something that happened only two or three times a year. Chunks of ice lay like shattered dishes all over the beach, and the green-grey surface of the sea now held a load of snow.

The hell with it. He'd been trying to work himself into exhaustion, and he'd almost cut off his nose. To spite himself. He laughed bitterly and gave up on the day, carrying his saw back to the cabin, stomping snow off his boots, and pulling the vodka bottle off the lowest shelf, where it was chilled but not frozen. It was the eleventh of January, his thirty-sixth wedding anniversary. A date certainly worthy of a drink, or a day of drinking.

Thirty-six years. He'd been twenty-two. This mathematics of numbers and dates added up to nothing more than a catch in the throat, an easily made mistake with a saw, a cultivated self-pity that surfaced on special occasions and yet was with him all the time. Thirty-six years. How could that be possible? He was fifty-eight, and so much of his lifetime had been devoted to Sophia, a woman he had lived with little more than a year. If only his devotion had been before the fact instead of after, he could have freed them both. Now he was forever in her debt.

He never thought of Sophia as she would look now, a woman close to sixty years of age. A Russian babushka, like his own in the village, probably a heavy woman with a lined face, a headscarf. No, Sophia would always be Sophia: black-haired, dark-eyed, like a Moldavian, a southern girl with a long dark braid and the slenderest of palms and funny-shaped little toes that bent sideways. He remembered a trip they took to Crimea, lying on pallets on the pebbled sand of the Black Sea, sunshine and sand on Sophia's bare legs. "Don't look at my toes," she said. "They're so ugly. If you see my toes, you won't love me anymore."

He raised her foot to his mouth and kissed each toe as tenderly as a mother kisses her baby's head.

"I'll always love you," he answered.

"Even when I'm old?"

"You'll never grow old." Kolya the prophet.

Now it was as clear a picture as though he held a snapshot in his hands: her fingers trailing through his own curls, which were sandy then instead of grey; the red of the sun against the back of his eyelids. If he shut his eyes, he could feel the sun baking, he could put his nose against her leg and smell the salty life of her skin. Nick closed his eyes and tasted Sophia on his tongue. He opened his eyes and saw his cabin, frost obscuring any view but making lacy patterns on the window, like the curtains of the room they'd shared on Lityenny Prospekt. He poured himself another drink.

Six hours of daylight passed easily, a series of motions: opening the door to the woodstove, poking and stoking, loading more wood, pouring vodka into the glass again and again. But the numbness he wanted wouldn't come. He lit the kerosene lamp and put leftover soup on the stove but forgot it until it burned and stuck to the pan. He hated his own indulgence, the compulsion to drag up every memory, to savor and suffer and pity himself and damn himself for what he'd done. But the vodka, which he relied on at times like these, refused to do its duty, to grant him relief and oblivion, so that he could wake up tomorrow as though from a fever and go on.

At seven someone knocked on his door. He was wrapped in a quilt in his armchair, still drinking slowly. He was surprised but unmoved by the thought of a visitor.

"It is open," he called without getting up.

Allie entered, swathed in down, a blue wool hat, and a scarf covering her mouth and nose, holding aloft a bottle. She glanced around at the cabin's unusual disarray, the bottle of vodka at his feet. "I brought you a present," she said, pulling the scarf off her face. Her hair crackled with electricity.

"Very nice."

"Nick, maybe I should come back another time. You want to be alone?"

"Not at all," Nick said. He'd thought that was exactly what he wanted, but he was glad to see her now that she was standing there in his doorway, her face red and the cold air emanating from her clothing, a reminder that there was a world beyond his chair. "Allie, you are here to play chess? I cannot play today. You would beat me too easily, and I would be shamed."

"Beat you? That'll be the day." Allie hung her jacket on a hook by the door, removed her boots, and put on an old pair of his slippers that he kept for visitors. She stopped to study the game in progress on the chessboard by the window. "Who's winning?"

"I, of course. I am always winner when I play against myself."

"Or, always loser."

"You are pessimist, Alinka. You cannot be such pessimist

and be chess player." He was amused to hear himself playing teacher with her, philosopher of optimism that he was. The need to instruct her in the arts of living, to bestow some gift on her, forced him up out of his chair and his mood. Why was it that such an unhappy creature as Allie could always bring about that change in him?

"Who said I was a chess player?" she asked.

"You are." He was pleased with how quickly she'd learned the basics. She was a passionate competitor and would take endless time to figure out her moves. Her major weakness was that, contrary to her claims of recklessness, she concentrated too much on protecting the position she had. He wanted to coax her into taking the risks necessary to an effective offense, to convince her that she could not win by defense but only by venturing forth.

Nick set Allie's glass on the table and beside it a plate with bread, his own pickled herring, and the two bottles. "You will have vodka or bourbon? If you have vodka today, you must drink it Russian style."

"What's Russian style?" She sat down at the table across from him.

Nick poured out two glasses of vodka, clinked Allie's, said "To your health," and knocked his vodka back in one gulp. He breathed out, took a bite of bread. "If we have no bread, we say, it is enough to have your company, and we sniff our sleeve. So. And you?"

Allie knocked back her glass, coughed, and bit a piece of bread. "Have you been doing this all day?"

"Yes. But without bread. You drink like true Russian, Allie. Alinka. You are Russian girl. Tell me about your Russian grandfather."

"There's not much to tell. He died when I was little. I remember my grandmother, though. All she talked about was how the Cossacks came, and she had to hide in the neighbor's cellar. She never got over it. She always thought they were coming back, even in Boston. She remembered the 1905 revolution. She was out on the street with everyone celebrating, and then there was shooting and she had to run home."

"Like Isaac Babel in Odessa. Those were hard times . . . Many times were hard times." He poured two more glasses.

"Nick, why are you drinking like this?"

"It is for me holiday." He gulped down another glass. "Today is my wedding anniversary."

"Your anniversary? It's hard to think of you married."

"Why? Most people are married at one time or another. Even you will be someday. But I was married many, many years ago. It is such an old story. Let us drink to your marriage of the future, okay?"

Allie rolled her eyes, as though that were an inconceivable thought. "Vivian wanted to marry you, didn't she?"

"Sonny told you that?"

Allie nodded, gnawing on a piece of bread, watching his face with her dark eyes. He was touched that she was actually interested in the details of his life.

"You know, when he was on my boat he talked very, very little. He was very quiet boy. So, Vivian. Yes, she would have liked to marry, but I could not." He hadn't thought of Vivian in some time, although when she'd first left, he'd noticed her absence and hoped without really believing it that she was surviving well in Juneau. Sometimes she even came to him as a longing, a lust that crept in and rattled his bones on cold nights.

"Why, because of her drinking?" Allie asked, interrupting the flow of his thoughts.

Why what? Oh, yes. Why hadn't he married her. "Perhaps if I married Vivian she would not drink so much. No, it was something else. Because of her sadness, maybe. Alinka, Vivian is very strong woman, and it is great tragedy to see her fail now. I knew her many years, before Sonny's father drowned and after, when she was raising those kids alone. It is only in past year or two that she is drinking so much. She is beautiful woman in her way, Allie. No, I did not marry her because I know that I am not good man for her. I could not give her what she needs. You understand?"

"No. Why couldn't you?"

Nick waved the question away with his hand. "Let us speak of *your* affairs of the heart. How does it go with Sonny these days?"

Allie's face fell. She was so childish with her moods, so transparent. "Terrible. Didn't you know he's gone? He left for Denver or somewhere."

"Ah, and you are sad. Do not worry, Alyusha, your Sonny will return. I am certain. Come, we will drink this time to the spring, when your Sonny will return and you will again be fisherman."

Allie stared into her glass. "It feels like spring will never come. I can't even remember what it's like, fishing. I just feel like I've been carrying drink trays forever. You know, people don't have names to me anymore. I just think of them as seven and sevens, Jim Beam straight up, or whiskey sours. Everything's all screwed up. I don't even know why I'm here. Sometimes I go sit on that old cannery dock, the abandoned one by the supermarket, and I look around and I don't know what the hell I'm doing, Nick. The mill's clanking away, steam coming out, and the boats are going away out there by Siligovsky Island. And I think, There's so much ambition. All these people who settled here must have wanted something. I mean really wanted something they could name. They cut down trees, made street signs, got a boat, or a bar, or a goddamn laundromat."

She looked at him urgently over her glass to see if he understood. He did. Hadn't he moved across continents with the same confusion, open-mouthed in the face of other people's ease of definition? It had taken him years to settle such questions for himself.

"Nick, how did they figure out how to put a name on what they wanted? When I came here, I wanted to fish so bad, and I really tried. I wanted to know all about it, to know how

240

people lived, to learn what mattered. At night I even dreamed about salmon. I don't know what happened to me. Now all I think about is Sonny, and he's not even here. I'm just like all those Vladimir women who sit around waiting for their men to come back to town. I'm worse, because I'm waiting and I don't even have anyone to wait for."

Again, he understood: waiting for someone who wasn't there to wait for, as Sophia had waited for him. As he waited now. A waiting that became an end in itself. He'd always thought he'd made his own peace, accepted his limitations as he had accepted Vladimir as his home. He was looking for no other place, but he had fooled himself, because all along he'd been waiting. Not for something to begin, but for something to end.

"Is it so bad to be like Vladimir women?" he asked gently.

"I don't *want* to be like that! I want to care about something important. I want to *do* something, but I don't know what. There's no point in caring about Sonny when he doesn't care about me, but I seem to have gotten caught up in it and I can't stop."

Nick wanted to put his arms around her, to rock her like a baby and tell her not to worry, that he understood and she would figure it all out eventually. Sonny wouldn't mean much to her as time went on. Her destiny wouldn't end here. She was so young, a third his age, and she looked so much like Sophia it hurt. He filled their glasses again and wondered just how drunk he'd become.

"I think Sonny does care about you, Alinka. But I do not think Sonny is what you really want. You deceive yourself. Tell me, if Sonny said, 'Allie, I love you, I want to marry you and put you in little house and make babies with you,' what would you say? Would that make you happy? I do not think so. You are not ready for such life, and when you are ready, I do not think it will be Sonny that you want. You want him now because you cannot have him. He is like fish that you cannot catch. He knows that. He is not stupid."

"You make it sound like I'm just screwed up and using him as an excuse or something. But I really love him. I think about him all the time."

"No, I do not think you are using him. I simply do not believe that Sonny is what you are after. Sonny is name you put on, as you say, name on what you want. It is okay."

What did she want, he wondered. There was something missing in her that she kept trying to find in the outside world, in Sonny, in fishing. Something that came from simply believing she had a right to live on this planet, a right to be loved.

Allie leaned forward on her elbows, hands under her chin. "You know, Nick, you're the only person here I can talk to. I could never talk to Sonny like I talk to you, even if you always make me feel stupid." She grinned.

Nick laughed. He was willing to accept the compliment, the favorable comparison with the younger man. "Alyusha, I admire you. You possess something very beautiful. All this searching has another side — it means hope. You are filled with endless hope." Everyone admired in others what they didn't possess or what they'd lost. It was what he'd seen in her that had reminded him of himself, of who he'd been. Did all love come down to such egotism?

"You know, this vodka's really getting me drunk," Allie said.

"Good. We will be drunk together. It is not crime."

Allie stood up and went over to the frosted picture window. She scraped off a little circle with her fingernail and put her eye close to the glass. "It's real clear out there," she said, blocking the cabin's light with her hands. "I can even see stars over the bay. You know, when I look up at the stars, I always feel scared."

"What is there to fear up there that is not here?"

Allie turned back and sat down again at the table. "It just seems so big and empty and makes me feel lost. I was afraid in the skiff, too. Sonny was always saying how I had guts to go out there, but I was scared. I'm afraid every minute of my life."

He considered offering her some bromide about courage — that brave people act despite their fear, not because they are not afraid — but he couldn't stand his own pomposity, his need to have answers for her.

"You want to believe that I am not afraid, Alinka? You will be disappointed. I am not afraid of ocean, or of stars, but I am also afraid. I am afraid of past." The words sounded grandiose and ridiculous. He pushed his glass back, got up to put more wood in the stove, and realized he was lurching. He had to put an arm on the chair to steady himself. He was truly drunk now. When he sat back down, he saw that Allie's face was flushed from the heat of the room and the vodka. Her black hair fell around her shoulders, and she'd unbuttoned her sweater, exposing a red turtleneck. Her features seemed blurry, not quite Allie anymore but more Sophia. Cheekbones, black hair, lips. This was what he feared, right here, not living and dying alone but that Sophia's face could rise at any moment to point a finger at him, to remind him of what he'd done.

"Nick, what happened to your wife in Russia?"

Could she have read his thoughts or had he said something? He was too drunk now to remember. But there was no reason not to tell her. He wanted to, so that she would know who he was, know him for what he was.

"Her name was Sophia. She was pretty girl with black hair, like you. A student also, in my institute. We married. Simple. Then came war, I was prisoner as I told you. Sophia was in Leningrad when I left. You have heard of blockade of Leningrad? For three years fascists surrounded city, cut it off. So many died. They had no fuel, no food. How did they live? I of course heard all this later . . ."

"She died there, in the blockade?"

243

Yes, he thought. Why not? She could have died in the blockade. It could have been like that, so simple. He put his head down and said, "Yes."

"That's awful. You must have thought if you were there you could've helped her, but of course you had no choice." She reached across the table and put her hand on his. A soft hand, despite the fishing. A hand like Sophia's.

"No," he said. "I am lying." He hit the table and the glasses rattled. "Why I am lying to you? We have no secrets, Alinka. No, she did not die in blockade. She survived. I received letter from her. I do not know how it got to me in France, but I have it here still. I will show."

He stumbled across the room to the dresser beside the bed, dug around until he came up with the small wooden box that held his most private things. He found the letter in its yellowed envelope and thrust it into her face. Allie opened it, looked at Sophia's letter, turned it over, looked up at him with a questioning, confused expression.

"I can't read it," she said. "It's in Russian."

He slapped his forehead and began to laugh wildly. "Of course." The letter was in Russian and Alinka couldn't read it. He was a great fool. He sat down again in his chair.

Allie looked at him. "Tell me what happened."

"You want to know everything? But when you know you will not know. Okay, I will tell. Sophia survived and I ran away. I did not write her. I did not want to do her harm. You must remember, this was still in time of Stalin. She would not renounce me, as was required, and she wrote me. For this she was judged traitor. I was also traitor, but I was not available to punish. She was. I did not learn what happened for long time, but information always finds you. They took her away. Prison, then to camp. Because of me, do you understand? Because I wanted like you to see world, to see what I had not seen."

He lifted the letter, found his place in the writing he'd read a thousand times, read aloud: "Kolya, if you cannot come to

244

me, I will find way to come to you. I am your wife forever, and I will never forget you or believe that you have forgotten me." Nick put the letter down. "You see, I *had* choice! She was only twenty-three years old."

The sobs surprised him. One moment he was reading the letter and the next he was crying, his back shaking, the sobs ugly and humiliating. It is the vodka, he kept telling himself, the vodka. He felt Allie's touch on his arm, but he couldn't stop now. Thirty years and he'd never spoken of this, and now that he'd begun, he couldn't stop. He wiped his eyes with the back of his hand.

"Alinka, since I tell you everything tonight, I will tell you one more little secret. In Russia there is lovely ancient town with beautiful churches and prison where prisoners were held, even in czar's time, before they were taken north. You know what is called this town, this prison? It is called Vladimir. Vladimir! And road they had to walk, to Siberia? Vladimirka. It is my little joke."

"Nick," Allie said. "It wasn't your fault. How could you have helped her if you went back and were shot? She chose to write you, that was her choice, not yours. You can't blame yourself after all these years."

But he could! He wanted to. It had given his life a shape. What life would he have had without Sophia's memory to accompany him? He didn't know. He looked up and saw Allie staring at him, her eyes wet, and he reached and took her hand. "Allie, Alyusha, sometimes I see her in your face." He reached up and touched Allie's cheek, then leaned forward and kissed her on the lips. Allied jerked back, alarmed. Nick felt suddenly weary, weary and ashamed. Who was he, an old man, to be placing his own history over this young girl's face like layers of paintings on an icon? It was Allie who was alive and real, not Sophia.

"You will forgive me. I am very drunk and I have talked too much, too stupidly. I am sorry, Alinka. We are still friends?"

Allie sat rigid, but she nodded.

"Now you will go home, I think is better. We will play chess another day, okay?"

"Nick, are you sure you're all right?"

"Yes. Please, forgive me. Go."

He held his head in his hands while she rose, pulled on her boots and jacket, and slipped out into the freezing night. He thought, Sophia, forgive me, but the words had no resonance. It was Allie's forgiveness he sought. The word *Sophia* suddenly had no power to call up hurt. He couldn't understand it. What filled his mind instead was the softness of Allie's cheek, of her lips when he'd kissed her. Allie, alive, sitting across from him, listening, wanting to understand. He sat in wonderment. Fool that he was, had he fallen in love with the girl?

THE GIRL with the broken front tooth Sonny met in the bar took him to a place in the mountains west of Boulder. Needleland? Netherland? Nederland. They climbed and climbed through a winding canyon, the ragged engine of her old Impala groaning against the strain of the drive. In the dark he could see snow heaped in banks along the sides of the switchbacks. From time to time the car skidded on patches of ice, and Sonny's heart rose into his throat as he imagined the fall over the edge into darkness, but the girl didn't seem concerned. She kept one hand on the steering wheel, the other on his knee, except when she had to shift, and she hummed to herself the whole time.

She was a thin, stringy-haired girl who'd gotten a kick out of the fact that he was from Alaska, and a bigger kick when she heard he was Indian. He'd gone with her because he'd been drunk and he wanted to see the mountains without being on a tour bus. Nederland, she said, was a far-out place. He didn't know what he'd expected; maybe a ski lodge where people sat around a fireplace drinking hot toddies and signing each other's casts. What he got was a tumble-down shack lit by kerosene and a couple of bodies sacked out on a mattress on the floor.

He slept with her on a sagging couch and woke to a bearded goat staring him in the face. His head ached. When he waved a hand the goat shied away, then wandered back to study him, its lower jaw rotating as it ruminated. Its eyes were large, yellow, and dispassionate, slit by a brown line. Creepy eyes. Sonny looked away. The girl — Mona, he remembered — slept like she'd never wake up. Loneliness and dim bar light had made her seem reasonably attractive last night, but now the sight of her broken tooth, greasy hair, and sallow skin repulsed him. He must have been in bad shape.

He sat up carefully and looked around. The single room held a plank table, a couple of armchairs leaking stuffing, a woodstove, a refrigerator decorated with swirls of red and orange that looked like a child's finger painting, a hand pump sink filled with dirty dishes, and a child's crib. On the mattress by the wall, a couple of lumps under a dirty turquoise sleeping bag stirred, contracted, but didn't rise. As far as Sonny could tell, there was no bathroom in the house. When he stepped outside, the goat pushed past him, clattering down the broken front steps. Barefoot, freezing, Sonny peed off the porch into a snowbank.

The air was cool and dry and crystalline, the sky azure. The cabin was surrounded by pine forest deep in snow, branches bent under powdery weight. The sun glinting off the snow hurt his eyes. It was just as he'd imagined from the photographs in *Rocky Mountain West,* except that in front of the cabin, a sports car lay rusting in a snowbank between Mona's dirty white Impala and an upended couch. The snow in the driveway was stained yellow by goat pee and littered with wisps of hay and piles of goat droppings. The wrong place.

Sonny patted his wallet, checked its contents quickly, and hid it away. He wished he was back in his hotel room taking a shower, brushing his teeth.

It occurred to him that he could walk down the driveway until he hit a road and hitch his way back to Denver. He could even hire someone to drive him to his hotel; he had over twelve hundred dollars in his wallet. But they'd arrived in the dark, and he had no idea where he was. And he had a terrible headache. He couldn't get motivated to do more than go back inside, sit down, and watch Mona sleep while a second goat nosed through an overflowing paper sack of garbage and a two-year-old in a sagging diaper played marbles with a pile of goat turds on the cabin floor.

When Mona woke, she offered him a beer and lit up a joint, and Sonny found himself letting the day slide. A man and a woman emerged from under the turquoise sleeping bag. The man was bearded, grotesquely thin, and wore his hair in a waist-length ponytail. His jeans hung low, exposing the bony plates of his hips. He gave Sonny some kind of elaborate triple handshake but said little beyond "Hey, man." Bobby was his name.

The woman, Trudy, was plump with a lot of frizzy brown hair, which she kept pushing off her face. Sonny tried to look away when she pulled up her men's thermal top to nurse the child. Rainbow — Sonny couldn't make out if it was a girl or a boy — looked old enough to have been weaned long ago. He-she sucked noisily, toying with the distended nipple of Trudy's other breast. Sonny's stomach turned, a strange mixture of desire and disgust.

There was some vague conversation about buying groceries, but nobody left the house. Bobby sat at the table rolling joint after joint. As soon as one was rolled, it was passed around. Even the child was stoned. A pot of chili appeared and everyone ate out of it without really sitting down to a meal. Sonny watched everything with a foolish grin that he couldn't seem to wipe off his face. His headache was gone, but he felt dreamy and cut off from everything, like an observer, floating somewhere above the dirty little cabin, this last outpost of hippiedom. Maybe all of the mountains were full of such cabins, such people.

Mona lay on the couch, emitting high-pitched giggles as she turned the pages of a fashion magazine. "Can you feature this?" she said, holding up a picture of a runway model in a black strapless satin dress that reminded Sonny of the dress he'd picked out for Allie in Juneau. Allie, Juneau, Vladimir. They took shape in his mind as a series of pictures — Allie in Macher's department store, the Juneau boat harbor, the kitchen of his own house in Vladimir — but he was looking at them from a great distance, or seeing them as though flipping through the pages of a magazine. *Alaska Magazine.* At home they sold it in the drugstore. He could go somewhere in Denver and buy it and look at pictures of his own life.

"Look at this one. She looks like a fucking poodle that's been clipped!" Mona said.

"You shouldn't spend money on those magazines," Trudy chided. She was busy changing Rainbow's diaper, filling the cabin with a terrible smell that seemed both insistent and far away, something bad that Sonny had once encountered. "You're just giving money to those advertisers who exploit women. And those cosmetics. Don't you know they kill whales to make that garbage?"

Kill whales. Killer whales. The killer whales came into the bay, and you could watch them from the Takine River Inn. Black and white, dipping, leaping, cavorting as though there were joy in movement itself, as though their own musculature were a pleasure, and they moved through the elements carelessly, intelligent and brutal. He was suddenly, thoroughly homesick for a place where killer whales danced in the bay, where the ravens made jokes in the treetops, where he knew everybody and everybody knew him. He wanted to go home, only he didn't know where home was. It seemed impossibly far away.

"Lighten up," Mona said, and Sonny thought she was talking to him.

Lighten up, but the light was already fading, the cabin windows filled with a golden late afternoon alpenglow. Then it was dark, and a Coleman lamp was lit. Sonny wasn't sad anymore; he was intent on watching the swirls of cigarette smoke trapped inside the beer bottle he was using for an ashtray. An inch of beer remained at the bottom, and the ashes he'd dropped into it had turned to a grey slush, but the smoke spiraled around and around inside the green glass. Ghost smoke. Even though the top was open, it didn't know how to get out.

The door opened and a man entered, stomping snow off his boots, bringing cold air into the room. The man was dressed in ragged fur, coyote or dogskin, with a twelve-gauge shotgun and a large set of snowshoes slung over his shoulder. He dropped the snowshoes with a thump and set the gun against a chair.

"Jack!" Mona said, jumping to her feet. "Wow. You came back!" She glanced over at Sonny, and he read fear in her bony ferret's face. The man didn't answer. He allowed Mona to help him out of his shaggy fur coat, his hat with ear flaps.

Sonny thought he saw something pass between Bobby and Trudy, some kind of look, but he was so stoned he might have been imagining it. Maybe he was imagining this guy in the door, a man dressed like a Vladimir logger: wool pants, red suspenders, a plaid wool shirt. A logger apparition, as though he'd summoned up a vision from home. He hadn't known his mind had such power.

"Who's that?" Jack said, narrowing his pale grey eyes at Sonny. The skin had been stretched too tightly over his blunt features. His face lacked all capacity for kindness, a face made all the more brutal by a scar running above one ear. It looked like the guy had been hit in the head with an ax and sewn up with steel cable.

"That's Sonny," Mona said nervously. "He's from Alaska. He's just, uh, hanging out."

"That so?" Jack said. "Alaska? Far out."

"Sonny's a Indian," Mona said ingratiatingly.

Jack raised a palm and winked. "How," he said to Sonny. "I thought you was a Mex."

An asshole dressed like a Vladimir logger.

Jack turned to Mona. "Hey, babe, I'm starving."

Mona scraped the remains of the chili out of the bottom of

the pot and sat at Jack's feet while he ate with the gulping frenzy of a dog. When Jack was done, he handed his bowl to Mona and began to clean his shotgun with great attention, plumbing the barrel with a brush, wiping the steel with an oily rag.

Sonny settled himself with another beer.

"So you're from Alaska?" Jack asked suddenly. Sonny looked up. Jack's voice sounded strained, gravelly, like someone who'd damaged his larynx by screaming too much.

"Alaska," Sonny said. "That's right." What a pretty word it was when you thought about it, but it was also a kid's joke: What does Mrs. Sippi want? Idaho, I'll ask her.

"Alaska." The man shook his head thoughtfully. "I'm planning to head on up there myself pretty soon. As far as I'm concerned, Alaska's the only place left on this fucked-up planet for a free man."

Sonny smiled.

"What's so funny?" Jack knit his brows suspiciously, put down his oily rag. His grey eyes clouded with an undistilled emotion. Sonny thought of chemistry class: anything could precipitate out of that murk, depending on the catalyst. Mona began to chew busily on a fingernail.

"Nothing's funny," Sonny said. "Nothing's funny at all." But he could feel his smile lurking just under the surface, a smile that said, You fucking fool. It didn't matter where you went. It was the same all over. And he resented the way this Jack was taking over the room. Everything was dreamy and easy, and then all of a sudden here was this guy emitting high frequency anger vibes. Jack was as much of a mood changer as a drug. All his life, it seemed, he'd been around guys like that, who got everyone else to accept their picture, their scene, because they believed so much in their own power. Sonny was tired of it, and at the same time, he felt himself being drawn in, seduced.

Trudy and Bobby whispered busily in the corner of the room. Bobby stood up. "Me'n Trudy are going to the store

252

for more beer and cigarettes. You guys want anything?" His voice sounded high and shaky, the voice of a skinny little rabbit — scared. Sonny thought, I ought to go with him, I ought to just get up and go with him, and when I get to the store, wherever that is, I'll put out my thumb and hitch. But Jack was like an interesting movie he was watching; he wanted to see how the story would end.

Bobby and Trudy went out, letting a blast of cold air in the room. Sonny listened to the low-battery groan of the Impala's engine turning over and over, but finally it caught with a roar. Bobby gunned it with a heavy foot, trying to keep it alive. Then the crunching sound of tires on snow. Sonny felt both too weary to move and belligerent. If he got up to go, this Jack would win.

Rainbow, who'd been quiet all day and hadn't even uttered a whimper when his parents went out, suddenly set up a nerve-wracking wail.

"Can't you shut the kid up?" Jack turned to Mona.

"It's not *my* kid," Mona complained, but she got up and went over to the child and gave it a sip of her beer.

"Man can't find peace in his own home," Jack said. "See what I mean? In Alaska, I wouldn't have to put up with this shit. Here it's all fucked. Petrochemicals everywhere, raping the land. You know what they say about this state? They say, 'Don't Californicate Colorado.' But it's already too late. You seen what they done to California?"

Sonny shook his head no. California wasn't where he wanted to go.

"Same thing they're doing here. These mountains are still pretty to look at, but they're dead. They're already blasting them apart for oil shale, and there's condos coming up like boils on the face of the earth. This land's diseased. God's left this place to die. There's apocalypse coming, and this is going to be one of the places that go. This is the future — *boom!*"

Jack grinned, not prettily. He resumed wiping his gun. "The only place left now is Alaska. The way I see it, they haven't got around to ruining it yet. It's still pure land, you know? The chapel of the firmament, where God resides. I got to get up there soon."

Where God resides. Sonny pictured his mother in Juneau, the AA meeting in that drab yellow basement at the Catholic church. He had a clear, brilliant image of the orange windsock that woman was knitting with huge needles. The chapel of the firmament and the higher power, for those who needed their little dream. He'd had his little dream too, Denver, but now he knew better. He could live without a dream. He could live without surrender.

"God don't live up there," Sonny said evenly. He felt a surge of superiority, a wave of triumph.

"The fuck he don't," Jack said. "Who the fuck are you to say?"

Sonny peered back into the beer bottle. The swirls of smoke had died. He shrugged, and the grin took shape on his face again. "You're kidding yourself, man," Sonny said. "God don't live in Alaska." Maybe he did once, before the white men came, maybe in the time of the legends, but not anymore.

"You don't know shit," Jack exclaimed. "You don't know shit."

"I know what I know," Sonny said stubbornly.

"You don't know shit," Jack insisted. "I don't believe you even come from there, anyhow. I know you're jiving me, because if you really came from up there, you never would've left and come down here." He nodded his head knowingly. "Look's to me like you're just some overgrown Mex who made up a good line of shit to pick up my woman. Lying about being from Alaska. Bet that noble savage line really works, really gets you some action. Huh, Tonto?"

Sonny understood this game. If you didn't agree with a guy like this, you didn't exist; his reality was stronger. It was funny to be accused of *not* being Indian. The old no-win. "Right," Sonny said. "You got it all figured."

Jack leaned forward in his chair. The emptied shotgun slid

down his knees, broken open. Jack reached for it. "Let me ask you something, brother." His grey eyes narrowed with menace. "How'd you like fucking my woman, if you don't mind me asking? I mean, we're all pals here, right? Share and share alike. Was she any good?"

"Jack," Mona wailed. "We didn't do nothing!"

It always came down to that, somehow. Fucking someone's woman. Sonny wanted to say, It was a mistake, really. I didn't even like her.

"And you," Jack said, turning to Mona. "I should've known what to expect from you. Don't think you got me fooled."

"You're the one who split on me, anyway," Mona whimpered. "How was I to know you'd come back?"

Sonny smiled. They deserved each other. How had he ever got himself in the middle of this? It was too ridiculous, someone else's problems.

"You know," Jack said, leaping up. "I'm getting sick of that smile you got on your face. You come here, fuck my woman, and try to jerk me around about Alaska. But you got it wrong, brother. This is *my* place. You can't pull that shit on me."

Sonny looked beyond Jack, to the door. Somehow this all wasn't real. He supposed he could still get out if he moved fast, but there didn't seem to be any point in going anywhere. He'd already gone far enough. It was all just a movie.

"Get up!" Jack said. "I'm talking to you, man."

The child began to cry again, but it sounded far away, like a dog howling in a neighbor's yard at night. Why was the child crying?

Sonny blew across the top of his beer bottle. A soft flutelike tone rang out, low and pretty.

"You fucking greaseball!" Jack stamped his foot in frustration, like a kid losing a game. "Get up!"

Sorry, Jack. It was too late for that. Jack was making such a big fuss about nothing, Jack who was going to find God in Alaska. It was funny.

255

Mona's voice was far away, a shrill little squeal. "Cut it out Jack. Cut it out. Lay off!"

Sonny grinned with satisfaction, with the joy of knowledge. All his life he'd been scared, and now he wasn't anymore. All his life he'd been running, and if only he'd known, he could've had peace. The point was to sit still and wait for it to come to you, as Jack was coming now. He was as mesmerized as a deer caught by the dazzle of a jacklight, but it was curiosity, not fear, that held him there. It wasn't that he couldn't push his weight around if he had to, it was just that it didn't matter. That was the truth, the word of God after all. He started to laugh, a laugh that wouldn't stop, a laugh that was triumphant. If only he'd always known what he knew now, it would have saved so much time, so much feeling.

The stock of the shotgun swung into his line of vision, gleaming and oily, and behind it Jack's raging face, distorted, a face that looked tremendously familiar. Sonny felt nothing, not fear, not even surprise. He'd been waiting for this all his life. He heard the crack of his own splintering bones and the light danced, shattered. Sonny said "Oh," surprised after all. Then he was lost in the darkness.

ALLIE SAT across the table from Nick, an array of knives, chisels, gouges, and sandpaper spread out on newspaper between them. Nick bent over his work, engrossed in polishing a raven's head bowl inlaid with abalone shell, a design based on a picture from a book of Tlingit art. Allie envied his concentration as well as his carving, envied the certainty of his hands. Her own project, a simple spoon lying on the newspaper before her, looked awkward, rough, and lopsided, a spoon nobody could love.

Through the frosted window, glittering under brilliant midday sun, the bay lay covered in ice. It reminded her of an Earth Science illustration of plate tectonics, the great frozen sheets overlapped and layered, broken upon themselves by the competing forces of tide and wind. This was the time of year when it got so cold that the fog lifted and everything looked sharp-edged and fragile.

Sunlight cut through the cabin window, striking Nick's face and startling Allie with the sight of deep lines fanning around his eyes, the network of feathery cracks and fissures across his cheeks. In the harsh light he appeared suddenly old, distressingly mortal. She looked away with the same sad wave of fear she'd felt when she'd caught sight of brown spots on the backs of her mother's hands.

Allie picked up her spoon, selected a sharp, thick-bladed knife with a green plastic handle, and pushed the knife against resisting wood, trying to make it go straight, struggling to keep the right angle so that she wouldn't take too much away. She wanted to make the neck of the spoon thinner, a more graceful curve to the rounded bowl. It was hard work. She bit her tongue, breathed hard. She would ruin it if she wasn't careful.

If it came out well enough, she might make a set and send it home to her mother — proof that she'd learned something useful, a reminder that she was alive. But then she could hear her father's voice, see the sneer on his face. Spoons. Send fucking kids to private schools, send them to college so they can clean fish and carve spoons. Why not basket weaving? Why not shoveling shit against the wind?

Allie pushed harder, sliding the blade too far. It hit a knot and bounced off, gouging the place where the bowl joined the neck, the spoon's jugular. The blade jammed, stuck in the gash. "Shit," Allie said. She laid the spoon down in disgust. Nick looked up, blue eyes flickering with a question, but he said nothing.

Allie picked the spoon up again, scowling. She held it in her left hand, the knife in her right, trying to twist it out, forcing the blade. What did it matter, since it was already ruined?

"Not like that," Nick said. "That way is danger —"

But it was too late. The knife came free suddenly, splintering through the broken wood. The blade sliced down across the palm of her left hand, leaving a red stripe that opened into a gaping mouth. Blood welled, quivered, spilled over. Allie stared down at her hand. Her face went white, her heart pounded.

Nick lunged toward her. Instinctively, she twisted away, cringing, and raised her hand in front of her face to ward off the blow.

Nick froze, then slowly sat down. "Allie," he said softly. "Let me see what you have done."

She looked at him. His hands gripped each other on the table as though to restrain themselves or to prove they wouldn't do harm. From far away, with someone else's eyes, she saw that his eyes looked watery, pained. Why was he sad? She clutched her cut hand tight to her chest, drawing shallow breaths that wouldn't fill her lungs. Blood ran down her wrist, onto her jeans. She was stupid, stupid. How could she be so dumb?

"Alinka, please."

Nick. It was just Nick, with his pale blue eyes, with the crepey lines on his face.

"Allie, is accident. Only accident." His voice sounded strange to her, thick. Slowly he got up and moved around the table. Allie surrendered her cut hand. She allowed herself to be led to the sink and stood quietly while Nick held her hand under the jug. The water ran, mixed with the blood, turned pink. Nick poured out alcohol. She looked at the cut with curiosity, the layers of fascia, an illustration in an anatomy book, not something that belonged to her. She could feel the pressure of Nick's fingers, then the tightness of the bandage as he wound the gauze around and around, but her hand had no feeling.

"You need stitches," Nick said. "I will take you to hospital now."

"No." She pulled away.

"Okay, okay. No hospital." Nick tied the gauze in a knot, cut it with scissors. "I do not think you have cut tendon, but you will have scar, like souvenir." He smiled. "When you are old, old woman, you will look at scar on your hand and you will remember — once I was young girl and I lived in Alaska. You will be proud. You will show it to grandchildren."

"I can't believe I did anything so dumb," she said. "I'm such a jerk."

"Allie, accident is accident. You do not think I have done such things? Look." Nick turned his palms over and displayed a tracing of white lines, raised welts. "Every fisherman has put hook through hand. I many times. Now you sit and rest. I will make for us tea. Sit, sit over there by stove."

Allie sat down in the chair. She felt weary, shaky with the aftereffects of shock, the ebb of adrenaline. Her hand hurt now, a steady, aching throb. She was ashamed that she'd cringed in front of Nick, allowed him to see that part of her, that reflex, that conditioned response. Playing in the garage as a child once, she cut her shin on a boat trailer. She was so afraid of being punished she hemorrhaged a blood vessel in her nose. When her mother drove her to the hospital emergency ward, they had to cauterize and pack her nasal passages with gauze to stop the gushing bleeding before they could stitch her leg. "It was an accident," she kept saying over and over to the intern, as though he would be mad at her too.

Nick bustled around, making tea on his gas burner, setting out cups. He carried the tray over, placing it on a folding table beside Allie, and sat down beside her in the second armchair. Along with the tea he set out a jar of smoked salmon, sliced bread, pickles, a plate of cookies. "So," he said. "Eat."

Allie wasn't hungry.

"Eat. Eat just little to be strong. The body must eat after shock. You lost blood." He made her a sandwich and held it in front of her until, just to accommodate him, she took a bite. Surprisingly, it tasted good, perhaps because it came from his hands, something he'd made for her like a solicitous mother. She smiled at the thought of Nick as a mother.

Her own mother hated to cook and never woke up in time to make breakfast, too lost in her own sorrows to care. No, Allie thought, sipping her tea, that wasn't fair. Occasionally, when she'd stayed home sick from school, her mother would come out from behind the closed door of her bedroom, emerging from her depression to play a record of the *Grand*

Canyon Suite — "Hear the donkey? And the storm?" — and make a wonderful dish of rice with milk and sugar, a miracle of white on white on white, with a lovely pool of floating yellow butter. Allie remembered eating it slowly, gratefully, every sugary grain's sweetness the sweetness of unaccustomed attention.

Nick raised his teacup and took a swallow. Allie could hear the distinct gurgling roll of his Adam's apple. She'd never before noticed how the body was so inescapably present, so much tissue, gristle, and bone. You didn't think about it, and then suddenly it was there with its wrinkles, leaking cuts, its betrayal. It was only the flesh that made a person vulnerable — to other people, to their bigger fists, their demands. If only she could escape her flesh, she'd be free.

Nick put his cup down. "Allie, you made horrible mistake."

"I know. I was really dumb. I'm sorry for being such a pain."

"I do not speak of your accident. That is nothing. I mean, you made mistake to think that I would hit you. I would never, never hit you. Not everyone in this world hits. You know?"

Allie shrugged. Probably everybody hit, if you got them at the right time, in the right mood. She didn't want to talk about it. She'd already learned her lesson with Sonny, a lesson she'd known all her life but had made the mistake of forgetting in Juneau: keep the family secrets. Pretend.

"You do not believe?" Nick shook his head, got up, opened the cast iron door to the stove. The logs had burned down. He stirred the embers with a poker, wedged in another chunk of wood, sat back down. Allie sipped her tea. He sat quietly for a while, then stood up again, agitated.

"I would never hit you, Alinka. I am not such man who hits women, children. You have known something of that ugliness, I see. I also know something of what men do. I was soldier, prisoner, remember? Still, you must believe, Alinka, that it is not all ugliness or you will lose everything. You must believe that I would never hit you, ever. I am your friend."

Allie chewed her sandwich. She didn't want to argue.

"You do not believe, I see." Nick sighed. "I want to tell to you story, Alinka. You are in mood to hear story?"

"Okay."

"So. When I was prisoner in Germany, sometimes at night in our barracks we told to each other stories, something to pass time. One night Misha told story. He was good-looking boy, Misha, simple boy from small city, Pskov, not ignorant peasant but ordinary man. Pskov is very ancient and beautiful city, many, many times conquered. I read that Pskov was almost completely destroyed by Germans. Maybe is now rebuilt?"

Allie waited, willing to be lulled by a fairy tale of an ancient city. She raised her bandaged hand, tried to get comfortable.

"So," Nick continued. "Misha entertained us with tale of our beautiful homeland. One evening in Pskov, he was at party with his friend, some Sasha, perhaps Alyosha. I do not remember name. Maybe was some holiday. At party they met woman. All three were very inflamed with passion, with vodka. They went to bedroom, excuse me, Allie, they made sex. When they were done, the woman said to Misha and his friend, 'It is all good for you boys, but what about me? You have not satisfied me. I need more.' Misha looked at his friend, and almost without words they understood each other. Like brothers. Excuse me, Allie, but they took vodka bottle, jammed it inside woman so hard it broke, and cut her very badly."

Shocked, Allie leaned back hard in her chair. Why was he telling her this? To show her that she wasn't the only one who'd ever been hurt? To prove that he'd seen more brutality than she would ever see? She didn't need to hear it. The hell with him.

Nick frowned. "Is not end of story, Allie. So. What do you

suppose was reaction of my fellow countrymen, my comrades, when they heard such story?"

Allie shrugged, slouched lower in her chair.

Nick stubbed out his cigarette. "First, you must picture me, my fellow prisoners. We sit on bunks without mattresses, heads shaved, starving wretches who would kill for peel of potato. We have lice, dysentery, we stink. In one bunk is man dying of typhus. At any moment we miserable creatures can be shot by German guards, at any moment they can put their boots on our necks, push our faces in the mud, for pleasure, for sport. We are nothing but garbage. Now tell me, Allie, what do you think was reaction of my fellow prisoners to this disgusting story?"

Allie sat still in her chair. She hated him for this.

"I will tell you, Allie. They opened their mouths and they laughed. Yes, they laughed and laughed. They experienced true joy, Allie. They slapped their miserable, skinny thighs, they said to Misha, 'Brother, you were right! You really gave it to that bitch!' They received great, great pleasure from story of this unfortunate woman. You understand? They were perhaps miserable, helpless prisoners, but they were *men!*"

Nick lit another cigarette. "I see that you do not like this disgusting story, Allie. I also did not like, although I am certain that I am man as they were. I looked at them, Allie, and I thought, 'For this I am soldier? For this I fought?' These were my comrades. It seemed at that moment that ugliness of men was simply too much. In world where men got pleasure from such story, I did not want to live anymore. I decided — now I will walk out. The camp was surrounded by electrified fence, by guards in tower. If I walked to wire, either they would shoot me or I would put my hands against wire and electrocute myself. You see, I simply was tired to live."

Allie began to breathe again. Without realizing it, she'd been holding her breath. "You didn't do it," she said. "You lived."

Nick smiled. "Yes. I lived. I will explain you. When I walked to door, I saw it was snowing. Big white flakes filling air. I could not even see wretched frozen mud in yard. I could have been anywhere. Under snow it was so pure, so pretty. I stood there in door, looking at snowflakes. I remembered when I was little boy, I lived with babushka in village after revolution. I remembered looking at snow through window, and my babushka saying, 'Kolya' — that was my nickname, for Nikolai — 'Kolya, when it snows, our Lord makes world clean, he wipes away sin.' I remembered so clearly my breath against glass, and feel of her hand. She had such large, rough hands, but very gentle. Standing there in that prison barracks, I remembered it all. And I felt such terrible, terrible homesickness. For my babushka, for birches beyond window, for my land. You know, it is funny, but I wanted to live. Even in world full of rotting corpses, with such Mishas, such guards. You understand? Not because I remembered someone who loved me, perhaps, but because I remembered that *I* loved. I wanted to live."

Nick got up and looked out at the frozen bay. The sun still spilled through the cabin window. It seemed impossible to Allie that it could still be daylight, midday. In this world of winter darkness, the sun had turned round on its axis and already the days were lengthening. Even while it got colder, by some mysterious process spring was coming.

At the table, on newspaper stained with her blood, the tools lay spread about and Nick's bowl sat upended, burnished cedar embellished with abalone shell, an ancient design. On top of the woodstove, the kettle hissed and blew a fine cloud of steam. Nick turned to her. "You understand, Alinka?"

She wanted to understand, but she didn't. She didn't know how.

Nick sighed, went to the bookshelf, and pulled down a book. "Let me read to you something. Maybe this says to you better what I want to say. You know the poet Akhmatova?"

Allie shook her head.

"She suffered very much under Stalin. They took her husband, her son. This poem, called 'Sentence.' I even have here translation. I will read to you first Russian, then English."

He leafed through the book, bent it open. He read in a loud, cantorial voice, chanting the rich Russian words as she imagined a priest would intone the service in a Russian Orthodox church. But the words in English sounded simple, plain:

> "So much to do today:
> kill memory, kill pain,
> turn heart into a stone,
> and yet prepare to live again."

Nick closed the book on his thumb, holding his place, and smiled, his face full of terrible, insistent hope, and something else, an emotion she could barely acknowledge because it was so terrifying: love. "It is lesson, Allie, for you and for me."

Allie wanted to receive the gift he was trying to give her. She wanted to believe in a world of babushkas with gentle hands who wiped the world free of sin with snowstorms, but all she could think of was the story of her own grandmother giving her mother a bath, the story she'd told Sonny.

Her mother, who loved to tell of drowned men in hurricanes, to recount every marital humiliation, had told Allie the story the last time she'd been home. They were sitting together in her mother's darkened bedroom in Massachusetts in the late afternoon. Outside the window, snowflakes blew upward, it seemed, light and airy and sparkling in front of the streetlight. Her mother turned to her, her face dreamy, childlike, and said, "And now every time it starts to snow I think of my mother giving me that bath and I feel happy. Isn't that silly?"

Allie answered breathlessly. "You never told me that one. Mama, why didn't you ever tell me that one?"

Her mother reached out and took her hand. Allie went rigid with the unfamiliar touch, with the necessity of holding herself apart from her mother, because all she wanted in the world was to lay her head in her mother's lap, to be tiny again, this time in a world where her mother knew stories with a happy end.

"Aha," her mother said, smiling mysteriously. "And you thought you knew them all."

Sonny woke to a cushioning softness, then the taste of blood on his tongue, metallic, salty, and a terrible aching heaviness in his head. He groaned.

"Hey, it's okay." He thought for a moment that he was dreaming — he was little and this was his mother wiping his face with a damp cloth — but he opened his eyes and saw the dirty white thermal undershirt, the long brown frizz of Trudy's hair. He closed his eyes again. He was lying with his head in her lap, leaning against her great soft breasts. He felt weak, grateful for her touch. If only he could climb back into sleep and make the hurting stop.

"I was really getting worried," Trudy said. "I didn't know what to do about you. Me and Bobby didn't want to have to take you to the hospital, and since Mona took the car, there wasn't no way to get you there anyhow."

Sonny tried to sit up. Mona. Jack. He had to get out of there. He struggled up, holding a hand to his throbbing head. Bobby was at the table, rolling joints. He said, "Hey, man. Thought you were out for the count." The baby sat on the floor with a spoon in its mouth.

Sonny patted his hip pocket. He looked around wildly. His wallet was gone.

"What's the matter?" Trudy said. "Take it easy."

"Somebody took my wallet," Sonny said. His voice sounded plaintive, a child's whine.

Trudy shrugged. "That's Jack and Mona for you. Sometimes they can do some fucked-up things. The two of them split last night after he smashed up your face. Well, at least all he got from you was money," she added philosophically. "He probably knocked up Mona, or gave her the clap."

Sonny's head whirled. Last night. Mona and Jack; he'd been ripped off. And now it was sunny again beyond the cabin windows, the middle of the day. How did he know that Trudy and Bobby weren't in on this, that they hadn't done it themselves? He backed toward the door. "I got to get out of here," he said.

"Suit yourself," Trudy shrugged. "But you're going to have a hard time getting a ride looking like that."

Looking like what? Sonny went over to a slice of broken mirror hanging over the sink. His eyes were swollen and black underneath, his nose thick, lopsided, obviously broken, and gashed and scabby across the bridge. It was enough to make him sick to his stomach. He felt weak, but he had to get out of there. He looked around the room desperately again, as though the money, his wallet, was just hidden somewhere, and if he tried hard enough he could find it. He thought of ransacking the place, of forcing Trudy and Bobby to give it back. But he was too weak. It probably had been Mona and Jack. Trudy and Bobby didn't look like they had the energy or initiative to do something like that.

He found his jacket, drew it on.

"Hey man, be cool," Bobby said. "You want to light up first?"

Sonny shook his head, and a little flash of light followed the motion, like a picture shot with low speed film at night. Maybe he'd broken his skull? It didn't matter, he had to split. He walked out onto the porch slowly, carefully, like an old man with a cane, afraid of breaking a hip. The goats pushed against him, and he avoided their yellow eyes. Trudy stood in the open door, watching him go. "Turn right at the mailbox and then another right at the highway," she said. "Sorry it was such a bummer for you. You ought to come back sometime."

Sure, Sonny thought. Sure.

His leather boots slipped on the icy ruts of the drive, and the cold cut through his leather jacket. There was nothing to do but keep walking until he hit the highway. He went about two miles before a car even passed, and that was a pickup with a rifle rack, carrying two rednecks in cowboy hats. The pickup actually veered at him, then veered away, the two men laughing at the sight of Sonny scared. Sonny swore and kept walking.

He stood on the highway, shifting his weight from one frozen foot to another, until after what seemed like hours, he was finally picked up by a kid in a salt-spattered Volkswagen. The driver, barely old enough to have a license, had blond curls and the peach fuzz look of someone not ready to shave. "Hey," he said, opening the door to Sonny. "Looks like you got on the wrong end of something."

"You going to Denver?" Sonny asked.

The driver shrugged. "Why not?" Sonny clambered in. He felt so weak he could barely close the door.

"You know how VW's are," the kid said amiably. "Air tight. They'd float if you drove into the river, but you can't get the doors to shut." He reached into a paper sack in the back seat, drew out a Budweiser, and offered it to Sonny.

Sonny knew he shouldn't drink with a head injury, but as soon as he took a sip, the pounding in his head let up. He sat in silence while they careened along the mountain curves doing fifty, the little car straining and huffing. The farther away he got from the cabin, the better he began to feel. The question was, what should he do? At least he still had his airplane ticket in his suitcase back in the hotel room. He could get a flight to Seattle tomorrow, sleep in the airport until he got an Alaska Airlines flight to Vladimir. On the other hand, how would it look, showing up in town broke, his face a mess, after only ten days away? He couldn't go back yet. He'd have to cash in his ticket. It was worth over five hundred dollars. He'd have to find a cheaper place to stay, get himself a job. There were a lot of possibilities.

Sonny accepted a second beer, watching the trees slide past, nodding his head so he wouldn't have to answer as the kid chattered on about how he was planning to drive his VW all the way to California, soon as the weather got good. By the time they got back to Denver, it was nearly dark.

At the pawnshop, the man only gave him seventy dollars for his gold nugget ring and leather jacket. When Sonny tried to object and hold out for more, the man invited him to sell somewhere else. Sonny left the ring, bought a ragged olive drab army surplus coat for five dollars, and took his suitcase to the Y, where they put him in a room with four cots and told him he couldn't hang out there during the day.

He hitched to a construction site outside of town and asked for a job, anything from pounding nails to hod carrier. The paunchy, red-faced foreman studied him from under the brim of a baseball cap, then exchanged a sly glance with a carpenter who'd stopped measuring a window frame to look at Sonny. "Sorry, Chico, it's all union here," the foreman said.

At the employment bureau, an annoyed looking Mexican lady in a red sweater that was too tight looked over his application and frowned. Her nails were long, curved like talons, and painted a glossy crimson that matched her sweater. "Fishing?" she said. "The only fishing we got around here is for trout. You know, you ain't gonna find no respectable job with your face like that. You better wait 'til those cuts heal, then you come back."

When his seventy dollars were gone, Sonny went to the Denver blood bank. There he sat on a plastic chair against the wall in a lineup of black and Mexican winos who'd come in to sell their blood for the price of a couple of bottles of port. A pale, overweight nurse covered in freckles led him to a hospital bed and hooked him up. "Okay, honey," she said, returning to take away his blood. "You just rest here a minute and have a donut." Sonny wanted to cry at the soft touch of her freckled hands, her gentle voice.

Afterward, he sat on a bench in a small park, sharing a bottle of port with a geezer who'd asked him to chip in for rotgut. Weak winter sun played on the pavement where pigeons pecked for crumbs. Outside the park a Kwik Lunch truck pulled up, and a skinny girl in tight jeans got out and started selling sandwiches to a road crew setting out a curb.

Sonny couldn't remember why Kwik Lunch seemed so familiar. Then he did: Allie, the night Bob and Gina were singing about humpback salmon at the Takine, the night he'd taken her home. Suddenly, sitting in that dirty little park in the midst of melting snow, he felt such desire for her, for the simplicity of that first evening, an urgent lust that made him weak kneed.

The Kwik Lunch girl stood on one side of her truck making change while a couple of men in coveralls ripped off pastries in the back. A Kwik Chick, a Goody Girl. At least Allie had found a job. For some reason that struck him as funny, and he started laughing out loud. The geezer on the bench beside him looked up from his toe-grooming operation.

"You're a good-natured boy, ain't you. What's your name, sonny?"

"Sonny," he said, and laughed until he got rotgut up his nose.

He cashed in his plane ticket the second week. He figured he could always get a bus ticket to Seattle and take the ferry from there to home, but he needed the cash badly now. He intended to buy his bus ticket first, but somehow the cash was gone in a few days, and then he had no money and no ticket.

One night he was stopped by a couple of black guys on a dark street downtown. When they saw the two dollars he had in his pocket, they started to laugh. "This dude's hard up," the taller one said. "Let him keep it." Sonny stood there in shame as they ambled off.

He got a job washing dishes at the Elite Café on Larimer Street. The busboys were all Chicano, and the kid who swabbed the floors was black. All of the waiters and waitresses were white. The waitresses wouldn't even give Sonny a glance. Although his black eyes had finally faded, the scabs on his nose were taking forever to fall off. The busboys and the floor swabber spent all their time talking about how they wanted to fuck the waitresses, and all the ways they'd do it if they got a chance. Sonny didn't pay much attention. When he got off shift at eleven, he'd buy a cheap bottle of wine or a six-pack, which he'd take to a movie or a peep show or a strip joint. The parks were too cold at night, and he couldn't drink at the Y.

He liked watching the girls at the strip joints gyrate, although it used up too much of his cash. What he liked most of all was the way he could just look at them without having to meet their eyes. It made everything so simple. He didn't care if they looked at the audience with disdain or even hatred. He could understand that.

One night, when he was cutting through an alley on the way to a movie with his paper sack, a wino slumped in a doorway reached up and touched his leg.

"You spare some change?" the wino asked. He had some kind of rag wrapped around his head like the hood of a burnoose, and although it was freezing outside, bare skin showed in the space between his ragged pants and his sockless boots.

"Sorry, partner," Sonny said. He was in no shape to give charity these days.

"Come on," the old man whined, "help me. I need it bad."

Sonny sighed, reached into his pocket and pulled out a quarter. The wino took it, but he still clutched Sonny's leg.

"That ain't nothing. What's the matter with you? I need help. You got a bottle there? Gimme!"

"Let go of my leg!" Sonny said.

He tried to pull away, but the old man had him clutched in a death grip. Sonny jerked his leg and the old man jerked with him, wrapping his arms tighter. In a sudden fury, Sonny bent over and slammed his fist into the man's face. Sonny leaned back and punched again. He couldn't stop himself until the man's mouth was mushy with blood, caved in. Breathing hard, Sonny backed away.

The man whimpered faintly.

"I told you to let go," Sonny said, rubbing his raw fist. "I told you! But you wouldn't listen. You asked for it!"

Down the street he heard voices echoing, the clatter of footsteps, a single high-pitched laugh. He turned and ran, his shadow stretched behind him on the alley walls.

A T THE TAKINE, Allie tried to push past two mill work-ers, Bobby Duffy and Joe Conan, with her drink tray. Obliv-ious to her loud "excuse me"'s, they shouted threats at each other, faces flushed red, cords standing out on their necks. Joe swung at Bobby, sending Allie's tray clattering to the floor. She swore but nobody cared; they were too busy pulling Bobby off Joe Conan's throat.

She was beginning to hate these men with their rabid faces, their anger. It seemed there was a fight almost every night now. A woman had been accidentally cold-cocked by brawl-ers on the Takine's dance floor two days ago, and only a week before, Allie had been standing near the bar at the Anchor when a man had gone flying through the front window, show-ering her with broken glass. She was amazed at how quickly she moved to the other end of the room, at her instinct to get out of the way. A few months ago, it would have seemed glamorous to her, a scene from a western movie, but all she felt now was fear and disgust.

In the ladies' room at the Takine, she leaned over the sink, splashing water on her sweaty face. Looking up into the mir-ror, she saw Brenda in the reflection. Brenda leaned against a toilet stall, arms folded across her chest, head tilted back. She was wearing her Black Hills of Dakota T-shirt again, and she appeared to be glassy-eyed drunk.

"You look like a Indian but you talk like a schoolteacher," Brenda said. "I always hated schoolteachers, 'cause they think they're better than everybody else."

"I don't think that," Allie said wearily.

"You think you're better than me, but you ain't," Brenda said. "You're just some fucked-up white girl trying to play Indian, wearing that Tlingit bracelet." She walked behind Allie, who watched her warily in the mirror. Brenda stopped at the door. "Sonny never wanted you," she said. "Nobody wants you here."

The door slammed. Slowly, Allie pulled a paper towel from the dispenser and wiped her burning face.

Linda and Allie rode out to Nine Mile in Linda's beat-up Volkswagen, bouncing over the potholes and puddles past banks of dirty, melting snow, past muskeg forest where the trees were sinking, green and creepy and moss-covered, and turning over in the bogs. Through the passenger window the ocean glittered between the trunks of the spruce trees, flickering like an old movie or the view through the slats of a picket fence. Motion gave the illusion of continuity, but it was merely an optical trick.

Beyond the bulldozed and graveled gash that marked Nine Mile, the clear-cut slope was barren of trees, littered with stumps: Vladimir Island was being logged. Linda pointed the Volkswagen toward the sea, away from the distressing view, put the car in neutral, and let it idle. She was afraid if she turned it off, it wouldn't start again.

From Nine Mile they could still see the curl of mill smoke rising over town. A flat swath of evening fog crept up the sides of the mountains across the strait, hiding the delicate perfection of spruce lining the shore. Just below them, a raven picked through seaweed on the low tide rocks, and in the channel a troller chugged along through the glassy still water, trailing a perfect curling wake.

It was April and the trollers were headed out. Nick had been gone for weeks and Allie missed him. Watching the troller glide by, the faint glimmer of its running lights in the twilight, she was filled with longing; she wanted so badly to be on a boat, to hear the engine start up, feel the vibrations, cast off the lines, and slide away. She craved the *chug-chug-chug* of a diesel, the sea beneath the wet black planks, the pitch and glide and roll.

It would be another month or more before the Seattle and Oregon boats clogged the dock and the crews filled the bars, and two months before the start of the net-fishing season. She was tired of waiting — waiting for the season to open, the net to come in, the set to end, the men to return from the sea, the mill whistle, her shift at the bar to be over, for Sonny to come home. Back in the winter when he was seining for herring, she used to imagine herself inside Sonny, going out to sea. He was taking her there. Now he was landlocked far away, and she was stuck inside barrooms, filling the hours with whiskey, waiting for her life to begin.

"I'm bored," Linda said, interrupting Allie's thoughts. "I've got to get out of here." She spoke in a rapid staccato between cigarette puffs. Behind her oversized glasses, her round, usually amiable face looked tense.

"Do you know what I do every day? I go pick up my mom and drive her to my gram's. Or I go pick up my gram and drive her to my mom's. We drink our tea and eat our dessert. Then I drive them home. I mean really. There's got to be more. I'm drying up here. Like an old maid. I'm already twenty-four. My gram said, 'Linda, you need a new romance.' I said, 'Gram, tell me about it!'"

Linda put the car in gear, gunned it. The tiny engine roared. The sun hovered just above the peaks across the strait, back-lighting the mountain in a halo of rays. Linda popped the clutch and they bucked forward. "I think I'll go up to Fairbanks," she said. "Get in on some of that pipeline money.

Why don't you come with me? There's nothing holding you here. It's not like you got family."

What was holding her here? Allie asked herself that question fifteen times a day. She *did* have family, and sometimes she suspected that they, as much as anything else, kept her in Vladimir. Back on her riverboat, the letter from her mother lay folded in its envelope, a letter she'd read again and again with amazement and disbelief.

Her mother was planning to leave her father. There was no real explanation, beyond the fact that Allie's brother would graduate from high school in June and Allie's mother would be done with her familial duties. She wrote that she'd gone to visit her sister, Allie's aunt Ellen, and played symphonies on the stereo, getting up to conduct the orchestra in her nightgown every morning. Now she knew she couldn't go back to live in a house with a man who wouldn't allow her to listen to music, a man who insisted she turn off that "damn noise and quit sucking on a cup of coffee." To Allie this all seemed as unlikely as a woman waking from a coma after twenty years.

She wanted to believe that the letter was real, that after all these years her mother really could leave the house, leave her father, but she feared it was nothing more than a fantasy her mother had cooked up. She was almost afraid to believe it could happen. If it was true, and her mother really was going to leave her father, where would she go? How would she live alone? Allie simply couldn't imagine her mother surviving on her own without her, and she couldn't go back there because her mother would need her too much.

She couldn't go home. What other options did she have? To go to Fairbanks, as Linda suggested? She was holding Fairbanks and the pipeline in reserve — the next place she could go to when she needed to go somewhere — but the truth was that it didn't really appeal to her. It would be a world of big-bucks construction jobs, rough men, more fights in the bars. And she wasn't drawn to the frozen Arctic as she'd been drawn to this land of wheeling gulls, fishing boats, and fog that crept into her heart.

She was beginning to suspect that wherever she went wouldn't be much better than where she was. So she was staying on in Vladimir, biding her time. In the summer, perhaps, it would be all right. On the right boat she could fish again — not as somebody's girlfriend but as a regular member of a crew. And when seining started up again, Sonny would surely come back.

"I might go on up to Fairbanks if things don't work out here," she said doubtfully.

Linda glanced at Allie, then back at the road. "You still waiting for Sonny to come back?" She shook her head. "Some people never learn."

Allie shrugged. "What are you going to do up in Fairbanks? Try to get on a construction crew? I hear they're hiring women to hold up road signs. You want to get rich playing red light, green light? It sounds pretty dull."

"I don't know. I'd probably work in a bar. It's mostly just to get out of here. Light me one of mine, will you?"

Allie lit a Parliament from Linda's pack and handed it over. "Did you ever think of doing something else? Some kind of work you'd like?" Allie asked.

Linda blew out smoke with disgust. "I always thought I'd just stumble on it, but I know I won't here. This place is dead for me, Allie. I don't even see how beautiful it is anymore. You know, if I met a man I cared for now, I wouldn't even remember how to act."

They splashed along through the puddles. The sun dropped out of view in a last blaze of glory, bloodying the water. Linda put on the headlights, glanced at the watch on her narrow brown wrist. "It's eight already and still not really dark. I guess spring's here. What should we do? Should we go to the Tak?"

"Where else is there to go?"

"We can leave early," Linda said.

"That's what we always say."

They parked in the rutted lot. Before they even came in the door they could hear the band playing a loud, off-key version of "I Shot the Sheriff." Allie lingered at the cigarette machine in the entry. It was her third pack, and the night hadn't even begun. Her lungs felt blistered all the time from too much smoke, and she woke up in the middle of the night with racking, phlegm-filled coughs. She sighed, pulled the knob, and the pack of Marlboros fell into her hand.

In the narrow aisle between the coat racks a logger dressed in a ridiculous cowboy outfit — fringed jacket with pearl buttons and a ten-gallon hat — stood with one palm against the wall above the shoulder of an extremely short girl in a white knit dress whose teased, bouffant hair gave her an added eight inches. Allie thought of boys in high school, the way they stood over girls in the halls with their arms against the wall, that possessive way they had of making themselves large. The short girl looked up at her cowboy and said, "If you're nice."

There was so little to look forward to now: a dance or two; fighting off the advances of various drunks; gossip about who'd gotten a "Vladimir divorce" — the local term for when a husband came home, found his wife in bed with someone else, and shot them both; a cribbage game with Henry if he felt like it, if he wasn't already too drunk.

Allie entered the room, glancing around to see if Linda had nabbed a booth, then stopped, dizzy with surprise. Sonny sat on a bar stool between Henry and Frankie, his head thrown back as he laughed. At first she thought she was mistaken — it must have been someone else. His hair was too short, and when he turned on his chair, grinning, his face looked lopsided, something about it was wrong. But it was Sonny, wearing his usual white shirt and jeans and motorcycle boots, as simple as day, as familiar as breathing.

Allie turned on her heel, ducked into the ladies' room, and locked herself in a stall. She wasn't ready. She'd gone over and over how she'd feel, what she'd say, every time making it dif-

ferent, practicing. She'd be prettier, nicer, better dressed —
someone else. She leaned her forehead against the cool Formica of the toilet door. She couldn't go out there now.

She heard the click of heels on tile and then Linda's voice.
"Allie? Why are you hiding?"

"I don't know. I don't know. I don't know what to say to
him. Maybe he's still mad at me for what I said."

"Don't be ridiculous. It's only Sonny. Just say 'Hi.'"

Sonny, Sonny, Sonny. Allie followed Linda into the room,
up to the bar. Sonny put an arm around Allie's waist and drew
her close, offered his dazzling smile.

"Hey. I can't believe you're still here." He shook his head
in wonder. The short haircut made him look younger. He was
thinner than before, and something had happened to his
pretty face. His nose was flattened, pushed to one side.

"Of course I'm still here," Allie said, keeping her voice
smooth. It was important that he not know how much he
mattered, important that she not scare him off. "So how was
Denver?"

"Denver?" Sonny looked at her questioningly, as though he
didn't recognize the name of the place he'd been, or he
couldn't make sense of the question for a moment. He looked
back at his drink. "Denver was great. They sure got some
good-looking women down there." He looked up again,
squeezed her around the waist, grinned. "You know, you
aren't looking so bad yourself. What are you drinking?"

Allie accepted Henry's proffered stool, the drink Sonny
bought her, and basked in the glow of Sonny's presence. He
was back. Now everything would be all right.

"Hey, did you make it to Vegas?" Frankie wanted to know.

"Uh-huh," Sonny knocked back his glass of whiskey. "I was
a rich man for a couple of hours."

"Yeah? How much money did you make?"

Sonny grinned. "A shitload. But I lost it all. Bad luck." He
signaled the bartender for another round.

Frankie's mouth hung open at the thought of showgirls,

casinos, the brilliant details of Sonny's life Outside. "How about the whores down there? D'you check them out?"

Henry glanced protectively at Allie. "Frankie, we got ladies present, remember?"

"Yeah?" Frankie said. "Where? I don't see no ladies. You mean Allie? She don't count."

"Up yours," Allie said, but she wasn't even annoyed. Frankie didn't matter. Sonny was all that mattered. She had so much to tell him. How sorry she was for what she'd said to him that night in the bar, how wrong she'd been, how much she'd missed him. She only hoped that when the bar closed, he'd want to go somewhere with her, down to her riverboat or up to his house. She couldn't wait until they were alone together, because it was only when they were that Sonny was really hers. He'd tell her everything then.

Allie sipped her drinks, chain-smoked, watched Sonny the conquering hero. All of Vladimir wanted to buy him a drink, welcome him home, hear his tales of a fortune won and lost in Vegas, of gorgeous ski area girls. But he was drinking in a way she'd never seen before, chugging them down fast and hard. Usually he was careful, usually he stuck to beer. And as the evening went on he began to repeat himself, as the electric waterfall on the clock advertising Olympia beer repeated itself, falling and falling. Allie tried to concentrate on the flow of blue tinsel water over brown tinsel rocks while the hands on the clock spun around. Eleven, midnight, one.

The band turned off their amplifiers, sprawled around a table drinking beers, and went home. Somebody threw money in the juke box. Johnny Cash droned unconvincingly, "I Walk the Line."

"I could've been a fucking rich man," Sonny said. "I had fifteen thousand dollars in my hand." He leaned back in his chair, eyes half closed, dipping his shoulders. At first Allie couldn't figure out why the gesture seemed so familiar. But then she realized: Vivian. It was the way that his mother moved when she was drunk. Allie wanted to call him back, but he was far away, farther away than Denver.

Frankie bought Sonny one for the road and headed out. Henry lingered, looking back and forth between Sonny's and Allie's faces, hoping against hope that Allie might somehow change her mind and go with him. Finally, he gave up and went home. Linda had disappeared long ago. Mel, the relief bartender, a silent, pale-haired Norwegian with washed-out eyes, was rinsing the last of the glasses, stacking them on the bar. Allie felt uneasy in his presence. One night Mel had slipped a ten out of the register and into her pocket; she'd never been sure what the money meant — charity? seduction? Sonny sat slumped with his elbows on the counter, head down, mumbling to himself.

"One thing I didn't like down there. They got too many jigs. Fucking jigs. A bunch of cowards. They wouldn't fight in Nam."

"Sonny, I can't believe you're talking like that. You never used to talk like that before." What was he talking about? It wasn't as though he'd been to Nam himself. And who was he, an Indian, to be racist?

"They're yellow," Sonny insisted loudly, pounding the counter and making the stacked glasses rattle. Mel glanced over at them, kept wiping. "They're fucking cowards," Sonny said. "Now I got a lot of respect for your people. I always said that. They don't take no shit. Kicked out those fucking Arabs, one two. That's the way I am. I'm fast. I know I'm fast. I can throw my weight around if I have to."

"Hey, welcome home, buddy," Smiley Ferris called out as he stumbled toward the door. Even he was calling it a night. The bar was empty. Allie put her jacket on, stood beside his stool. She didn't know what to do. Sonny was too drunk now, and none of it was as it was supposed to be, not the way she'd imagined.

Sonny turned to Allie, his eyes cloudy, bloodshot. "Hey,

where you going? Aren't you gonna be my date tonight?"

She stared helplessly at her own sneakered feet, her legs in jeans. "If you want me," she said. If he wanted her. She didn't want him like this, but this was the way he was now, and he was Sonny. She'd waited so long.

Sonny stood up, stumbled, pulled bills out of his wallet, and dropped them on the floor. Allie glanced nervously at Mel, ashamed before him. Mel shrugged.

Out on the street it was drizzling again. Sonny kept turning around to look behind him, ducking his head, mumbling to himself, grunting and uttering incomprehensible animal noises that made her cringe.

He lurched against her shoulder. "Hey, you got to watch out for Indian boys and whiskey. We just can't handle that firewater. Whoooeeeee."

"Sonny, why are you doing this? Please, don't." He was acting like a drunken Indian, playing out a stereotype, reducing himself to that. This wasn't the Sonny she knew.

"Please, don't," he mimicked, then turned to Allie, grasped her face between his hands, smashed his lips against hers. His fingers slid down, pressed against her windpipe. "Did you miss me?" he demanded.

"Sonny, stop it, you're hurting me."

Sonny released her. "I told you, you got to watch out for Indian boys and whiskey. Didn't I tell you that? I warned you, a long time back."

He stumbled over to the boardwalk, sat down on the damp planks, his head in his hands. Allie lingered for a moment in the middle of Front Street. The street was empty, the streetlights glaring down at intervals, the shops dark and closed. Then Buzzy's cab, the only cab in Vladimir, an old black Cadillac with tail fins, came splashing through the gravel and pulled over. Buzzy, a short-haired, deep-voiced woman in a lumberman's jacket, rolled down the window.

"You need a ride? Last chance."

Allie considered. She wanted to be in a car, driven away

somewhere, but there was no place to go. She shook her head. Buzzy shrugged, rolled up her window, and drove away, tail-lights streaky red as the Cadillac bumped over the potholes. Allie walked over to Sonny. "Sonny, are you all right?"

"It's all shit," he said, shaking his head. "It's all gone to shit."

What was shit? Vladimir? His trip? Her? As drunk as he was, she still feared his judgment, feared that he wouldn't want her and she'd be left all alone.

Sonny looked up, his eyes full of drunken sorrow, maudlin love. "Allie? I can't believe you're still here. The little Indian girl from Boston. I was sure I'd never see you again."

"Oh, Sonny." Allie sat down beside him, pushed her face against his cheek. She might have been able to walk away from meanness, but meanness mixed with affection did her in. She knew this part of herself. Like an alcoholic picking up a drink after long abstinence, or a fish that had taken the hook: she was already caught.

"Sonny, let's go home." Gently, she helped him up and led him, supported him, down the long slippery boardwalk to his swampy yard, into his house, up the stairs.

It wasn't supposed to be like this. It was supposed to be slow and gentle and full of pauses. They'd laugh and wrestle and hold each other until they fell asleep. But it was fast and hard and ugly, and in the middle of it, Sonny passed out on top of her, and she had to struggle to get out from under him. She lay in bed a long time with her eyes wide open in the darkness, listening to his ragged breath.

During the night Allie dreamed that she was running down Front Street, but instead of the Potlatch and the Five and Dime, she passed bars and honky-tonks and bordellos, swinging western saloon doors, girls in feathers and fishnet tights. She ran from door to door, looking into rooms of screaming, drunken people, where green and red lights swirled. Nick appeared in a doorway. "You're going to learn a painful lesson," he warned before turning his back on her.

When she woke Sonny was still sleeping. Dim morning light cut through the curtainless window, illuminating the peeling wallpaper, the horrible rock posters, the broken dresser. Why was it that they always slept in his brother's room? She didn't even know what his own room looked like. He'd kept it from her, another of his secrets.

She studied him carefully, as though his face would tell. His nose had been broken; a scar ran across its bridge. There were puffy dark bags under his eyes. Sonny slept as though he were in pain, grimacing and clenching his teeth. A totem face. The totem image made her dislike herself; she was as racist as Sonny, who hated "jigs." But all she'd ever wanted was to see Sonny's face set loose and free, to see him unafraid. What had she done?

The sky lightened, a brighter grey marking daylight. Outside, an insistent, ratchety noise could be heard over and over. *Eh-eh-eh-eh. Eh-eh-eh-eh.* Allie slid out from under the covers and went to the window. Across the street on the damp new grass in front of the Catholic church, a small boy lay on his belly making machine gun noises and throwing rocks at birds. She pulled the window shut.

Sonny slept on and on and Allie grew restless. She climbed back in bed and tried to force sleep, but every time she shut her eyes another shameful image surfaced, one she couldn't escape. Last night, when Sonny leaned forward in bed to pick up dropped cigarettes, she'd seen something familiar in his long, dark, naked back and buttocks: a picture from *National Geographic,* a picture of natives squatting in mud.

On a balmy day in late April, when the springtime sun beat down intense and unimpeded, drying the puddles on Front Street and allowing everyone to take off their wool jackets for the first time all year, Nick ran into Vivian at City Market. She stood in line at the next register, her back to him. He recognized her instantly, knew the curve of her shoulders, the flirty little dip of her head as she chatted with the cashier.

Vivian turned to lift a bottle of bleach from her grocery cart and he was moved, after all these months, by the sight of her wide Tatar cheekbones, her coral lipstick, bright and jaunty against her dark skin. She wore a fluffy grey angora sweater, which swelled over her breasts and made touching little bulges above her waist: Vivian in the flesh. He experienced an odd lurching sensation, not unlike that emptiness in his stomach when the boat was caught by a maverick wave and he hung for an instant in the air.

"Hey, you want this stuff delivered to your boat or what?"

Nick turned back to Bettina, a thin woman with a pencil stuck in her marcelled curls and a large ink stain down the front of her pink smock. Bettina drummed her fingernails on the register, annoyed.

"I said, you want this stuff sent to your boat, Nick?"

"Sure, sure."

"Before seven okay?"

"Okay."

Vivian had already paid for her groceries and was wrestling with three overstuffed paper sacks. "Put it on charge," Nick told Bettina. Feeling like a teenage boy who ought to know better, he hurried out to intercept Vivian as she went through the electric doors.

"Hello, Vivian."

Vivian stopped in flustered surprise. "Well, hi, Nick." She smiled a tentative, cautious smile, yet her face looked somehow softened. Perhaps it was a reflection of her angora sweater, the way her set hair curled gently around her face, or just that she'd put on weight. She looked good.

"May I help you to carry? My hands are empty." Nick opened his palms.

"Well, all right."

Nick leaned forward, nearly encircling her as he clasped the grocery bags, shifting the weight to his own arms, an awkward little transfer that made them both laugh nervously. Her sweet perfume filled his nostrils: the same as before, pungent, dizzying. She was wearing pearl clip earrings that matched the artificial pearl buttons at her throat.

"There," Nick said, juggling the bags.

"You didn't have to take all three. I can carry one."

"No, no. Allow me."

"Still a gentleman," Vivian said. Without the bags, she didn't know what to do with her hands. She dug in her purse for cigarettes, lit one quickly, and puffed it as they walked along, squinting in the spring sunshine.

A child careened down the boardwalk on a tricycle, imitating the sound of an outboard engine, forcing them to step apart. Inside the Potlatch, Dottie, holding a Pyrex coffee pot aloft, glanced out at them. They could see her puzzled face, her mouth a gaping little O behind the glass: something for the last of the afternoon coffee drinkers to talk about before they got off their stools and headed home to cook their desultory suppers. Nick glanced sideways at Vivian. She stared ahead.

A green and white pickup with Nevada plates hauling a silver, blimp-shaped trailer drove slowly past the false-fronted clapboard shops, a heavyset man in a cowboy hat sitting at the wheel beside his grey-haired wife. Tourists off the ferry. Soon there'd be hikers and backpackers unloading from the ferry, heading out to Kutl Park. It was all starting again, like the birds flying north.

Vivian said, "It sure is nice weather today. Makes you believe summer might really come after all."

"Yes, is very nice." Now that he'd impulsively forced them together, he didn't know what to say. There were so many tricky topics to step around yet so much history between them that idle chatter sounded intolerably false. What was it he had wanted to say to her?

"So, how's the trolling?" Vivian asked.

Nick shrugged. "Not too good. Tell me, how you are, Vivian? You enjoyed your stay in Juneau?"

"Enjoy?" She laughed. "I don't know if I'd put it that way. Let's just say, I learned a lot up there."

At the turnoff to Vivian's house, at the corner past the Anchor, Vivian stopped and reached for the bags.

"Thanks, Nick. I can get them from here. You're probably headed down to the dock, so I don't want you to go out of your way."

"Is no problem."

They continued up the hill. Her house looked even more dilapidated than he remembered, badly in need of paint, with an exposed wire dangling across a window and a hole in the clapboard covered with flapping plastic. A house in need of a man. He felt annoyed that Vivian's two grown boys had done nothing to fix the place. Even the slatted chicken walk was broken, the boards squelched into the mud underfoot.

In the kitchen, Nick set the bags on the counter and looked

around. The big white washing machine still stood gleaming amidst the drab peeling wall paint and broken chairs. The room smelled of leaking gas, as before. But there was none of the clutter he remembered — no dirty dishes on the drain-board, no clothes on top of the chairs. Vivian had imposed order upon chaos, a clean little space inside a house that was falling apart.

"Well, thanks," Vivian said. "It would've been hard, drag-ging those bags up here myself." She wiped her hair from her eyes with the back of her wrist. "You want a beer or some-thing? I mean, before you go?"

Nick considered. Although she was giving him an out, showing that she assumed he'd be running off, he was still afraid to do anything she might interpret as encouragement. There was really no point in starting up with all that again.

Vivian leaned back against the counter. "It's just a beer, Nick."

Her chin had raised a notch at his hesitation. This was hard for her, too, he realized, perhaps much harder than for him. She was the one who had offered him love last year, even if her love had been distorted by need, and he'd been the one who had turned away from her.

"Why not?"

"I think I got some here, if those boys haven't cleaned me out." Vivian rummaged around in the refrigerator, came up with a bottle of Oly, which she poured out for him, and a can of Coke for herself. She opened a bag of pretzels with her teeth, set the bag on the table, and took a chair across from him. He watched her chug down half the Coke and refill her glass. He wondered if she was drinking Coke for his benefit, if it was simply a performance. No, that was unfair. Vivian had always been honest. She'd never pretended to be more than whatever she was at the time.

"The kitchen looks . . . nice." Nick gestured at the drab but tidy kitchen. What it really needed was paint, hours of repair.

"Oh, God. Don't get me started. It's tough trying to keep it up with those two boys. They've really been getting out of hand." Vivian sighed. "I don't expect much from Mikey. He's always been wild, but now Sonny's raising hell. I never figured on this from him." She stubbed out her half-smoked cigarette and lit another. "I just try to take it one day at a time, but it's rough. I can't help feeling it's my fault. I made it so hard on him all those years. He was always so good."

Nick was struck by the strange balance of forces between mother and son. Here was Vivian sitting across the table drinking Coke instead of beer, and now Sonny, who'd returned from his trip not long ago, seemed intent on becoming a drunk. It was almost as though there wasn't enough health to share between them, and one's rise determined the other's decline.

"Sonny is grown man," Nick said. He regretted his words instantly, hearing in them the echo of his fight with Vivian on the Fourth of July. He looked over, expecting to see her face darken, but Vivian merely frowned and stared at the point of her cigarette.

"You're right, Nick. I got to remember that. I'm really powerless over him."

They sat for a couple of minutes in silence. A car without a muffler rounded the corner and headed out toward the power plant, its exhaust shockingly loud. Vivian and he both reached for the bag of pretzels at the same time, their hands colliding. Nick laughed. "You are looking very well, Vivian. Juneau must have been good to you."

"Yeah?" She looked up into his eyes, her own black eyes flickering with a question. A sharp little crease formed between her brows, as though she thought she might discover, by sheer concentration, what his words meant, why he was here. Nick felt ashamed because he didn't know the answer. He didn't want to toy with her.

Vivian sighed, turned away. "I got fat up in Juneau. It's always some trade-off. Well, I guess I ought to start putting something together for dinner, just in case the boys show up.

I'm trying to play good mother these days. You don't have to rush, Nick. Finish your beer. I'll just throw something in the oven."

She pulled a package of ribs from one of the grocery bags, bathed it in bottled barbecue sauce while Nick drank his beer. The last of the afternoon sun cut through the window, caught Vivian's shoulders in a golden stripe, made a halo of her fluffy sweater, but left her face in shadow as she bent over the sink. He watched her move from the refrigerator to the counter to the oven. There was something comforting about sitting at the kitchen table while Vivian hummed to herself, slamming pots and pans. A man was supposed to live like that, in the presence of a woman.

He wanted to stand up and put his arms around her from behind, to feel the softness of her sweater, to run his hands over her breasts and kiss her neck . . . He stubbed out his cigarette. He had to go. If he didn't, she'd ask him to stay for supper; if he stayed, it would be all the harder for him to leave afterward. He wanted to stay, to sit with her thigh to thigh on the couch watching the news on TV, and then to climb the stairs to her room. No. Better to cut it short, keep it simple. There was no point in starting the same old futile song and dance. He had no right to hurt her further.

Vivian washed her hands, wiped them on her slacks. "Well, Nick," she said. "I got to run now. I've got to get to a meeting. Thanks, you know, for the help."

"To where you are going?"

"AA. I go pretty much every day. Don't look so surprised." She turned away, taking her jacket out of the closet. "It saved my life."

"No, no. no. I did not mean . . . I mean, I think that is wonderful." Nick stood up hastily, knocking over his chair. He bent to right it, the blood rushing to his face. It wasn't AA that amazed him, although that was astonishing enough — he was flabbergasted with himself. Vivian hadn't asked him to stay, she hadn't even intended to. What he felt wasn't relief after all, but disappointment. He, who knew his own heart like he knew his hands!

Nick spent an evening playing chess with Eddie Ellis, a troller who lived with his wife, Irene, up by the power plant, and it was after midnight by the time he headed home. Eddie offered to drive him back to the boat harbor but Nick declined. He liked the spring nights when the mist was soft and warm against his face, enjoyed the walk around the curve of the boat harbor. The tide was out and the streetlights shimmered over the wet mud where the derelict boats lay heaped on their sides, exposed.

Around the harbor, the mill whistle blew, signaling coffee break for the graveyard shift. The smoke hung bright and ghostly against the dark sky. Night and day, the mill churned out lumber for Japan. Almost everywhere he trolled now, he couldn't escape the great gashes in the forest where the clear cutting left the hillsides as bare as a prisoner's shaved head.

Fishing was worse than he'd ever seen it. He kept a log of every fish caught — where and on what bait — and this spring the fish weren't out there. When net fishing started, it would get worse. Last year, in July, Fish and Game had closed all net fishing for ten days, the first time anyone had heard of such a thing. There were rumors going around now that if the spawner count was too low, they might shut down longer this year. It didn't look good.

Nick sighed at his own pessimism. It was all a matter of perspective. When the timber was gone, the loggers and mills would go broke, and the forests would grow back. When there was no more profit in fishing, the fish would return. Of course, a man's life could be twisted in the process, but only if he counted too much on things staying as they were. Nick prided himself on not confusing what he'd lost with what he still could lose. But there was also the grim possibility that the abuse might be too great, the damage so severe that the land would never recover. There was always a point of no return.

At Olson's boatyard, a huge steel seiner loomed up from the cradle like a shining beast too large to live on land. Across from the boatyard, on the top of a small hill in a cluster of firs, was the grave of Chief Kutl, the last chief of Vladimir Island. A broken rail fence surrounded the hillside, and two crumbling killer whale totems guarded the grave. Nick stopped there, looked up. The leaping whale carvings seemed to shimmer and vibrate in the reflected lights from the boatyard. There was a certain magic to the spot, but not in daylight. Once he'd climbed up to examine the carvings and found broken beer bottles, toilet paper, and a used condom.

Someone coughed and Nick whirled around at the sound. Out of the reach of the streetlight, shadowed by a fir, a figure sat on the rail fence. He could see the red point of a cigarette glowing in the dark.

"Good evening," Nick said.

"Is that you, Nick?"

"Allie?"

"Yup."

"What you are doing here? You are not afraid of ghosts?"

Allie snorted. "No. I like it here."

"You want company?"

Allie glanced over her shoulder down the muddy road, then back at him. "Okay."

Nick went over and leaned against the fence, pulled out his pack of Pall Malls, and lit up. "You come here often?"

Allie laughed. "That sounds like a pickup line from a singles bar. No, I never came here before. I was at a party and I kind of got disgusted and left. Now I'm a little sorry I did."

"You can go back," Nick said carefully.

"I know."

"You are waiting to see if he will follow?"

"He won't," Allie exclaimed angrily. "He's so fucked-up

294

drunk he probably doesn't even know I'm gone. I don't know why I even went. I don't like those parties anymore. I don't even know what I'm doing sitting here. I had to get away, and now I'm sitting here, waiting for nothing. I'm fucked up too." She kicked her feet violently against the rail. The fence swayed, threatened to collapse.

"Careful!" Nick put out a hand to steady her. She'd had too much to drink. He could see it in her reckless motions, hear it in the desperate bravado in her voice. He felt angry at her, still drowning herself like that.

"You know why I like it here, Nick? Because this is what it's all about. This is really it, isn't it? A couple of crumbling totem poles guarding something nobody cares about anymore, something no one believes in. I can relate to that. I mean, the dream's gone, right?"

He wanted to laugh. She was talking of history with the arrogance of one who saw only a reflection of her own life in the sufferings of nations. To her, the extinction of an entire culture, a people, was just a metaphor for her romantic disappointment with an Indian boy. She possessed the narrow self-importance of a child. Instantly, he forgave her.

"Alinka," Nick said gently. "You have walked away from stupid party, that is all. It is good sign. It means you are already smarter girl." He dropped his cigarette into a puddle. "Come, Alinka. You will catch cold sitting here. We will walk together back to dock, and you will climb into your bunk and go to sleep. Or, if you like, I will make for you tea."

Allie looked at him, shook her head. "I don't think so, Nick. Thanks anyway, though. I think I'll hang out here."

He felt his own hands hanging uselessly at his sides. He had nothing to entice her from the path she had chosen. She'd walked away from Sonny, who seemed intent on obliteration, and instead of seeing it as an accomplishment, she needed to punish herself. Punishment was the only thing she understood. He couldn't help her — she didn't want his help. Sighing, Nick headed back to the road. The mist no longer felt warm. The dampness had crept into his bones while he leaned against the fence, and his legs belonged to somebody else. He felt years older than he had half an hour ago.

"Nick?"

He stopped, turned to see Allie huddled on the fence rail, knees up.

"Can I still come with you?"

Although her voice was small, it filled him with relief. She hopped down, slid on the grassy bank of the hill, and splashed through the puddles to join him. They walked along in silence around the curve of the boat harbor, past darkened cabins, crumbling totems, and wet glossy ferns, in and out of the glow of the street lamps. No cars passed, and the only sound was the slight suck of their rubber boots, the distant, gentle lap of the tide on the mud. They turned onto Front Street.

"You want to hear something funny?" Allie said.

"Sure." He would love to be delivered by laughter, a convulsion that had seemed so foreign to him lately he wouldn't know it from a sob.

"Today's my birthday, Nick. I'm twenty-one, a real grown-up. Pretty funny, huh?" She looked up with a rueful grin.

Nick was filled with a surge of wild springtime hope. Perhaps the damage could be reversed. Perhaps they could all travel back from the point of no return.

"Happy Birthday, Alinka."

JULY
1975

———◆———

Sonny woke and knew it was too late. He was supposed to be down at the Ketchikan dock by nine, and in the drear light of the flophouse room, his watch read ten forty-five. For all he knew, they'd pull out without him. He dressed quickly. The red-haired girl was still asleep, mouth open; rumpled sheets revealed a long thigh and a belly slashed with stretch marks. She had kids. He remembered that much, but he couldn't remember her name. When he turned on the water to splash his face, averting his eyes from his own image in the cracked and spotted mirror, the girl woke. She looked at him once, then rolled over and faced the wall.

"Got to move it," Sonny said. She didn't answer. He hurried out, patting the breast pocket of his denim jacket, where his wallet nestled safely. The hall was dark, lit by a few low-wattage bulbs dangling on wires, and a pile of vomit lay on the rug in front of the elevator. He chose the dank stairs, clattering down them two at a time, every step a jolt to his pounding head.

On the street he was assaulted by honking traffic, streetlights. The dusty store windows were full of soapstone, bowie knives, and sealskin jackets for the tourists. The concrete sidewalks were littered with broken bottles and passed-out drunks. A cold breeze blew up from the channel, swirling the trash on the street. Sonny stood in a doorway to light a cigarette with shaking fingers, peering out at pedestrians who seemed to lurch instead of walk. They all looked like escapees from a carnival side show or a bad dream — men with smashed, battered faces; grotesquely fat women with mammoth thighs quivering under improbably bright stretch pants.

A tattered banner stretched across a main intersection: WELCOME TO KETCHIKAN: ALASKA'S THIRD LARGEST CITY. POPULATION 10,000. THE SALMON CAPITAL OF THE WORLD. They'd have to revise their sign now that the human population had shifted north with the pipeline, and the salmon population seemed to have disappeared. Sonny hated Ketchikan, a goddamn town set out in one long street five miles long and two blocks wide at the base of an eroded clear-cut mountain that threatened to slide into the bay, drowning them all.

He passed the bar where he'd picked up the girl last night and shuddered. Frankie, Henry, and Duane had been there with him. Had everyone gone back down to the boat while he and the girl headed up to a room with a sprung cot, grey sheets, and a stained mattress? He hoped he hadn't caught anything from her. He needed to stop and buy something — a beer, at least, to cut the shaking in his fingers. He was so late now it couldn't matter that much.

In Vladimir the bars didn't open until noon, but in Ketchikan they swept out the drunks at five A.M. and opened again at seven. Sonny ducked into the darkness of a dive called the Home Port and took a stool. A kid with a crew cut was pinging away at a pinball machine, slapping it so hard that Sonny wanted to get up and kill him. The bartender, an elderly man with glasses, sat by the register, engrossed in trimming his curved yellow fingernails with a pocket knife, letting the horny cuttings fall on the bar. The old man sighed with annoyance, put down his knife, and came over to take Sonny's order. Sonny asked for an Oly, drank it fast, and ordered another. The radio was on and blaring the morning's list of arrests for DWI, aggravated assault, murder — the usual Ketchikan news. Sonny patted his wallet in his breast pocket and breathed relief.

The only other drinker in the Home Port sat two stools away, a middle-aged guy with a week's worth of stubble, sloping shoulders, and a belly that drooped onto his knees.

"I don't know what she gone and done it for," the man said sadly. He leaned over to peer at Sonny, squinting out of one brown eye, and Sonny saw with a little shock of revulsion that the other eye was blue, fixed in a gaze, and certainly made of glass, or plastic, or whatever it was that fake eyes were made of. It struck him as pathetically low. If Sonny had a glass eye, at least he'd make sure it matched.

"What she gone and done it for, huh? What for? You tell me," Glass Eye whined.

"Can't help you, brother," Sonny mumbled. He couldn't help himself, for that matter. He was a fucked-up drunk Indian in Ketchikan. It was twelve-fifteen already. He ought to just leg it on up to the ferry terminal and buy himself a ride back home. He didn't want to go down to the dock. He couldn't even remember the day of the week, but he knew there was a seine opening, and they were supposed to be heading out to the grounds. Today? Tomorrow? Twelve hours? Twenty-four? All they'd done was haul water last time. Bill would be ripped, ripped that the fishing was so bad, ripped that Sonny hadn't shown up. What was the point of going down there? To haul water, get screamed at? He ordered another beer.

The kid had given up on the pinball machine, and Sonny's headache had eased a notch. He regretted not ordering a tomato beer for his hangover. Could you call it a hangover if you'd been drunk for the past five months?

"You know what I'm gonna do?" Glass Eye inquired with sudden determination. "I'm gonna timber the bar." He reached up from his stool to grasp at the string dangling from a bell that, when rung, signaled free drinks for everyone. The underage pinball player perked up his jug ears with interest.

"It ain't hardly timbering if there's only two of you," the bartender commented dryly.

"Hell it ain't," Glass Eye said. "I sure as hell can timber the bar if I feel like it. I'm a generous man." He reached up and gave the bell a good hard pull, filling the dark barroom with a raucous clang that hurt Sonny's head. It struck Sonny as some kind of noble, futile gesture: the right intentions but the wrong moment. On the other hand, maybe he was just cheap.

Glass Eye sat back on his stool, winded and drained. He'd expended the whole of his energy ringing the bell. "I just timbered the bar. Don't tell me I ain't a generous man. That's what I told her, I'm a generous man, but she still gone and left me. Get my friend here whatever he wants." He gestured toward Sonny.

The bartender put his hands on his hips in a show of put upon patience.

Sonny lifted his Oly can and shrugged. Whatever he wanted? That was the beauty of it. His hangover was lifting, and he no longer wanted anything at all. He forgave the guy his bad taste in glass eyes, his pitiful, grandiose gesture. He was a generous man, too.

Sonny stood at the top of the dock ramp, looking down at a brilliant panoply of tumbling colors, intricate motions, and competing sounds that left him dizzy and impressed. Everywhere boats were pulling in, pulling out, their masts, trolling poles, booms, and suspended power blocks tangling up in his vision. Rumbling diesel engines, whining outboards, and screeching gulls confounded his ears.

The ramp to the floats was steep and felt like a trampoline beneath his feet. Sonny gripped the rail. Even on the level he seemed to be tilting, and he had to concentrate to keep an even keel. The black water showed through the cracks between the planks, reminding him of that children's rhyme: step on a crack, break your mother's back. He couldn't seem to avoid them. Damage was inevitable, as usual.

He finally found the *Nancy M.* tied to the gas dock, engine running, the power skiff snubbed up on top of the piled seine. Frankie, Henry, and Duane were lounging on deck, looking useless. They glanced at one another but didn't say anything when Sonny climbed aboard. Sonny spotted Bill by the pumps, talking to the gas man. When Bill saw Sonny, he walked over. Duane whistled low. "Can it," Frankie hissed.

"You're off the boat," Bill announced.

"Hey." Sonny smiled ingratiatingly. "Hey, man. I'm sorry. It won't happen again."

Bill frowned at him from under the visor of his fisherman's cap. Sonny had never before fully noted the ridiculousness of Bill's muttonchop whiskers. It was funny how guys grew more hair on their faces when they started to lose it on top. Bill probably wore his fisherman's cap to bed. Vanity. The thing to do was to appeal to Bill's vanity, to work him around and finesse his way back on board. Sonny dug into his mind for something Bill would want to hear, but nothing sounded right.

"It already happened too many times," Bill said. "Get your stuff and get off." He gestured toward a green duffel bag flopped beside the hydraulic winch. The duffel was stuffed with his belongings — a bad news bulletin.

"Hey, Bill, give me a break. Everyone makes mistakes, right?"

Frankie, Henry, and Duane were no longer looking at Sonny, but in every other possible direction. The hell with them. Some friends. He didn't need friends. He needed a beer. A beer would give him back the good feeling he'd lost, or at least a feeling better than this.

"C'mon, man, I'm sorry. Hey, you know how it is. You chased a little tail in your day, right?"

Bill turned away, lifted Sonny's duffel, and threw it over the rail onto the gas dock. "You don't work here no more," he said. "Henry, get those lines. We're casting off."

"Hey, man," Sonny called after him. "Hell with you. You got no sense of humor."

Bill didn't turn back but merely shook his head in disgust as he disappeared into the galley. Henry came over and offered Sonny a what-can-you-do shrug. He reached a hand up to Sonny's shoulder.

Sonny twisted away, lurched, regained his balance. "Fuck you all." They weren't going to make any bucks anyway. The fish weren't out there, and everything had gone to hell.

IT WAS tour boat day at the Takine, a day that Allie hated. The *Princess Eleanor*, a Canadian ship, had docked for its regular ninety-minute scheduled stop in Vladimir, where it was welcomed by the Vladimir High School band. The tourists, mostly middle-aged and elderly ladies in pastel raincoats and accordion plastic rain hats, with a sprinkling of retired gentlemen sporting trench coats and complicated cameras, filed up and down Front Street in search of gift shops and photographs. After forty-five minutes, they'd had enough. Vladimir, although it rated high on the quaintness meter, offered nothing to buy that they hadn't already seen in Ketchikan.

By six o'clock all the booths by the picture windows were full of tourists. The band, this week an argumentative threesome from San Bernardino called the Tracy Trio, was paid to come in early to play a set, allowing the widows and divorcées to take their turns spinning around the dance floor in the arms of Oliver, the boat's social director, a smarmy little effeminate man in a toupee. Oliver flirted outrageously with his ladies, bought them all drinks, and rolled his eyes campily at Allie and Linda, as if to say, "It's awful, but we're all in it for the tips, aren't we, girls?"

Allie despised Oliver as she despised the tourists — outsiders who came into town, knew nothing of its life, and left with their superiority intact — because she secretly feared she might be like them. Last week she'd been walking down Front Street when a husband off a tour ship pointed her out to his wife and loudly announced, "Look honey, a klootch!" He'd probably just learned the term from Louis L'Amour's *Alaska*. Allie had thrown back her shoulders in her best imitation of native pride and sneered.

She'd wanted to tell that story to Sonny, to hear him laugh as he'd laughed in the Baranof in Juneau. It had been a long time since she'd told any stories to Sonny, a long time since she'd known how to make him laugh. When she saw him on the street or in the bar now, he still had the power to take away her breath, but it felt more like emptiness than love.

Later the incident haunted her, made her ashamed. She could afford to get a kick out of playing squaw in the face of foolish tourists precisely because she wasn't Indian. Her outrage was a sham. If she'd been truly Indian, it would have been pain or hatred she'd have felt, not the relief that came from playing at being someone else. She was tiring of the game of mistaken identity. It wasn't fair to hate the tourists. The truth was, she could easily imagine her own mother as one of them: a frightened divorced lady trying to make the best of being alone.

For forty minutes Allie ran around delivering Manhattans and whiskey sours and blender drinks that matched the pastels of the ladies' raincoats. Nick had come in and taken a seat at the end of the bar. After the tourists left she'd go over to talk to him — a reward for good behavior, for not snapping at anyone. She kept reminding herself that she had only five more days of this. Soon she'd be on a boat. A boat at last!

The skipper of a cannery tender from Ketchikan, a packer boat, had finally agreed to hire her on as deckhand. It wasn't as good as fishing, but at least there was a woman cook aboard, so she wouldn't be expected to play girlfriend. Her skipper-to-be liked to hire women deckhands, he said, because they were more reliable. They didn't get tanked up in town and then not show up when it was time to leave port. Allie suspected he hired women because he could pay them less, but she didn't care.

Linda couldn't understand it. Since the pipeline construction had started up north, they were all making money off the trickle-down effects of Alaskan oil. It seemed half of the men in Vladimir — loggers, mill workers, tug crews — had headed up to Fairbanks and Barrow where they made so much money in a couple of months they'd have to quit for a while in order not to raise their tax brackets. They came back to Vladimir for R and R and threw their money around in the bars. Tips were great, but tips didn't matter to Allie. What mattered was the chance to stand on the deck of a boat again and glide out of town.

It wasn't the same as last year, when she'd worked in the Takine's coffee shop and mooned over the fishing boats through the window. She no longer believed the fishermen spoke a secret language and that they would teach her something she needed to know. She simply couldn't stand what she was doing, and she craved the relief of motion. If she was still prey to the belief that it would be better somewhere else, it was now a diluted version. "Better" only meant the novelty of change; escape was merely temporary. A boat would give her the pleasure of feeling wet lines between her fingers, the roll of ocean underfoot. She knew it wouldn't tell her who she was, just where she'd been. A boat was better than nothing.

At six forty-five, Oliver looked at his watch, clapped his hands, and ushered his brood out the door. On the bar he left twenty dollars apiece for Allie and Linda. The band immediately stopped playing and put down their instruments. Allie went over to clear the empties from the booths.

"The ladies leave you anything?" Linda asked as Allie came up with a tray piled with ashtrays and glasses.

"The usual." Allie's change belt clanked full of change that wouldn't amount to more than five or six dollars. On package tours, the women seemed to feel they didn't have to tip.

Linda pushed the twenty at her. "Well, here's yours."

"I'd sure hate to have his job," Allie said, first inspecting, then pocketing her money.

"Oh, Allie. I wouldn't mind it. It's not any worse than what we do. He's giving them a good time."

Allie sighed and pushed her hair off her sweaty forehead, went over to finish cleaning the booths by the windows. Through the window, the water was glassily calm, the bay a smooth sheet of grey-green, and fog climbed in tiers up the sides of Siligovsky Island. The enormous, dazzling-white *Princess Eleanor* appeared in her line of vision, swung smoothly around and headed — eagerly, it seemed to Allie — west to its next scheduled stop, Sitka or Juneau. Kids in speedboats raced around the ship like dolphins, jumping back and forth across the big boat's surflike wake. Allie pressed her face to the glass and imagined the spray flying up in their faces, their screaming, arm-waving joy.

She carried her empties back to the bar. Digger had come in and was sitting at the bar beside Nick, talking animatedly in that booming voice she knew so well and still disliked, although now he was a minor irritation since he had no power over her. He was just another drinker, someone who tried to pick her up when he'd had too many whiskies.

"You hear what happened yet?" Digger demanded. Up close, Allie saw that his dirty white fishing cap had slid half off his head, and his eyes were wild. He looked as crazed as the time she'd fallen asleep on watch last summer, when she was gill-netting on his boat. Instinctively, she moved out of hitting range.

"The goddamn game's over," Digger said. "They shut it down!"

"What?" Allie looked into the blank faces of Linda and Nick.

"They fucking shut it down," Digger said. "They fucking shut down all net fishing until further notice. Gill netting and seining both. You believe that shit? They might not open up again this year at all. They might never open up again."

Stunned, Allie turned to look at Nick for confirmation.

Nick shrugged.

"Nobody knows yet," Digger said, "but I got a friend up in Juneau who works in Fish and Game. They're going public tomorrow. Fucking shit."

Allie put her elbows on the bar and rested her head in her hands. If it was true, her job on the packer boat no longer existed. It was all over. She knew that it also meant a disaster for Vladimir — the cannery shut down, half the town out of work — but her own loss loomed much larger. She wouldn't be going anywhere. She'd be stuck here, trapped.

"That ain't the worst of it," Digger said furiously. "Wait 'til you hear this. I might not even get a trolling license next year. If they put through the grandfather clause to cut out half the boats, trollers are out too. If you didn't have gear in the water steady for the past five years, forget it. You're out, cold. I put in one season on a tug to make cash for gear, and it fucks up everything. Is that fair? I'm a fisherman, and they won't let me fish. We ought to have a fucking rebellion, that's what we ought to do."

He turned to Nick for agreement. Nick remained impassive, staring off into some private middle distance.

"Yeah, what do you care?" Digger spat. "You had a license for years, so it's all the more fish for you. But what about me? I ain't going to take this laying down. We ought to just go on out there and shoot any Fish and Game asshole that tries to stop us. It's time for war!" He pounded the top of the bar, making the glasses rattle. "We ought to have a fucking revolution!"

Nick stood, put a five on the bar, and walked out of the Takine Inn.

Allie looked wildly at Linda, threw up her hands, and ran

309

out to the street after him. "Nick," she called. "Nick, wait."

It was raining, a chill summer rain falling straight down into the Front Street puddles.

Nick stopped and turned. His cap was spotted with rain, his down vest dark across the shoulders.

"Nick, please. I'm going to lose my deckhand job if they shut it down. Let me fish with you, please?"

Nick shook his head. "Allie, you know I fish alone."

She grabbed his sleeve, spoke in a rush. "You didn't always. You took Sonny out with you that time. We're friends, right? Please, Nick, take me with you. Everything's shutting down. I won't have a chance to get on any boat, and I can't stand hanging out in this bar anymore. Help me get out of here, please."

Nick looked at her for a long time, his blue eyes moving over her face so thoroughly she could almost feel them. His eyes flickered, and she saw again the strange blue-black prismatic shift deep within his irises, then his angular face contracted, hardened. She knew he was going to say no. He didn't want her.

"Allie," Nick said. "Allie, you humiliate me. Am I so old you do not have to consider me like man? You know my boat. She is no ocean liner. You think I could eat, sleep, dress beside you and be stone? You think we could wake up beside each other every morning and go to sleep like that? You could, of course, but I could not. I would want you, Allie, and it would be very wrong. I am three times your age, perhaps. But I am still man." Nick touched his dripping cap, turned, and walked away down the middle of Front Street, shoulders stooped, head down.

He didn't want her because he wanted her. Once again her body was to blame. Even to Nick she wasn't a deckhand but a girl deckhand. She would never escape. Clutching her bare wet arms, shivering, Allie trudged back into the Takine Inn.

W HEN SONNY walked out onto Front Street, the sun made him wince. Everything had too many edges; he preferred the fog, the softening grey of an overcast day, the usual rain. When it was foggy, you couldn't see the tops of the mountains, and the islands seemed farther away — a vista of endless depth. The sun made everything shrunken, too close, too real. He was getting to be like those old-timers sitting in the window of the Anchor Lounge glaring out at the sunshine — a bunch of slugs.

Ravens squawked at him from the trees, tossing insults, clucking their tongues. Did ravens have tongues? He didn't know. They looked down at him with their black beady eyes, turning their heads from side to side. "Get out of here," Sonny said, picking up a pebble and taking aim. The ravens flapped up awkwardly, beating their wings, screaming obscenities. Sonny threw the stone at them, cursing. Don't talk to the ravens, his grandmother had warned.

At the platform over the dock, Sonny stopped. A flock of gulls were fighting over fish gurry thrown from the stern of a halibut boat. A float plane taxied through the channel, its roar hurting his ears. It was too noisy today, everywhere static clogging his senses, too many competing signals, nothing coming in clear. He spotted Henry below on the dock, standing in his flat-bottomed river skiff pumping gas from a red tank through a rubber hose to the outboard. Duane and Frankie putted up in a second skiff and idled alongside. Sonny squinted down at them, gripping the railing.

The ramp seemed steeper than it ought to. It couldn't be low tide now; you couldn't get over the flats by the mouth of the river at low tide. He knew something after all. But his fingers were shaking. The cold of the six-packs in the paper sack under his arm made him ache like a sore tooth. He needed the beer fog that would shade his eyes and make the pound in his head go away. He didn't want to go upriver. He didn't want the banging of the skiff across the shallow flats, and the glare of sun on water would be too much. But here he was, and Henry, Frankie, and Duane were waiting.

"I see you dressed for it," Henry said, grinning. Sonny looked at his black motorcycle boots, new leather jacket, and white shirt. He'd never undressed last night.

"I just want to make a good impression on those moose up there." Sonny smiled weakly.

"Hey, Allie!" Henry called out. She was walking toward them from the other end of the dock. "Allie. We're going upriver. You want to come along?"

Allie was wearing jeans and one of those loose white embroidered Mexican blouses. Sonny narrowed his eyes. She looked exactly like some Mexican señorita. Still wearing costumes, still playing games with his head.

Allie put up a hand to shade her eyes. "Well . . . I've got to work tonight. How long will you be gone?" She glanced at Sonny questioningly, waiting for some kind of encouragement. He looked down at his boots. He couldn't stand that way she had of looking at him: those big cow eyes, always full of disappointment, reproach. What the hell did she want from him anyway? The trouble with the girls in this town was that they wanted too much.

"We'll get you back by dinnertime," Henry urged. "C'mon.

We're just going to zip on up to the hot springs and soak our blues away. Nobody's got anything better to do anymore, right? We got some wine here." Henry lifted a bottle out of a paper sack. "It says Riunite. But I just call it Real Neat." He smiled his happy little kid's smile.

Allie frowned. "Can you wait a minute while I grab a sweater?"

"Make it snappy," Frankie said. "Those hot springs are calling my name."

Allie ran up the dock toward her riverboat. Sonny climbed into the bow of Henry's skiff, reached into his paper sack, and popped open a beer. It sprayed up, a steamy little fog of cold bubbles caught by the sun. He sucked it down gratefully.

Allie returned and climbed into Henry's skiff. They cast off and headed out into the channel between the fishing boat floats and the tugboat dock, chugging along slowly with Frankie's skiff right alongside, until they were past the shrimp cannery and into the bay. Then Henry let her rip and they shot forward, tossing up spray. Frankie and Duane passed them, cutting across their bow. They slammed into Frankie's wake, leaped into the air, plummeted, leaped — a roller coaster ride. Up ahead, Frankie and Duane were laughing, guzzling beer.

Across the water to the west, Siligovsky Island stood out sharply in the sunshine. Northward, ahead, the mainland mountains rose up like an icy white jagged wall. Sonny had the strange sensation that he was being sucked into them, as though the mountains were magnets and the little skiff an iron shaving. He felt a sudden rush of fear — the hair on his arms and on the back of his neck prickled. Don't think of that, he told himself. Don't look.

He turned to see Allie leaning into the rushing wind like a dog sticking its head out a car window. She squinted her eyes, stuck out her chin. It was a relief to see her black hair whipping around her tanned face, her white blouse flapping like a sail. He felt contrite and moved close to speak into her ear.

"I was heading down to see you last night but things kept getting in the way. You know how it is."

"I know how *you* are."

"Can't make everyone happy," Sonny said. He tossed his empty beer can into the glinting water, where it leaped into the air, caught for a second in the wake.

"Oh, Sonny," Allie said. Her voice sounded far away.

Then the beer started to work, and he got under the fog. He didn't know why everything had gotten so twisted. He'd had some nice times with Allie. It was peaceful for a while. Maybe he'd even loved her. If he'd stayed around last winter instead of going so far from home, maybe they could have kept going the way they were before the Denver business screwed it all up. No, something had happened that made that seem unlikely, but he couldn't remember now what it was. He'd said something or she had . . . People were always saying something. Like his mother with Nick. No one really wanted to be happy. If they wanted to be happy, they wouldn't go around saying things. He felt wise and on top of things and full of understanding.

But lying around talking to Allie in bed up at his mom's house had been nice. He remembered how she liked to play with his Alaska ring, trying it on. She would joke about stealing it from him, although it was too big for her finger. Sonny smiled at the memory, looked down at his hands to admire his ring, and saw that it was gone. He jerked up in his seat in panic. Shit! He always wore that ring, never took it off. He frantically searched the bilgy floorboards around his boots, then glanced over at Allie in sudden suspicion.

Allie looked back at him, puzzled. Innocent, Sonny decided. She hadn't taken anything. He must have simply left the ring somewhere. He'd been so many places lately, and he didn't remember any of them very well. Oh, well, there was no reason to sweat it, no reason to ruin his mood. He could always get another one. Still, it was funny how you could lose things without noticing until they were gone. And once they were gone they kept haunting you so that it was the loss that mattered, not the thing.

Sonny sighed, leaned back, and popped open another beer. He shut his eyes against the glare, but bright lights danced under his lids, dazzling squiggles of color. It seemed that his own electrical impulses, his brain waves, were being projected onto the back of his lids like on a movie screen. He smiled at the idea of tuning in to his own private channel. Sonny began to hum.

The skiff bounced and shimmied over the waves. Allie pulled her flapping, windblown hair out of her face and turned to steal another look at Sonny. His eyes were almost closed, as though there were nothing of interest to look at out here in the middle of a sunstruck sea. At first he'd been smiling, happy with himself, and then his expression had changed to alarm. Now he looked simply vacant. His eyes, which had been darting under the lids, were still, cast down.

Dead eyes, that's what he had. The sudden knowledge made her shiver. Sonny's eyes gave out no light but sucked it all in, compressing every bit of life into a dense dark absence, a black hole. Even when he looked at her, she didn't exist for him. And yet here she was, rushing toward snowy mainland mountains with four drunken men, just to be near him again. Now she knew her mistake: Sonny wasn't a presence but an absence. It wasn't Sonny but the absence she'd loved.

Dead eyes. They were so, so familiar. Every man she'd ever been with had dead eyes — men whose eyes turned away from her before the door even closed, men in whose eyes all life had been extinguished. All her life she'd been saying, "Look at me," but their eyes couldn't see her. Her father had eyes like that.

Her father's eyes were beautiful, flecked dark green with

315

straight thick lashes, eyes that never met Allie's face but always looked away, preferring to settle on her body or down into some private emptiness. Allie's mother said she had married Allie's father because his eyes were so sad. She wanted to save him. "You have to forgive your father," her mother counseled, "he's an unhappy man."

Allie had forgiven and forgiven, and all the time she'd been waiting for the day when he would open his eyes and see her. Waiting for him to rescue her from this false life, this twenty-year bad dream. Waiting for him to release her from exile, to take her home.

Her father would never come.

Allie didn't want to go on this river trip anymore, she wanted to go home. She looked across the expanse of bay, the mountains rising larger and larger, and she was filled with a terrible emptiness. She was alone.

Henry held up the bottle of Riunite and called out to her over the roar of the engine. "You want some?"

She accepted the bottle of wine from him, took a swig. They passed the Takine Inn, the ferry terminal, the beach with Nick's cabin. Allie wished she was there, on shore, playing chess with Nick instead of sitting in a skiff with Sonny, sucking down bad wine at ten in the morning. It was too late now.

They crossed the line where the milky, silt-laden river water met the darker sea and headed over the flats at the river delta. Henry slowed the skiff, picking his way carefully over sandbars and reefs, reading the depths by the color of the water. Frankie pulled up close to follow Henry's lead. Then they were racing over the shallows into the broad green mouth of the river, into another, inland world.

Leaving the ocean behind was like moving from black and white to color, the change was so immediate, so intense. The Takine River was a roaring expanse of icy fresh water carrying millions of tons of silt, yet soft as a dream with secret gurglings. Half-submerged chunks of glacier ice and whole upended trees sailed along beside them in the greeny water. Henry headed straight for the snags, then veered away at the last moment.

The banks of the river were dense with shrubbery, deciduous trees, and flowers — alder, red fireweed, blueberry, high bush cranberry, devil's club. Cottonwoods dropped fluff, perfuming the hot summer air. Above them, waterfalls spilled down the stony flanks of steep cliffs in paths like forked lightning. The sound of running water was everywhere, water running down to the sea.

Allie had never seen a place more beautiful, more wild. Let it fill me up, she silently begged. Let it be enough for me now.

Henry turned into a narrow side slough. The water there was so shallow, so clear, they could see every pebble delineated, even the trout darting beneath the skiff. Beyond the alder thickets, the land opened into grassy meadows, wild pastures for moose and deer.

Frankie shouted, pointed up. They slowed. Far above them, a black bear ambled across a snowy slope. Frankie pulled out his pistol and fired into the air. The bear took off in an awkward, shambling gait. Frankie howled with laughter.

They ran deeper into the forest, finally stopping to beach the skiffs on a mucky shore backed up against a thick wall of devil's club, Sitka spruce, and white fir. A big, old, round wooden tub, a vat for dyeing gill nets, had been set up on a wooden platform, and the waters from a hot spring had been routed into the tub through plastic tubing. Henry carried the paper sack full of wine bottles up to the platform. Duane immediately stripped, exposing his blubbery belly and dangling penis, his reddened, flaccid behind as he clambered into the tub. Sonny and Frankie looked hard-muscled, brown. Henry, in deference to Allie or out of self-consciousness, got into the water wearing his clothes.

Allie hesitated on the platform. She didn't want to strip.

Frankie was watching her over the rim of the tub. She finally decided to take off her jeans but to leave her blouse on. As soon as she climbed into the hot, steamy water, settling between Henry and Frankie, her wet white blouse clung to her, as transparent as gauze. She sank down to chin level. Across from her, Sonny sat with his head back, eyes half closed. His brown chest was as smooth, as hard as ever. It seemed strange that his body could still look so healthy and young. Henry passed her the wine bottle.

"Hey," Frankie said. "Remember Mickey Duffy? Remember that?"

Henry said, "Poor sucker."

"What happened?" Allie asked.

"He was poaching deer in December right down this slough when his skiff swamped," Frankie said. "He knew his river, but he was greedy. They found the skiff with three does on it. When they picked Mickey up he was a regular icicle. Frozen solid. They took his body up to the hospital for the autopsy and thawed him out. Doc said his Timex was still ticking."

"Jesus," Henry said, "that's sick."

"Hell," Frankie said, "it'd make a good ad."

Allie giggled. The heat and the wine were going to her head. She felt a hand on her thigh under the water. She glanced quickly around at their faces, but they all looked serene, nobody showed anything. She moved her leg away and frowned.

Duane leaned back, groaning in pleasure. "This is the good life, all right. I better enjoy it while I can."

Frankie said, "Hey, with no fishing, you can come here every day."

Duane shook his head. "Nah. I'm gonna head on up to the pipeline. I can't wait around to see what happens with fishing."

"You're going to have to get in line behind us," Frankie

said. "They're hiring natives first. Allie here could pass, but they won't take a big fat honky like you."

"I ain't going to no pipeline," Henry said. "I don't care what kind of money they got. I got everything I need right here. It don't matter to me if fishing shuts down forever."

"Yeah, right," Frankie said. "Henry'll just live off poaching deer. He took twenty-three last season."

"With only twenty-four shells," Henry said proudly. "And they all got eaten by people who needed 'em."

Sonny said nothing.

"Hell," Frankie considered, "I might go up there and check it out. Vladimir's going to be dead without fishing, and I don't want to go work no green chain in the mill."

"There's big money to be made." Duane splashed at the surface of the steaming water. "You might as well get your share before it's gone. Get in on the gold rush."

"Hey, Allie." Frankie smirked. "I hear the whores up there are making a fortune."

Henry said, "Don't talk to her like that."

Allie grimaced. "You know, Frankie, they probably could use some male prostitutes up there too. Maybe that's your true calling."

"You gonna teach me how?" Frankie leered.

Under the water she could feel the hand on her thigh again. She punched at it. "You wish."

Sonny still said nothing.

Frankie rose from the steaming water, giving Allie a faceful of his behind, and ran howling down the path to jump into the slough.

In the skiff again, Allie and Henry drifted, engine off, spinning gently in lazy circles down a wide, slow-moving tributary of the main river. Alder leaves rode the current, little green Viking ships. Allie looked across the gleaming water at Sonny, who was sleeping in Frankie's skiff. He'd wake with a four-star hangover, she was sure. The wine was already gone. Real Neat.

Across the river the mountains rose steep and dramatic, pale rocky cliffs so high they blocked the sky, although the sun beat down intensely directly overhead, making the water sparkle. Disney mountains. She was spinning downriver in the middle of a nature film, through countryside too gorgeous to be real. Allie, she told herself, this is your life. You are in a skiff, drifting down a river in Alaskan wilderness. She didn't believe it. "It's so beautiful here," she said softly.

Henry looked pleased, as though she'd complimented him. "You know, Allie, I've spent a lot of time up in these mountains. Hunting goat. I could go up into this country any day and live all right. I love to hunt. I don't kill for fun, but I love to do it, long as you do it right."

She remembered Sonny's words last summer, about the snow geese, and why he couldn't stand to hunt anymore. How he didn't believe in taking away their freedom, and how they struggled to live right up to the last moment.

"Henry, why don't you just live out here instead of in town? You know, get a cabin?" There were people who lived like that, in houseboats on the river, or in shacks. They came into town every few months to buy staples. Wolf trappers, homesteaders, people who couldn't stand even a Vladimir version of civilization.

"Oh, you know how it is. Can't live with town, can't live without it." Henry shrugged. "I got family and all. But I'd never live anywhere else besides this part of the world."

"How do you know if you've never been?" she said, although she really couldn't imagine Henry living anywhere else.

"Oh, I went Outside once. The BIA sent me down to Chicago to go to mechanic school." Henry raised his eyebrows. "I don't know why they couldn't find a mechanic school in Anchorage or Seattle, but what the hell, BIA was paying.

They sent me with this Eskimo kid from Barrow. He was the meanest little SOB you ever met. Always looking for fights. I guess he must've had a chip on his shoulder about being little.

"Jeez, it was hard keeping him out of trouble on that train. He was always going for the biggest guys. But when we got to Chicago, he got homesick for Barrow and turned around and went home. I figured I might as well stick it out and learn something new. I roomed in this house but the landlady wouldn't let me talk to her kids. She told them I ate whale blubber and lived in a igloo."

Allie pictured a young Henry alone in Chicago, a Tlingit Indian from Vladimir, as alone as Sonny must have been in Denver. How was it that Henry had survived? "What a bitch," she said.

"Aw, she didn't know any better. It was okay. And there was this orphanage down the street. They let me take the kids out. Every Sunday I took a different kid to the zoo." Henry looked happy at the memory. "Hell, I had more fun than they did."

Allie smiled at him. Sweet Henry, with his gentle chipmunk face, his round blue eyes that always looked surprised, his courtly ways. In Chicago he'd managed to find what he needed, children and wild animals, even if they were in cages. Why couldn't she have fallen for someone like him instead of Sonny?

"Chicago was okay," Henry said. "But after nine months, I came home. This is where I live. I never wanted to be a mechanic anyway." He reached across the distance to touch her hair for a second. "You're a real nice girl, Allie. Easy to talk to. You stay around until fall and I'll teach you how to hunt."

"Thanks, Henry." He was offering her his greatest gift, but she couldn't accept it. She looked over at Frankie's drifting skiff, where Sonny still slept on and Duane and Frankie were sharing a joint. "How come you're always so nice?"

"Hell," Henry said, embarrassed. "I ain't nothing. I don't

321

want nothing and I don't give a shit about nothing. Hunt in the fall, fish in the summer, set my traps when it snows."

Allied trailed her fingers through the water, looking out at the brilliant, heartbreaking pageantry of wilderness, the dark green forest, the rocky cliffs where Henry's mountain goats lived out their shaggy, risk-filled lives. It wasn't enough. It was beautiful, but it wasn't hers.

They beached the two skiffs and sat on a hill of heaped white sand as fine as a Cape Cod beach, beside a wide, slow spot in a back slough — the swimming hole. Duane, Henry, and Sonny shared a joint. Now it was Henry who slept, passed out in a little childlike ball, his face on his arm. His nose looked sunburned. Allie touched her own cheeks and felt the tightened skin. Too much wine, too much sun reflecting off the water. She felt dizzy. It was already late afternoon and she had to work tonight; she couldn't work a shift drunk and stoned. It was time to lay off, time to head back home.

She got up and walked to the edge of the water to clear her head, dipping a toe into the pool where minnows darted. To them, she thought, her foot must look like a giant monster, yet in the midst of this forest, this wildness, she knew how small she was. "I'm not as big as you think I am," she said softly to the little fish.

Frankie appeared beside her. He smiled amiably, then shoved her hard, backward into the water. Allie came up spluttering and mad. Her clothes had been wet all day and had finally dried out while they were drifting in the skiff.

"*Very* funny," she said.

She started to clamber out, but Frankie grabbed her shoulders and pushed her down again. This time when she came up, she backed away, knee deep in the water, glancing over at the sandy shore where Duane and Sonny leaned toward each other, intent on their joint.

Frankie looked over his shoulder, then back at her. "Sonny don't care," he said.

It was true, but it made her angry to hear Frankie say it. She tried to dodge past him, but he leaped forward and wrapped his arms around her, forcing her down again. His hands pressed against her breasts.

"Cut it out, you bastard," she hissed.

Frankie laughed. In his grinning, drunken face, his blood-shot eyes beneath the hooded epicanthic folds of his lids, she saw something new, something she hadn't recognized: real malice. Frankie was willing to do her harm. Allie's heart began to race. She glanced at Sonny again and knew it was hopeless. There was no one to help her. Henry was the only one she could trust, and he was out of it. She'd made a mistake. What was she doing with four drunken men in the middle of a wilderness with no way home? And Frankie had a pistol. Under the waves of fear she felt a terrible sadness, a piteous loss. She might never get home now.

Slowly, cautiously, she started to walk parallel to the shore in the shallow water. Frankie followed, crouching and waving his arms like a basketball guard. In sudden desperation, Allie lunged at him, grabbed his shirt, trying to take him by surprise and knock him off balance. He was too strong. He twisted her arm behind her back and forced her down so that she was kneeling, her face touching the water, her nostrils filled.

"Leave me alone!" Allie screamed, wrenching away. Her voice echoed off the cliffs — high pitched, straining — and was swallowed by the dark wall of the forest. A startled sand hill crane flapped up from the shallows, dragging its long, ridiculously-hinged legs behind it into the air. Allie watched it rise. Don't leave me here, she wanted to cry after it.

"Hey, Frankie," Duane called out placidly. "You want the last hit of this number?"

Frankie let go of her. Panting, Allie scrambled up. She

ducked away and went over to stand by Sonny. Her chest hurt. Her mouth tasted bitter, acrid with fear, and she thought she might vomit.

"I got to work tonight, remember? You guys promised you'd get me back in time. I think we should go."

Sonny gazed up at her. His lips looked thick and rubbery, parted in a stupid grin. "The thing is to get your own boat so you don't have to work for nobody else," he said. "That's what I'm gonna do. Get my own troller like Morgan and work for myself."

"Sonny," Allie pleaded. "I've got to get back for work. I want to start back."

"That's the trouble with women," Sonny said. "Always after you about something. Can't let a man just sit in peace. All right. All right." He rose and brushed the sand from his jeans. "You want to ride with me or Frankie?"

"With you," Allie whispered.

She kept an eye on Frankie while they gathered up their trash and hoisted Henry into Frankie's skiff. Why was it taking so long to start the outboards, to tuck sweaters and paper sacks under the seats? They were all tumbling about like actors in a Fellini movie — Duane dropping his shirt into the water, Frankie stopping to pee. She would scream if they didn't leave. Finally, Sonny sat down at the wheel of Henry's skiff, and Allie climbed in beside him.

"You want me take the wheel?" she asked. She wondered if he could handle it, if he wasn't too messed up.

Sonny said, "Hey, I'm the skipper here."

They started out slowly, putting along through the narrow slough, ducking the low overhanging branches, their backs brushed by leaves. Allie tried to force herself to relax. Frankie was safely at a distance in the other skiff. In two hours she'd be back on Vladimir Island. They still had to get across the flats, which could be tricky if the tide wasn't right and the wind blew up. Flat-bottomed skiffs were no match for waves, especially when piloted by drunken men. Stop worrying, she told herself. Up here, inland, the air was calm, the river glassy. It was still a gorgeous, perfect day.

Sonny turned up the throttle to full speed. They shot forward, whipping around corners and curves. Branches snapped overhead, broke against the bow of the skiff. Allie ducked too late. A twig hit her cheek, and the wind filled her eyes with tears.

"Can't you slow down?" she shouted. "There's snags, you know."

Sonny yelled back over the roar of the outboard. "I'm the skipper. This is *my* boat now."

"Sonny, please slow down!" Allie's words were swallowed by the engine, the rushing wind.

At the wheel, Sonny looked inordinately happy — mouth open in pleasure, white teeth bared.

The slough cut sharply right, the last turn before it spilled into the roaring rush of the main river. Sonny spun the wheel but he couldn't make it. They lifted up off the water, planing. The engine lost its resonance, sounded higher, as they skittered diagonally across the surface of the slough, out of control.

Allie wasn't scared. All she felt was the joy of defying gravity, the thrill of sliding on ice in her father's car. Time slowed. How lovely the water looked, reflecting golden afternoon light. It took forever to hit the tree. Allie studied the patterned bark, the arching bower of branches. She'd never known anything so well. She felt oddly peaceful, filled with relief: it was finally out of her hands. As if on its own, her left arm went up, a small gesture of self-protection. The skiff's bow splintered in her face.

Everything stopped. Such sudden silence. She could hear a light breeze rustling leaves, the hushed roar of the main river like voices in a faraway stadium. Sonny sat still beside her, holding the detached steering wheel in his hands. He smiled absently and blood ran down from his forehead, his nose. Allie's own left arm was bleeding. The split, broken skiff turned a lazy circle, drifting with the current toward the mouth of the main river. Cold water spilled in through the shattered bow, filling the hull, swirling around their knees. The cold came as a surprise, almost an insult. Allie woke from her reverie.

"Sonny! We're going into the river!"

Sonny smiled vacantly.

The skiff sank lower. Allie lunged for the last jutting branch on the bank at the mouth of the slough, but the current spun them away teasingly and into the gargantuan roar.

They were in it now, a giant cement mixer of water and silt, pulling them into its vortex. The broken skiff buckled under the current's pressure, the two halves splitting further, spilling them into the breach. Allie went under and the broken hull banged over her head. So this is all it is, she thought, nothing more than green water filtering light. It came as a disappointment. She'd been here before — a wave that lifted her, then sucked her down one brilliant day at a Cape Cod beach. That day she felt such panic, the sand at the ocean's bottom sliding beneath her nose as the undertow dragged her away, and then the wave tossed her back on shore like a stranded fish.

The skiff passed over her and Allie bobbed up gasping. The blue splintered stern was right there in front of her face. She caught the shaft of the propeller, pulled herself to it, and hooked her elbows over the transom. Only inches away, Sonny dangled off the starboard rail. It was so cold. She never would have believed it could be this cold. The cold climbed inside her, made everything sharp, her head clear and aching to the back of her teeth. Her nostrils filled with the obscenely sweet perfume of the cottonwoods. In detail so sharp it looked microscopic, she noticed cottonwood fluff floating on the water and spidery insects skating along gaily, oblivious to her struggle, supported by surface tension.

Around the angled cornice of the stern, Sonny slipped down. His head appeared low in the water, bobbing like a buoy, a round thing afloat.

"Sonny, hang on!" Allie urged, twisting around to see him.

His mouth touched the water. He coughed, sputtered, raised his head an inch. One of his arms trailed behind him. He'd let go one hand.

"No! Sonny!" Allie tried to reach him with her right arm, to grab his shirt and raise his head, but her left arm couldn't hold onto the skiff. She let go of Sonny and grabbed the transom with her right hand again. "Sonny, hang on!" she screamed. "Sonny!"

Up ahead the gnarled roots of an upended cottonwood jutted into the air. It came closer. It wasn't floating as they were, but stationary, a snag. If they could just get close enough, she could grab on as they went by. Allie thrashed with her feet, trying to steer them closer. Her legs were frozen, numb, they wouldn't move. She wanted to cry. All the will in the world, and her legs wouldn't move. But the current, following its own rules, suddenly swirled into a side eddy and spun them into the tangle of roots. The skiff's shattered bow jammed, held fast. Gasping, Allie pulled herself over the skiff, onto the trunk of the cottonwood. The sun-baked wood felt wonderfully warm against her frozen cheek, as warm as clothes fresh from the dryer, as warm as a day on the beach. She would stay here forever, like a lizard, sucking in heat. Her teeth were chattering, her whole body shook. Then a wave of euphoria swept over her. She'd made it.

She remembered Sonny. The broken skiff was there, bumping repeatedly against the snag as the current pushed it up into the roots, a crazy little dance, but it was empty and Sonny was gone.

Allie scrambled to the top of the cottonwood trunk, looked downriver. All she could see was the broad expanse of surging, silty green water, the cliffs far away on the other bank.

She put a hand up to shade her eyes, searching the shrubs along the right for a spot of color, for Sonny clinging to another snag farther down. Nothing. Nothing but the empty river and the glittering, sun-dappled leaves.

She was still screaming Sonny's name when Frankie, Duane, and Henry found her.

Nɪᴄᴋ sᴀᴛ on the bedside chair in the hospital room, watching Allie sleep. She was under sedation, and the nurses wanted to keep her that way for another day. They didn't think there was any reason for her to attend the funeral, since she wasn't related.

Allie slept on her back with her broken arm in its cast jutting out over the sheets. Her nose was sunburned, and there was a large scabby scratch on her cheek. Someone had put a red plastic headband, the kind that schoolgirls wore, into her hair to hold it away from the wound. It was something she never would have chosen. She looked like a dark-haired Alice in Wonderland. Allie in Wonderland. What had she seen through the looking glass, under the water, down in the kingdom of fish?

A vision of his own carved chess set with its kingdom of miniature salmon, shrimp, and halibut danced luridly before Nick's eyes. Toys and games to fill the hours, a life of pretense. He shook the mocking image out of his head. He'd been up all night. Allie slept peacefully, her chest rising faintly, her face relaxed. Eventually she would wake up into horror, into a truth that couldn't be taken back. They had a covenant, he and she. Survivors. Let her wake up during the day, not the night, Nick prayed. Let someone be here with her then.

Eleanor appeared at the door, frowned. "Visiting hours are over, Nick."

He stood, reached out to touch the tips of Allie's fingers, which dangled limply from the open end of the cast. Her fingernails, he saw, were bitten low, the cuticles chewed raw. The sight pained him more than her scratched face and broken arm — distressing evidence of the small daily damages she wreaked upon herself. So much impulse toward destruction. Was it only luck that had allowed her to surface like a cork, to come back, while Sonny had been swept away? It was an old, familiar question.

And what about you, Sophia? How long it had been since he'd thought of her. Sophia who hadn't come back. Or had she? That was a lie he'd been harboring as long as he'd harbored his debt to her. He'd never been certain of Sophia's death. It was possible that somewhere, on the other side of the planet, there existed a Sophia who had survived ten, twenty years in the camps. A Sophia who could only have emerged broken and bitter. How could a woman who'd been forced to slave among criminals, at the mercy of guards, in hunger and cold, survive at all, let alone as the woman he'd known? How could she forgive him for abandoning her to that fate? Better for both of them that she had been taken away and shot from the start.

Perhaps that was only his arrogance, his guilt speaking. Who was he to judge the value of another person's life? People survived against the greatest odds. There were miracles of human will, resilience. There were chances and chances. There was the indomitable hunger for life itself. Redemption in every breath. Even his old babushka, when she was dying a torturous death from cancer, had prayed, "Please God I should live." It was possible. Sophia might have lived.

"Nick." Eleanor tapped her foot impatiently. "You don't have a right to stay here any longer. I only let you in because you said . . . You don't have a right, you know."

"Okay, Eleanor. Okay." He bent to kiss Allie's scratched cheek, and lines from a Roethke poem came back to him:

I, with no rights in this matter,
Neither father nor lover.

A teacher's lament for a dead student. Yet in a white room, under white sheets, with her broken arm and her child's headband, Allie miraculously slept. Allie, Nick thought, we are lucky ones. So many chances.

What rights did anyone have, beyond the prerogative of love?

No one answered at Vivian's when he knocked, but the door was ajar so Nick went in. She was sitting on the couch, staring at the dead TV set. Her hair was uncombed, and she was wearing a man's plaid shirt, something that must have belonged to the boys, perhaps something of Sonny's. Nick felt a waver of fear, a desire to retreat from the pain he was walking into.

Vivian didn't turn her head. Nick sat down beside her.

"Hello, Vivian."

"How are you, Nick," Vivian said in a voice that betrayed no feeling. "Everybody's coming. Emily and Bob are coming down from Juneau on the ferry tonight. The girls are on their way. I don't know where Mikey went."

He found her flattened monotone more horrifying than tears. This was going to kill her after all, he thought. Sonny's death would be hers. There were limits.

The phone rang. Vivian got up and went into the kitchen. She came back in and laughed a ragged little laugh that made him wince. "Wrong number," she said. She sat down again.

"Tell me, Vivian, how you are?"

"Oh, you know. I mean, what do you think?"

"I am sorry."

"Yeah," Vivian said. "Everybody's sorry. I'm sorry." She turned to face him. He was reminded of the way she'd looked that day in the hospital, after her D.T.s. Her face a fragile brown mask that might shatter into fragments, into dust. Her eyes were reddened, but dry, her mascara smeared.

"You know, I spent all morning thinking about getting drunk, Nick. I just thought, why not? There's a bottle in the cupboard, something Sonny left. All I could think about was that bottle. It was easier than thinking about Sonny, I guess. I would've done it if I thought it'd work, but the trouble is, it won't work anymore. Getting drunk won't really make the hurt go away." She smiled a lopsided smile. "Well, for a while it would. But we aren't talking for a while here, we're talking forever." She turned back to the empty TV screen. "What time is it?"

"Seven-fifteen."

"I got another ten minutes then. I got to go to a meeting. I been waiting for it to be seven-thirty all day."

She would survive this too. His relief was so great that when he reached out to touch her knee, he saw that his own hand was shaking.

Vivian shuddered at his touch, and her face began to crumple. "Oh, God. Nick, he never even had a chance. If only I knew what happened, really, it might seem real, but I don't believe it. I keep thinking that Sonny's gone fishing, that he'll be back when the boat comes in."

Nick sat silently, his hand on her knee. He felt so helpless. This was hers alone. What could he do for her? What could anyone do for anyone else? Loss banished people to exile, to a foreign country where nobody spoke their language, a land where nobody understood.

"You know how I feel?" Vivian turned to him. "I feel like some rock left on shore. Like I just been sitting here for a million years, and the tide keeps coming in and going out. And every time it goes out it takes away someone I love. That's how I feel, Nick."

332

She lit a cigarette, the sound of the match against the matchbook an angry rasp, and then the smoke curled up. He remembered the smoke rising from the ashtray in the empty pilothouse, the wheel turning by itself, that time he'd gone out to clean the windshield and had nearly fallen off his boat. Emptiness and motion. In a rush, Nick took Vivian's hand, the cigarette still burning in it, and brought it to his lips. He kissed her warm fingers, squeezing his eyes shut against the spiral of smoke.

"Vivian, please. You will marry me?"

Vivian began to cry.

At the funeral, the minister didn't take long to sum up Sonny's life. There wasn't that much to say. He'd been a fisherman like his daddy, who'd drowned before him. He'd been a great comfort to his mother in her earlier time of bereavement. He'd gone to the University of Alaska for a year, studying engineering. He was beloved by mother, brother, sisters, friends. His wonderful future had been cut short by cruel fate. God bless this frail flesh, amen.

Nick looked away when they lowered the casket. Standing between her daughters, Vivian never flinched.

Nick was awakened in his bunk in the middle of the night by the sound of someone coming aboard his boat. Footsteps on deck and then the fo'c's'le squeaking open. He sat up in the darkness.

"Nick?"

It was Allie. She stood in the dim galley, her white cast gleaming against the dark of her shirt and sling.

"Nick, can I stay here with you for a little while, please?"

Nick turned on the generator light by the bunks. He shut his eyes against the glare, then opened them to see Allie before him. Her shirt was buttoned wrong under her sling, her hair was tangled, the headband gone, the scratch a dark line running down her cheek.

"Of course," he said.

"I can't sleep. I keep having these nightmares about . . . about it."

Nick slid his legs out of the covers onto the cold floorboards. He was wearing long john bottoms and an undershirt. "I will make for you tea."

"No, don't bother." Allie fumbled with something in her breast pocket, drew out a cigarette, and awkwardly tried to light it with one hand. Nick pulled his lighter from the shelf above the bunk and flicked it for her. Her eyes looked hollow, illuminated by the small flame.

"Sit down, Alinka," he said, patting the bunk across from his. She sat down, her knees touching Nick's. "You want to talk?"

"No, I don't know. I just want to be here."

Nick got a blanket and draped it over her shoulders, set an ashtray beside her on the bunk. He waited. Allie sat silently, sucking at her cigarette, blowing the harsh smoke upward. Then she stubbed it out.

In a small, pleading voice she said, "Nick, can I get in with you for a few minutes? It's just that I can't sleep anymore."

"All right." Her request embarrassed him, but he climbed back under the covers, pushed up against the curving planks, and helped Allie into the narrow bunk beside him. She lay with her head against his collarbone, her cast on top of her chest. Nick rested his arm gingerly around her shoulder. I could be her father, he thought, her grandfather. I should have had a child, a grandchild, to comfort. In his whole long life he'd never held his own child.

"Nick? He just let go," Allie said. "He didn't even try to live. He let go."

Yes, he was sure it was true. Sonny had let go. And Allie would see pictures of that for a long time, as he'd seen pictures from the war, from prison camp. Pictures of Sophia.

"I never should have let him drive the skiff," she said with sudden conviction. "He was too drunk. I should have stopped him."

"Alinka, it was not your fault."

"I tried to get him to hold on, but he just let go. He wouldn't hold on, Nick. I'm so mad at him! That jerk! That bastard! He's such a jerk for doing it I want to kill him."

Allie began to cry. Gently, uncertainly, Nick stroked her hair.

"How come he didn't want to live?" she sniffled. "*I* wanted to live."

A question without an answer. Alinka, Alyushka. He'd wanted to keep her safe, to keep them all safe, all of them on some faraway island — Vivian, Sophia, Allie, Sonny, even himself. The ones who wanted to live and the ones who didn't. But he'd always been powerless to protect anyone. Instead he'd chosen this faraway island as his prison, his sentence, calling it home.

Allie pushed herself up with her good arm and pressed her lips to his.

"Allie," Nick said in surprise. "Sleep."

She kissed him more fervently, and her free hand ran down his belly, over his undershirt. Against his will, Nick felt himself growing aroused by her touch, the length of her body pressed against his. He pushed her away.

"Allie, you are upset. You are not yourself. What you are doing now is not right."

"Why? Why isn't it right? Who makes the rules for what's right? Remember, you told me I couldn't fish with you because you'd want me like a woman, remember? Well, I'm here now. I want to be with you. I don't want to be alone." She ran her hand down his belly to his groin, stroking with an insistent, expert touch that struck him as obscene.

"Stop it!" he said, thrusting her off him roughly, forgetting for the moment her broken arm, her cast. "Enough!"

Allie sat up. She looked perplexed. "What's the matter? Isn't that what you wanted?"

"You understand nothing," he shouted, his voice quaking with fury. "Nothing! You do not know what love means! You think you have to sell yourself for my love? We are friends. I love you without that. But you make it into something else, you make it ugly, Allie. You sell yourself because you do not believe in anything, you do not believe in me or yourself."

Allie's eyes welled up. She wiped her face roughly against her sling. "And what do you believe in, Nick?" she spat out. "Being pals, as long as you call the shots?"

Immediately, Nick knew what he'd done and the anger drained out of him. He'd gotten angry because he'd wanted what she had offered, because she'd tempted him. She didn't know what love meant, didn't believe he could love her without that. He'd been the one who had kissed her drunkenly, who'd said he couldn't fish with her because he'd want her like a man.

"Allie, forgive my words. Please. What you wanted, it is not right for us. You are too young. You have a whole life ahead of you, children. You would leave me, of course, and it would be right, but we would both feel bad. I would not want to lose you. Better that we are friends, Allie. It is enough. We will be friends, long after you are gone from this place. And . . . I, I am to marry Vivian soon."

Allie jerked as though shot. "Well, congratulations! I'm so happy for you. You want to save her now, because of Sonny? Now you're going to be a big hero, right? It doesn't matter if you love her or not. You prefer feeling pity for people. That's your favorite emotion, because you can pity without getting close. But what about me, Nick? What's going to happen to me?"

"You said you wanted to live," Nick said wearily. "Allie, you will live."

Allie scrambled out of the bunk and stood at its foot, facing him. "You're full of shit!" she shouted. "You're full of shit, and I never want to see you again." She turned and ran up the fo'c's'le stairs, her feet pounding on deck, the boat rolling as she leaped from the rail to the dock.

Nick leaned back against the hard planks. He hadn't intended this. What a mess he'd made of it all. She'd come to him for comfort, and he'd ended up hurting her. He thought of going out on the dock to look for her but decided against it. Allie's anger would pass. She would be back and they would forgive each other, as she had forgiven him the time he'd kissed her. He had to trust in that. Allie was childish, but she was smart.

A frightening thought came to him. Perhaps Allie had been right, had told the truth about him in her anger. What if he was marrying Vivian out of pity, not love? So that he could finally think he'd saved someone. Nick the hero.

Stiffly, Nick clambered out of his bunk, pulled a bottle of bourbon out of the storage space beneath the galley bench, and poured a single generous slug into a cracked white mug. He threw it back. Then he sat down at the galley table, resting his chin in his hands.

From his seat he measured the narrow reach of his life: bow to stern, starboard to port. Sink, stove, bunks. A diesel engine for a heart. His boat, which he loved dearly, looked oddly cramped, constricted under dim generator light. It wasn't enough.

Allie was wrong. He wasn't marrying Vivian to save her, but to save himself. He needed saving as much as anyone. Pity wasn't what he felt for Vivian now, but respect. Love could follow. It was possible. Sometimes love was an act of faith, of willingness, as one needed willingness to believe in God. We believe not because we are certain, but because we need to believe. To fill a God-shaped hole in our hearts. We love because we need to love. He loved Allie; he would love Vivian.

For this he'd been spared.

Nick rinsed his mug under the pump, turned off the light, and climbed into his bunk. The Alaskan night, like the white Leningrad nights of his youth, was brief; already light filtered in through the portholes. He lay on his back with his eyes open, waiting.

ALLIE STOOD on the end of the dock where the outhouse used to be, looking into the black, murky water. She could do it, she thought. She could just step off and go under with her cast. Where the outhouse used to be — a fitting end to her life. Nobody cared, least of all her. Nick didn't care. He'd betrayed and humiliated her, after she thought he was her friend. Now she had no one.

But there was a disgusting film of gasoline on the surface of the water. Toilet paper and a beer can floated around the pilings. She didn't want to go in there.

It was a bad joke. She'd already ruined that one. If she'd wanted to kill herself, she'd had her chance. Like Sonny, she could have just let go. She wanted to live.

Then what? She had to do something to make the feelings go away. They would suffocate her. She looked down at the rough plaster of her cast, glowing white in the early light, and thought: she could hurt herself! She could crack her arm open again. She could break the cast. She could break the bone. She could cut herself with a knife, so the feelings would come spilling out. She could slit her throat.

No. She was back where she started. She didn't really want to hurt herself. She didn't need any more souvenirs.

Allie sat down on the end of the dock and looked across the water at Olson's boatyard, where a rusted old shrimp trawler lay in the cradle. To the left of Olson's were the pleasure boat docks, a maze of floats for fiberglass speedboats and skiffs. Their gay, unnatural colors — turquoise and orange and red — glowed faintly in the early dawn. Boats for fun, for thrills. For going fast.

She would go somewhere. She would go away, some place where she would never have to see him again, never see any of them. But where? It was Wednesday, and there wouldn't be a ferry for two days. A ferry north. She didn't want to go north. She was stuck. On the island, the road ended at Nine Mile. She'd have to turn around and come back. The wilderness offered no answer.

There was nowhere to go.

It was ludicrous. She'd stomped down so many docks — away from Digger, away from Steve Tucker, away from Nick, and every time she got to the end of the dock she'd had to turn around. And here she was again. There was no place to go but back to herself. She should have learned that when Nick took her around the island.

Two weeks ago he gave Allie a ride on his boat to see the spawners going up Kutl Creek, but instead of just returning the way they'd come, he decided to take her all the way around the island. A full circle. For a year she'd lived on Vladimir Island, but until she went around it, she hadn't really appreciated that it was an island. She'd ended up back where she started.

At Kutl Creek, Nick dropped anchor and wrestled his little dingy down from its place on top of the pilothouse. Together they rowed across the channel and beached the skiff on the rocks at the mouth of the mainland creek. The rain forest was thick and lush, hung everywhere with moss and enormous leaves, rich with struggling life. At the mouth of the creek the water was black with the backs of salmon waiting in the shallows, gathering strength for the leap up the series of falls that rose five hundred feet above them where the creek tumbled through the trees. Thousands of salmon, wriggling like sperm in a high school film on reproduction. In the falls they leaped upward, bashing themselves against the rocks, falling back in the rush of water. Bald eagles swooped overhead, talons out, diving for the easy catch. Across the water, a black bear scooped fish with a long-clawed paw.

She was shocked by how many salmon there were. Fish and Game had shut down net fishing until further notice, and here was a creek full of spawners. "There's so many," she said in an awed, hushed voice.

"Yes, not so many as before, but there are fish. I think they will open again," Nick said. "It is not yet over."

He plucked a handful of fat ripe blueberries from a bush and handed them to her. She bit into them; a wild sweetness filled her mouth.

"You know what it is I miss, Alinka?" Nick said. "It is such small thing, silly. Once, many years ago, I visited San Francisco. There was Russian church there. I went to see icons, to breathe incense. When I sat on the grass, I realized they must have imported seed. It was Russian grass! Softer, more friendly than grass here. I sat there long time on that Russian grass, and I missed my home. You never know what it is you will miss, Alinka. It always surprises you."

She could see now his familiar pale blue eyes, his bemused expression. He'd never meant her any harm.

What did she miss? She missed living in a place where the sun rose up out of the ocean in the morning instead of falling into it in the evening. She missed her part of the world, which was small, tired, and bounded by stone walls, by fences and highways, by an Atlantic that was brittle and blue. Where in July heat hung in the air, mirages formed on the asphalt, cornfields shimmered, and the maple leaves were lush and soft and full of moisture.

She missed her mother.

She would miss Nick when she went home.

Last winter, in a tender moment, Sonny had said, "I'll think of you a long time after you're gone." But he was the one who was gone now.

Allie struggled to her feet. She walked slowly up the dock, between the line of moored gill netters and seiners, boats that had been shut down, boats without purpose. How beautiful they still looked with their tall masts, their networks of rigging, their bows jutting up from the water. They swayed gently and the planks echoed under her boots.

Allie climbed the stairs to the pilothouse of the *Emily Jane*. She sat in the old riverboat's captain's chair, spun the brass-fitted wooden wheel, and flicked at the compass. Through the dirty pilothouse window, beyond the corrugated aluminum roof of the shrimp cannery, the sky was brightening in soft purple streaks. Morning again. The compass lolled, charting no distance, pointing no way.

Her broken arm ached. She must have hurt it when Nick pushed her off his bed. She hadn't understood what he'd been trying to say: he loved her as he would his own child. "I'm sorry, Nick," Allie whispered. "I didn't know."

She cradled her injured arm with her right hand, like a baby, like the baby she must have once been. "Poor little arm," she said aloud, turning to look behind her, embarrassed at her own tender words. But no one was there to mock her. Reflecting back from the pilothouse window, her own face, above the gleaming cast, looked benign.

She was tired now. Allie rested her broken arm on the riverboat's wheel and lay her cheek against the hollow plaster. Pressing her ear to the cast's white shell, she could almost hear, not the roar of the ocean, but the silent mending within.